FIC

Wetl S0-BKZ-504

Morning

MORNING

Fiction by W. D. Wetherell

Pantheon Books

New York

MORNING

W. D. Wetherell

North Richland Hills Public Library
6720 N.E. Loop 820
North Richland Hills, Texas 76180

This is a work of fiction. Any resemblance to persons
living or dead is entirely coincidental and unintentional.

Copyright © 2001 by W. D. Wetherell

All rights reserved under International and Pan-American
Copyright Conventions. Published in the United States by Pantheon Books,
a division of Random House, Inc., New York, and simultaneously in Canada
by Random House of Canada Limited, Toronto.

Pantheon Books and colophon are registered trademarks
of Random House, Inc.

Library of Congress Cataloging-in-Publication Data

Wetherell, W. D.
Morning / W. D. Wetherell
p.   cm.
ISBN 0-375-42088-6 (HC)
1. Television personalities—Fiction.   2. Triangles (Interpersonal rela-
tions)—Fiction.   3. Television broadcasting—Fiction.   4. Fathers and
sons—Fiction.   5. New York (N.Y.)—Fiction.   6. Massachusetts—
Fiction.   7. Biographers—Fiction.   8. Murder—Fiction.   I. Title.

PS3573.E9248 M67 2001
813'.54—dc21   00-057457

www.pantheonbooks.com

Book design by Johanna Roebas

Printed in the United States of America
First Edition
2 4 6 8 9 7 5 3 1

The author would like to thank
the American Academy of Arts and Letters
for its support during the completion of this work.

Television is going to be the test of the modern world,
and in this new opportunity to see beyond the range of our vision
we shall discover a new and unbearable disturbance of the general peace
or a saving radiance in the sky. We shall stand or fall by television.
—E. B. White

Contents

Part One

OPENING THEME

One

Morning wasn't morning until McGowan came to town. This would have been the early autumn of 1950, that difficult corner year between then and now. He'd done well with his evening show in Chicago, but he was convinced that nighttime would be the slums of TV, and in any case his affairs had caught up with him and it was time to move on. New York, summoning him like that, seemed the providential next step. Yes, he had done well in television. No, he had not forgotten the great romance of his life. Yes, he still had lots left to prove. On that late September day when he got off the train in Grand Central, tipped the porter to carry the one bag that was all he had, walked up the ramp to daylight, stood there staring at the slick bronze of the skyscrapers, as awestruck as any rube, he teetered on that most appealing and vulnerable of points: a young man on the verge of making it in the big splashy American way.

For what was morning before he confronted it, seized it, spun it all around? An intermission between night and day, the neutral ground separating nightmares from daydreams, reality's launching pad, hope's fragile hour—the one moment in the day when if you felt courageous and energetic and hopeful the sun backed you up. It was a time when people went first thing to appraise the weather, suck in fresh air, stoop down to touch the dew, rise again and stretch. It was a time when chores were still performed before breakfast, cows milked, sidewalks shoveled, faces scrubbed behind the ears. Wives pulled on robes and went outside to cut flowers for the breakfast table, waved to neighbors doing the same, then went in to break eggs into cast-iron skillets with thick cuts of ham. Kids played outdoors, got shouted at to get ready for school, propped their bikes up with kickstands, ready to zoom off the moment they finished. Cats scratched at screendoors to get in or out. Dogs fetched newspapers. Roosters still crowed. The city, the town, the village came once again to light.

Morning was the cards you'd been dealt by fate. You woke up and felt lonely, circled your hand around on the sheets trying to summon up a genie who would rescue you, then forced yourself to plunge back into another day alone. You woke up beside someone you hated, bitterness a sandpaper collar around your neck, cutting off your breath. You woke up beside someone you loved, and reached for that familiar warmth and pulled it closer, no hurry now, content to linger in the sweet, lazy hollow of awakening. And yet even here you felt a little hunger, if you were lucky. Just enough vacancy in the heart for the day to fill.

There was radio, but it was only music, or farm reports, or weather, nothing that stopped you, made you sit down. Seven now and you were showering. Seven-thirty and the first swallow of juice. Eight and the morning paper. Eight-thirty and outside to the car or the station or the tractor, joining the mainstream, everyone in lockstep, eyes squarely forward on the day. But until you left home all you wanted from the rest of the world was to know it was still there, and you could get that in those little sounds and rumors that leaked in from outside. Birdsong in elms. School buses changing gears. The clink of milk bottles on the stoop. Sun edging through curtains. The soft summoning whistle of trains. Everyone did morning differently, and yet everywhere it was the same. You woke up to who you were in your narrow, most essential denomination, who you were when you were alone, the larger world for ninety minutes be damned.

All this was in morning until McGowan regarded it, sensed everything was not well there, turned it to his purpose. A morning so rich and textured and unbroken, and yet all it took was for the right man to come along at the critical moment, stare fixedly out into its depths, clear his throat to its deepest baritone, peer down those horn-rimmed glasses, talk, and it all shattered apart.

Hence this biography etc.

Explain here in intro how he's remembered, but barely now. Aging boomers mostly, the ones who as kids pressed close to the screen as they waited for breakfast, hoping the picture would stop rolling, squinting at the fuzziness to try and make it go sharp. They remember the chimpanzee, of course. They remember the clumsy sidekick, Chet Standish, and all the beautiful *Morning* girls, including Lee Palmer, prettiest of all. They remember the window on 49th Street, the people outside mugging, waving, holding up little signs with the names of their hometowns. They remember how McGowan met his end. A good many claim they saw it happen, were actually watching that last morning, and there are those who still remember how it seemed to change everything from make-believe to all too real. The early shows weren't taped, so little did anyone regard them, and the later ones, on Electronicam or Kinescope, were either destroyed when more modern taping methods became available or dissolved into acid while in storage. What survives is barely a thousand feet of film from four years of programming. As the film disappeared, as even smoother, more relaxed hosts succeeded him on the program, the memory of McGowan disappeared, too, and so only someone in their late fifties is old enough to actually remember what he looked like on the tube.

Alec McGowan? Sure, the one who started the Morning *show, the man with glasses. Talent? Nothing obvious. Looks? Interesting, our mothers used to say, with a certain look in their eyes. There was all kinds of stuff. The chimp in diapers. That Chet guy stumbling into things, getting his words wrong. The clocks showing what time it was all over the world. The smart lady with the warm smile and the short hair, the one who was so obviously nuts about him. His slogan, the sign-off everyone imitated. A lot of educational stuff, too, though it's hard to say just what. Our dads put it on when they got up in the morning and our moms turned it off when it was time to go to school. Only when we left they turned it back on again, because we caught her once and she blushed all red.*

The fifty-year-olds grope, they squeeze their hands into fists and reach, as if to pull from the ether what it was they found so compelling, and yet only the shrewder ones come close to pinning down the secret of his extraordinary success. A lot of people have spent their lives staring at a television screen, but Alec McGowan was the only one who devoted his life, right down to its brutal last seconds, to staring intently back out.

Support this with quotes. Intro blending into first chapter. Starting with Jay etcetera and so forth. Thumbnail bios or blend right in?

Barbara Jay (1922–). Came to KDKA in Pittsburgh after stint with radio ad agency in Evanston, then moved to New York with network. Head writer, *Morning,* 1950–53. Later formed independent production company. Emmy for writing/producing documentary "Behind the Mask" exposing obstetricians without licenses, 1963. Adjunct professor Columbia Graduate School of Journalism 1965–92. Interview of 5/9/99.

Living out on Long Island like so many from early days. Southampton, house built by bootlegger on bluff above pitch pine. Bright morning, wind bringing in sunshine with surf, tossing both across rocks. Tall woman as in pictures, only in pictures seems somehow older thanks to flouncy skirt/thick lipstick/high heels; 1950 in drag (save that line). Now jeans/leather vest/short hair, coming to door with boxer puppy in arms, scolding it and kissing at same time.

Seventy-seven, she says right off. Horny as ever and backs this up with grin. Strong forehead and chin are what's left from picture, except everything in between has gone leathery. Voice burred by too many cigarettes—a voice that snaps/crackles/bangs like an old manual typewriter.

What you have to remember, she says, is that smooth didn't work in those days. The resolution was terrible, the matrix. Put on one of these pretty boys you have nowadays and it would have been like watching scrambled eggs. Crude didn't work either. There was this big thing about how we were being allowed into people's homes and you had to look a certain way to pass muster. The educational function, too—we took that very seriously. If you go back you'll notice the first ones who made it big looked like professors with bow ties and hankies.

That's who Abramsky was searching for. A host who could be seen through the blur, someone handsome in an unusual way and more or less intellectual. Namely, McGowan, who had made a big splash in Chicago. He had a forehead that would have done justice to Einstein, but below that his shoulders were wide as DiMaggio's, and no one, *no one,* ever looked better in a double-breasted suit. He had a sleepy expression—only a little more awake than you were yourself, and that went down easy.

His glasses were the big thing, of course. His trademark. He had horn-rims, which must have been among the first pairs—everyone wore rimless before that—and it made him interesting right off the bat. He didn't need them. He needed them, but only tinted because the klieg lights were so strong. They were big with the audience right from the start. He put them on, it was like he was putting on the entire McGowan. In the Chicago days sometimes he took them off on camera, like he was thinking and the only way he could do that was suck on the earpieces. He was thinking, I can vouch for that, only in those days it was about whether to screw the script girl or the assistant grip. But it was the sexiest thing you ever saw, like he was taking his clothes off right there on camera. Those were the days when most TV sets were still in bars, and they claimed the moment he took them off you could stand outside any dive on the Loop and hear dozens of women moaning simultaneously as they came. The same thing happened on

Morning. Women loved him. Here was this sexy, intelligent, soft-spoken man appearing in their homes when they were all alone. The show became—maybe it still is—the biggest grosser in show business history, and those glasses were a big part of why.

Study door opens, woman enters with tray. Black coffee, raspberry scones. A younger woman, not by much. Spry in the old-fashioned way, vest just like Jay's, only of velvet. Smiles as Jay rumples her hair. My partner, she says proudly. The coffee. The scones. The window open, breeze coming in. The iodine smell of seaweed and salt.

She talks on with her partner behind her. Explains how hard it was writing cues for him. He'd ad lib all over the place, go off on his own for five minutes at a stretch, and the writers would despair, throw their hands up, but then he would wink and come out with it—how this new musical called *Guys and Dolls* was opening on Broadway that night and they'd woken the chorus up early to do their final dress rehearsal right there in the studio. He always hit the cue, but it would drive them crazy the loops he took to get there.

But I'm wandering, she says. What I wanted to say about those glasses, those horn-rims, was that they cut through the fuzziness. Watching out in Peoria at the far end of the cable, using only rabbit ears, that's all you could see sometimes. It wasn't like there was a man on the screen at all, only those square black frames and they centered and held the picture like nothing else could. He'd push them back on his nose, kind of tuck his head in like this and squint down through one lens. People picked up on that after a while, all the impersonators. "Well, old tiger." They picked up on that, too, though even the best of them never got his purr down, the way it came out.

People in the business were slow in taking him seriously, deciding whether he was a visionary or a huckster, but I think both were pretty evenly balanced. You know what grace means, in the old Latin sense? *Gratia*—favor. Favored by the gods. He was favored all right, for those first years. You thought about Hemingway's grace under pressure, too, seeing what he had to deal with just in the way of getting the show on. Of course there was that telegenic quality—he was blessed with good bioelectricity. But I wasn't kidding before, what I said about his staring back out through the camera. You wouldn't notice it sitting in the studio, but what I used to do was take sponsors or network bigshots and pull them around to the monitor, which, don't ask me why, was located right next to the ladies' john. There it was obvious as soon as I pointed it out. Alec wasn't trying to see out of his glasses—they were just transparent glass. He wanted to see out through the *camera,* wanted to see who was watching and why, see right into their souls. He had this wonderful curiosity about people that wasn't fake at all, just as strong when he died as when he started. Look at *me,* that's what all the pretty boys are saying if you watch them today. Study Alec, if by some miracle you can find some tape, and you see it's just the opposite. Look at *you,* he's saying, and that's why people responded to him right from the start. He wasn't just bringing the world into ordinary people's lives, he was bringing ordinary lives out into the world, and that's what made him larger than life, a true hero, goddam his sexist soul to hell, even to me.

Michael Rinaldi (1924–2000). Deli clerk, Broadway Charlie's, 1948–54. Owner Broadway Charlie's, 1956–82. Fast-food franchise owner, Fort Walton, Florida. Interview of 6/18/99.

Tan, fit-looking, black T-shirt over plaid golf slacks. Sucks in what little he has for gut, punches to show how tight. Enough hair left to brush straight back from forehead, like bobbing crest of little bird. A contented man, pleased to be found.

Yeah, yeah, sure. People still come up to me, even down here. Mike the Muffin Man! Sometimes I correct them, sometimes I don't. It was always Mike the Muffin, no man. I was short and plump in those days, my hair had kind of a raisin-bran color, and so it was Mike the Muffin almost from the start.

We always had a show-biz clientele. People said, Mike how come you're still a deli clerk at your age, you who were in the merchant marine, saw action. You'd think it would be boring schlepping around sandwiches. Boring! Jesus, it was anything but. We were right up the block from the old Met, and a lot of opera people liked to play cards and were always ordering these big platters of cold cuts. Pinza, Merrill, Melchior—I knew them all, and they used to slip me tickets for the matinees. Great days, let me tell you. Used to go to the fights at the old Garden, boxers like Jake LaMotta, or Sugar Ray Robinson, who everyone knew was the best tipper in town. It was a good job for a kid like me, always hopping, right in the thick of things, the biggest deli on the greatest block in the greatest city in the world.

So okay, it's just before Christmas 1950. I don't usually go in early, but I'm in early for some reason and old man Myers behind the counter puts down the phone and yells, "Order out to Forty-ninth Street, anyone in the mood?" It was a short walk through snow, though that was the days before cardboard trays and you had to balance things on your arm and coffee was always spilling down your wrist so you had to be a juggler to be any good.

A doorman lets me in. This is Rockefeller Center, okay? I glance down at the note I had stuck in my glove. "I'm looking for someone named McGowan." He points me toward the lobby. "I'm looking for McGowan," I say, this time to an older guy in a suit. He points me through a door. "McGowan?" A cute blonde this time, sort of a Patti Page type, and she pulls open these thick padded doors and points me down an aisle. Now it's getting interesting, because there are all these guys in shirtsleeves with earphones over their heads, all these armored cables I had to skip over. "Anyone here named McGowan!" I yell, top of my lungs. I was getting impatient and all, knowing the coffee was getting cold. You deliver it cold, you get stiffed every time.

I'm about to shout again when this gentleman comes up to me with a clipboard, puts his hand on my arm. Distinguished-looking, kind of a rabbi type. "Hey, father," I said. "Where is this guy McGowan at?" He looks me up and down, kind of auditions me with his eyes, thinking for a minute, then pushes me gently on down the aisle.

So there I go, suspecting nada. All of a sudden it got hotter than hell—it was like the sun had come up indoors. When my eyes cleared out, there, right in front of me, sitting in front of this low desk under some clocks was a big man in a double-breasted suit. He had glasses on, and he looked hungry, I remember that part. He looked like any other guy who had skipped breakfast and was waiting for a delivery. "There you are!" he says, with this slow, lazy kind of grin. I hand him over his bag, he fishes in his pocket for some change, then he starts talking to me like it's the most natural thing in the world. About where the deli was, how busy we were with Christmas coming, whether it was a good job or no. I talk back, cracking some wise-guy jokes like I do, not thinking anything of it, not until funny stuff starts happening behind me. There's a big guy in the background where it's dark and he has a big microphone on a pole and he's holding it over us, straining to keep it from conking us on the head. There's this other guy behind a huge camera and he's pedaling in closer like a kid on a scooter. There are more lights, people standing around doing nothing, and then it hits me. Hey, television! This is television and you, Mike Rinaldi, are goddam on it!

A roar that shakes the entire condo, sets the plates to rattling, vibrates the couch. B-1, Rinaldi says. Stealth bomber, not so stealthy, huh? Explains about big air base across the bay, how the sky got dark with bombers during the Gulf War, and how the pilots, when they came back, always made right for his restaurant for burgers and fries. Goes on from there to talk about the lousy winter so far, how he loved it, him being the only retired guy in Florida who didn't like sun. Slow to get back on track, then talks even faster to make up for lost time.

That's how it all started. Yeah, yeah, sure. One thousand three hundred and five shows straight. I was part of it all, just like the cameramen and the ladies who cleaned up and the mailman and the Western Union messenger and everybody else he brought on camera. At first those days he was coffee or sometimes cream soda and corn muffin. He had it in his head that cream was healthy and that corn was his fruit and vegetables. Later he switched to bagels, and that was the first time anybody outside New York ever heard of them and look at bagels today, I wish I had stock. Chet Standish would always get a fried egg on a roll, only he wasn't much of a tipper, no offense. Lee Palmer only got tea—I guess she was so trim and all she couldn't risk things like muffins. Then his guests would order things, like Benny Goodman or Bogart or even once Ike.

Freddo the chimp liked Dutch loaf best, only it took them months to figure this out. They tried everything—knishes, doughnuts, ham and cheese. Freddo was wasting away right on camera and they got letters from all over the country suggesting different food. McGowan used to hand-feed him on his own, this Dutch loaf he tore in strips, taking out the olives. He loved Freddo, always clucking him under the chin, holding him on his lap and so on, even when the cameras turned off. Great thing to see, makes you think he would have been good with a son.

But anyway, it was just Hello, Mr. McG., how are you today? and Hi, Mike, what's the word, old tiger? At least at first. Then he gradually got me talking about other things, not just my folks out there in Queens, not just what it was like being a deli clerk on Broadway, but what I thought about things happening out there in the world. Like Korea. Well, Mike, he'd ask, the camera boring right in. What do you make of this mess in Seoul? Mess is right, I said right back. No Korean ever did anything bad to me, and besides don't we have enough problems here at home? That's a quarter for the coffee, fifteen cents for the muffin and you owe me a buck from last week. He didn't just ask, either. He was interested in what you had to say. He'd get Chet or Lee Palmer to interview the bigshots, but it was him who always talked to the likes of me.

After a year or so I got a bright idea I'm still not totally proud of. All those people lined up outside the window on Forty-ninth Street staring in at the show? They always looked so cold and hungry. I got the idea of starting up a little coffee service just for them. It hit, right from the start. I'm talking a couple of hundred people some mornings, most from out of town. That's how I saved up enough to buy the deli. I was a celebrity and they were always asking me about what everybody was really like inside the glass, and in the meantime I'm selling them coffee and crumb buns for twice what they'd pay at a deli.

The first year I came on the show early, but then later it was always the last thing. Okay, so what happens. It's July 3, 1954. I go to the deli,

I'm putting together the usual, when old man Myers waves me out back. He looks—what's the word? Distraught? Distraught all to hell. Mike, he says. I don't think you're going to make the delivery today. What are you talking about? I say. You crazy or what? One thousand three hundred and five shows straight, you think I'm going to quit on him now? Mike, he says, I don't think you want to go over there—only now he's crying and I noticed back in the kitchen the TV is on and everyone is crying or looking shocked or going over to take a swipe at the rabbit ears, and there's this siren going by outside on Broadway, lots of sirens, and then it hits me. Something's happened, something real bad.

You know that part. You don't want to know. But you're asking me about McGowan and I can tell you this. He made something of me. Here I was, a stupid no-nothing kid from Queens and he made something of me just by letting me do my job, saying what I had to say. I don't buy any of the crap you heard about him. For me, for always, a true gentleman and one of those demigods. Yeah, yeah, sure. Kind of my slogan, my pet phrase. People come up to me today, want me to say it. Yeah, yeah, sure. Yeah. Sure. Brings it all back—even, you'll excuse me, the tears.

Martin C. Slisco (1921–). Head cameraman, *Morning*, 1950–54. Levittown, New York. Interview of 4/23/00.

The famous suburb, growing old. Burglar alarms on every house— a forgotten, quietly desperate feel, even with the primness. Noon and no one outside. Smaller house than neighbor's, beside barbed-wired municipal pool. On the lawn, rusty hand mower covered in oak leaves, the wooden shaft splintered and gray.

Younger-looking than expected, though moves with arthritic slowness. Strong arms, shirtsleeves rolled up to white forearms purpled with veins. A gray fuzz on his cheeks where sideburns used to be; deep eyes inside dark saucers. Unsettling—a moody, dangerous raccoon. Round face, almost Asian. The crowning touch, high and tight against his eye sockets: black horn-rimmed glasses circa 1954, lenses greasy, corners taped.

It's been eight years since anyone came and now two in the same week. Years ago lots came. Cultural historians they called themselves, bigshot phonies from Columbia and Yale, each more pretentious than the last. What a scam. Television has no history, not what was live. Since there's no surviving tape of him, McGowan is dust. What Kinescopes we bothered making were all dumped in the harbor to save storage costs. Same with the two-inch tape. Kinescope sucks, anyway—a film taken of a TV screen. But I knew you would come searching anyway. You or your type. Grave robbers pissed to find the coffin is empty, settling for someone you wouldn't ordinarily even notice, Martin Slisco in person. But I'll tell you what I told the other one. Even if I had some Kinescopes, I wouldn't sell them. I see what your kind does to people. He's better off dead.

He knew the cameramen were everything. Right from the start he treated us special, fought hard to get us raises, more time off. We were part of the show—we turned the camera on ourselves, let people see how the magic worked. Your pal Chet Standish never learned the facts of life. Bit of the snob, Chet was. We fixed him over time. That reputation for clumsiness, where do you think it came from? We always kept him just a little bit out of focus, and that's how it started about him being blind. We jiggled the lens every time he moved and made him clumsy. Why so many mediocrities flourished and so many talented ones bombed? It's because of what we did or didn't do, not because the cameras were lousy. The cameras were sharper than the Jap crap they use now, and had to be, the cable was so bad, the ghosting. Standish fucked us over and we turned him into a fool.

You want to ask about the monkey. Everyone, that's the first thing out of their mouths. Oh tell us about Freddo, he was such an adorable little critter. McGowan hated its guts. I don't know how many times the goddam thing bit him, right on camera. There was a special first-aid box just to make sure he didn't get rabies. He knew how important the monkey was, and that didn't help his ego any. Ratings stank before Freddo. Here McGowan had worked and slaved to make the show what he wanted and the whole thing was going down in flames around his head and what saved him was a five-dollar monkey that needed twelve diapers a day. He was always asking people to kill it for him. People thought he was joking, and I was the first one who figured out he was serious. You know how hard it is to buy arsenic in Midtown Manhattan? I went to a dozen drugstores before I found some. But it worked. I slipped some in its coconut juice. They announced it was a stroke, but it was arsenic, and as far as McGowan was concerned, after that I could do no wrong.

I had other jobs. Waking McGowan up was one of them. He'd be partying all night. Not drinking. Girl partying. He was all fucked out by morning, dopey, and it was hard to get him awake. Cough medicine worked best. The ones who came over from radio were always concerned about their throats, so I convinced him to take some, only it was mostly codeine. That woke him up all right. For ninety minutes he'd be dynamite. Martin, my throat's a wee bit scratchy this morning, what do you have? And that's the way it was for four years solid until that bitch Lee Palmer convinced him to go straight.

I was there when he first auditioned. A big reputation in Chicago, but that meant nothing in New York. The uppity-ups demanded a test for him, just like a beginner. It was in studio 8-H, which had no windows, hardly even a ventilation shaft. Toscanini rehearsed there and he was from Italy and he liked it hot. Lights were everywhere. You needed a ton of light to begin with, and a lot more banks were added at the last minute, so what they ended up with was probably 25,000 watts of incandescent pointed at him from a distance of ten feet. I'm not sure on whose orders. He had enemies right from the start. No reason. This is television, okay? Half the people there were hoping he'd fall on his ass. Abramsky had enemies, too. I was told to keep adding lights as the audition went on and Abramsky knew something was up but didn't say squat. A lot of people didn't think McGowan had what it took and they wanted to fry him right back to the boonies where he came from.

Write this out.

The network had booked him a room at the Waldorf Astoria, but on that first day in the city McGowan was in no hurry at all to get there. As anyone who watched the show knows, he was a devoted walker. In a story he liked telling on himself, he strolled down Madison Avenue toward where the skyscrapers rose thickest, forgetting the porter was still following with his bag, so it was like a great white hunter followed by his faithful gun-bearer, a short, respectful distance behind.

How far did he walk that first day? Later on he claimed it was all the way to the Battery and back again uptown. He didn't feel he knew a city until he knew it in his legs. Friends who walked with him say he would close his eyes half the time, soaking up the smells and sounds, so you were sure he'd be demolished by a bus or cab. And yet somehow his instincts were certain and they carried him through even the busiest intersections unharmed.

When he got back to the Waldorf there was a message waiting from Abramsky saying he should be at the studio at seven ready to go to work. That must have surprised him. He had been a celebrity in Chicago, used to calling his own shots, and now here he was in the smallest, cheapest, dampest room the Waldorf had to offer, with no one having come to meet him, being ordered around by penciled notes slipped under the door. Did he sense they were hedging their bets? Whatever his doubts, he forced them away, showered, polished his glasses with toilet paper, dressed, went down to the Automat on Forty-third Street, grabbed a sandwich, then found a cab for the short ride uptown.

No one waited for him there, either. He pushed through the entrance, beginning to feel a little sorry for himself, whistling "Always," (his theme song from Chicago) to keep up his spirits. Studio 8-H had a door that would do justice to a dungeon. When he pushed, it creaked open and there on the other side, like a convention of hangmen, sat the network brass.

Peter Abramsky was almost certainly the only one he recognized— at fifty-seven, the network's miracle worker, at least when it came to programming. He walked over holding out his hand, with that expression of patience and just barely controlled cynicism that was so characteristic. But even Abramsky kept his distance once the first niceties were over. McGowan would always remember how alone he felt—and how he had to accept that and get over it or else he was finished. Barbara Jay was there that night as Abramsky's assistant. "You could cut the proverbial tension," she remembers, "with the proverbial knife. A butter knife at that."

Before the ring of brass was a similiar ring of cameras, pointing like big-bored cannon ready to shoot. An assistant director stepped out, pointed McGowan over to a metal stool which was the only prop on a stage designed to seat a symphony orchestra—the same man leaned over and slapped a slate board in front of his face. There were four types of lights bearing down: key lights, which were bright enough to illuminate Ebbets Field; fill lights to take care of the shadows thrown by the key lights; back lights to make his head and shoulders clearly discernible from the studio walls; background lights to take care of the shadows cast in back. Each of these was doubled, making eight lights in all. Stronger men than McGowan had been known to melt under these. There's a story, not necessarily apocryphal, about Chet Standish sitting down to do a beer commercial, reaching for a long golden sip from the glass beside him, swallowing—discovering the beer had reached the boiling point, but discovering this only as it went down.

McGowan sat on the stool, his elbow up high as if the stool had a back on it, his legs crossed, his body turned half around, so he had to bend his head back to face the camera. It was a posture he admitted stealing from newsreels of General Montgomery, "Monty," and yet it quickly became identified with him. His expression was relaxed, curious, pleasant. As people would later notice, he always seemed on the verge of smiling, but rarely did so. His massive head could seem too weighty for his neck, which was one of the reasons he craned it around like that, tucked his chin down. His hair was sandy then, and he wore it in a great shock over his forehead, so it almost touched his glasses, his glasses that were an immediate challenge for the cameramen: how to penetrate their glare, keep the picture from flaring. His eyes were blue—even in black-and-white (people swore) they were unmistakably blue. Cliché eyes, the critics called them. Cliché the way they sparkled, caught whatever light was around, set it sparkling.

And there he sat, perfectly comfortable and calm. Three minutes went by—in the heat from the spotlights it must have seemed much longer. Finally, a low, stentorian voice called out from the darkness behind the cameras, "So talk!" (Robert Blaisdell, network usher, his celebrity days as a reporter still ten years in the future, happened to wander in at this juncture, and ever after claimed the voice was that of General Sarnoff himself, or "General Fangs," as he was known to his subordinates.) The sound of it, flaring out from the silence, was like another spotlight, the harshest, most unsparing one yet.

For maybe a full twenty seconds McGowan acted confused. He brought his chin up just enough that his glasses caught most of the light, raised those eyebrows, put on that absentminded expression that was already a deliberate part of his charm. Casually, tilting his body the slightest fraction, he reached deep into his jacket pocket ("For his ticket back to Chicago, is what we figured," Barbara Jay recalls), fumbled there for a moment, then brought the hand back out—*empty*. What gives? everyone wondered. Then, in an even smoother motion, he tilted his body the opposite way, reached into the other pocket, fumbled with his left hand, drew it back out closed around something no one could see.

"Has more contentment ever been wrapped up in such a small package in the history of the world?" he said, his fist still closed. Bringing it forward and higher, he opened his fingers to reveal a square little packet that lay flat on his opened palm—at mouth level and a little to one side.

"Gum they call it—a homely, lovable little word that makes you feel good just saying it out loud. A substance that's been chewed as long as man has walked this planet. The extract of trees in the olden days, resin treasured for its soothing resiliency, its syrupy sweetness, its medicinal properties, which were and are considerable. Not food, certainly, but not just bark either. Something in between, and so oddly satisfying, right from the start. Food not only for cavemen, but philosophers and kings."

What's this? everyone wondered, really taken aback now. Someone, maybe even Abramsky, gave a signal and klieg lights no one even suspected were there flashed down from the ceiling, doubling the intensity. In the circle of onlookers, everyone sat sweating. Men plucked their shirts out away from their chests, fanned themselves with leftover symphony programs; a woman, one of the script girls, leaned forward with her head between her knees so as not to faint.

In the center of this, under the circle where the beams converged, McGowan seemed unaware there were lights on at all. He wasn't sweating, not the slightest bead. He reached for his collar, and everyone assumed he was going to unloosen his bow tie ("Uh-oh, bad move," Blaisdell decided, sweating bullets himself), but all he did was push the knot even tighter, as if he were chilly. A second later he took the gum packet, made it twirl somehow through his fingers, tossed it to the other hand, and carefully started peeling back the foil.

"Listen here, old tigers, and you shall hear, of the many fine stories that revolve around"—pause—"gum. Many heroes, titans who walked the earth oh not so many years ago now. Messrs. Beechnut and Wrigley and Spearmint, not to mention that new kid on the block, Mr. Bazooka. There was generous inspiration in these men. To hit upon something you can chew for a contemplative few minutes, then park conveniently on your cap or beneath your hair. Something you can swallow if you must, say if the teacher catches you at it, without suffering any undue harm. Something that works as glue in a pinch, and you all recall the story of that army tank on Okinawa that got moving again thanks to some Wrigley applied to the carburetor and how it took out a Jap blockhouse that was holding up our advance off the beach. A versatile piece of equipment indeed."

By now the temperature in the studio was over a hundred degrees Fahrenheit and rising. The cameramen hung limp on their cameras, even as they dollied in closer. An olive-colored steam rose from the ventilation shafts and made it seem hotter. Insulator wires (Blaisdell claims) sizzled and burst. Abramsky, sliding his chair closer to the edge of the light, stared with a peculiarly intense kind of fascination—he was the only one of the onlookers who wasn't sweating.

McGowan, almost smiling now, placed the wafer of gum in his mouth as daintily, as formally, as a priest giving himself communion.

"Humble Mr. Gum. And yet what happened? We had a war, some of you may remember. A little number called World War Two. And what do we remember about it? The lonely times when we hunched down low in our foxholes trying to see through the night, or leaned over the rail on our tanker, looking down at the sea for the blunt-nosed wave of a torpedo, the miserable duty when we faced Panzer tanks there in the Ardennes snow. Even stateside—those tough, boring, someone's-got-to-do-it jobs that made victory possible. What got us through? Gum, natch. How it wasn't much solace, but sometimes it was all you had, brother, and it made all the difference in the world. Made a difference to the kids you ran into along the way, you betcha. The starving kids in Italy with the heartbreaker's eyes. The soulful waifs there in the Philippines looking like they didn't know what it meant to smile. Even Jap kids playing in Tokyo's ruins. What did they demand when they ran into you, the first words out of their mouths, the only English they knew? Gum, chum? Got any gum?"

All the while he talked, barely perceptible but just perceptible enough, McGowan worked the gum back and forth in his mouth—not too intently, but not too casually either, finding just the right balance to suggest how satisfyingly sweet and sticky the gum tasted. He talked while he did this—but now he left off talking and right there under the worst of the heat, at the very moment when people in back were gasping for breath, the lights burning his forehead bright red, he puckered his lips together as if he were about to lightly, halfheartedly kiss someone invisible, then widened them and blew the largest, pinkest, roundest, most perfect bubble anyone had ever seen . . . big . . . bigger . . . then, a perfectly timed second after it reached its fullest possible expansion and totally hid his face, popped it with his pinky to stand revealed where the bubble had been, smiling as evenly and coolly as before, but with his glasses tilted down now, winking toward the camera and blowing it the lightest of kisses goodbye.

According to the legend this quickly became, there were two minutes when no one said a word. A camera, panning back from the right, short-circuited up a plume of bluish smoke. The cameraman cursed, but then it was quiet again for another, even longer minute, until from the deepest part of the studio the same hoarse voice as earlier rang out once more.

"Genius!"

The lights flared out, withdrew toward their plum-colored centers, and instantly McGowan was surrounded by network executives, ad reps, the publicity people, all of whom were trying either to shake his hand or slap him on the back. A script girl ran up with wet towels and began mopping off his forehead, even though it wasn't wet. Another stood by with a change of clothes, though there was no reason for him to change. All the faces that had been so hard and skeptical and malevolent now radiated nothing but the purest goodwill . . . and off to the side, taking no part in this, watching McGowan even more intently than he had earlier, as if the real test were only now beginning, Peter Abramsky slowly shook his head, looking (as Robert Blaisdell puts it) "not happy or proud at all, but like that bubble had ruptured something essential in his heart."

Take up the story with *Collier's Magazine* interview of 1/6/54. Last ever published? Verbatim with edits. Pertinent parts spaced throughout entire bio, but go easy here at start. Who A.M.? Himself? Fits in with his sense of humor. A pun? Possibly Albert Munz, gossip columnist on *Herald Tribune,* wenching companion/procurer/fairweather friend.

A.M.: *I take it you had a great deal of affection for Peter Abramsky?*
MCGOWAN: *He was a sick man, even then. He had a yellow silk handkerchief and he kept pressing it to his mouth like he was trying to keep his life from pouring out. The 21 Club was his favorite restaurant. He'd been exiled from*

Berlin in the thirties, and places like that, cozy and expensive, made him feel nostalgic for home.

A.M.: *He'd been around some.*

MCGOWAN: *Theater, films, radio. The kind of mix that's getting rarer. Young & Rubicam hired him because they wanted someone who could do it all. He was Jack Benny's producer, of course.* Song Parade *was his idea for Chesterfield. Then the network hired him away, partly for that same kind of versatility, only now he was looking for something much more serious. What people forget is that Mr. Abramsky was a great visionary, a great innovator. Half of what we do on TV came out of the ten or eleven brainstorms he had every hour. Unlike a lot of radio people, he grasped the potential of television very quickly.*

A.M.: *You talk about vision.*

MCGOWAN: *Mr. Abramsky was the last person in television who could speak of an audience's soul and mean it.*

A.M.: *Some would claim that can be said about you.*

MCGOWAN: *(Laughs.)*

A.M.: *Tell us about the early days, when the two of you first thought up the idea of the show.*

MCGOWAN: *There's not much to tell. Lots to tell, but it came slowly at first, in drops. As I said, we went to 21 that first night and he let me do all the talking. I told him about Chicago, the good and the bad. I explained that I thought nighttime television would always be trivial escapist fare. You know. The baggy-pants guys, the seltzer bottle, the pie in the kisser. People coming home exhausted after work and what they wanted was a circus. Mornings, that's different. Morning you can do something to educate people, elevate them, if you do it right.*

A.M.: *I have wax in my ears. Did you say elevate?*

MCGOWAN: *You have to remember how revolutionary a concept this was. Nothing was on in the morning before that. Nothing, not even cartoons. Heck, not even test patterns. Some stations played music and people would turn it on like they played the radio, but if you looked at the screen all you would see there was a cold gray blank.*

A.M.: *Did he talk specifics that first night?*

MCGOWAN: *A few. He originally wanted to call it* The Rise and Shine Review, *which was his one bad idea. He wanted it to be mostly heard, not seen, so we could mimic radio and steal its audience. Like the first cup of coffee in the morning—a habit, once started, it would be hard to break. Other than that, he could be infuriatingly vague. When reporters asked him what the new program would be like, he'd make that contented cat grin and say in his best Von Stroheim accent "a kaleidoscopic phantasmagoria," just to watch them gape . . . He had a lot of trouble convincing the affiliates to start operation that early. His brilliant idea—and this sold the network—was letting the local stations insert their own five minutes of news, sell ads around it . . . He was pretty modest, by the way. At Christmas he sent all his friends a book called* What I Know About Television, *and it was entirely blank. But he was on solid ground with the program. I remember him saying it should be a coverage program that would tell early risers all kinds of things they should know as they faced the day. He was fond of saying a man's conversation is our only clue to his soul—that interviews would be a big part of what we did.*

A.M.: *And so Abramsky. Excuse me.* Mister *Abramsky had the details already planned?*

MCGOWAN: *Not that first night, no, I don't think so. What he had was the end of the program. That's the way he always worked. Backwards. He could see the end quite clearly.*

A.M.: *Which was?*

MCGOWAN: *Me signing off. Me sitting alone in front of the camera, signing off with a closing line that would become my signature. He was very clear on this. A lot of people in the industry thought I was nothing more than a glorified disc jockey, and he knew they'd require convincing. I needed something memorable to go out with, the way all the big-time announcers did. Lowell Thomas.* So long until tomorrow. *H. V. Kaltenborn and what he does. Murrow's* Good night and good luck. *Mr. Abramsky was giving me twenty-four hours to come up with it and we would develop the show from there.*

McGowan enjoyed telling intimates the story of what happened next. He went back to the Waldorf in the company of a writer named Bud Schlossberg who had been assigned to him as a combination watchdog–publicity man–factotum. Well past midnight the two of them sat in facing chairs in the small cramped box of his hotel room, McGowan trying out one sign-off after the other, gauging how they registered by the expression on Schlossberg's face.

"They were ludicrous, most of them," Schlossberg recalls. "We were drinking scotch—at least I was, and maybe that made them seem even crazier. But Alec was sweating, there was no doubt about that. He may have passed the audition all right, but this was much tougher. Twenty-four hours and the clock was ticking."

McGowan was obviously very concerned to establish just the right coda for what he wanted to do, something that came naturally enough to him that he could say it from the heart. But all this was nebulous and he couldn't put it into words. None of the ideas were usable. There were folksy ones like *Great day to you!* or *See you soon, hear?* Old union tags they decided were far too pinkish: *Take it easy but take it! Fight the good fight, brothers!* Ironic ones floated out just to be rid of them: *Hail and farewell! Don't give up the ship!* The one they liked best, but realized was still inadequate, was: *Go easy with the day.* Or even, in desperation: *Goodbye.* None of them worked; if anything, each seemed more contrived than the last.

An exhausted, brain-dead Schlossberg quit around two. At three, McGowan called for room service and tried a new round of sign-offs on the startled bellboy. He tried sleeping after that, but the adrenaline must have been pumping, because he was up, showered, and dressed well before dawn. He went down to the lobby, bought a morning paper, stuck it under his arm, went out to Forty-ninth Street, and sucked in a deep breath of that metallic, potent, exhilarating Manhattan air.

What happens next—and he was never shy about painting it as such—is the defining moment of his career. He looks to the right, looks to the left, shrugs, starts walking crosstown, his stride taking him at a pace that's double any of the other pedestrians who are up and around. Hookers, panhandlers, derelicts, cops. These are the ones he walks with, and it's not until Madison Avenue that he starts seeing ordinary people, men and women going grim-faced to work. He walks to get to know a place, soaking in its sights, sounds, and smells, but for serious thinking he favors another mode of travel, and without really making a conscious decision, compelled now by instinct, he walks down Fifth Avenue to Thirty-third Street, then cuts west past Gimbel's toward Pennsylvania Station.

In 1950, Penn Station still rose proud above the street, a domed, expansive temple of great slanting shadows and crepuscular shafts of light. At eight it's crowded with commuters—with men in fedoras and topcoats carrying briefcases; with women in high heels and long sheath dresses, swinging their pocketbooks like machetes to clear a way. Within the mass of them are several discernible streams, the broadest moving toward the subway stations, the smaller channeling toward the escalators that lead up to the street.

McGowan walks against the grain toward the ticket counter, but here the stream is too thick to go further, and he finds a concrete pillar, puts himself on the upstream side, leans there with his arms crossed watching the parade of humanity that sweeps past.

He plays a game with this. He picks out the grimmest, most serious faces, sometimes from the men, sometimes from the women. He catches their eye and smiles. If they smile back, he gives himself a point. If they don't, he subtracts a point. In five minutes, no longer, he reaches a hundred, laughs out loud, then pushes through a gap in the stream to the nearest ticket booth and the grouchy, cigar-chomping man who sits there with his ear cocked to the little window.

"Round-trip ticket to the farthest place you go."

"This is the Long Island Rail Road, pal. You want far, try the Santa Fe."

"I've got to be back in town by six."

The man reaches behind him for a ticket, wets his finger, slides it across the tray, pulls in McGowan's money. "Eight fifty-seven, track number twelve."

There's no one else on the train except the conductor. The straw seats are still warm from the commuters who rode in on them, and there are newspapers folded over the backs like improvised doilies. McGowan, in telling this, would always pause here, explaining how alone he felt, there in the railroad tunnel deep beneath the city. Whether he sensed it then or whether it colored his memory in retrospect, it was clear that this would very likely be the last chance he would ever have to be alone like this, alone as in forgotten, overlooked, neglected, and he found this exhilarating. Almost immediately, even before the train emerged into daylight on the other side of the East River, he knew he had done a smart thing—that somewhere between the beginning of this journey and the end an answer would be waiting for him, the slogan he needed to define himself, launch his new career.

This was the era when conductors still called out the stations, and even though McGowan is the only one in the coach the conductor still makes a point of coming to the door and shouting each time the train stops. *Val*ley Stream! *West* Hempstead! *Am*ityville! *Bab*ylon! Exaggerating the first syllable, drawing it out like a yodeler with a Brooklyn accent, leaning far out the door to scan the platform, waving to the engineer to go ahead.

McGowan sits with his face close to the window, noting the look-alike houses with their patches of brown lawn, the waiting lines of traffic beyond the striped crossing gates, the kids on their balloon-tubed bicycles waving as the train passes—noting these, but hardly considering them. The motion of the train is what occupies him most—the slight back and forth wobble noticeable even on the straightaways, the added torque when the train leans into a curve, the perfect, incremental way the train slows, stops, and starts. This brings it all back to him, the function trains had played in his life until then. How they were his escape, his university, his (in his own favorite simile) *Niña, Pinta,* and *Santa María.*

Everyone who came into contact with him soon learned of his passion for trains. The only thing in his North Shore mansion that wasn't rented was his model train layout (027 gauge, Lionel mostly, some imports), and if you weren't among the privileged few who got to see this, then you were likely to hear the joke he enjoyed bringing out on any and all occasions. "Of course I became interested in trains," he would say, bringing up his eyebrow just so. "You're born on the wrong side of the tracks, you get adept at dodging the locomotives."

Only a few friends knew how deep this went. He had left his hometown of Springfield, left it for good, on the evening of September 11, 1941—the Mohawk Express for Albany on the tracks of the old Boston & Maine. Pearl Harbor was three months away, but already men were being drafted, and he wanted to enlist in a city where he could get a fresh start. No one was at the station to see him off, which wasn't surprising since he hadn't told anyone he was leaving—hadn't, until that afternoon, known it himself. He threw his cardboard valise in the overhead rack, settled down against the window with a beer he had bought at the canteen, stared out at the Connecticut, which shone in oily black ripples against the darker ribbon of the autumn sky. West of the river were the Berkshires, then the thick obscurity of night, and then somewhere east of Albany, as he stared intently at the somber reflection of his own defeated face, his youth came to an end, discarded like it was a hot cinder tossed from the tracks to go hissing out onto the dusty pile of cinders that lay there from earlier heartbreaks on earlier trains.

Springfield had broken his heart. A girl there. Leaving, he felt a despair so deep and essential the weight must have seemed molten, forming at the bottom a grim kind of exhilaration—that he could take even this pain in and not be shattered. Yes, for all his pluck, his vivacity and passion, he had lost the girl, which for him—and not just temporarily—meant losing everything. Yes, he was running away from home, the home he had outgrown spiritually so long ago that staying on had nearly crushed him. Yes, he was going off to be a soldier in a war where millions of young men would die.

But he was not without resources of his own—this is what he discovered on that first short train ride to the west. Though he couldn't put it in words (though it's a hard quality for a biographer to judge), he was drawing strength from what was undoubtedly the most unusual trait in his entire character: that at twenty-three, just barely a man in the world's estimation, he was armored with the kind of world-weary wisdom known to seventy-year-olds. He knew, that is, how fleeting life is, giving you only one brief chance, and knew there was still time to do something about this, not bitterly rue never having acted. Okay, his heart had been smashed—how could he have avoided that, considering who he had fallen in love with?—and yet he knew on some level that it was supposed to be smashed, that he was over with that now, and, like a suicide who has botched it, he still had another chance at life, never mind he would always be crippled by powder burns, knife thrusts, scars.

"*Patch*ogue!" the conductor calls, recalling him to the present. The doors open and close on the quick scent of burning leaves. A vendor staggers to the door under a huge pile of string-tied magazines, throws them out toward the platform to a newsboy who staggers in catching them, almost falls. "Board!" the conductor shouts. The train moves on.

That first night he spent near the Hudson in a flophouse filled with tubercular old men who tried fondling him under his one thin blanket. Once morning came, he climbed down to the river, did his best to clean up by splashing water over his face and hair, then walked past the malt-reeking breweries to the recruiting office on Parnell Avenue. After basic training in Georgia (and high marks on the IQ test), he was assigned to Officer Candidate School at the Aberdeen Proving Grounds in Maryland. This was smart of the army, smart of him—in the rough and hazy conception of himself that was forming, coming out of the war as an officer was an integral part.

Most of the graduates were headed for ordnance, but whether through the luck of the draw or because he had somehow run afoul of one of the commanding officers, McGowan was assigned to what was generally considered one of the worst jobs in the entire army: graves registration. But even here there was another dark joke to be played. In early 1942, GIs weren't dying anywhere, at least not in any numbers, and it was decided to send him, not overseas, but on a different mission entirely.

In the panic attendant upon Pearl Harbor, in the very real fear of Hitler's unstoppable troops, the civil defense authorities in Washington began planning for an invasion that didn't seem farfetched but a serious and imminent danger. One of the things that occurred to them was that there would very likely be immense civilian casualties, and that planning had to be done to insure there would be mass graves available when and if this happened. Among the officers assigned to finding proper sites for these was the newly minted Second Lieutenant Alec McGowan. By the summer of 1942, the first invasion panic had subsided, but soldiers soon began being killed in the Pacific and North Africa, and the decision was made that, unlike in World War One, bodies would be shipped home for stateside burial. This changed his job only slightly—to search out the proper sites, talk to local authorities, draw up maps and file reports—and even toward the end of the war it remained largely the same: finding the proper locations for the immense veterans' cemeteries whose creation was part of the GI Bill of Rights.

"I was good at it," he would tell Barbara Jay and the other writers and directors who made up his circle of friends. He wouldn't say this in a boastful way but a marveling one. "They pretty much left me to my own devices. You'd call ahead to alert the local civil defense people you were coming. What you were looking for was an old farm near town that had gone bust during the Depression but still had lots of acreage. You'd go out and examine it, talk price with the farmer, remind them of their patriotic duty, even threaten eminent domain if they got greedy. Views, too—you always tried picking places that had nice views. Shade trees, views, drainage, no clay. At night I'd draw up reports, send them in, and next day I was up early on my way somewhere different."

As conscientious as he tried to be, it was obvious no one was bothering to read his reports; decisions about cemeteries were being made by mayors, and chambers of commerce, and local congressmen, men who considered what kind of money mourners could bring in after the war. McGowan was never one to become bitter over hard political facts; if that's how things worked, fine. But at the same time, it soon became apparent that in the workings of the army's huge bureaucracy this particular second lieutenant had been almost totally forgotten—that he could pretty much do what he wanted with the war and no one would care.

Faced with this kind of freedom, many men would have turned themselves in, asked for reassignment, preferring anything than to be left alone and uncertain. Others would have found a comfortable refuge somewhere, sent in faked reports, lived it up. McGowan was not this kind of man. He continued with what he was doing, acting as if his reports and surveys were still an important contribution to the war effort. He spoke with the mayors, the retired colonels, the Red Cross ladies, the ministers, rabbis, and priests. He bargained with farmers. He took soil samples, climbed hills to appraise the scenery. He traveled to every state in the union (except Massachusetts—he took long detours to avoid Massachusetts), and in doing so, learned what he had to learn, impressed the country on his bones, printed it on his muscles, engraved it across his heart.

To what purpose? Apparently at this stage he wasn't yet sure. He had seen enough of the country on that first sweep across that its sense was starting to come to him, acting as a stimulant on an ambition that was sizable enough already. He was one of those men who, having known great hurt in childhood, and possessed of a compensatory energy and drive, find their ambition takes on a continental kind of scope and they want to find a way to seize America whole. In another century these had been the railroad builders, the robber barons, the industrialists—and yet McGowan wasn't any of these things, sensed that they and their type were old-fashioned and done with now and the time was ripe for a different kind of dream altogether. What kind? That's what he would discover, thanks to those open-ended orders, the magic pass that would take him anywhere. Just because he had no idea what form his ambition would eventually take he sensed the force of it all the more intensely; there were times, riding trains not very different from this one (out to the east now, rolling along Long Island's lower flank, the tracks high enough that he can make out the whitecapped sea), when he felt that, given even the slightest hint of what destiny had in store for him, he could reach through the smudged window glass to the blurred landscape and make it his.

He traveled in the mornings because this was the only time the crowded wartime trains had any room. His pass was of such low priority any officer or enlisted man with more urgent orders could bump him from his seat right back out to the platform. The earlier a train left town, the better his chances of remaining on it to his destination, and so even when he had stayed up late, he forced himself from the barracks or hotel room or the YMCA, thumbed a ride to the station, waited there in the heavy, compacted mist for the distant headlight to pierce it, yellowing it apart just enough to admit the locomotive in all its black indisputability, his ticket to the future, the next installment of the crash course in that unknown something he meant to be.

This is how he learned about morning. In the South the heat would be waiting when he stepped off the train, making it seem like a smothering muslin blanket had been draped over the tracks, and the only cool spots were where the oaks and magnolia held it up higher, so there was air. He knew cold mornings, too, times in the Dakotas where the wind that came with sunrise was so intense you couldn't walk straight down a block but had to detour into one store and then the next, warming up by the woodstove before getting up the courage for another dash outdoors. He knew about mornings in the Rockies, the eastern edge where the sea of the prairies broke apart into rock— knew how the sun brought it all to color, the even brown of the flatland being lifted and shined, chopped into walls, cubes, and pyramids, the vertical thrust of them sandblasted all to gold. Mornings in cities, the medium-sized ones that were the country's heart: Knoxville or Syracuse, Bangor or Topeka, Stockton, Des Moines, Charlotte—how each factory or warehouse or garage would accept color in a way that was oddly intimate and endearing, so you didn't have to see the sunrise there at all but could watch the morning move from the pavement toward the rooftop, brick by blushing brick.

He learned about the predawn hour that was hardly morning at all, a thinning in the blackness you had to sense with your instinct, your hope, because there was nothing visible to the eye alone. The morning that lay just past this edge—not first light but the first suggestion of light. The gray that came after this, the half-hour when nothing stirred, not even in the busiest city—the hopeless four-o'clock hour, nurses told him, when most people died. And sunrise, of course. The classic yellow, the startling red, the cliché gold, the make-believe purple or pink. Sunshine in a thousand different variations, nowhere the same, seen so often, from so many vantage points, that in some moods it didn't feel like he was riding trains at all but acting as the advance crest of the sun's leading rays, its emissary, Mr. Alec Sunshine, coloring the landscape with his thoughtful, miss-nothing gaze.

Full morning, morning shared and celebrated—he knew this, too. Breakfast in buffet cars or station cafeterias or trackside cafes or river-front dives. The day walled off a bit, the future put on hold by that most pungent and characteristic of American aromas: bacon, eggs, and coffee, and how this could shine like another sunrise, especially on cold dark mornings when the sun wouldn't come. It was often his only meal until nighttime, and so he always made a ceremony of it, taking his time, flirting with the waitresses, regarding those who sat on the next stool with a grave regard, nodding seriously at everything they said.

"How are you, General?" they would begin. "How's the war going, huh?"

Welders coming off the night shift, armament workers going in. Farmers up for hours, taking their first break, talking crop prices and weather. Salesmen traveling the back roads even during wartime, ever lonely, ever ready with their jokes. Truck drivers with hard-luck stories about why they weren't in the army, how they envied him, the way girls went nuts over uniforms. Conductors, ticket takers, engineers, swiveling around to constantly check the tracks behind them, as if afraid they'd be stolen. Soldiers' wives crying over their far-too-early beers. He liked especially to watch people as they first came in—see them dust the snow off their hats or wipe the sweat off their foreheads, demonstrate by their posture and expression what the weather was, how they regarded it, whether they were the kind to be braced up by it or beaten down. In the morning they talked their heads off, filled his ear, unloaded. Meet the same men in the same cafes at night and no one said anything, each sat wrapped in what the day had done to them, with no energy left at all.

These cafes were his graduate school, and he was a serious and attentive student. The first lesson he learned was the gift of small talk—of being able to talk to anyone about anything for thirty minutes at a stretch. The second was a voice. Unconsciously he mimicked the inflection of everyone he talked with, to the point where his voice became a blend of accents. (Listening to him on television, people would always be convinced he was from their own part of the country.) The third lesson is harder to explain, but it came from the distances he was so aware of, the enormous, umbrella kind of quiet that seemed, in these first morning hours, to shelter even the cities, making them hardly more than inconsequential specks on the vast and patient green land. He learned to put this kind of quiet, this recognition of space and solitude and emptiness, in his own manner—his look, his eyes, his voice—or rather it inserted itself there without his being aware the process was going on. He always took his time before responding, then let his eyes do much of the answering on their own; later, when people said something trivial on camera, the merest commonplace, it would, by the time he responded, seem to have grown in importance to the very edge of profundity via a trick many critics commented on and yet none could fully account for. "Space comes first," he once said in advising a younger colleague on interviewing technique. "Pretend the words are coming to you over mountains, over desert or plains, and you have to squint with your ears to make them out."

These were his mornings, small talk and travel. Afternoons would be busy with the requirements of graves registration, and then there was often still time to visit the local radio station, pay a kind of courtesy call from one professional to another—at least that's the way he saw it. To those working at the stations it was something a little more manipulative and forced.

"Sure, I remember him," says Alan Gilum, station manager at the old KSTP radio station in St. Paul, Minnesota, on the early rungs of a career that would later see him running the network affiliate in the Twin Cities. "He came in one afternoon looking like General Patton, his uniform so tailored and crisp. Said he just wanted to meet us, look around. Kissing ass was more like it. He was on his way around the country, kissing ass with everyone in the business he could find, getting ready for the end of the war when he would need a job. Networking we call it now. You couldn't help liking him, even though he tried too hard. We let him take a turn at the mike. This great big RCA saltshaker and he worked it close to his lips like a crooner. His voice was perfect for radio, of course. I noticed he made sure everyone in the station, right down to the secretaries, learned his name. That night I ran into him waltzing down Main Street, a blonde on one arm, a redhead on the other."

It was at one of these stations, a little mom-and-pop operation in Lafayette, Indiana, that McGowan first heard the word *television* pronounced, not like something futuristic out of Buck Rogers, but as a force that had to be considered, one that would be there the moment the war ended. He wrote it down, the single word. He wrote it down on a stray piece of paper, tucked it away in his uniform pocket, and thought no more about it.

As the radio people who ran into him all attest, his nights were given over to the pursuit of what he termed, without irony, "feminine companionship." This would not have been difficult to find—for the most part, feminine companions always found him. In the war years, for a handsome young officer given the run of the country, available women were everywhere. Waiting in line at movie theaters. Sitting opposite him on trains, or coming up to him in stations to ask a pretend question. At USO canteens or even the kind of church dinners officers were always being invited to by motherly types who saw it as their duty to introduce them to nice wholesome American girls. Many of these were hardly out of their teens, looking for a good time pure and simple, but many were a few years older, young wives whose husbands were overseas and who couldn't face the loneliness a single night more.

Several factors seemed to be at work here, driving him on. His heart had been badly burned in Springfield, and he wanted to smother this under the sheer weight of fucking. He was flattered to be the focus of so much attention—to be wanted so openly, honestly, directly. And astonishment played a part. Astonishment at how beautiful American women were turning out to be, a second landscape to superimpose over the terrain, one that was composed of curious eyes, perfect complexions, supple bodies, cheeks and lips so fresh they needed no makeup, hair done peekaboo style over the forehead, or cut short and boyish along the neck.

That many of these women had husbands fighting in Europe or the South Pacific occurred to him, but it didn't stop him or even slow him down. If there was guilt, the unwritten law was that it would be dealt with later, time being too short to worry about that now. Everything was intense, everything was temporary—no one needed to spell that out. At night you fed each other lies like you fed each other cigarettes or whiskey, neither caring if they were true, and in the morning you tried to deal with the hangover, the burnt heavy feeling in the back of your throat. He would wake up in the furnished room or the farmhouse or the hotel and often the woman would already be up and getting dressed, putting back on the life she had for one night abandoned. It was his favorite moment, more compelling by far than that nighttime seduction. What was the eroticism of undressing a woman compared to the eroticism of watching her get dressed? He could wax eloquent on this. Being able to see only her hair at first, and then only because it was near enough to a mirror to catch what light chevroned in through the blinds. Black hair this time, detached silky strips of night that had unaccountably survived the dawn, and which were now being reassembled by a comb that went up and down with a speed and steadiness that seemed beyond what a girl's hand could do alone. How the light would come in and give the hair more shape, draw it inward, down her back, then spread it out again just above the curved line where her nakedness merged with the fabric of the chair. He favored small women then, their shoulders never very wide, and at his touch they bunched and shivered so as to all but disappear, and yet below them her back would be broad and full, a woman's, ending in the matching swellings, inward and out, of her slender waist and high white buttocks.

Far more gently than he was capable of himself, she would lean forward, lift and pull her panties up her legs. The fabric made a taut line across the small of her back, separated the whiteness above from the new darkness below. Then she (the Laura, the Margaret, the Betty) would take her bra from the little dressing table formed by her knees, bring it with a grave gesture behind her back, turning her arms in, fastening it, pulling the fabric down over her nipples, then, reaching again, shimmy her slip down over her head, smoothing it with the loving, intricate gestures of a sculptress putting the final polish to her own perfect form.

He loved watching them dress, remembered as a boy wishing he could be invisible to witness women doing just this, act as the collaborator in their beauty, their secret audience. Was a beautiful woman beautiful with no one watching? Yes. Invisible, as good as, he had his proof.

"You're funny," they would say, glancing around now, smiling shyly. "So serious, and me getting ready."

"There's time."

"Easy for you to say. I'm a working girl, Lieutenant Alec. None for the road. But you take care of yourself, hear?"

In the end the lesson he took away from those years wasn't erotic at all. What he learned (and explained frequently to friends) was how lonely these women inevitably were, an emptiness that seemed to have nothing to do with the fact that their men were away; it predated that, as if they were the inheritors of a plague of loneliness that had fallen over the country God knew when and possessed it to that day. What accounted for this? The fact so many were descended from women who had been dragged west against their will? The fact they were surrounded too often by men who did everything for them except like them? The exhaustion from the Depression? Hollywood, with its cheap and empty dreams? The sense the country was moving, always moving, only now with a new and dangerous speed, and they were all in danger of being left behind? The foreshadowing of what would come when the war ended, the riches, and how all that, as much as they longed for it, would quickly turn to ashes in their hands?

Wherever it came from, it was there, and for that matter it was present in most of the men he met, though in them it was hidden deep in swagger and bluff. For four years solid he traveled the country planning where these women's husbands would one day be buried, visiting radio stations in the afternoon as a way of taking care of what he still thought of as his calling, even while he grew into the sense that it was this loneliness where his true vocation would reside, trying to assuage it, and not just by fucking it out of existence one isolated woman at a time.

This is almost certainly why, faced with the crucial moment, he had decided to board that train for the ride out to Long Island—to put himself back in contact with what he had taken from those years. The train goes slower now on older, less traveled track. He paces the aisle, stands by the door and stretches, strikes up a conversation with the conductor, disembarks briefly as the train coasts to its last, easternmost stop. "*Mon*tauk!" the conductor calls, even though McGowan is the only person in the car. It will be there for ten minutes before starting on the long ride back to the city—time enough for McGowan to walk along the platform, smell the salt air, hug himself in the chilly mist, glance around looking for the famous lighthouse, the continent's eastern tip, then, not seeing it in the roll of bluffs, contenting himself with patting the MONTAUK sign hanging from the station's roof. He buys a Hershey bar, then gets back aboard, this time sitting on the left side of the train, the window that will command the best view of the sun as it crosses the horizon and begins to set.

Create aura here that in some measure lasts the entire biography. End chapter with him at his most immaculate and appealing. Who the Gods would destroy, etc. Get a coda going/rhythm of memories/bass note similar to what he himself must have sensed as he leaned against the window staring out.

Mornings in Vermont, the soft light from barns. Mornings in Eastport, Maine, walking out to the headland, the shingle of beach, stopping by a little striped stick where, when the dawn touched it, you became the first American the sun shone on that day. Mornings in Portsmouth, going down to the docks, knowing that the dives where the fishermen waited out the weather had the best coffee, the freshest doughnuts and rolls. Mornings in Atlantic City, the hotels turned into hospitals, expressionless soldiers wrapped in blankets pushed along the boardwalk by smiling nurses in sweaters, the wheelchairs looming against the flat gray ocean. A morning in Charleston watching a black woman suckle her baby in a park by the harbor, oblivious to everything except each other, the woman in a cheap cotton dress, shifting position so the sun, in rising higher, would stay warm on her baby's head. Mornings in Virginia, the Blue Ridge, missing a train and hitching a ride with an old farmer who had fought in the last battle of the Civil War, rolling up his sleeve to the pucker mark a bullet had left in his arm. A winter morning in Pittsburgh, where he watched from the distance a woman walk out onto a pier behind a warehouse, stare down into the mercurous water, press her arms rigid to her sides, jump in.

Mornings in Lubbock, Texas, a silver field of B-17s, the clean, light smell of their oil. Mornings in Colorado, the air cinnamon-colored and sweet, forest fires burning everywhere, no men to fight them. Morning at the First Brick House Built Between the Mississippi and the Rockies, the kind of tourist attraction his irony could never pass up (the Exact Midway Point Between the Equator and the North Pole, the Desert of Maine, the Tree in Provo the Brakemen Watered That Grows out of Rock)—locked and boarded for the duration, putting his head to the window, seeing a play of light and shadow that could only be ghosts. Mornings in New Orleans, sipping coffee near the cotton mart, joking with the whores. Mornings in Chicago, the sun off the lake climbing the buildings along North Michigan, slabbing them with a bright lemon wash.

Mornings along the high line in Montana, the towns that were the most forgotten and forlorn of all he had visited. Mornings in the Idaho wheat fields, the variegated rusts and coppers and fawns, the wind like a finger, an invisible thumb, digging deep into a thick auburn plush. Mornings at the Kaiser shipyards on the Columbia, the cranes and derricks hoisting the sun by brute force. Mornings in San Diego, stepping over the drunken soldiers who lay curled on the pavement clutching each other in the chill. A morning in Salinas when he came upon a hobo camp near the tracks, bums in the old style roasting spuds over a fire of kerosene-soaked tires, kindly, polite, addled by Sterno, most of them unaware there was a war on at all. A morning in Detroit when the race riots errupted, watching, as in an evil slapstick, a mob of whites armed with baseball bats chasing a black kid around a corner, reappearing seconds later, chased by a bigger mob of blacks armed with tire irons. A morning in Baltimore when, by some trick of light, some weakness of memory, he woke up beside a woman he thought was Lee. Mornings in Washington State, the spit of land beyond Grays Harbor, the outermost beach, or at least that's what he imagined, standing there facing west, taking a grave and solemn satisfaction in having the entire continent at his back.

He remembers all these, or at least the compacted, seamless blend of all these, as he sits against the window of the train speeding back toward New York, sensing the word or words he's been reaching for as his sign-off are now very close. Ahead of him the sun goes down in a thin wash of pinkish cobalt, and yet even here it mimics morning, so there is nothing in the scene to wrench him from his mood. There comes a stretch where the neat little houses give way to factories and the tracks become surrounded by rough black walls of cinder and ash topped by enormous billboards, but even here the grade rises enough that he can make out the clean, hard, indisputable line of skyscrapers

NORTH RICHLAND HILLS PUBLIC LIBRARY

in the distance dead ahead. His first Manhattan sunset—the finest sunset in the world—and yet to him, lost in this mood, it only looks like another dawn, the yellow window squares appearing against the sky in jigsaw flashings that make it seem as if morning is assembling itself piece by golden piece.

This is his real arrival in New York, these last few moments before the train plunges into the tunnel and deposits him on the same concrete platform he had left eight hours before. All the distance there ever was in him peaks in an overwhelming sense of certainty, though the slogan itself doesn't come until the very last moment, when he faces an expectant Abramsky in the blazing camera lights for his second, more stringent test. And then he has it, the gesture and word that will soon become so familiar a part of the new landscape he's creating, imitated by comics and twelve-year-olds and wise-guy teenagers, trotted out by joking salesmen, admonishing parents, cynical fraternity men, folksy politicians, none of them bringing it off with quite the right panache, since none of them has the miles he had, the lonely sixth sense of who is watching.

The right hand upraised from the elbow, palm outward, fingers together, like a cop stopping traffic, a witness swearing an oath, a president at his inauguration, a chief at a powwow. Eyes on the camera trying to see into the soul of whoever is watching, the simple word said a full beat after the hand goes up, said quietly so the viewer has to lean in to hear . . . the unimpeachable hand, the soft voice, the eyes staring out through miraculously clear glasses, the single word that comes as a pledge, a promise, a benediction, all wrapped up in a sound so deep and solid it seems to emanate from the upraised hand itself.

Truth.

NORTH RICHLAND HILLS PUBLIC LIBRARY

Two

Morning in late October. Sun up slow, right smack into clouds. Morning of gray rain, slick driving, jaywalking kids. Morning when the leaves came down without any wind, wearily surrendering, putting up no fight. An institutional kind of morning. Morning of cracked Styrofoam cups, rush-hour traffic, the drab morning news. Morning fit for remorse and apprehension. Morning of what promised to be the hardest, blackest, most miserable day of my life.

There's nothing like self-pity to set you up first thing. I'd had forty-six years' worth heaped on me, or, in a fraction that seemed stenciled on my forehead, forty-six fifty-seconds of my life. That was the primary reason I'd left home so early—I didn't want to inflict my misery on Kim or the kids.

I'd made myself some coffee, left a note about the furnace man coming, hesitated, procrastinated, then grabbed the only prop I could think of to make the trip easier, or at least the return part of the trip: a blanket, a soft one, the kind you would use to swaddle a baby. Just what a would-be biographer needs for protection, I decided, taking a grim satisfaction in the way it draped over the seat—fuzzy irony, fuzzy comfort, fuzzy warmth.

It's a three-hour drive but seems much longer. You can't get anywhere fast in Massachusetts. We've got such an inflated sense of ourselves it infects the distance, so trying to make time through the western part of the state is like trying to take a shortcut through Texas. For the first half-hour I listened to public radio from Amherst, but once I got to the turnpike the Hartford stations crowded it out and it was either listen to the garbage or try to feather in on the station and see what Terri was up to on her show.

I felt bad about this—I'd vowed not to listen during what I still pretended was my sabbatical—but once I turned to it I became curious to see how long the reception would last. I drove through the Berkshires, the kind of enveloping hills that can soak up a signal fast, but through some trick of the elements, maybe even the dampness, I could hear Terri clearer than I sometimes can at home. She was up to her usual— soft rock, contemporary jazz, her crazy Neapolitan songs—and the music stood out from the uniformity crowding in on its edges like a flower in the midst of weeds. That was the other reason it sounded so clear: no commercials, or damn few. We had a flower all right, a rose growing out of a desperately thin, malnourished soil.

The signal whispered its way into static behind Greylock, and the only thing I had left for company then was the hills, or the lumpy clouds that passed for them. I'd buried a lot of mistakes in those hills. A gentlemen's college I walked out on early, quitting my sophomore year to take my chances with the draft. Two brain-numbing years spent typing orders in Germany, pathetically grateful it wasn't Vietnam— and then a winter playing Thoreau in a borrowed cabin while I leached the army out of my bones. A marriage so ill conceived, so short-lived and bathetic I feel sick with shame to even think of it. A year spent pretending I was an investigative reporter for a rag pretending to be a newspaper, struggling, for a little while longer, against the notion of inheriting the family business. Mistakes, false directions, blunders—and here I was going through the hills on my way to one more.

I got off the pike below Pittsfield, detoured through a quiet corner of Connecticut and entered New York. A big sign announced a construction project for the new century, but the sign was already soggy-looking and faded, and it didn't appear as if work had ever begun. The land, the terrain, surprised me and didn't surprise me. It was more rural than I had pictured—ridges with big transmission towers, rusted farm machinery sitting in the middle of stubbled fields, the peeling, wind-tattered remains of drive-in movies. It wasn't as chic as Westchester, and it wasn't as quaint as New England; it seemed to be exactly what it was: a forgotten strip where the state could dump its most intractable problems and no one much would care.

The town itself was attractive enough, in a ramshackle Victorian way, and most of the houses were decorated for Halloween. Downtown was a triangle formed by a discount drugstore, a fast-food restaurant, and a gas station. Dominating everything, visible behind every house, was a huge industrial laundry, steam pouring out of its three black chimneys as if it were working full blast.

My mouth had gone dry and then some by this stage—I stopped in the drugstore for cough drops, then got back in and studied the directions that had come with the packet of release material sent by the state. The correctional facility was down a gated access road to the right; the geriatic and rehabilitative center was a little farther up the main road. I had thought about driving close enough to the prison to at least see it, come to terms with it, stack it up against forty-six years' worth of wondering, but found I couldn't do it now that I was so close. When the turn came I kept on straight.

This was my second surprise of the morning—how neat and well groomed it all turned out to be, and for the first few seconds I had the feeling I had entered upon the campus of an elegant small college.

Matching pillars on either side of the driveway, a lawn strewn with poplar leaves, the parking lot shaded by old pines. The building itself was a low one of weathered brick, darker and heavier-looking than it should have been at that time of morning, but otherwise respectable enough, with no bars visible on the windows. Not a college exactly, not at this point, but perhaps an exclusive kind of recovery center where a brooding Gothic quality was a vital part of the treatment.

The only spot to park was the handicapped slot, and after driving around three times I took it, deciding that if he wasn't handicapped, who was. All through the drive I had been searching for the right attitude, or at least some attitude, and I had one now. Walking up the cinder pathway, trying to look through the windows and yet not through them, I felt, of all possible things to feel, *stern*—felt as if I had brought from Massachusetts the hardest, most Puritan side of my nature, and what in hell was I going to do with that?

A guard sat at the entrance behind a grade school desk—he checked my name off on a list and waved me in deeper, into a lobby of some sort, dominated by the smell old linoleum takes on when it's been splashed with disinfectant. Toward the center stood the kind of signboard you never see anymore, with candy-white letters neatly arranged across felt.

I read each line without learning which corridor was which. I thought about going back to ask the guard, but he had his head down on the desk, as if he were taking a nap or being punished. A short way down the hall from him, blocked before by his shoulders, were three old men dressed in robes sitting on a metal bench. They looked toward me but didn't see me; they gave the impression of being lost in a dense fog, lost there together, each responsible for his own share of haze. Which one had been the murderer, which one the rapist, which the child abuser, it was impossible to say. Past them, under a porthole-sized window, was another desk similar to the guard's; another old man sat there, but this one was well-dressed and dignified-looking, like one of those gentleman volunteers you see in hospitals.

I tried the largest corridor, the one that ran off the lobby at an oblique angle toward what seemed the only pocket of activity. Halfway along it a small intense woman in a lab coat stopped me with exactly what you'd expect to pop out at you in that environment, a crisp yellow form.

"Here for a release?"

"I'm here to pick up Chet Standish. Chester Standish."

"Relationship?"

"Son."

She stopped her pen just long enough to look up at me with surprise, the beginning of interest. "Hello, Mr. Standish," she said, jabbing out her hand.

I'd been expecting this, too—first awkward moment in what promised to be hundreds. "It's Brown," I said, doing my best to smile. "Alec Brown. My mother changed our name."

Most of the interest was already gone from her eyes. "A lot of people do that," she said crisply. She scribbled something on the form. "I knew your sister from all her visits. Lindy. I gather she changed her name, too."

"Yes. Back again to Standish. She was devoted to him."

I didn't need her grimace to impress on me the obvious; if Lindy had been a hero of devotion, I had been a bum.

"It was sad, when I heard it," she said. "Bad timing, too, just when he was about to be released. He took it very hard. She didn't leave kids?"

"No kids. No."

"There's that. Wait right here."

The buzz of activity at the end of the corridor was coming into focus now. Nurses, aides, orderlies—not much different from what you would find in an ordinary hospital. You had to think about it to remember how strange it was. Men beat and harried all their lives, treated so tenderly at the end. I remembered reading about how in the old days they would revive would-be suicides in order to drag them to the gallows.

"Mr. Brown? I'm Doctor Obrioni. Let's duck in here."

A resident, judging by his age—was it some deal by which he got his education paid for, working a stint in prison? Boyish, brisk, likable. Even more likable when, once we got seated in his cubicle, he got immediately to the point.

"You're going to have your hands full with the meds. I've put the prescriptions in this envelope here. The other is the blood work, his latest EKG. He'll be due for another chest X-ray soon—secondhand smoke is bad, as you can imagine. The big problem is his prostate. It hasn't metastasized yet, but it will. I'd have thought the liver would be the most obvious spot, given his history."

He glanced down at the paperwork. "He had a major depressive episode six years ago. Shock therapy when the antidepressants didn't work. There may be some memory loss attendant upon this. Your sister's death could have thrown him back, but apparently it hasn't. There's all kinds of stress that comes with release."

"I was going to ask about that."

He leaned back in the chair, put his hands behind his neck, stared up at the ceiling. "For most of them it's a difficult experience. He's what—eighty-eight? We've found that sometimes the really old ones do better. Freedom becomes a shapeless kind of blur to them, sort of an afterlife they don't have to be too involved with. Does that make sense? I'd try not to make him nervous over little things."

I'd learned one lesson in the few minutes I'd been inside—it was impossible to talk here except in clichés. "How much time does he have left?" I asked.

"Do you want me to prevaricate like they teach us in med school or do you want the truth?"

"A year?"

"Shorter. I would say your father would be extremely fortunate if he were to make it to the spring."

You could see he was new at this—tossing off grim facts—and it was turning out to be harder than he thought. Embarrassed, he began shuffling papers, clipping them together, sliding them across the desk. "He'll be staying with you?" he asked after I had signed yet another form.

"An apartment. It's not far away. They have nurses that come in." Then, when his expression didn't change, "We have three kids at home."

"He's not dangerous."

"Vigorous kids."

"I see. Well, you'll be glad to hear he's still covered by supplemental health insurance. The state is pretty generous in this regard. We *are* talking first-degree murder, after all."

Was this meant to be funny? "Great," I said, and "That will help immensely."

There was a regular changing of the guard after that. Dr. Obrioni got up and shook my hand, then waited by the door until another man entered from the hall. Obrioni saluted him—a make-believe salute, all exaggerated and crisp—and then the newcomer and I were left alone.

At first I assumed it was another doctor—he carried a manila envelope under his arm, the kind they put X-rays in. He was short and squat, with such a happy shock of wavy black hair he made me remember pictures I'd seen of Fiorello La Guardia. His suit was solemn enough, but his tie clasp was a little orange jack-o-lantern with pop-eyes that glowed.

"I'm Charles Daigle," he said. "I'm the CEO here."

I fell for it. "CEO?"

"Chief Enemy Officer," and he laughed so hard his cheeks turned purple.

Again, was I supposed to laugh too? I was so worried about etiquette. But by now he was back to looking nothing worse than genial, and he made a dismissive gesture with his hand, as if to put the funny stuff behind us.

"What they called in the olden days the warden. I wanted to make sure I was here when Chester checked out. Do you know I used to watch him on TV when I was a kid?"

"A lot of people did."

"I've gotten to know him well in the five years I've been assigned here. We've had many long talks in my office during free choice period. Deep talks, about everything and anything. Your father has a deep perspective. That's the way I would characterize it. Deep, the depths."

He picked the folder up from the desk, fanned his face. "I'm sorry the pardon didn't come sooner. The governor intended it much earlier, but there were the usual kinds of delays. A victims' group—they scrutinize everything. I'm sorry that it took, you know, the big C for him to get out. Frankly, I see no reason, speaking as a correctional professional now, why this inmate wasn't paroled twenty-five years ago."

He was interrupted by his cell phone going off—he pulled it from his jacket pocket, mumbled something, covered the mouthpiece with his hand. "Albany calling. Here, you go out and fetch your father. I'll be along in a minute."

I must have hesitated once I reached the hall, because he followed me partway, made a little shooing motion to get me started. Before, all I had been aware of was how much everything resembled a hospital, but there was no disguising the prison part now—the hall seemed to have grown longer, darker, and colder in the few minutes I'd been away.

I was nearly to the lobby when something stopped me. At first I was puzzled by exactly what . . . I glanced around expecting to see that the warden had come up to grab my shoulder . . . then realized the touching sensation came at me from the lobby. Even then I was still confused—I thought it was a cold burst of air, an actual physical presence or force. It was only after I stood there motionless letting it have its way with me that I realized the force was a voice. Not any voice, but *the* voice, so clear, so unchanged, so unmistakable, it could have been coming from a spool played backwards off time.

The easy part to describe is the register—baritone, masculine, clear, and yet with a velvety kind of collar around the edges that kept it from sounding too machine-tooled and stentorian. The inflection kept in fairly tight check, each word dignified by complete enunciation, even the consonants, making you think of an elocution teacher who didn't take himself too seriously. A surprising flexibility in a voice so deep— the trick of going higher and faster almost like an auctioneer's voice can, but only as a kind of lyric decoration. Absolutely no accent of any kind. A radio voice, one that seemed amplified even when it wasn't. A voice, at its loudest, you could imagine convincing you to buy a refrigerator. A voice, at its gravest, that might come from God.

I took this in with what I can only describe as the historian part of me. I was fascinated, intensely fascinated, but not any more than I had been in meeting other survivors from that era. For that matter, my reaction was what almost anyone experiences in coming into the presence of a celebrity—*My lord, these people really exist after all.* What the actual words were about still escaped me—again, all I was conscious of was their signature tone. But compared to the other sounds that might emanate from a prison hospital they sounded ridiculously tame, soft even, words someone might toss up conversationally at the weather.

The voice should have affected me even more. Hearing it, I had a very clear memory of listening as a child at a time when my mother had banned actually watching him, crawling across the living room floor like a sniper, using the sofa and footrest as cover, getting close enough to the television to reach out with my air rifle and press the on-off button, then scuttling back behind the armchair to listen, consider, and brood. But this is all I felt. Recognition, curiosity, a painless flash-back. Given the setting, the situation, the voice should have been a depth charge going off inside me, and what it was really like was a fire-cracker that popped harmlessly off my forehead and fizzled out at my feet.

Brushing my hair back, rearranging my glasses, I stepped out into the lobby to find the man the voice came from.

It wasn't one of the old men on the benches, the semicomatose bookends propping up the semialert one in the middle. It had to be the one who looked like a retired businessman, the one in the suit. He stood with his hands clasped behind his back talking to an aide who held a gym bag—the aide looking at him with the kind of respect the voice deserved. I could hear distinct words now, people's names, the words *tell them* coming as a kind of steady punctuation—and the words seemed like a carpet unrolled across the linoleum, one I only had to put my feet on and it would lead me infallibly to him.

He heard me before he saw me; it was only when he turned, tilted his head, and squinted that I remembered about his myopia. My first reaction was that an enormous mistake had been made, that it couldn't be him. He was bald, the rusty kind of baldness that comes to red-heads, and a prominent semicircle of warts drew my focus instantly to his forehead. Below it his flat baby's nose seemed much larger than it did in pictures, his cheeks having lost their buoyancy and sagged. His eyes, even when he was younger, had been far too small for his face, lost in huge sockets, always appealing for help; now, with his eyebrows having thinned to the point of invisibility, the effect was even more pronounced. The ears that had once been hidden by hair flapped out like phony rubber; his lips were pressed thin, looking like those bleached sticks that come in Popsicles; his skin, once so tight and manly, was halfway to translucency and gave you the feeling one touch would make it peel. It was a face with no defenses left to it at all, the face of Chet Standish only by name, a frail, mocking assemblage of the handsome man he once was.

Again, this was all from comparing him to photos. Even when I had snuck to the television I had been too shy to ever actually look at him. And yet there was a recognition that went much deeper than the voice alone, and it came when I brought my eyes lower to assess his posture, how he stood. I was struck by an overpowering sense of recognition, the heady, dizzy reaction you get when time snaps its fingers and forty years dissolve. His suit prompted this, his gray flannel suit—expensive, classy, the lapels wider than what was currently fashionable, the pinstripe light and beautifully draped, the sleeves and cuffs fitting perfectly, even now. It was the first description of him I remember ever hearing, what a sharp dresser he was, how clothes always enhanced him, and one of the few memories I had of actually being in his presence was once on a crowded Manhattan sidewalk, taken to see him for a reason I can't remember, wanting to get close enough to touch his suit and gather between my fingers the magic that people talked about, see for myself if it was real.

This was the suit he wore now, kept in storage for forty-six years, looking new and old at the same time, as if a piece of 1954, its very texture, woof and weave, stood before me, trembling, smelling of camphor, but in its essence perfectly intact.

A long description of a moment that seemed even longer. I knew I was supposed to get control of myself, say something, and yet what could I say that wouldn't seem obvious and insincere? In the old days I could have slapped him theatrically across the face, yelled "Despicable villain!" spun on my heels, and stomped majestically away. A younger version of myself almost certainly would have cursed him, yelled bastard and asshole and son of a bitch. Either reaction would have been better than the one I was stuck with. "Hello, Chet," I said lamely, and reached out my hand.

He stuck out his hand, but at least a foot wide of mine, so for a moment he was solemnly shaking thin air.

"I don't have much," he said softly.

Taking this as his cue, the aide came over with the gym bag, handing it to me along with a pair of rubber overshoes. "You take care of yourself, Mr. S. You stay away from those wild women."

"Yes, Henry. I will certainly do that, and you do that yourself."

We were alone after that, except for the old men and the drowsy guard, but before I could say anything else, the warden came up the hall waving the manila envelope above his head like a flag.

"You can't forget this!" he said, beaming. "Lots of people frame theirs when they get home." Then, when both of us must have look confused, "It's your pardon, signed by the governor himself."

Chet took the envelope, pressed it under his arm; a second later he glanced down to make sure it was still there.

The warden had a great time with all this. He took Chet by the shoulder, rubbed his fist into his suit sleeve, all but nudged him in the ribs. "Once more before you go? You know what I mean." He closed his fists and stuck his thumbs out, wiggled them back and forth by his hips. "You dirty copper. You're not going to make me take the rap on this, hear? There's no bughouse in the world tough enough to stop me, hear that, you lousy screw!"

There was just enough resiliency left in Chet's face to make his cheeks ride up in embarrassment; he shook his head the slightest bit, then looked over at me with an appeal I didn't let myself read.

"Oh come on, Chester, one more time, will you, please, huh? No one does it like you can. You dirty copper. You lousy fink screw."

The phone rang in the warden's pocket. He answered, put his hand over the mouthpiece—"Good luck, Chester! We'll stay in touch, okay?"—and then he was hurrying back toward the dark part of the lobby, all but skipping, trying a little Cagney click of the heels that made him stumble, nearly fall.

"A good man," Chet said, when the quiet came back. He looked down at the envelope, seemed to think about it, brought it carefully across his chest, and pressed it under his other arm where it felt more secure.

Nothing to do then but leave. His walk was firm, strong even—judging by his face you would have expected him to wobble. We were over to the front desk when the guard, so sleepy-looking, stood up as if to hold the door open. A nice touch, I decided—but this is not what he did. Looking down at the desk toward a form, hardly bothering to notice us, he brought his arm up stiff like a bar and laid it crossways against Chet's chest.

"Not until noon," he said gruffly. "Two minutes yet. You wait here."

Chet did not seem surprised at this. He stopped with his chin no more than two inches above the guard's arm, so the uniform fabric pressed against his throat—he stopped there, his legs and torso going rigid, like an old soldier snapping to attention. Above this his head was motionless; he closed his eyes, shut them hard enough that new lines appeared on their corners, where you wouldn't think there was any room . . . stood there as if he had withstood a lifetime of such arms, could endure one more if he had to, making himself into a zombie, going rigid . . . and then there came a double beeping sound from the guard's watch. He brought his arm down, held the door open, grinned, grunted "And don't come back!" and slammed the door on us with a loud and triumphant snort.

Outside, even to me, the wet autumn leaves never smelled so deep and pungent and intoxicating.

I walked him to the car. My original thought had been to stroll around the grounds a bit and let him acclimatize slowly, but the only motive I was conscious of now was wanting to get him to Massachusetts as fast as possible. He had some trouble bending down into the passenger's seat, but once settled there he seemed grateful for the blanket, using it as a padded backrest to hold him straighter.

We drove past the trailer parks where the guards lived, the access road to the prison, the old Victorian mansions, the puny strip of downtown, the huge laundry with its smokestacks, and before we could be free of them the rain began falling, sending up a yellow-gray mist that made it seem we were slipping out backwards from a dream.

Chet's reaction to all this was hard to gauge. He kept his face near the window glass, but with his myopia not much could have been visible. He could have been an old man taken on a Sunday drive, pleased to be out and about, though not seeing anything worthy of comment. He still clutched the envelope with the pardon—I noticed that much. He turned and looked at me once when I was making a turn, then quickly looked away when I caught him staring.

That left me my own reaction to try and figure out. If he didn't want to talk, that was fine with me, since my mind was racing. The good news was that we had gotten through the first impossible moments. If he had called me son, made any claim on affection, I would have walked out on him then and there; I had promised myself that during the drive over, and it was a promise I would have had no trouble keeping. I don't feel anything toward you, Chet, is what I could have said now. I don't feel hurt and I don't feel sadness and I sure as hell don't feel anger, though it would probably be better for all of us if I did.

You can think things so intensely they come out anyway, never mind words. We had ten miles left to the state line and I was looking for the next turn when he said something that surprised me, all but made me stop.

"I'm sorry," he said.

In his clear announcer's voice it sounded like he was apologizing for a technical glitch—which I suppose in a way he was. But for the briefest of moments I thought he was making the apology we both knew would be horribly inadequate and yet needed to be said—a moment, and then he put some softness in his tone, enough to let me know he felt embarrassed.

"I have to go."

I found a gas station on the far side of the highway, parked, went in to ask the attendant for the key. Chet seemed strong enough to get there on his own, but I pulled up right close to the curb. He was inside for at least ten minutes. On the way back he bumped into a trash can, and I could hear him apologize to it, gravely beg its pardon.

"Where's the boy who checks the oil?" he asked when I opened the door.

"They don't use them anymore. You pump gas yourself, check your own oil. If you want, you can wash your own windshield. You put air in the tires it costs you money."

He nodded a little too vigorously, as if he wanted to assure me he knew all about this. "I saw a poster in there," he said. "About the new century and how the oil company is going to make it wonderful. They're wrong, you know."

It was the first sign of animation I'd seen in him. "About making it wonderful?"

He shook his head. "About the new century. Everyone thinks it starts this year, 2000, when it really begins next year, in 2001. You see, the first year with Christ they didn't call zero, did they?"

"Yes, I've heard that."

"And it doesn't start on New Year's Day, either. A popular misconception. There were sixty-seven days lost when the Gregorian calendar was adopted. The new millennium doesn't really begin until March."

"Good point," I said, and "March when?"

His nose popped out from the pudding of his face. "The seventeenth. I'm looking forward to it with a great deal of anticipation."

Neither one of us said much after that. Chet, like every old-time announcer I ever met, cleared his throat a lot—it was like listening to a finely tuned engine trying to rid itself of sand. I took a more northerly route this time, hoping to save some mileage. The low hills steepened, then spread apart into a little valley that opened into Massachusetts. "State line," I said, pointing to the sign, and while he squinted, I don't think he saw anything. Fifty years ago McGowan had snapped his fingers and Chet had rushed off to join him in Manhattan, and now here he was going home to Massachusetts again, his New York adventure at an end. What could he have been feeling? Even for me, having gotten all this at secondhand, the irony was overpowering.

"I'm sorry," he said a few minutes later, just when I thought he had fallen asleep.

"Can you hold on for ten minutes? There's an exit coming up."

"Oh sure," he said, but I could see him start clenching and unclenching his fists.

The place we stopped at was a fifties diner called Glory Jean's. An Elvis poster hung over the door, plastic T-Birds dangled above the counter, and everything was lousy with neon, chrome, and Formica. It was quieter in back and the men's room was just to our left. Running along that wall on a metal shelf was a collection of vintage radios. Not the really old stuff but sets from the days when manufacturers had first gone wild with the possibilities of plastic. Pink radios intended for girls, radios shaped like baseball mitts or hot dogs, radios meant to be futuristic with twenty more dials than what you needed, stream-lined jobs, little-bitty ones designed for the beach. This was pre-import days, and the names on the sides were Majestic and Philco, Emerson, Sears and Roebuck, RCA. It was a good collection, the one authentic thing in the diner, and before we sat down Chet walked along the wall looking it over, managing to suggest, by the appraising way he squinted, that he wasn't someone visiting a museum but a professional trying to catch up on current trends.

We found a booth in the corner, leaned back as the waitress cleared off the dirty plates. A maple leaf had fallen on Chet's head on the way in and managed to cling to the one little curl of hair remaining. He seemed unaware it was up there and I was too impressed to tell him—impressed that all the stories were turning out to be true. This man attracted the ludicrous like a magnet attracts iron.

It was a good place to sit and talk. I think we both realized this. That whatever was going to be between us needed to start right now.

"Specials," the waitress said, handing us printouts to go along with the menu. Chet was still clutching the envelope, but now he placed it edgeways on the table between the sugar and the napkins, where it wouldn't get stained.

He sat rigid on the edge of the seat like a plebe at West Point—like someone who hadn't sat in a booth in decades and had lost the knack. Still, I could see at least a flicker of interest. In a modest way the diner must have reminded him of the years when he ate out in all the best restaurants, fawned on and flattered, never having to pick up a check. "I'll have the club sandwich," he said, savoring each word; the waitress, expecting an old man's voice, did a little double take and looked at him again.

"Yes sir," she said. "Right away."

Once she left he put his arms behind him, felt for the back of the booth, found it, settled in more comfortably. His eyes had been rheumy-looking before, the way they are in people with cataracts, but when he looked up this time they seemed much clearer, as if he were forcing the cloudiness away.

"Lindy would show me pictures sometimes, but they were old ones. Your eyes surprise me. They're quick eyes, interrogative. And a middleweight's square chin. The fair skin your mother had. The hair surprises me, too."

I did my best to smile. "That's my only claim to fame. The oldest redhead in America."

"How old?"

"Fifty-two."

He frowned, as if this computation were new to him. "You remind me some of Buzz Colgan. Buzz was my first cousin. His father was the biggest pirate in Springfield, but Colgan was okay. Your bone structure is identical. I have no idea what happened to him."

"He moved to Seattle, worked thirty-four years as a foreman for Boeing. I tracked him down there three months ago with some questions I had. We had a nice talk about the old days over the phone."

That really surprised him—surprised him and confused him. I felt bad at that, but it wasn't time to enlighten him further.

He pointed toward the radios on the wall, tried to hold back some on the eagerness, made the next question seem more casual than it really was. "How's the station faring?"

"Okay," I said, knowing he wanted the long story, opting for the short one instead. "We have a format that seems to work. Soft rock, jazz, folk. The news from the BBC. High school sports on weekends. Ethnic shows on Sundays, everything from Greek to Colombian. No talk. We're just different enough that people who can't stand any other stations think of us as theirs. We're lucky we are where we are, with all the colleges."

"Sounds great," he said, but his lips tipped down. "How's revenues?"

"Worrisome. I'm happy enough with modest growth, but who knows what modest means anymore. One of the problems is we can't find any sales reps who know how to sell it. We've gone down every quarter for the last nine."

He made his hands into little fists, arranged them next to each other just so on the table. "We were always solid in that respect."

I glanced up sharply. "Thanks to my mother. Yes, that's true. But even Mother would have trouble in this market, shrewd as she was. Would she give in and become like everyone else? Stay the course? I wonder about this all the time."

I didn't intend this as a question, but that's how he took it. "Your mother? Well I think . . . well, that's hard to say."

Of course it's hard to say, I felt like telling him. What remembrance could you possibly have of her? The high school brain, married to inject sense and stability into a man who had neither—married to rescue the family radio station from collapse. Did he remember the sober calculation that led him to this? Did he remember finding just enough passion toward her that he fathered two children before running out, leaving business and kids in her hands while he followed McGowan's star to New York? For a moment I felt the anger I had been reaching for and felt good about that—to feel anything toward this ludicrous old man at all.

"I remember when Alec, Lee, and I ran it ourselves," he said. "Eighteen. Yes, just the three of us and no one could say boo. Dad won the station in a poker game, do you know that? He was holding two pairs, but that's all it took. What did he care about radio, everything was lumber, so he let us run it the way we wanted. Goodman, Ellington, early swing. We had the brightest sound in Massachusetts, and don't think everyone wasn't cognizant . . . But that was the worst mistake I ever made. Leaving radio for television. Radio is pure. Radio is solid. Radio is going to be bigger than it ever was if you can just hold on a little while more."

Okay, this was partly an admission, the start of an admission, but the rest sounded plain crazy. My anger, cresting, settled back into the same passionless regard as before. The waitress brought our sandwiches and he stared down at his in obvious satisfaction—how long had it been since he'd confronted a turkey club sandwich face to face?—but then, rather than biting into it, he started in with what I'd been half-expecting: a passionate description of Lindy, how much she had meant to him, how for almost fifty years she had been his reason for living, his lifeline to the outer world, the unshakable pillar of his support.

"You know how many times she missed visiting?" he asked, his eyes going rheumy again. "Four times. Four times in forty-six years. Once she fell on playground duty and broke her left tibia. Another time her car broke down with a balky water pump. That was June 19, 1968. The first time was April 30, 1963. After that she didn't miss at all until September 4, 1997. She was sick a lot after that, but she never missed again, not until the last time. I sat there and I stared at the clock and I paced, but she didn't come."

He looked up from his sandwich—my turn to say something—but all I could do was nod. If mother was just a vague recollection to him, Lindy was just a name to me, a sister but not a sister, someone whose only role in my life had been saving me the worry of him for forty-six years. So I owed her something. I owed her the effort of trying to picture what those visits must have been like, the long drive to prison, the waiting on line, the making friends with the guards, becoming a regular, the little presents handed over for inspection, the conversations through the grill—"Are you well, Dad? You look pale." "I'm well, Lind. And yourself?" Lindy, the last of the spinster schoolteachers, building an entire life around what was never more than ten or fifteen minutes every third week.

We ate, we thought grave thoughts, we looked at each other at precisely the same instant, then looked away again, he busy with his sandwich, me with mine. Outside, the afternoon sunshine had opened up the gray, but what little made its way to our table only made it seem bigger, wedging us even further apart.

"I'm looking forward to meeting your family," he said, hunching over his plate so it would catch the crumbs.

"They're looking forward to meeting you."

"Tell me about them. Your wife for starters."

"Her name is Kim Rogario. She's a middle school principal, the best in western Mass. It's a brutal job, the way things are these days. She fights more battles in one morning than most people do in a month."

"I see. And your offspring?"

I couldn't help laughing at that—his make-believe sincerity, the moving-right-along stuff. I had forgotten the most important fact about him: he was a professional interviewer, a man who could make his voice sound concerned whether he felt it or not.

"You mean your grandchildren?" I let that sink in. "The twins are seniors in high school. Bonnie is an all-state center on the basketball team. She averages thirty-two points a game and there are colleges all over the country desperate to get her. Alan helps her with this. He's good with numbers."

"Basketball?" He thought about that for a moment. "I remember a player called Robert Cousy. He could pass the ball behind his back. I interviewed him once when he was just starting. They called him Cooz . . . And Lindy said you have an adopted daughter? I don't know the proper term. When I was younger it was 'Negro.' "

The anger again, a quicker, harder flash. "She's a little girl, age nine. That's what she is. Her name is Elise."

"Fine. I won't be in their way?"

"We have an apartment set up. Everyone is looking forward to meeting you, like I said."

He had to go to the men's room. Some teenagers sitting at the counter noticed his shoes, his old-fashioned wingtips, pointed and laughed, making me think of Catskill wiseacres snickering at Rip Van Winkle with his tricornered hat and pantaloons. Alan's sarcasm would have some fun there. I wondered if there was time to get him to a shoe store before driving home.

"You know, I was thinking about what you said earlier," he said once he came back. "About the station. It seems a new sales force is what's needed to add some pep. I still have contacts. I could make some phone calls for you, see who's out there."

It was ludicrous, his saying that. Not endearing ludicrous like his clumsiness, his nearsightedness, but irritating ludicrous—to be so far out of touch with the way things were. A lot of people I had talked to about the early days mentioned his tendency toward delusion. But it was one thing to hear someone reminisce about this in a nostalgic, cozy way, another thing to be sitting directly across from it.

"Yeah, great," I said. Then, "I'm not actually involved with the station right now. I'm on a sort of sabbatical."

That was obviously the last word he expected to hear from me. "Oh?" he said, still very much the interviewer, not letting it throw him.

"I'm writing a biography."

"Oh?" he said. It was as if his mouth was stuck on round.

"I'm writing a biography of the man you named me after."

That wiped the smile off all right—his mouth snapped from round and curious to hard, tight, and dumb.

"I'm writing a biography of the man you murdered."

He put his hand to his ear. "A biography you say?"

"I'm writing the biography of Alec McGowan."

It was like flinging an ax at someone—you put all your strength into it, really heave, then, divorcing yourself from the implications, look up cold-bloodedly to study what happens when it hits.

Nothing happened. Not a flicker of surprise, not a wince, not even a grimace. His face was set in the blank immobility I had seen back in the hospital when the guard brought his arm up, demonstrating what I should have understood then—that this is what he had learned in prison, to immediately smother every strong emotion the moment it arose, buy time with blankness, betray nothing, do your thinking behind a mask.

I don't know how long the silence lasted. He had to say something—he must have sensed that much. He looked over his shoulder, then lowered his voice as if telling me a secret. "Alec McGowan wasn't his real name."

"I know that. His real name was Philias LeBlanc."

"Pierre we called him. It would make him furious."

"Born February 28, 1917, in Holyoke, Massachusetts, the poor part, by the paper mills. Father an alcoholic French Canadian who drowned in the Connecticut River. Mother a Catholic of stern and inflexible faith."

"They lived at 63 River Street. A three-decker. I remember it well."

"Sixty-four River Street. Apartment 2A. It's still there."

"I discovered him. I brought him down to Springfield. I gave him his first break."

"Some Russian immigrants live there now. They showed me around."

"By eighteen we were running the station ourselves. What do you know about writing a biography?"

"Scar tissue. It's teaching me as I go."

Okay, this was something—a fast surge of memory we could ride on all the way to safety, never mind the bumps. But the waitress came over now, Chet's initial energy perceptibly sagged, and after she took away the plates the only gambit he had left was to trot out something automatic and stale.

"I did not kill him, not deliberately. I meant to scare him, that's all. All that was perfectly obvious on camera, but the DA had the Kinescope destroyed so as to obtain a first-degree conviction. I was told that personally by someone in the prosecutor's office."

"It's what you said at the trial. I've read the transcripts."

His face reddened, which was surprising—that there was enough passion left for color. "Of course it's what I stated. It's the truth, isn't it? I meant to protect Lee, that was the only thing I wanted. You have to realize what Alec had become by that stage, a kind of monster. It wasn't my fault the evidence was destroyed."

"There's hardly any tape left at all. Not from any of the shows."

He waved his hand. "We did it all live."

"I've got some leads about where to find some. A man I'm working on. In fact, a person I think you might remember."

Yes, I told myself, let's keep talking this way, pretend we're two collaborators solving a joint puzzle, nothing personal in it whatsoever. But he'd been in prison too long, had brooded too long, become too stuck in the cold groove of his justification. *Just to scare him. To defend Lee. The tape deliberately destroyed. The truth smothered.* These were the kinds of things you could hold so tight for so many years they became compressed into stone.

There was lots I could have said, of course—I was very conscious of holding back, not wanting to shatter the stone, not then and certainly not there. I looked at my watch, reached for the bill. "We have to get going."

He didn't budge. I remembered the other stories I'd heard about him, how stubborn he could be, and when I glanced down, trying to read his expression, I had a vivid flash of the Chet I knew from dozens of photos: the average Joe's face, the crewcut alertness that topped it, the clown's elasticity of feature, the deferential manner of the sidekick, the second banana—saw these even though everything in his expression contradicted them, demonstrating nothing but how foolish old men look when they try to pout.

"You think I'm going to help you," he said, more to his hands than to me. "The only reason you came for me is so I can spill the beans. I'm not talking about him, that has to be understood."

Spill the beans? "Oh, come on, Chet," I said. "I came for you because there was no one else to take care of you. Why pretend it's any deeper than that."

He got up, grudgingly, then surprised me once more. "Take my arm," he commanded. "I get tired and you have to hold my arm."

He tugged me to a stop when we passed under the radios, reached with both hands as if to gather them all in, thought better of it, let his arms fall, then allowed me to lead him toward the door. Once in the car he fell asleep immediately, his back against the blanket, his head lolling down on my shoulder. It was sharp there, like someone taking a knuckle and pressing it deep into my collarbone, but I didn't shrug him off. Out the window Greylock looked much larger and softer than it had in the morning, the afternoon haze swelling it double, confusing it, making it much more indistinct. Always before it had loomed like a welcoming portal leading to home, a good omen, but my mood was too jumpy and irritable now, and it seemed a portent of something massive, difficult, and prolonged.

We were thirty miles from the diner when I remembered the manila envelope with the pardon, realized we had left it on the table. I considered swerving around to fetch it, actually looked for a place to turn, but then something else kicked in and I drove on eastward, putting enough miles behind us that there was no longer any temptation. Here all day I'd been searching for an emotion, any emotion, to help carry me through with this, and now I had one—an overwhelming sense of childish hurt—and there was nothing to do but brood on it, take a small boy's revenge, picture the envelope with ketchup stains across the front, getting shoved aside by the next patrons, then finally thrown that night into the trash . . . to hurt him immediately, even while he was asleep on the seat. It was pathetic of me, cruel, wanton—and yet somewhere in the depth of that hurt was the crude outline of a beginning.

We drove into the apartment complex just as it turned dark. Leaves covered the pavement, shining gold in the spotlight. Posted on the front door was a brightly crayoned poster in Elise's handwriting, *WELCOME HOME G'POP!* and beneath it on the carpeting a broken piece of pizza crust curled upward in a grin.

Part Two

THE WINDOW

Three

One of the oldest, most venerable of industry legends is that it only took Peter Abramsky and Alec McGowan one single working day to devise, develop, and implement the entire *Morning* program. The truth is, they started at nine in the morning and finished by noon.

This was September 28, 1950—the Friday after McGowan arrived in New York. It had already been decided to use the old street-level studio facing Forty-ninth Street. All the time the two men talked, pacing back and forth in what was essentially a cold, dusty auditorium with the seats removed, there was a constant coming and going of carpenters, stagehands, and painters, trying desperately to get things in shape for the premiere scheduled for Monday. People who were there remember it all happening under the smell of sawdust and turpentine—remember, when they tell of it, how the two men seemed like carpenters themselves, doing their own hammering and pounding, only with words and gestures, grimaces and shrugs.

They made an odd couple—everyone agrees on that, too. Abramsky the Berlin intellectual, much shorter than McGowan, his appearance offering as many contradictions as his personality. Gnomelike, sickly, withered, wearing a rumpled jacket with fabric so thin you expected his elbows to pop loose any moment, and yet with a head that was leonine and handsome, a line engraved on his forehead for every hard year of the century, and above it the most luxurious sweep of silver hair in town. He had two styles when he moved: lethargic verging on world-weary, or, when an idea had possession of him, a nervous little dance, so like a marionette's you couldn't help glancing above him to see who pulled his strings.

Beside him, McGowan looked twice as big as he really was, and yet for the most part he deferred to the older man, making his posture softer than it usually was, cocking his head down so his ear was in reasonable proximity to Abramsky's mouth. The suit and bow tie were already so much a part of him that people were surprised at how he looked when dressed casually; one writer, remembering the impression he made with his tennis sweater, his elegant slacks with their wide cuffs, his loafers, compared him to a choreographer at rehearsal—very easy with himself, taking a deep physical pleasure in expressing the movement in his imagination through the movement of his arms.

A sizable crowd of kibitzers had gathered that morning; word had spread through the building that something was up, and almost every creative person on the payroll found a reason to saunter in. Television being television, most couldn't help feeling they might be needed—that their opinion would be asked. None of them were asked, and so none of them stayed long, and their subsequent recollections came in fragments and short takes, making it difficult to assemble them into one coherent picture. But all seem agreed on one point: that so casual and offhand were Abramsky and McGowan's manner that no one, absolutely no one, had any idea they had even begun their planning, let alone that momentous decisions had already been reached.

Take the matter of an audience, whether or not to have one. The head usher, a man named Sluggan who had been there forever, interrupted them, demanding to know how many tickets to print and when to start distributing them.

"Tickets?" Abramsky said, exaggerating his accent as if he had never heard the word before.

"An audience?" McGowan said, playing dumb himself.

Abramsky looked toward the empty space where the seats would have to go. "We want one?"

McGowan looked, squinted, shook his head.

"No tickets," Abramsky said, waving Sluggan away. "Leave us alone, you pompous son of a bitch."

And so it went. Would McGowan do the commercials himself?—Abramsky asking this like it was a test. No commercials, McGowan said, he'd keep himself free of them. Fine, that was settled, time now to move on to something else. Set? A sofa would look stupid, too much like a living room, something slightly more formal was needed, but what? A park bench? Too corny. A desk? Better, but what kind of desk? Wooden desk, him alone behind it? No, it would make him look like an angry principal or somebody's boss. Conference table? Too big and unwieldy. They grabbed a few stagehands, used them as markers, placed them in various positions trying to figure out how things should look. A long oval table facing the camera with enough room for three to sit comfortably? Yes, but who were the other two going to be? A man to do the announcing and a girl to act pretty—fine, that was settled, they would put a call out for them that very day. Two chairs off to the right to use for interviews? Okay, only with a little table set in between for coffee and books. Okay, and then we need a clock right above the desk so we won't have to keep breaking in with the time.

The stagehands bent down on all fours, Abramsky walked over, stepped onto the stockiest one's back, reached, drew a circle on the wall with his pen where the clock would go. McGowan, staring like a painter appraising a canvas, took off his watch, grabbed some masking tape off a ladder, and fastened the watch to the wall beside the circle, then did the same with one of the stagehand's watches, and then

Abramsky got the idea and added his own—have not just one clock on the wall but six, showing the time in every corner of the world. *Tokyo,* McGowan wrote in big fat letters. *Moscow, London, New York, Chicago, San Francisco.*

The most famous decision of the morning was McGowan's own, though it later became evident that the two of them had talked about it prior to the run-through. The studio was large, lined with acoustical baffles from radio days, and one of the first and most basic decisions that had to be reached in converting it to television was where to erect walls, where to position the cameras, how to hide the klieg lights and the overhead mikes and the cables. Tom Castor the head camera-man, the technical producer Connie Connors, Mitch Spellman the boy director (he was all of twenty-four)—all these were anxiously waiting just off to the side for their instructions.

Abramsky beamed now, absolutely beamed, and made a reaching kind of motion, as if he were serving their questions to McGowan on a tray—*Explain it to them, Alec.*

He did, very simply and directly, not wasting any time. Nothing was going to be hidden. No walls, no curtains, no baffles, no obscurations of any kind. They were going to show everything, the cameramen in shirtsleeves, the stage managers with their earphones, the lighting people at their consoles, even the writers at their desks. They were going to take the magic of television and make it visible, the structure laid bare, so people watching could not only see it all happen, but understand how it all happened, be part of the action. If a set had to be banged together, fine, they would turn the camera on the set being banged together. If a camera dollied in for a close-up, then another camera would capture the first camera dollying in for a close-up; if anyone needed makeup, then the makeup artists could be seen doing it just off in the wings. So far television had spent all its creative energy in disguising how its magic worked, erecting at ever increasing expense what was an ever harder illusion to maintain: that what people watched was anything but what it really was, an elaborately constructed artifice requiring the talents of dozens of people in an enormously difficult choreography supported by enormous resources of technology. In one bold stroke, *Morning* would cast all this illusion aside. It would be a program in progress, a program made visible, stripped of the pretense and thus more open and honest than anything attempted so far.

It's easy to picture the reactions this elicited from the courtiers. Their mouths falling open, the cautious glances to check out the reaction of the person standing beside them, the thinking this was madness combined with the worry that maybe it wasn't—the grudging, fence-straddling nods spreading down the ranks until they were transformed into enthusiastic grins that rippled back the way they had come as actual applause, everyone trying to create more sound than their neighbor and so be credited with climbing on the bandwagon first. Genius! Again!

Abramsky and McGowan paid attention to none of this, but continued their relentless pacing around the studio's perimeter. Despite the reversal in their sizes, they reminded people of a father watching his son take his first brave steps, nudging him forward with little pushes and smiles of encouragement. *Go on! Go on!* Abramsky seemed to say (among the onlookers were many world-class lip-readers). Others remember how alone the two men seemed, enclosed in the bubble of their inspiration where no one could reach them.

It was eleven now, and their sketching had reached the point where they required someone to write everything down. Mitch Spellman was summoned, told to take notes. Fifty years later he still has these, jotted down on a yellow network pad in rough shorthand, the speed showing in the way the letters crowd into each other across the margins. (Spellman himself only lasted three weeks as director; McGowan labeled him with the most damning of his indictments, "unimaginative mediocrity," and that was that, though he later went on to a successful career producing game shows.)

PETER ABRAMSKY: *The finish we have. Truth shmuth. What do we do before that?*

ALEC MCGOWAN: *I talk.*

P.A.: *Talk is easy. Long talk or short talk?*

A.M.: *Long. Closing monologue. I take my time.*

P.A.: *Before that?*

A.M.: *How long?*

P.A.: *Four minutes, five.*

A.M.: *Music.*

P.A.: *Accordion. I know the best.*

A.M.: *Quintet. Resident. At least two of them Negro.*

P.A.: *Say instructional before that. Show them how all this new garbage works. The pretty girl does this.*

A.M.: *Swell.*

P.A.: *Commercial. Stations identify. It is eight forty-five, before which . . . ?*

A.M.: *We visit.*

P.A.: *With film. At least now. You mean you visit?*

A.M.: *Later. Me walking. Travelogues for now.*

P.A.: *Get Peterson to see what is out there. The army has films, you know that? Pressure to use theirs. How about stock market? Ticker tape, you going over to read. Bad, frown. Good, smile.*

A.M.: *Garbage. The weather. Reports from all over. Record highs, lows—we go for the big picture. People down South like seeing snow. People up North like orange blossoms, cactus.*

P.A.: *We could use a map.*

A.M.: *Big one splashed across the wall, give whoever a pointer, draw in fronts, highs and lows.*

P.A.: *Something for snow.*

A.M.: *Cross-hatching. Something for tornadoes.*

P.A.: *Curlicues. What, people phone in?*

A.M.: *They could with a lot of things.*

P.A.: *Lovelorn? Bullshit. We are on weather. Weather. Your sidekick does . . . ?*

A.M.: *We figure that out.*

P.A.: *Talk here. Interview, Semiserious person, bigshot in news.*

A.M.: *Doing something that day. Can we stick to? Whoever has got to be doing something later that day.*

P.A.: *We make it a rule. I see fun before. Stunts. Lion tamers, circus clowns, cabaret.*

A.M.: *Something.*

P.A.: *Commercial.*

A.M.: *Everyone will go crap.*

P.A.: *Music again. This time a guest.*

A.M.: *Fine by me.*

P.A.: *Before?*

A.M.: *News. Two minutes' worth.*

P.A.: *Five. You want do yourself?*

A.M.: *Thanks, no.*

P.A.: *Then a man I know from network. A nebbish, but he will do.*

A.M.: *Serious person before that? Author or dramatist or similar?*

P.A.: *We are on first half-hour now.*

A.M.: *I talk for half that. Whoever wanders in I collar.*

P.A.: *Fine.*

A.M.: *Commercial, right? Jesus.*

P.A.: *Mazuma. Money. And I would like please some experts. News and views.*

A.M.: *Maybe. We'll figure that out later. I'm not giving up minutes.*

P.A.: *What else?*

A.M.: *I don't want to talk with the girl much. She does her part I do mine. We're friendly, chatty, but that's it.*

P.A.: *Top of the hour. How we open?*

A.M.: *That's exactly it. How the fuck?*

P.A.: *Spinning globe?*

A.M.: *Big calendar?*

P.A.: *Like an hourglass?*

A.M.: *Clock hands ticking?*

P.A.: *How the fuck?*

In twenty minutes, except for the vexing problem of the opening, they had the structure pretty well settled. They talked theme next— they had decided each day should have its own theme. It wouldn't be rigid, more like a framework around which they could organize the program, keeping things flexible so as not to box themselves in.

Monday's theme was going to be *Tolerance*—they apparently agreed on this at once. Having an integrated band was part of this, but only

part. Guests that day would be chosen because they were the kind
who could widen people's understanding of the larger world. Rabbis—they would find some rabbis, and some lay ministers, and cardi-
nals, and maybe even some patriarchs, whoever happened to be in
town. Politicians, too—Monday would be the only day they would be
permitted on, drawn strictly from the middle, no one extreme; everyone would have to fit in some way, implicitly or explicitly be preaching
toleration.

Tuesday would be *Laughs,* oddballs, comedians, out-of-the-way
stuff. Wednesday would be *Wild Card,* spur of the moment, feature
stories that needed more time, perhaps visits to places that got the
day started, like bakeries or power plants or newspapers. Thursday
would be *Courage,* people who had done brave deeds, rescued people,
withstood great hardships—sailors who had survived in lifeboats
for months in the Pacific, mountain climbers, test pilots breaking
the sound barrier, and—and here McGowan insisted—women who
weren't conventional heroes at all and yet had put up with great difficulty and heartbreak just going about their daily lives.

It was Friday that provoked their only argument. Abramsky apparently wanted to center it around *Wisdom,* with older men coming
on, the famous columnists, renowned authors, senior diplomats, men
whose careers had spanned decades, and would bring more breadth of
view than anyone who had been on earlier in the week. McGowan
insisted on *Innovation*—on having scientists who were doing up-to-the-
minute work, new entertainers or the younger writers, people whose
careers were still in front of them. He was certain about this, it was his
strongest instinct toward the show—that its primary focus be on the
day at hand, the day specifically, the day as in The Age.

Everyone could see them going at it—it was like an allegory of
Maturity versus Youth. Abramsky's temper was famous for the steady,
incremental way it worked itself up to its highest pitch, going through
all the stops between mild irritation and uncontrollable fury like a
flame racing up a fuse toward a keg of dynamite. McGowan, however,
refused to give in, even when it exploded; the angrier Abramsky grew,

the more wildly he gesticulated, the more rigid and tense McGowan became—and rigidity and tenseness, in a man so habitually relaxed, exerted a terrible pressure of its own. Finally, when the two men came to a stop by one of the pretend cameras (one of the stagehands down on all fours, eyes closed, wincing under the shouts) and it seemed that they could only settle it by blows, Abramsky made a bowing motion and smiled, smiled broadly. McGowan had gotten his way with the theme—*Morning* would wipe the slate clean each day, start fresh—and Abramsky got something even more important: the proof that his protégé was tough enough to watch out for himself, withstand all the pressures that would surely come.

That left one last problem: what to do for the show's beginning. A lot of ideas were floated out—Spellman kept writing furiously on his pad—but they were all so bad neither man even bothered to comment on the other's suggestion. Finally, just before noon and the lunchtime break, McGowan, in his restless pacing, came to a stop near the heavy gray fire curtains that covered the window facing Forty-ninth Street.

"Take a ladder," he said, to no one in particular. "Pull those back and let in some light."

The curtain probably hadn't been opened since before the war—it took three stagehands straining on each end to pull them apart. A half-century later Mitch Spellman still remembers the rusty shriek of the runners, the cloud of dust that descended, how all the network executives shrank back from the sunlight like vampires confronted by the dawn. The window, standing exposed, was huge, fifty feet long and ten feet high, divided by vertical metal strips into three sections, and even greasy and dirty as it was it still commanded an expansive view of Forty-ninth Street, right outside the glass at street level.

It was nearly noon, the street was crowded with businessmen carrying briefcases, office girls on their way to lunch, the usual tourists; the weather was warm, so the men were coatless, the women still in dresses and frocks. At first, none of them noticed anything different in the streetscape—obviously most of these were pedestrians who had walked this way many times before—but then one man, shorter

than the others, quicker-looking, dressed in a baggy zoot suit that
seemed a leftover from the war years, noticed a reflection of light
where there had never been any before, and in no particular hurry to
be anywhere, strolled over, cupped his hands around his temples, put
his face against the glass, and stared in.

Could he see anything? It was hard to say, it was dark in the studio,
but if he could what he saw was approximately eighty-five stagehands,
senior producers, assistant directors, and technicians staring back out
at him with even greater curiosity than his own. The man glanced away
for a moment, said something over his shoulder ("Hey, Manny, get a
load of this!"), and another man came over. Two people looking in
now—and then a third, this one a stranger to the first two, and then a
man with his family, out-of-towners, and then some pretty shopgirls,
going up on tiptoe to see over the first ones there, until within five
minutes there were at least two hundred people standing out on the
sidewalk straining to see in through the glass.

Inside the studio no one said a word—as if any sound, any motion,
would spoil the perfect rightness of the moment. Abramsky broke the
silence first; he waved Spellman over, shoved the stagehands around
to establish where the cameras would go, started issuing commands in
the quiet voice he used when he wanted results fast.

"You got this, Mitch? I want a camera lens right here in the middle
of the glass they think is the real one. A dummy. Slap some letters on
it, and while they stare at it, we get two cameras panning in from the
sides to catch their faces . . . Let us get this window clean, use something strong on it, acid . . . We need a rail out there so they do not
crowd too close. What is the focal length on that, Connie? You with
me on this, please, Alec?"

"We'll need titles superimposed over the glass. Can that be done?"

"Of course, of course. Titles over the glass. Someone see to it, cut
the reflection. Faces at the window, no title . . . title . . . then slowly pan
over to Alec, sitting—"

"Standing."

"Standing here, coming into view, please, the camera swinging around this way until finally it is Alec with the window at his back, yes? Our start?"

"Our start," McGowan said—and then he turned slowly around, moved toward the window glass, rubbed his hand on a filthy section, spit in his palm, rubbed hard, harder, harder yet, spit again, rubbed, kept rubbing . . . stepped back, stared out at the people, the newly cleansed mass of them, nodded and smiled.

That's Friday.

Pause/breather/back in two etc.

Good place for 1950 after research completed. Abbreviated for now, then bring to life with splashy anecdotes/telling details/curious facts/salient observations/humorous asides. Avoid decade clichés, i.e. usual 50's crap. Instead how 1945–50 was era of its own, all but forgotten now etc. Life and times, Alec me boy. Life *and* times. Statistics, including 30% of American homes have no bath or shower, 26% no indoor toilet, 28% no electricity. Two million adults never went to school at all. Per capita income is $2,989. Over one million acres of land still open for homesteading. Of all employed women 78% work in "female only" jobs. U.S. first nation in world in production of petroleum/coal/steel/electricity/copper/cotton/lumber/agriculture, contains 80% of all the machines in the world. Baby boom stats: four million kids a year by 1950, over 30% more than 1945. One school attributes to returning GI's wanting instant families; others, the "great expectations" school, thinks better economy means people more confident about future, less concerned about extra mouths to feed. Birth of mass man explain why. Historian Eric Goldman: "when community life turned into one vast gurgle." Ten most popular boys' names: Robert, John, James, Michael, William, Richard, Joseph, Thomas, Steven, David; girls' names: Linda, Mary, Barbara, Patricia, Susan, Kathleen, Carol, Nancy, Margaret, Diane. Over 48,000 die in automobile accidents, over 19,000 in train accidents, 8,576 in accidents involving horses or mules. Nineteen lynchings in course of the year,

Alabama the leader, Georgia second, Mississippi third. Drivers roll down windows and stick arms out windows when changing lanes. Film takes two weeks to develop. First class letter costs three cents to mail. Women wouldn't be caught dead appearing in public in pants, men ditto in shorts. Winston Churchill the most admired man, Eleanor Roosevelt the most admired woman. Families still sit on front porches after dinner. *When we arrive* the favorite expression; *Conformity* not yet a dirty word.

Quotes, including Fred Vinson, Truman crony: "Americans are in the pleasant predicament of having to learn to live 50% better than they have ever lived before." *Life* magazine: "A nation is tired when it ceases to want things fervently—the habit of insatiable desire can be as much a factor in maintaining social vigor as the dedication to ideals and holy causes. Being greedy for something better is one of the main-stays of our dynamism." William Levitt: "No man who owns his own house and lot can be a communist, he has too much to do." Lewis Mumford: "There they are, a multitude of uniform, unidentifiable houses lined up inflexibly at a uniform distance, on uniform roads, in a treeless communal waste, inhabited by people of the same class, the same income, the same age group, conforming in every outward and inward respect to the same common mold manufactured in the central metropolis." Someone else (lost source, make up name?): "In 1950, America was a country lousy with greatness." John Gunther: "Here in the first gaunt years of the Atomic Age, lies a country more favored by man and nature than any other in history, now for the first time attempting with somewhat faltering steps to justify its new status as a mature world power. Here is a country blessed by an ideal geography and perfect natural frontiers, by incalculable bulk and wealth and vital-ity, by a unique heritage in democratic ideas and principles—a country deliberately founded on a good idea. The United States is the craziest, most dangerous, least stable, most spectacular, least grown up and most powerful and magnificent nation ever known. A lucky country, with an almost obsessive belief in the happy ending. What will happen next? Having come so far, will it yet fumble the brightness of these morning hopes?"

My own conclusions; choose one of following as in 1950 was America's last chance to be young and undefeated forever, or America wasn't to the dream yet, but damn close, and close to a dream has always been the position where Americans are at their best. Or, the United States at mid-century: might, power, swagger, exuberance, confidence—and yet it's a nation one-quarter of whose population still craps outdoors.

Atomic Age etc. Bizarre short-lived phrase where nuclear weapons become folksy and fun, *atomic* being catch phrase for anything new/ exciting/sexy. A burlesque theater in Nevada features "Atombomb Dancers." Cereal company offers "atomic viewers" premiums. Atomic hamburgers/pizzas/gum/umbrellas ("The natural repellancy of a mushroom-shaped cloud"). Children, taken to shoe stores, step onto platforms to have feet X-rayed inside new shoes to check fit—work in my own memory of this, the way I felt naked and ashamed. Fun phase ends in late 1949, a grim President Truman announces Soviet Union has detonated at least one nuclear weapon, immediately millions of young American children learn how to "duck and cover" under elementary school desks—and my own memory here, too, if fits. The bomb was the American invention, ultimate expression of our genius (say some such), created in a kind of horrible but perfectly natural spontaneous generation out of love of ingenuity/love of bigness/ negligent power, yet for all this it's the *wrong* invention, one that really doesn't express U.S. genius, not then, not in the bright new dawn of 1950. Americans waiting for something better to come along, the main event, an invention they can fall in love with en masse.

Television. Do careful detailed history going back to 1829 when devices called Fatanscopes/Phenakistiscopes/Zoetropes utilized drawings around spinning slotted discs. 1858 invention of primitive sealed glass vacuum tube glows in electric current, ancestor of cathode ray. 1884 Paul Pilnowi, German, invents more sophisticated spinning disc, turning research in wrong direction, i.e. all mechanical system. The Thomas Edison of all this, the Alexander Graham Bell, a brilliant loner and prophet without honor in native land: Philo Farnsworth. Self-taught kid genius, at 21 (1927) invents first electronic TV picture.

Big radio companies, sensing a killing, immediately challenge him to long costly patent fights; RCA's own white hope is Russian émigré Vladimir Zworykin, he who in 1930 invents iconoscope TV camera. First programs are ready for 1939 World's Fair, though picture remains primitive; "Fred Astaire's face not only came and went," one unimpressed reporter wrote, "it came and went underwater." Tempting to get lost in technology etc. yet difficult to understand. Were these men alchemists? Mystics? Gum-chewing plain-talking no-nonsense engineers? Farnsworth a Mormon kid from Idaho who liked tinkering with machines—the whole modern world invented by Mormon farm kid from Idaho who liked tinkering with machines (good line). Sketch basics out now, come back later if more details needed. Point is people wanted TV to be magic, cared little for details. May as well say God said let there be TV and there was TV.

Tele-vision. Greek and Latin roots meaning *distant seeing.*

War slows down, though first five-inch screens available for $600. By 1946, back on track, with first New York–Washington transmission via 225 miles of "coaxial" cable. Image Orthicon camera sharpens image. Technology in place/advertisers wake up to potential/picture grows less fuzzy/price of sets drops. Network executives decide not to pussyfoot anymore, but promote it aggressively; worried before about killing off lucrative radio, but now decide to replace it immediately. First big story that goes nationwide is when four-year-old Kathy Fiscus plunges 237 feet into a pipe near her home in San Marino, Calif. Local station KTLA plugs into network, broadcasts uninterruptedly for 27 hours until girl's body brought to surface. In 1948, one in ten Americans had *seen* a TV picture; by 1950, eight in ten *owned* one, steepest, most dramatic rise in ownership of anything in Twentieth Century. Polls show 92% of respondents listened to less radio than before, 81% cut back on moviegoing, 59% read fewer books, 48% fewer magazines, 33% gave up daily paper.

NYC as center of all this innovation. Something like: In 1950, New York City stood alone as the capital of the world. Who could challenge her? London a shell of what it had been before the war, Tokyo and

Berlin still in ruins, Moscow a riddle wrapped inside an enigma, Paris still shamed. The U.N. Secretariat Building soon to billow like a huge glass sail along the East River was the extravagant physical confirmation of what was a plain and simple fact: New York was the world's golden city and 1950 was its golden moment, though no one knew how long this would last. Perhaps for the first time before or since, New York of that era was a very American city, the one that was not only both the summation of everything good and bad the country offered, but the original stimulus for much of it, simultaneously the country's fountain and drain (one cynical observer etc). Cities have their imperial moments, their centurions and storm troopers, and NY's was going to be protons/electrons/unstoppable cathode rays etc. P. G. Wodehouse: "Being in New York in 1950 was like being in heaven without going to all the bother and expense of dying." John Mansfield: "New York City is a gladness, the romantic, beautiful city, the queen of all romance cities." Another Brit: "If Paris is the perfect place for starting a romance, New York is the perfect city in which to get over one, to get over loving, to get over anything." Jan Morris: "Ask anyone who remembers Manhattan at mid-century and they recall it with proud nostalgia, even if they were poor and lonely. Few cities in the history of the world can have stood so consciously at a moment of fulfillment, looking into a future that seemed so full of reward."

Do the usual, including financial center of world/more Jews than in Israel/Irish than in Dublin/Italians than in Venice/blacks than in Alabama. Nine of ten tallest buildings in world; metropolitan area greatest concentration of humans on globe; three major league baseball teams, the fights at Sunnyside or St. Nicks; Triborough Bridge, Empire State Bldg. etc. 90% of New Yorkers polled say their lives are "happy." Put all this in, the city, the era, a kind of historical roulette wheel, set it spinning, stops on one innovation that seems to sum up all that is best about city: The Automat. As for instance: It was a time of great nightclubs, the Stork Club, the Cotton Club, Toots Shor's, but for most Gothamites these hardly registered, or if they did, it was as in the same category as nirvana or Valhalla, places they'd heard of but had little chance of ever visiting. No, for the ordinary Manhattanite the eatery that characterized the age was the Automat, the magic Horn & Hardart's—a miracle of technology that worked on a human scale as well. Spacious in size, often reached by going downstairs below street level, cozy, with all kinds of nooks and crannies you could lose yourself in, the Automat seemed to sum up all that was best in 1950 New York. You put down a dollar bill, whereupon the change lady slid over some tokens not much bigger than what you used in the subway. After that it was over to the opposite wall and the little glassed-in slots arranged one on top the other in four horizontal rows; each slot, each little window, had behind it a steaming plate of baked beans or a thick dish of rice pudding or chicken pot pie, the perfect brown crust cascading down around the sides; put in your token, lift the little white knob, reach in your hand (tapering your fingers, pinching down on the plate's blue rim) and the dish was yours. The food was good, plentiful, cheap; the coffee was the best in town (pour it yourself from brassy dolphin-headed spouts). You could spend a whole afternoon parked at a table talking ball scores or fights or philosophy or politics and no one would say boo . . . and so on, incorporating being taken there once myself. Third person, as in, This biographer remembers being taken there as a small boy, his father with him for once, and while patrons were staring at him even *more* people stared at the other man who accompanied them—a man of whom fifty years later all he remembers is the glint of light off his glasses, the width and strength of his shoulders, the way when the boy strained to reach a plate of cherry pie in the window too high for him, the man softly laughed, bent down, boosted him so he could put in his token and pull out the dish—the moment of empathy required for this being too much for the boy's father to come to on his own. Include this. The strong hands under the boy's arms, lifting him toward pie in the sky. Alec McGowan—the first adult who had ever bothered to console him, even over something so small.

Brings it around full circle. Automat on 54th Street where much of this early planning goes on. Impromptu conferences there, more formal ones back at RCA Bldg. Saturday, the mad rush to get things ready for Monday's first show etc., including bringing in lights, camera, hiring newscaster (Frank Stannard, hold off for now), announcer (Billy Benson, hardly bother), pretty girl (Barbara Tyler, already famous from commercials for toasters). Don't bog down in details here—if anything, ratchet up the pace. They all thrive on pressure, can-do kind of improvisational spirit. Show how it's possible. Insert technical details, but also a sense of *play* as part of their drive. Decision is made to broadcast first two weeks in New York only, postponing national premiere until kinks worked out—takes some pressure off, but even so, etc. Personal stuff now or save until he hits it? Lead up to Sunday of infamous Waldorf banquet.

Write this out.

With everything else to worry about that weekend, McGowan couldn't have been enthusiastic about the prospect of attending a formal banquet Sunday evening. But somehow word was passed to him that his attendance was expected, along with assurances that the evening would end early, allowing him to get a good night's sleep before Monday's premiere. The dinner was at the Plaza, hosted by the famous advertising agency Smachs, Smolinsky and Sunshine—a testimonial to William Bruce Featherstone, a revered name on Madison Avenue, the man who eighteen years earlier had invented the idea of putting toys inside cereal boxes, thereby earning fortunes for four different food companies, three radio networks, and Messrs. Smachs, Smolinksy and Sunshine.

New York being New York, a wide range of types showed up that night—advertising men, television executives, theater people, writers, reporters, critics. One of them was Louis Barbour, a syndicated gossip columnist ("Rita Hayworth had a rumbly in her tumbly last night while at Sardi's. Word is the divine Rita is in the grip of the grippe") who turned out to have kept a remarkable diary that was published after his death. Called *City Smart,* it's in turn malicious, shrewd, observant, and catty, and gives one of the best pictures we have of Manhattan nightlife in the late forties and early fifties.

"Dug out the monkey suit and made the long trek uptown . . . A bar twice as long as usual, people lined up four deep shouting orders. First person I bump into is old Featherstone himself, looking chipper, ready as ever to tell the story of how he got the idea of putting tin rings in boxes of shredded wheat . . . Surprised to see P. Abramsky there, one of two men in city whose good opinion I give tuppence for. Surprised myself by actually primping in his presence, trying to sparkle. Lost on him. Looking ill, as in severely so, white, stooped over with stitch in his side, like all the infighting, all the sniping, has gotten to him at last . . . Accompanied by one Alec McGowan, the great white hunter imported from Chicago to accomplish great things. Pleasant enough lad, with a kind of sleepy sexuality the dames should go for, if they can keep him awake. Stays close to Abramsky's elbow, gives impression of being shy and contemptuous both . . . The alcohol lake showing signs of drying, we shuffle toward our tables. Second surprise of the evening. Across from me sits Ned Custer, nephew of the famous general, or so he claims, and why not, since he looks like him, take twenty years off his age, give him long hair and a Stetson. Surprised because we all thought he was dead. No longer the celebrated Village radical I take it—his tux looks a lot newer than mine. I find myself trying to remember the names of his plays, but can't, and so end up stuttering. As we talk, watching his eyes flit away from me in boredom, I become convinced he's telling the truth about the Custer connection—yes, this is a man put on earth in order to badly overestimate his abilities. A man you can't think of without appending the adjective *nearly* to him: nearly a success as playwright, nearly a success as critic, nearly important, nearly profound. Does he realize this himself? I would think a lot hinges upon this. Shaving in the morning, does he see himself as Dr. Goebbels or Thomas Mann? . . . Appetizers served. For a centerpiece, a blownup replica of Featherstone's first cereal toy and a bronzed, turd-sized square of shredded wheat."

Barbour's attention was taken up by the man sitting next to him—a handsome young gate-crasher who wanted to land a job in show business. Barbour flirted with him through dinner, arranged a rendezvous, and it wasn't until dessert that his attention switched back to what was happening up on the dais—the dais constructed to resemble a television set.

"Featherstone gets up and tells the story of his invention. Impossible not to like the old gent and he gets a standing ovation. Mr. Smachs speaks next, then Mr. Smolinksy, then Mr. Sunshine, who turns out to be dark, morbid, and saturnine. There seems to be a changing of the guard in progress, F'stone from the glory days of radio, everyone else from television, and you can see how ripe and succulent the word tastes on their tongues. Sunshine introduces Carter Goodell, network vice-president, which is to say, the right-hand man of God, God himself not deigning to make an appearance. Everyone expects his to be the main speech, and we settle in for the long haul, but his remarks are all introductory and he announces the featured speaker: Ned Custer... Gasps of astonishment, literal gasps. I swivel around. Custer gets up from his chair with the slow, chilly exultation of a dead man rising up out of the grave."

The speech that followed was destined to become famous—quoted extensively at the time, cited extensively in histories of those years, valued as a summation of the attitudes toward television's future prevalent among its pioneers. There's no doubt it made a big impression on all those in attendance that night; even Barbour, the professional cynic, found himself gradually won over by the intoxicating sweep of Custer's inspiration.

"At first [Barbour wrote] he still resembles a cowboy, albeit a more dignified one than his Custer namesake. He leans on the dais like the leader of a wagon train peering off into the middle distance. He clears his throat, sweeps back that white-streaked hair, turns his craggy face a bit to the right so as to make out his notes, then—thirty seconds gone by and him not having said a word—fixes us with a stern and serious expression that would do justice to a Puritan minister, staring down from the high prow of the dais as if from the deck of the *Mayflower,* the matching red spots on his temples bulging toward us like horns."

"We stand tonight," Custer told them, "on the shores of a wide and unknown ocean. Ahead of us lies the Indies, the verdant New World. How we navigate and explore this new territory is the most momentous question posed to mankind since Columbus defied the intellectual naysayers of his day and sailed west toward glory. Those of us assembled in this room tonight have a virgin landscape beneath our feet that is every bit as real and promising and fertile as any discovered by those early explorers, only ours rolls before us without limits, without bounds. The advent of television is ultimately of more importance to the human race than the Industrial Revolution, the splitting of the atom, the development of automation; it has more immediate impact on society than psychiatry or even medicine; it will, if we approach it correctly, remain true to our vision, be the one redeeming invention of our age, the one we can look back upon proudly and say, Yes, I was part of it, I brought it to life. Brought what to life? The complete and instantaneous transmission of actuality."

This went down well with the audience; Barbour described how you could literally hear the sound of backbones snapping as everyone sat taller in their seats.

"If I speak in epochal terms," Custer went on, hardly bothering to scan his notes now, "it is because we stand at the dawn of a new epoch. The other seas, the traveled routes that have done so well by mankind in its long journey through the ages, are now bankrupt and stagnant. The world of literature, the sphere of poetry, traditional journalism, even theater—they are exhausted now, bereft of ideas and vitality, cared for by an ever shrinking coterie of specialists, littered with icons that are increasingly irrelevant . . . We have television in being now, and the whole world waits to see what we will do with it. With the advent of this new power, the combined emotional results of both seeing and hearing an event or performance at the instant of its occurrence creates a magic new informational force to be reckoned with, and it will make for a much greater force than that aroused by audition alone. The emotional appeal of pictures to the mass of people is everywhere apparent. Indeed, ninety percent of our learning comes through seeing. We have only to regard the success of motion pictures, tabloid newspapers, and modern picture magazines to be convinced of this. We, the custodians of this pictorial power, must not ask too much of it too soon—but after the much-needed experimental stage is over we must ask much of it, apply the very highest standards we may possibly apply. Television is as expansive as the human mind can comprehend, and so this one point becomes of paramount importance: television must not merely deliver the worn-out entertainments of a sterile era; rather, it must learn how to deliver, creatively, its own."

He was in full stride now, his words coming in a liquid, self-assured cadence as irresistible as surf. Someone had lowered the lights in the overhead chandeliers, and in the soft nicotine yellow that hung over the television-shaped dais, his was the only figure visible, the other guests having disappeared into the blackness that framed and bolstered him on either side.

He extolled television's community values, described how in thousands of neighborhoods across the country millions of people were even then gathering to share this new experience of sight and sound, watching together; then he went on to explain how television combined this community virtue with something much more personal ("Television presents the first strong approach to the public with the advantages of mass dissemination technique plus the benefits of the private, purely individual approach"). He made broad claims for it as something that would revitalize democracy ("The most outstanding contribution television can be expected to make is to further democracy by its unique usefulness as a generator of public information"), claiming, in effect, that it would make it impossible for politicians to lie ("When the eye has seen something, no amount of piety or wit can call back that single subliminal flash of misinformation . . . There will be no furtive hiding on TV. The eye, any motion, the whole attitude of the body—phoniness of certain types cannot survive visual presentation"), and then, having sounded all these notes to increasing and sustained applause, went on to the part of the speech that is quoted most often.

"No art can be pulled out of a hat overnight. The primitive days of
the baggy pants and seltzer bottle, the pie in the kisser, are already
behind us, though I would never want to see this Rabelaisian humor
ballasted entirely. We must remember that while Shakespeare's master-
pieces were being performed at the Globe Theater, outside its walls the
plaza was noisy with bearbaiting and cockfighting and Punch and Judy
shows, and there was a vital, natural connection between these two
worlds. Yes, television must have its bearbaiting, its Punch and Judy, its
penny dreadfuls, but it must also have its singspiels, its pageants, its
mass . . . The audience we should cultivate and aspire to is the one that
consists of the high middle ground. We will not lure them into our
web immediately—indeed, the high middle ground may not yet exist
in the form it will come to have, making it incumbent upon us to educate viewers until they reach this level and we advance together toward
television's natural, most comfortable plateau . . . Thus, to those priests
of high art, those intellectuals who not only dwell in ivory towers but
towers made of fairy gossamer, artistic bluff, and priestly mumbo-
jumbo, I say let us go now our separate ways, we to the largest audience any art form has ever reached, you to an age of increasing
irrelevance . . . Television has felt the need of and created a new type
of celebrity—the ordinary human—and the coming decades will see
the closest answer we have ever come to, to the question 'What is
humanity really like?' Television, if it does nothing else, will be the
window to our souls, and it behooves us to make its standards as
proud and exacting as we can . . . And so, in conclusion, I do not advo-
cate that we turn television into a twenty-inch complaint box where
intellectuals constantly bemoan the state of our culture. But I would
like to see it deal occasionally with the adamantine realities of the
world in which we live. The instrument can teach, it can illuminate, it
can even inspire. But it can do so only to the extent that humans are
determined to use it to those ends. Otherwise, my distinguished audience, ladies and gentlemen, it is merely wires and lights in a box. It is
the moral responsibility of those gathered here tonight to make of it,
truly, the dawn of a miraculous New World."

This was greeted with tremendous applause—everyone in the ballroom was up on their feet. Even Barbour joined in ("Hating myself," he wrote, "but work is work. Why, when I looked up at Custer accepting the handshakes, the rabid slaps on the back, did the name Vidkun Quisling occur to me so distinctly?"). When the tumult finally subsided, Carter Goodell went to the microphone to make the second surprise announcement of the night. The network had established the position of director of broadcast standards—an executive who would report directly to him, and whose job would be to see that network programming adhered to the very highest, most rigorous standards of taste, truth, and responsibility—and that the person selected to occupy this new position, starting immediately, was Ned Custer himself.

"More applause," Barbour wrote in his diary. "Enough was enough for me, and before calling it a night I thought I'd go over and say hello to P. Abramsky, who I noticed standing alone and forgotten by one of the exits. His protégé is there, but he seems to have deserted him, too. I see him staring up toward the dais where Custer accepts a new round of handshakes; the expression on his (McGowan's) face showing admiration and awe—is he about to change masters? . . . I go over to Abramsky, trying to think of something clever to say . . . I get close enough to see he looks even paler and sicker than before . . . when he makes a little chuttering kind of sound, closes his eyes, pitches forward on his face, knocking over a plant . . . Instant confusion, at least in the tight, crowded circle immediately around us. McGowan kneels down to cradle his head, someone else tries clearing a space, one woman starts screaming for a doctor. This gets carried to the front, until there's a waiter standing at the mike, yelling "Is there a doctor in the house?" Everyone in the audience, not knowing what's happened, lubricated from the free booze, thinks it's a joke, a Marx Brothers' routine, and starts laughing—people really hilarious, everyone yelling and laughing and hooting—"Is there a doctor in the house? Repeat, is there a doctor in the house!"—and the man that finally comes over, the only one they can find until the ambulance comes, is an ad rep for a pharmaceutical company, and all he does is fan his portfolio back and forth over Abramsky's motionless form."

Abramsky was rushed in an ambulance to Lenox Hill Hospital,

McGowan riding with him, still cradling his head. Barbour, sensing a scoop, grabbed a cab, along with the waiter who had called for help in the first place and one of the network's ubiquitous assistant directors. By the time they got there, Abramsky had been taken to a closet-sized room just off the emergency room—the doctors, after their first frantic efforts, seemed just waiting for him to die.

"The four of us make the room too crowded; I think of the scene by Lincoln's bed . . . Abramsky's face has color now, but it's a terrible thing to see, his skin purple-black, as if it can no longer keep the blood back, the lines of his forehead already rigid and hard. Nurses had cut his shirt off with scissors—his chest lies black and bare. Strange to say, but I've never seen him look so unmistakably Jewish, so very stricken by the bitter weight of the ages . . . The waiter—Dominic turns out to be his name—asks whether there is family to call, but McGowan shakes his head, kneels by the bed, wipes his forehead, talks so softly we can't hear . . . Doctors coming in and out, then not bothering anymore. We seem to be waiting, not so much for death, but for any last words, and after a long string of them none of us can make out, mostly in German, we finally get them, sort of. 'Do you know what happened?' he asks in English, straining upward, the terror showing. No accent now, the words piercingly clear. No idea what he's referring to, except it must be something big to scare him so. Nazis? Stalin? Hiroshima? . . . 'Do you know what *happened?*' . . . We look at each other, dumbly nod, McGowan saying, 'Sure we know.' This seems to satisfy him, at least for a moment, then he starts struggling again, angry this time, enough that the red in his lips starts burning away the purple. 'Do you know what *is* happening?' Perfect English, like a drill he's reciting in naturalization class . . . What's he mean? Korea? These red-baiting turds? Yahoos firmly in command? . . . Again, McGowan speaks first. 'Yes, we know.' A few moments of calm, then he's straining upward, unable to use his arms, doing it all with his chest, like a man in a straitjacket, the fear coming back. 'Do you know what is *going* to happen?' . . . McGowan looks at him a long time, squints like he's trying to see into a future that must be so clear to Abramsky, finally nods, his voice solemn. 'Yeah, we know.' And it's only then that the old man sinks back to the bed, waving all of us to leave, all but McGowan, whom he tugs by the jacket sleeve in a gesture pathetic to behold."

Barbour waited outside the door with the two other men, feeling shaken and confused by what Abramsky had been shouting, fighting down the all but irresistible urge to put his ear to the door and listen. McGowan and the dying Peter Abramsky were alone in the room for more than two hours, interrupted only by the occasional doctor or nurse; no one knows what they talked about (what happened, is happening, will happen) or whether they talked at all—and outside the door, too, as deaf and frustrated as Louis Barbour, waits any McGowan biographer, powerless to penetrate it, unable to invent anything, inches away from a key moment in his life but permanently barred.

Four

Peter Abramsky died three hours before dawn on Monday October 1, 1950. At 7:00 A.M., Alec McGowan, apparently showing no trace whatsoever of his all-night vigil, stepped before the cameras for *Morning*'s premiere.

Months later he confessed to Laura Shelton, the third of the *Morning* girls, that this was the hardest thing he had ever done. Nothing was said during the program of the producer's passing, at least not directly—this was very much in keeping with the show-must-go-on spirit Abramsky himself would have admired. No tape is known to exist of the first show, though it can be partly reconstructed by going back to the reviews that appeared in the New York papers the following day. These ranged in tone from guarded skepticism to measured approval, and at least one of them contained a shrewd estimate of the show's potential.

Here is a portion of Milton Cassidy's evaluation in the old *Herald Tribune:*

"It's hard enough that we ink-stained wretches have to stay up all hours viewing the capers of roller derbymen, aging cowpokes and hackneyed has-beens from burlesque, but now we are asked—nay, positively commanded!—to rise from our slumbers at the ungodly hour of seven, this to watch what is billed as a grand experiment in television, *Morning,* featuring a much ballyhooed up-and-comer from Chicago named Alec McGowan.

"He's a pleasant enough, soft-spoken, bespectacled young man who comes across as a combination of Will Rogers and Fred Allen, with, so help me, a dose of the young FDR thrown in for good measure. He meanders through a well-produced show, sort of a grand goulash that goes down easy, though there was enough meat on the ribs for those wanting heartier fare.

"Mary Martin and Ezio Pinza showed up early, dressed in their coats as if they had wandered in off the street. Mr. McGowan 'invited' them to linger, and they just 'happened' to break into a duet from *South Pacific.* They were balanced with Ralph Bunche, the famous Negro, speaking on the U.S. role in the UN. What came next was a man from Vermont who claims to have the world's largest maple leaf collection, then a feature on how to change sparkplugs (McGowan, to his credit, plunging his hands right into the Studebaker that was wheeled out from the wings), and then, after a short presentation of the day's news, an interview with, of all people, Alexander Kerensky, the first premier after the Russian Revolution, now living in obscurity downtown.

"What else? Well, talk, lots of talk, especially when mechanical glitches arose with the film segments and host McGowan was forced to fill in. The subjects he waxed eloquent about included 1. Parrots; 2. Nazi war criminals; 3. Fountain pens; 4. World Series chances (he favors the Phillies); 5. The shortness of human life; 6. The relative merits of suspenders versus belts; 7. Truth (well, at least truth was *mentioned*, if not dwelt upon at length).

"A decision has apparently been reached to make the show a demonstrator's model of sorts—there was an embarrassing openness to it all, as if they couldn't be bothered building a decent set. To one reporter's eyes this came across, not as daring, but as cheap—who wants to be presented with an unshaven, slope-shouldered, suspender-wearing cameraman at *this* hour of the morning? And while old tiger McGowan is as smooth and polished and relaxed a personality as television has yet discovered, his charm is largely wasted at such a ridiculous hour. It's a good bet the program won't last into winter. Morning is simply too busy for most folks to be watching *Morning,* and, like the passersby outside the window on Forty-ninth Street which opens the show, most viewers will take a glance in now and then out of curiosity, but then proceed on down the sidewalk to the busy demands of their regular lives."

The unsigned review in the old *PM* paper was shorter and shrewder:

"Industry savants were predicting *Morning* would fall on its kisser long before yesterday's premiere, but it is off and running now, with a brave and possibly revolutionary piece of programming. Alec McGowan is an interesting host for the camera to follow, and he looks into the lens with more real sincerity and interest than any personality so far. He is surrounded by a supporting cast that is more decorative than substantial: a stolid Frank Stannard reading the news, a silly Billy Benson looking badly out of place, the familiar Barbara Tyler, whose job seems to be merely to look fetching, and a quintet led by the mellow clarinet of Terry Hodges.

"One segment, apparently spontaneous and unrehearsed, demonstrated the show's potential as a lively slice of life. A Western Union 'boy' walked in with congratulatory telegrams wishing the show well, and McGowan talked to him on camera for a good five minutes. Named Johnny Temple, he is hardly a boy at all, but a man of 54 who has been delivering telegrams for thirty years; particularly poignant were his stories of delivering telegrams during the war telling parents their sons were wounded or killed.

"The bare-bones set with its stripped-away façade, the camera film-ing other cameras, the no hiding the structure—this is as risky an experiment as television has yet seen, and it works wonderfully, making the show *part* of the show . . . Alec McGowan cannot quite seem to make up his mind whether to play it for light amusement or high seriousness, and there is some danger he may fall into the no man's land of irrelevance that waits in between. But you get the sense he recognizes this, and though the next few months will undoubtedly be a shakedown cruise, allowing McGowan to become acquainted with his audience and his audience to become acquainted with him, *Morning* seems to be under capable captaincy for a very long voyage indeed."

Enough? Keep in mind what reader already knows. Not least of bio's attraction will be "explaining" how a show everyone knows came into being. Thus emphasize similarities and differences, including a short list of early fuck-ups. Camera catching Tom Piersal with finger in nose. Lights so hot drinking water sends up steam. Guests from theater not getting it, how to act on television, coming across as ridicu-lously pompous/flowery/melodramatic, especially against AM's easy-going smoothness. Infamous Billy Benson, talking to woman whose husband due to clerical error had been stuck in army ever since war ended, her joy at his finally being released, Benson asking, "Tell us— how did it feel to hold your husband's discharge in your hands?" Cam-eramen cracking up, Benson not getting it, asking blushing wife same question again (vouched for in person by Piersal and Tyler's book). Or BB thinking mike is off, making voice go falsetto, telling AM about how moment show's over he's going to go up to Harlem to get a hot piece of ass. Frank Stannard's face supposedly red even on black and white from video sunburn; his notorious reluctance to read a roll cue. Film on, say, anti-American demonstrations in Guatemala, Stannard saying "Meanwhile in Central America, another demonstration took place protesting U.S. support for . . ." and then instead of reading roll cue, him frowning, scratching his head. "There's *supposed* to be some film here, but I don't know *where* it is."

Technical stuff, where applicable. Remote cameras apparently the program's own invention, run on automobile batteries, no tachometers to indicate speed, so sometimes Keystone Kops souped-up effect. Going right from optical sound to magnetic sound, big innovation, so program sounded sharper clearer than anything else on TV, the overlooked secret of early success. Will Jimbo know much about this? (call at station). The improvised graphics, i.e. a clay map and toy soldiers for Korea.

How gaffes become part of the show's fascination, one of reasons people watch, at least at first—to see what can go wrong next. Open studio format helps here. See, we hide nothing, not even our mistakes. Ditto AM's sign-off, immediately famous. Describe different ways he says it. Wry/earnest/tragic/sincere. *Truth.* Legend is many people watch *just* for this, tune in *only* at end.

Explain how each regular came to be so. Was Salvatore Chin first? Pint-sized garbage man. Second day or not until show went national? Wanders in to pick up trash, AM spots, waves over, talks to—his signature combination Italian/American/Chinese slang. McGowan refers to him as *sanitation man,* which is apparently origin of term, to point union adopted it, became common parlance etc—see if dictionaries acknowledge this. Maura Davidovana listed in Yellow Pages as "travelling seamstress" who they call in to fix BB's suit pants when they rip on camera. How funny she is, way she fusses over everyone, tells them they should eat more, critiques stars' dresses right to their face, asks them where did they find *that,* and so on. Mike Rinaldi thought she's still alive, living in Florida—any way to trace? Insert Muffin Man again. And Johnny Temple comes back too. "A telegram, Mr. McGowan!" shouted off camera becomes another catchphrase.

Explain how, with Abramsky dead, AM takes all creative direction onto himself. Piersal used as errand boy/traffic director keeps things flowing, but all big decisions AM's own. Fires Billy Benson. Fires Barbara Tyler, then after three weeks fires her replacement. Legend quickly grows as impossible to work for, a perfectionist, far too demanding. Get some quotes to back this up. Odd contrast between soft-spoken demeanor and sudden ferocity of judgment—speculate on why. Codeine at this stage or straight?

Laura Shelton (1923–). Originally from Cedar Rapids, Iowa, with farm-fresh complexion to match. Started on radio, then got job as Grover Whalen's assistant official greeter in NYC. AM met at reception, offered her job as third *Morning* girl. Later worked as actress on various sitcoms (*December Bride, Father Knows Best*) before retiring at an early age to raise family. Interview of 10/13/99.

Alone now, living in retirement community east of San Francisco. Comes to door with big smile on pixie face, so my first thought is Peter Pan. Happy and content, like so many from early days. Shows me photos of her family. As we talk, doorbell keeps ringing, men, widowers, stopping by to ask if she needs help with her storm windows or whether she wants them to pick up her mail. Treats them all gently—a natural-born sweetheart.

I lasted six months, three days, forty-five minutes, which was the record until Lee Palmer came along. It was part of the show's attraction after a while, people watching just to see how the new girl would do, whether or not she would be "it." Now a lot of this had to do with Alec's demands, how he was never satisfied—we could talk all afternoon about why he wasn't. But it was a hard role to fit yourself into. For instance, poor Barbara Tyler, the first one. She got it all wrong, and why not, since there was absolutely no model to follow. She thought—well, I'm an actress, I'm on television, I should act. How she acted, that was the problem. She was all flirtatious, to every guest that came on, trying to vamp them—she had a habit of putting her hand on Alec's arm every chance she got and that didn't go down well at all. What you have to remember is that all these women were watching in the morning, all these young mothers whose husbands had gone off to work and left them with the kids. They liked fantasizing about Alec in an innocent kind of way, and the last thing they wanted was to have to compete for his attention with a busty blonde. It took a while for everyone to understand this, and by that time another *Morning* girl had come and gone.

Me, I was supposed to be the brainy one. *Be yourself*—that's all Alec told me, and the next thing I knew the cameras were on. Now, it's one thing to be yourself when no one is watching, something else when there are millions out there. It warps you. I knew I was flubbing it, I hated myself, and yet I couldn't help wanting to be mainly . . . can I confess it? . . . *pretty*. It was all I thought about. If you ever manage to dig up any tapes, you'll see my voice sounds about three octaves higher than it really is, and it goes all fluttery. Lord, what was I thinking? That Davidovana seamstress, bless her heart, had me pegged early. You act like a librarian who's seen too many Greta Garbo movies, she said, right on camera, and I knew she was right. Alec was very gentle when he fired me—this was during a commercial and we stood behind the weather map where no one could see us. We're going with someone else, he said, like it pained him. No explanation really. I started to say something and he grabbed his head, like I mustn't, it was hurting him—he turned his back on me and stomped off . . . I was cleaning out my things later that afternoon when he happened by, looking exhausted as he always did when a show was over. What he said surprised me, though it shouldn't have, given his reputation. He asked me out on a date, and though I was cursing him for a hard-hearted insensitive bastard just a moment before, I said yes . . . This all happened about the time he hired your father and the show took off.

The hiring of Chet Standish. Abbreviated version now, then blah blah blah to wit etc. and so forth later. Reader will sense my holding back and be alert for that, so keep relatively straightforward, informational, as for instance: While the distaff side of the program would remain shaky, the male side began rounding into shape. Frank Stannard, other than his notorious stubbornness over roll cues, worked out fine delivering the news; his craggy Montana features, his two-note range of expression (bemusement to concern and back again), his clear and commanding voice (one reviewer described it as "Listerine sharp") won him instant popularity and a career on the program that lasted forty-one years. Billy Benson, on the other hand, was fired his second week, which set up an opening for another male. McGowan interviewed applicants himself and none of them met his qualifications. What he wanted was someone flexible enough to do the promos and commercials, weighty enough to interview the politicians, friendly and outgoing enough that he could fill the on-air role as McGowan's sidekick and best friend.

Tom Piersal remembers talking it over after yet another out-of-work actor packed up his clips and left.

"I want an everyday kind of person," McGowan said, pointing, as he always did when at a loss, toward the street. "A regular guy."

"You got someone specific in mind, don't you?" Piersal said.

"He's a kind of genius."

"We don't need genius."

"A genius of normality."

"Yeah? Where's this genius live?"

"Springfield, Mass. But I think he'd come if I called."

"What's his name?"

"Chester Standish. There's genius in his vocal cords, too." McGowan hesitated, then flashed Piersal the most dazzling and irresistible of his smiles. "The only thing is, he's nearly blind."

The two men went back a long way. When Philias LeBlanc's father drowned, his mother, fiercely ambitious for her only son, changed his name to one she hoped could power him through the world toward the success she craved: Alec McGowan—and she didn't stop there. Forging tax receipts, inventing an address, spending all her savings on a sports coat and suit, she talked him into the best high school in Springfield. One of his classmates there was a good-natured boy named Chet Standish, whose father owned the paper mill, under the reeking effusion of which the young LeBlanc/McGowan had been raised. The two boys hit it off; for all the differences in their upbringing and characters, both shared an impatience with provincial tameness and mediocrity, though in McGowan this burned in fierce, unpredictable flames, in Standish, like ashes that smoldered. Then, too, Standish recognized there was real ability beneath McGowan's swagger and bluff—he was the first one to defer to him, worship him, give him his due.

When Chet was seventeen, his father won a local radio station in a poker game—a Springfield legend that turns out to be essentially true. Not interested himself, searching for a career that would suit his well-meaning, somewhat plodding only child, he gave Chet the station the way other fathers would hand their son a jalopy, telling him to make of it what he could. Chet, in turn, immediately enlisted Alec McGowan's help, and so while they were still seniors in high school they were running what quickly became known as the most up-to-date, innovative, and interesting station in town.

When the war came and McGowan left to enlist, Standish felt abandoned and badly out of his depth. He married a classmate named Margaret Pebble, who had all the business acumen and firmness he himself lacked. Declared 4F because of his eyesight (he suffered from macular degeneration—an erosion of the central part of his vision normally seen only in seventy-year-olds), he brooded his way through the war years, unhappy, but not talking about it, seemingly as stolid and content as ever. When McGowan, whom he hadn't been in contact with for nine years, called out of the blue one morning with his offer, Chet had two young children and was on the verge of settling into a premature, restless middle age. Intimidated by his wife, terminally bored with Springfield, still hero-worshiping the idealized version he remembered of his friend, possessed by the feeling that he needed to grasp life instantly before it passed him by forever, he leapt at the chance—and twenty-four hours after hanging up he had moved to New York for a trial period on the show, renting a businessman's efficiency on Seventh Avenue just across from Carnegie Hall.

Right from the start it worked out wonderfully, at least as regards the program. McGowan and Standish had developed a lightly teasing way of relating to each other during their days on radio, and it translated well to TV, where nothing like this informal and relaxed interplay had been seen before. Viewers responded to Standish's well-meaning earnestness, even his squareness, especially how it contrasted with the vaguely Bohemian quality that underlay McGowan's smoothness. Standish was the straight arrow, the friendly neighbor, the one you could count on, everyone's uncle. His voice seemed much larger than anything his body could account for, and he used it to great effect on the commercials—it was a voice you couldn't imagine being enlisted for anything but the strictest truth. His eyesight, the problems with it, weren't obvious, at least not in the early days, when he would arrive at the studio an hour before anyone else to walk around and around until he memorized where everything was located. By the time his trial period ended, it was obvious he was the perfect man for the job, the humble foundation above which McGowan's talent could soar.

Even with the cast settling into place, the show went through a rough patch during that first winter. The primitive ratings system showed a declining number of viewers—the evidence suggested that people turned television on out of curiosity in the morning, but that's all they would do, everyone being too busy getting ready for their day to actually sit and watch. Even worse, there were indications that people used the program only as background noise, something to turn on while shaving and then ignore, and that there would have to be much more in the way of visual appeal to break them of this habit. Doubting critics, skeptical advertisers, executives in the network who had been dubious all along—there were many who would have liked nothing better than to see the program fall flat on its face. Then, too, Abramsky was no longer around to run interference, and the rumors were that if ratings didn't improve by Easter, *Morning* would be scrapped.

On March 5, 1951, one of the guests was a lion tamer from the Ringling Brothers Circus named Hercules Strong. As a kind of tease, he brought along his "pet"—not a lion, but a young male chimpanzee named Freddo, wearing a diaper. Freddo was a hit, right from his first appearance. He had a wide, bemused smile, a friendly way of smacking his lips, the trick of putting his arm around anyone who sat beside him in fraternal goodwill, and the even better trick of sneaking behind whatever bigshot politician was on, snorting, making a face. Phones at the network began ringing the moment his first show was over, people asking how they could get pictures of Freddo, or demanding that he be brought on again. It was more calls than they had ever gotten. Had a corner been turned?

Piersal wanted Freddo as a regular. McGowan, the one person who had never lost faith that the program would catch on, hesitated, for the obvious reasons. Here he had been trying to set a certain tone for the show, a deliberate way of regarding the world, and while this included humor and even zaniness, he couldn't help thinking a half-naked chimpanzee might be going too far. While he brooded, the advertising people were putting all the pressure on him they could, but this only made McGowan dig in his heels. Weeks went by—Strong threatened to take Freddo west with him when the circus left town—and the only break in the impasse came when Piersal had the bright idea of sending McGowan to talk it over with Ned Custer.

No one was at the meeting besides McGowan and Custer, but it's possible to reconstruct much of their conversation from what McGowan later told Laura Shelton. As proof of his importance, Custer was installed in an office on the forty-seventh floor, immediately adjacent to the general's. BROADCAST STANDARDS read the sign on the door, and this is what he was called by everyone in the network, half in respect, half in fear. *Have you cleared this with Broadcast Standards?* writers and producers would ask each other. *Broadcast Standards okay this yet? You get BS yet on this or no?*

He had changed since the night of the speech. The soft tweed jacket had given way to a blue pinstriped suit, and he'd gotten a crewcut, one that left his silvery hair vertical and stiff, like brain waves made visible. His office, smelling of wintergreen, featured blond mahogany furniture, wall plaques from B'nai B'rith and other organizations, a sand-filled ashtray with *Stork Club* engraved on the side in flowery script.

"I hear wonderful things about you," Custer said, when the two men sat down.

McGowan, who was getting used to flattery, modestly smiled. All the evidence is that he'd been tremendously impressed by Custer's speech, especially the part about making television the ordinary man's medium.

"Yes," Custer said, tapping his fingers against the Dictaphone machine on his desk, "I hear you throw the most wonderful of parties."

This took McGowan aback; at a loss, all he could think of was to invite him to come any time he wanted.

"Oh, no, no," Custer said. "I'm too old for such foolery." He smiled, disarmingly. "And I hear you're having trouble with an ape."

McGowan outlined the situation. Custer listened patiently—he explained this was exactly the thorny kind of problem he'd been hired to attend to—and only once did he interrupt with an actual question. "Will it soil itself?" he asked—and, assured that Freddo wore a diaper, he smiled and wrote something down on his pad.

"I think we have to keep one important factor in mind," he said, when McGowan finished. "Your show, your concept, is one that is going to revolutionize television. You're bringing the world into people's homes for the first time ever, and not only that, but as it is happening. You're expanding their concept of what their domain is, making them citizens of a much larger, more complex, and much more rewarding kind of world."

"Yes," McGowan said, flashing a smile that was as self-deprecating as Custer's own. "And now here we are asking to bring a chimpanzee into that world."

Custer let this go past. "I'll be frank with you, Alec. What you're setting out to do won't be easy. There are those who would like to see television used for a very different purpose indeed. Not to elevate the masses, but to lower them. There are merchants of greed out there purveying the slickest of lies, legions of them. I would like to think their moment in the industry will be brief, but there you are—they are a factor not to be denied. Certainly, it's incumbent upon us to present the issues of our times with enough showmanship that most people will be eager to watch. But let me say this. I would like you to know you have a friend here in this office you can always count on. Someone who understands what you're doing and applauds it. I haven't been shy in expressing these views—the general is getting weary of hearing me out. Any difficulties, any gray areas that arise, you come in and talk it over with me and we'll see what we can do."

Custer got to his feet, ran his hand back to preen his crewcut, led him over to the door. It was only later, when he took the elevator back down to the studio, that McGowan (telling the story to Shelton) realized he'd been given permission to use the chimp.

Freddo became a regular the next morning and ratings immediately soared. Everyone who had watched the show admired and respected it, but now everyone *talked* about it: asking their friends if they'd seen what Freddo had been up to that morning. Bouncing on Chet's lap, leaping up on a camera and pounding his chest, begging candy bars from stagehands, riding his little scooter or tossing his toy football. Freddo, as one reviewer put it, "took a somewhat static show and hurried it into motion, cranking up the speed and immediacy so everything buzzed."

Kids loved him, of course—they were sitting at the breakfast table demanding their parents watch. Mothers loved him even more, and it was thought this had something to do with the fact that Freddo was in diapers, a charming detail baby-boom mothers could relate to. In the early days, Freddo had real charm, and toward the end of the program he would bounce up on McGowan's lap and put his arm around his shoulder, nuzzle his chin, as if comforting him after a hard day's work.

Morning's chimpanzee phase didn't last long. As with many stars, success soon went to Freddo's head and his behavior became increasingly erratic. He started biting people, including his trainer, Hercules Strong. (Strong responded by pulling him off camera and socking him in the jaw.) He had discovered Chet couldn't see very well, and he took great delight in swiping props from right under his nose. The final straw was the show of May 16, which became an immediate TV legend. Freddo started the morning by lifting up the skirt of a woman novelist and sniffing, followed this by biting the visiting March of Dimes boy on his knee, then climbed up on the overhead lights and tore his diaper off to crap.

Something had to be done about this, but Piersal was afraid that if they "fired" him public reaction would be overwhelmingly negative. He was kept on for another month, under heavy sedation—it was a mellower, less interesting Freddo everyone saw now—and this phased him out so gently there was hardly any comment at all when Chet Standish came on camera in June to say, sadly, that Freddo had passed away and been buried out in a quiet, grassy grove on Long Island.

He had done his job. Those three months saw *Morning* go from a novelty not many people knew about to an integral part of the American day. By April, *Morning* had an 80.7 share of the viewing audience, as measured by the three ratings systems then struggling for dominance (Hooper, Nielsen, and Trendex)—an unheard-of figure, even if the morning competition at this stage was largely test patterns and cartoons. And by May a curious phenomenon began to be noted—that more children than ever were arriving late for school, and not only that, but more of the workforce was arriving late, too, white-collar types and blue-collar in equal measure, right across the country. Critics wondered how to account for this. A declining work ethic? People exhausted from trying to grab too much at once? Only gradually did the answer become clear (an answer immediately trumpeted at full volume by the network publicity people): they were staying home as long as possible to watch *Morning*.

It wasn't just the chimp. In those early days McGowan accomplished what he and Abramsky had set out to do: convince a majority of Americans that their day couldn't be said to be under way until they watched at least a portion of *Morning*. Before, the tendency had been for people to think of the overnight hours as an intermission during which nothing of any significance happened; thanks to *Morning's* news reports (before this, news had always been the property of the evening, even on radio), which emphasized what had happened in Europe and Korea and time zones to the east, the notion was conveyed that something very important had indeed happened during the night and the only way to find out about it was to turn on the TV immediately upon wakening ("the town crier effect," critics called this). This was combined with the other half of the program's strategy: the emphasis on the events that would be happening in the course of that particular day, so that watching the program became as automatic as glancing at your calendar or appointment book, only on a larger scale. Suddenly it became important to know that President Truman was due to speak before the American Legion in Indianapolis that afternoon, or that Judy Garland was going to open at Radio City, or that the world's second-highest skyscraper was going to be topped off in Chicago with a special ceremony.

Everywhere now the talk was of Alec McGowan—everywhere people were imitating the slow, earnest way he raised his hand and signed off. There were real, calculated reasons behind his success, but, as always, much of this was ultimately unaccountable—why a great number of Americans suddenly decided that this man so perfectly embodied all they liked best in their own era. He had accomplished the first part of his goal, getting a sense of the country, and now the second part was accomplished, too, getting his hands on it, grasping it, looking it squarely in the eye, and now, just past his thirty-third birthday, with everyone telling him, if he didn't already sense it, that the world lay at his feet, he could concentrate on the hardest, most dangerous and tempting of his challenges: what to do with this morning power he so triumphantly had won.

Evidence of his personal life from this period is difficult to come by. He rented a studio apartment in a shabby neighborhood on the West Side, though he was working so hard he barely spent any time there. He had no real male friends until Chet Standish arrived, just buddies from the show, cameramen and writers he enjoyed having a few drinks with. Someone must have told him he was working too hard, needed some relaxation, because that first full summer saw him renting an old mansion on the North Shore of Long Island right on the water, spending his weekends there, weekends which soon became famous thanks to his parties.

The most reliable surviving witness from that year is Laura Shelton. Their first date had gone well; he had taken her to his favorite musical, *South Pacific,* and she had cried at exactly the moment he expected all his dates to cry, Ezio Pinza singing "This Nearly Was Mine" (a piano

version of which was *Morning*'s new theme), and then after a late dinner they had taken a taxi over to the East River.

As much as I enjoyed the show, the rest of the evening was even
better. One of the first guests on the program was a Venetian gondolier who had brought his boat over on a freighter and was offering
rides along the river. It was wonderful—Alec and the gondolier talked
to each other in pidgin Italian and Alec kept asking him all these questions about Venice. He was a reader, people forget that—it's one of
the reasons he could talk to anyone about anything . . . Alec was very
sweet on a date, very much the gentleman. He never wore glasses
when he went out, which made him look boyish, so I think women felt
protective. Boyish and yet a bit world-weary, too. He had invented
himself and he had to keep inventing, and he was already tired of this.
Without glasses no one recognized him—he could have walked into
the Copacabana and no one would have blinked. With the glasses on,
headwaiters saluted. He didn't care anything for celebrity, though, not
even a little. He was a real romantic about things, and while I found
this enormously appealing, it made me frightened for him, too, being
in such a business. He had a way of withdrawing from all common
concerns, focusing inward—the right to do this was the only privilege
he ever demanded. I think he would have been happier as a creative
artist working in solitude rather than a performer, but that's what he
had to do—try to fit himself into a role that was nowhere near as natural as he made it seem. There was a side to him that was different, of
course—the huckster part. But you had the sense he was trying to
smother that, use it only when absolutely needed, in self-defense . . .
Anyway, there we were in the gondola all by ourselves on the East
River, and it was chilly out and we had a blanket and when I got shiv-
ery I could look up and see the silver lights up high in the blackness,
and to make a long story short, by the time we got back to the pier I
was head over heels for him, head over heels bad.

She remembers, most vividly of all, summer weekends at his mansion on the Sound. He would be waiting at the station when his guests
arrived Friday afternoon, driving an oversized roadster from the twen-

ties that had come with the rental, wearing a yellow planter's hat with a turned-down brim, tennis clothes that were too big for him, and the heavy black boots of a lobsterman. The sun had freckled up his face, so he looked younger than he did in New York, lither, quicker on his feet; he would stand on the running board waving to each face he recognized as they stepped down from the train.

The house itself had once belonged to a bootlegger, and it was surrounded on all sides by an expansive lawn landscaped, according to McGowan, to give its former inhabitants a clear field of fire. Before the war this had been the richest part of the Shore, the one with the most lavish mansions, but times had changed, and a new highway out to the suburbs now cut through many of the oldest properties, chopping them up until the houses rose like obsolete castles set on scabby promontories in a wasteland of cement. McGowan's house managed to escape the worst of this; set beside the Sound, it enjoyed both a glorious view over the water and the freshness of the late-afternoon breeze.

One of the best things about these weekends was that you never knew who you were going to meet there, McGowan apparently having had the habit of inviting anyone who appeared on the show. A great many took him up on this. Laura stood by the tennis court one night watching some athletic young men throw an old football back and forth across the net, when she realized the man closest to her, the one who threw negligently and gracefully at the same time, a cigarette drooping from his lips, was Joe DiMaggio.

Celebrities from show business, politicians in the news, jazz musicians, ballplayers, TV people—they were all there that summer, helping themselves to McGowan's booze, waiting on line at the long buffet table, eventually, many of them, running down to the beach, tearing their clothes off and plunging in. McGowan took special pains to invite his growing band of regulars. Violet Shugrue, the one-armed typist. Manuel Ramos, the industrial cleaner. Danny O'Fallen, the sandwich-board man ("I'm in advertising, Mr. McGowan, but I done it all"). Mordecai Stern, the professional matchmaker, sent on originally by McGowan's friends as a joke but quickly an audience favorite. They all brought along their families, so there were plenty of kids running around, even when the parties grew wildest, so one-half the mansion would seem like the changing room at Jones Beach, the other half like center stage at a Roman bacchanal.

There were some oddities, too. Laura saw Broadcast Standards there once, wearing tennis flannels softer and whiter even than McGowan's, looking lordly, like it was by rights his mansion and he was puzzled to see anyone else there. Chet Standish came, too, making a happy fool of himself over the girls. She felt sorry for him—it was as if he'd never had any fun in life and was trying to make up for lost time. He had already become the butt of jokes because of his eyesight, and the one that made the rounds that summer was how he was only interested in big-breasted women, flat-chested ones not even registering on his radar as female. McGowan, if he caught wind of any of these, immediately lost his temper, yelling at whoever was joking to shut the hell up. He was fiercely loyal to Chet—you discovered that in a hurry, or else you were told to leave.

Most of the fun was innocent, at least compared to what happens today. (Laura speaking again.) Yes, couples would disappear into the house for ten minutes and come back looking coy. Drugs, too. A lot of those jazz men were serious, though I don't think Alec was—his problem was codeine, and that came later. No, it was mostly booze, scotch or bubbly. I remember one night toward the end of summer. We were dating, I made no secret about how I felt about him, but always just when I felt something finally melting in him it was like a cold surge would take over, the shadows dropped down again, he grew moody and backed away. He was terribly polite about this, of course, but somehow that only made it worse.

Labor Day weekend saw the last of the parties. Laura and Alec walked down to the shore just past midnight, sat against the low seawall, staring out past the sand at the scattered buoy lights forming a red necklace across the Sound. There was something ghostly about the scene—not a scary ghost, but the kind of ghost image that early TV

pictures were prone to, where everything seemed echoed by a doubling of its own image. She blamed this on the booze. They had both
been drinking, but she had the feeling McGowan was acting drunker
than he really was in order to evade the obvious issue. Between the
early autumn air, the sadness the alcohol brought, and the occasion,
the night, in her words, seemed stained with farewell.

"Okay," she said, after they had sat there for a time, their shoulders
nestling. "Who is she?"

Alec pretended not to understand. "Over there is Massachusetts,"
he said, slurring the word for all it was worth. "I've been watching it all
summer. It's moving closer."

"I've seen it before. No, Alec, I don't mean Mass-a-chu-setts. I
mean when a man has a woman he can't get over. A lost love. Someone
he puts up on a pedestal and erects a wall around and casts in bronze.
We could stay together for years and I could never find a space beside
her . . . I don't think you owe me a detailed explanation, but just out of
curiosity I wonder who she is."

He tried putting his arm around her shoulder, but when she drew
back he grabbed a handful of pebbles and threw them angrily toward
the Sound.

"Worst place in the world, you know that?"

She sighed, braced herself for what was coming. "What is?" she
said wearily.

"Massachusetts. Biggest snobs in the world live there. They go to
Hahh-ved and Amherst and Mount Holy Yolk and they think they
own the goddam world. You know what their motto is, the word that
defines them? Impunity. They feel armored by a sense of impunity. It's
where they live. Full Impunity, Massachusetts."

"Aren't you exaggerating?"

He spread his arms apart, as if he hadn't even begun. "That's on
one side of town. On the other, you have your Frenchies living in
slums, little more than white niggers, always talking about going to
duh grocery tore, or duh five and den, kowtowing to priests, dreaming
about their son becoming a priest or their daughter a nun, like virgin-

dom is the greatest thing that could ever happen. You throw in those Irish mediocrities, the real crooks like Joe Kennedy, the textile bosses, the pompous assholes like Lodge, and you give all of them, without exception, a swelled head, and you have what I call the worst fucking place in the world."

"You don't mean that."

"They framed Sacco and Vanzetti. Made their fortunes shipping slaves. Coolidge was mayor of Northampton, how do you account for that? Puritans sucked the joy out of the country before there even was a country. Indian killers by the score. Did I mention slaves, Sacco and Vanzetti? What's the one common denominator here? Come on, tell, me, only you don't have to because it goes without saying. Massachusetts."

He said this with real vehemence, something she hadn't seen in him before—this surprised her and in an odd way flattered her, to see one wall down at least. She listened to him rant and rave, listing all the terrible things he could think of to heap on the state's head, stopping only to take another swig from the whiskey bottle between his legs or hurl another fistful of pebbles toward the Sound—she listened, thinking, well this is over, it was fun while it lasted, and if what we're looking for now is a line to end this on it may as well be mine.

"Alec?" she said softly. "I hate to break it to you, but those lights way out there? That's Connecticut, not Massachusetts."

He looked at her in bewilderment, stared out toward where she pointed, squinted with a drunk's exaggerated concentration, rubbed his eyes, shrugged.

"Massachusetts' doormat. I hate Connecticut even worse."

She smiles remembering that—smiles and grows quiet.

That was the end of it, at least for us. I never saw him again after that weekend, except on TV. I was a smart young thing, but not that smart, and it was only later, after what happened, that I realized what he had been trying in his drunken way to tell me—that there *was* a great love in his life and that she lived in Massachusetts. Smart, right? We were all so stupid then . . . But you had the sense, being around

Alec that summer, that he had reached a dangerous plateau and reached it too early, and that he could only go down from what he had created for himself, yet at the same time recognizing there was still room for tremendous growth, if he could only get through the next few years . . . It's the question you should answer in your biography, if you do nothing else. Did your father cut him off just as his trajectory was rising again, or was he putting him out of his misery, delivering the coup de grâce? . . . It's really hard to try to describe him in words. If you could only find some film you would see for yourself what I mean. He was a man put on earth in order to be seen on television, or maybe it was the other way around—television was invented in order to present to the world a beautiful man like him.

There exists one surviving tape from *Morning*'s first year, a Kinescope of smoky opaqueness and fragile stiffness not much longer than fifteen or sixteen coils around the center of a tarnished aluminum spool. If you ask at the Museum of Television and Radio in New York, fake some academic credentials, the attendant will fetch it for you, or at least a videotape made from the original—you take it into a closet-sized room and watch on a little monitor.

What you're watching is a film made to promote the show to potential advertisers. There is no sound—the surviving footage is an outtake left over from editing. It's short, five minutes' worth, and very simple, showing the crowd of faces that came to Forty-ninth Street each morning to peer through the famous window. This is the shot that opened every show, faces near the glass, and then McGowan stepping in front of them to start the show off.

McGowan isn't on this tape—it's faces in the window alone. They're staring at a monitor just the other side of the glass where they can see themselves on television, and, just beyond this, the basic *Morning* set with the show in progress. The camera filming them is not the camera they're staring at but one just to the side, so their profiles are captured—this gives the feeling of taking them naked and unaware.

The tape must be a composite of several days' worth of programming; even with expert splicing, you soon realize the faces are changing, though the overall impression of the crowded, surging mass remains constant throughout.

Several things strike you when you first start to watch. The black-and-white image, for starters—how it seems much more real than color, giving you the feeling this is precisely the tint and texture 1951 would have chosen to go down in history with if given the choice. The clothes strike you, too; this is long enough ago that they seem not just dated but antique, especially the hats. Everyone wears hats. The women in cloches that seem like leftovers from flapper days, or extravagant concoctions with feathers that make you think of the Three Musketeers, or neat little caps copied from the latest Parisian styles. The men, without exception, in fedoras, their personalities revealed in how they wear them, cocked soberly down over their foreheads like gangsters, or rakishly to the side, with big-city panache.

Their naïveté is striking, too—these are people who aren't used to the camera lens and so are both shy of it and fascinated. No one knows to preen or strut yet, and so the effect is of simple, unjaded folk, media peasants, staring with excitement and awe at the first car to pull into town, or a flying machine, or their first train. Toward the end of the tape this changes—people are catching on very fast—and there are teenagers mouthing "Hi, Mom!" or mugging, as if in the course of those few weeks the camera has become the most natural presence in the world, and everyone has a little act prepared to trot out the moment they get their chance.

They seem gaunter than a modern crowd—not shabby, but examples of a leaner, faster, hungrier race of man. Many of them point to the monitor, laugh open-mouthed to see themselves pointing; some blow cigarette smoke, others blow kisses; the ones in back strain to see over the ones in the middle; many of the younger ones raise their fists over their heads like prizefighters; one old black woman makes a tsk-tsk motion with her lips; a young couple put their heads together and make a bouncy jitterbugging wiggle side to side; two secretaries smile coquettishly; a girl in back, like a frantic bobby-soxer, presses her hands to her cheeks and silently screams; men in hard hats chew rolls so large their faces disappear in crust.

Many of these are obviously New Yorkers, but increasingly they're joined by people from out of town—the *Morning* window quickly became one of the most popular tourist attractions the city offered. From that very first week people began holding up signs bearing the names of their hometowns, ranging from lipstick scrawled across handkerchiefs to elaborate placards up on sticks. The camera lingers on these, and if you watch with a pad and pencil, slow the playback speed, you can jot down the names. McKeesport, Pennsylvania. Sandusky, Ohio. Hannibal, Missouri. Paris, Maine. Guthrie, Oklahoma. Austerlitz, New York. Browning, Montana. Davenport, Iowa. Heber Springs, Arkansas. Nogales, Arizona. Kokomo, Indiana. White Pine, Nevada. Baton Rouge, Louisiana. Port Townsend, Washington. Sauk Centre, Minnesota. Enterprise, Oregon. Scottsboro, Alabama. Homestead, Florida. Nephi, Utah. Cripple Creek, Colorado. Meridian, Mississippi. Waco, Texas. Whittier, California. Los Alamos, New Mexico.

The signs—and then more faces, new ones pressing their way forward for their turn in front. A girl in a sailor suit with a Mona Lisa smile. A toothless old man whose mouth drops open in wonder. A bearish man with thick eyebrows wearing a Russian fur hat. Someone in a gorilla suit beating his fists against his chest. An exact look-alike of Marilyn Monroe, only retarded-looking, her eyes empty, her jaw slack. A child sitting on her father's shoulders swaying dreamily back and forth to the magic of her own image. A boy making a polishing motion with his hand.

They press close to the glass, ducking under the rail, the ones behind them press on them, still more are coming all the time, people are standing up on tiptoe, jumping, until the sheer weight of humanity makes the faces closest to the glass go hard and determined as they fight to hold their place. For a moment the balance is equal—but then the ones in back press harder, the close-up faces go soft and distorted in the beginnings of panic, and in the flattening of grayness caused by the crush, the window itself becomes visible for the first time, greasy from the flesh pressing against it, a thin membrane of dirty transparency, bulging inward, out and inward, a little further each time, until just as you wince, move instinctively back from the screen expecting it to shatter, the tape races through a last blur of illegible signs, skips over a black-striped nothingness, makes a wet snapping sound, flashes silver, darkens, dies.

Five

The window was everything to him right from the start. I would pull into the parking lot, climb out of the car loaded down with groceries and medicine, trying not to glance up that way but glance up anyway, see his face three stories above me in the corner where the brick wings joined—see Chet's face half in profile, a man mimicking a crescent moon, the pale orb of it sliced by the blinds into thick vertical bars. He would still be there when I let myself in, the back side of his head with its crown of warts, his nose pressed so tight against the glass I could see the misty smudge that doubled it from the warmth of his exhalations. What could he have seen there? A square of concrete, a few twigs of oak, cars, occasionally someone getting out of one, for excitement a stray cat or dog. Not much of a world, and yet, I kept reminding myself, for forty-six years he had put up with a smaller one, and for all I know he saw mountains there, prairies, stars.

The apartment itself was clean, warm, and anonymous, located where the city broke apart into the first plush suburbs, with the medical center only a mile away. It was no problem at all to arrange for a nurse to come in, set up a lifeline, take care of the basics. Beyond the basics? I came when I could, which was at least once a day, but he hardly left the window for me, the glass creating a sticky adhesive he was too old and feeble to break, even if he had wanted to. If he wasn't by the window, then he was in the bathroom, and if he wasn't there, then he was in front of the television, his face pressed as tight to the screen as it had been to the window, his hand on the picture as if he were afraid it would slip away.

Did he watch *Morning*? He did not watch *Morning*. The only programming that interested him was the Weather Channel, which he had on continuously. Did he remember, I wondered, that Alec McGowan had been the weather map's inventor, that he himself had been one of the first to stand before it with a pointer, casually limning out cold fronts, storm tracks, and tornadoes, updating America on the battering it was in store for—the what, the where, the when?

"Hello, Chet," I would say, putting the groceries down on the kitchen table, making my voice a lot more jovial than anything I felt. "Well, what's the verdict? Cold, hot, or in between?"

He wouldn't answer, not right away, but let his hand linger on the screen, as if there were a kind of Braille at work, or he was judging the temperature by his fingers. "Cold," he said, in his deep announcer's voice. "Bitter cold. In the Plains and the Texas Panhandle. Early frost in Florida. The orange crop is at risk."

"I've brought your new prescription. Are you still coughing? Doctor Herne says this will help."

He would get up, hitch his pants tighter, walk like an old baggy-pants vaudevillian across the room to the straight-backed chair he favored over the plusher ones, incline his face against the window, nestling it there, as if the glass had softened to the indentation of his

features. Bathroom—window—television—window. That was his circuit,
the locus of his days, making it seem the only task left to him in life
was to find out what fate was racing across the country toward us, then
go to the window to wait for its arrival.

Passive, beaten, catatonic. This is how I described him to Kim, and
yet it became obvious over those first weeks that there was more activity going on than I suspected. One of the things he asked me to buy
for him was some sketching pads and thick felt markers. Tacked to the
wall, pressed to the refrigerator, stuck in every available cranny were
notes he wrote himself in black sloppy letters big enough for his
myopic eyes to make out. With nothing better to do, faced with his
silence, I got in the habit of reading these the moment I got there,
updating myself on the new ones, looking for old favorites, trying to
decipher not just what they meant individually but what they meant en
masse.

One morning at a time! one read, taped to the back of the couch. *Keep
options flexible* read another, this one pinned to the curtains. *It's not the
destination but the journey* read a third. *Morning pills three with milk. Vincit
omnia VERITAS! Exercise where applicable. Hurricane special 9:00 Eastern.
Beware no man more than thyself! Be frank and open and manly with Dr. Thad-
deus S. Herne. A ROSE among THORNS is a ROSE still. Dinty Moore stew
the kind with potatoes three cans. WHAT FOOLS THESE MORTALS
BE!!!*

There were dozens of these, exhortations, reminders, injunctions,
proverbs, many of which I couldn't decipher at all, stare as I would.
The one I always came back to was tacked outside the bathroom door,
IN AN EMERGENCY CALL MY SON, and I would remain there,
staring at it, while behind the door Chet wrestled in private with what
the cancer was doing to his insides, me standing guard to make sure he
was all right, that it wasn't an emergency yet, that I wouldn't have to
call what must surely be another person, *my son.*

The only other thing that interested him was the lunch I brought,
more specifically the soup. He had become addicted to canned soup
while in prison, and now that he had his freedom he was determined

to indulge it every chance he got. And it wasn't going to be cream of tomato, either, but every kind of exotic variation I could find. She-crab soup from South Carolina, lobster chowder from Maine, imported bouillabaisse. I would take the cans out from the bag, open one, put it in a saucepan, and the smell would eventually draw him over to the kitchen, even put a smile on his face, get him talking.

"I sampled she-crab soup in Charleston once," he said. "We'd gone there to do a remote. They put sherry in and they put too much and they did it deliberately just to get me garrulous."

"One of McGowan's famous walking tours?" I asked, seeing an opening.

"Walking? He liked to walk?"

"You tell me."

His smile fell. "I don't remember."

"It was one city a month, wasn't it? San Francisco was first. San Francisco through his eyes, and it must have been 1951."

He didn't respond and we never went any further in this direction— a cautious tiptoe toward the past, then the little scurry of retreat, back to the steaming bowls in front of us, the artificial, overrefined taste of whatever we were eating, the appreciative smacking sound as Chet sucked it down.

He had been there three weeks, it was already the middle of November, before I let anyone else in to visit. There were what I considered to be good reasons for this delay. First, because I wanted him to get settled; second, because he had a brief flare-up of fever; third, because everyone was so busy I couldn't find the right day. As a backup, I had a reason that was even stronger: I didn't want my family becoming too close to a man who would be dead by Easter.

Or so I told myself. What seemed odd was that here was a total stranger, someone who was my "father" only by the most liberal interpretation, the kids' "grandfather" by an even greater stretch, and yet right away there was pressure to do the right thing. I resisted this because it angered me, and then I got to the point where I couldn't resist anymore, the family was giving me funny looks, acting like I was an insensitive ogre, so I started with visitors, and the first one I started with was Kim.

I arranged for her to come in the morning, when he was at his strongest—I went ahead early to get him ready—and so I was sitting on the sofa helping him tie his shoes when she knocked lightly on the door and let herself in. Partly because of where I was situated, partly because I intended to, I saw her for that first moment as Chet might have, someone completely new to me—saw, in other words, an attractive, alert woman in her early forties, dressed in a dark wool suit, ready for work that was obviously professional and demanding. Her hair is gray, worn long—years before, when it was fashionable to wear it long, she had worn it short—and this little note of rebelliousness goes down well with the intelligence that's immediately evident in her expression, keeps it from being too prim and severe.

What else? She's slender, fit, an athlete aging well. Her face is small-featured, the skin paler than she would like but completely unwrinkled, with the kind of sympathetic eyes that suggest the beloved elementary school teacher she once was. Along with this comes something that partly contradicts it—an ironic set to the mouth, a skeptical tilt of the head left by too many school-board meetings, too many political battles, too much fighting over too much that is petty and small—and then I had to imagine this through his eyes, his real eyes, her features smudged and blended by myopia, so the overall impression he must have had was of a slim band of maroon-colored light moving across the room toward him, a package held before it like the brightly wrapped gift of grace itself.

"Why, hello, Kim," I said very formally, as if I hadn't seen her in months, and "Come over here and let me introduce someone to you."

Chet smiled, then did his best to push himself up from the sofa, forgetting that one shoe was still off. He immediately slipped on one of his sketching pads that lay on the carpet, did a perfect slapstick pratfall, his arms windmilling through the air, then—just before falling flat on his face—caught his balance and walked over to meet her as serenely, with as much dignity, as a restaurant maître d'.

"It's a pleasure," he said, bobbing his head down in the general direction of her hand. "Alec here has been telling me so much about you."

This was a lie, of course—I'd said nothing beyond the basics. But I could see Kim was charmed by that—an old man's attempt to be charming. She was also taken aback by his voice, as everyone was; she was too young to remember him from TV, and the rich baritone produced by his frailness was not something she could have expected.

"It's wonderful meeting you," she said in return. "Is everything going all right here? The arrangements with the nurses and all? You won't be embarrassed to tell us anything you might need, okay?"

We went into the kitchen for coffee, Kim taking Chet by the arm so he wouldn't slip. The gift she brought turned out to be a portable radio, which really delighted him. "Still in the middle?" he asked, turning it on. "Still in the middle," I said, and so there we were listening to the station, the news borrowed from the BBC. Chet looked confused by the British accent, and yet unmistakably pleased, that the signal should be there right where he had left it fifty years before.

Kim, I noticed, was up to one of her favorite tricks: keeping up the pleasantries while boring in on someone with her eyes. I hadn't seen her give this look at full strength in years—the look of a mother evaluating someone as to whether or not they posed a threat to her children. Chet must have passed the test, because by the time we finished our coffee and he began showing signs of tiring, most of her critical glances were directed squarely at me.

This was the subject that interested her now—her trying to figure out what lay behind my silence, the moody way I sipped at my coffee, her looking from me to Chet and back again trying to pick up a connection that was obviously not there. Was I just interested in this sick old man because of what he could tell me about McGowan, or was I hoping for something deeper?

For all that, this first visit went well. By tossing various names at each other they finally managed to come up with someone in Springfield they both remembered—an old, one-legged janitor who had been a fixture in town for years. It was a bond between them that pretty much left me out in the cold, and, frankly, I wasn't sorry when it came time for her to leave. She had a symposium on school violence to go to; before she left, Chet excused himself to go to the bathroom and she and I had a few whispered seconds by the door.

"He's a charmer," she said, glancing around at the pasted notes.

"That's exactly what I was afraid you'd say."

"We need to talk."

"I'm stuck with his urology appointment."

She tilted her head a couple of inches past irony. "No, I don't mean that kind of talk. I mean a real talk."

I was about to try and feel her out on what exactly her subject might be when Chet came coughing and wheezing back into the kitchen, black felt marker all over his nose where he had leaned down to write a note.

"It's been a real pleasure meeting you," Kim said, wiping it off for him with a napkin.

"I hope you come back again often," he said. "Alec's been implacable keeping you away."

I smiled, feebly.

"I have an idea," Kim said, before I could stop her. "Why don't you come to Brenda's first basketball game next Friday night? It's against Bishop O'Meara. It will do you good to get out."

I expected him to say no, was all set to back him up with extra excuses, but he surprised me by nodding, blowing out the dry sliver of his lip. "That would be fine. I remember once meeting this player named Robert Cousy. Cooz they called him. He could pass the ball right around his back without looking. I remember describing him as 'a diminutive giant.' "

Kim smiled. "Brenda has her own tricks. You can see for yourself next week."

Elise's visit came next. She was excited and nervous, asking me all sorts of questions about him, most of which I couldn't answer. Kim's father died before we were married, and so none of the kids had ever known a grandfather, a loss that seemed to weigh especially heavy on Elise. Like a lot of adopted children, she takes a real interest in family history, is always asking about who begot who, where the in-laws came from, trying to make connections even stronger than those we can spin out of love alone. Then, too, she had insisted on coming over to the apartment by herself, riding the bus; we had argued with her about this, but as always, faced with her precociousness, we reluctantly gave in.

Chet was sitting near the window, folded into his morning stare when she arrived. Again, as with Kim, I tried to distance myself from the visit, see her through his eyes, though with Elise this was damn near impossible. Still, I tried playing the game—saw a girl of nine emerge sideways through the door, wearing white jeans and a plain blue T-shirt, her hair short in back, only with orange ribbons that drooped down like surplus ponytails, flouncing behind her as she walked. Her cheeks were still a baby's, round and high, and set between them was a nose just wide enough to hold up the enormous pair of sunglasses she wouldn't leave home without. Her skin is the richest, darkest black it's possible to imagine, and it seemed to take on added lustre set against the drabber black of the huge, overstuffed backpack she wore looped over one shoulder. On her ears were the little gold hoops she was so proud of, having just had her ears pierced. On her feet she wore sandals, her toes polished in alternating flashes of silver and pink.

All these things I saw first, which was backwards, because the most obvious feature a stranger would notice I hardly saw at all: a girl of nine who wasn't much over four feet tall and yet weighed 120 pounds.

"Hello, Grandpop," she said, stopping right in front of him. She snapped off her sunglasses, peered deep into his eyes. "When were you born?" she demanded, like a reporter who didn't have time for the niceties. "Daddy told me January, but I could see he really didn't know."

Chet looked at me, then back at her, made kind of a groping, shrugging motion, but couldn't find the wit to answer. It was obvious he was startled at what he saw, and I hoped for his sake it was only her size that threw him, not her color. Even allowing him that, I was furious. *Say something,* I felt like shouting, *and say something quick.*

"I'm a little short of supplies," he mumbled, eyeing her warily.

Elise was giving him a pretty thorough appraisal herself, her eyes going up, down, and across his face as if they were slabbing on paint. Satisfied, she put down her backpack, reached inside for a pencil and paper. "What are your earliest memories of Springfield?" she asked. "I mean, from a completely different epoch."

Chet looked at me again—why did he seem at such a loss? It was a good question, not so different from the ones I wanted to ask myself, but it seemed to overwhelm him, so instead of answering he forced himself up from his chair, walked disconsolately toward the kitchen, finally remembered to turn and wave us in after him.

"You're probably hungry," he said.

We sat down and let him play host. He opened a box and put five doughnuts on the table—Elise immediately grabbed three of them. He stared down at the plate where they had been, grimaced, then without saying anything reached over and pulled two of them back. Elise, hardly giving it a thought, and acting like she was at home, reached to take them back again. Chet stared down at her, made kind of a feinting motion with his head, then swept them back to his side. Four times they did this until Chet, frowning like a chess player, reached, put the doughnuts back on the saucer, arranged them just so, then bore down on them with his thumb and index finger, crushing them to smithereens.

"I'm rationing here," he said, with enough severity to startle even me. "One per customer, that's the rule."

Elise looked a question mark at me, but I couldn't help her, not then and not there. Shrugging, she got up, went into the living room, came back with her backpack, unzipped the top, turned it upside down over the table, shook out six candy bars, three cupcakes, two apples, and enough oatmeal cookies to entirely cover the table, doughnuts, crumbs and all.

"I always tote along some extras," she said. "Now. When did you say you were born?"

Chet, thoroughly checkmated, blurted out the date.

"April seventh?" Elise's eyes blinked in disbelief. "That's when Daddy was born. How come you never mentioned that, Daddy? You were both born on the same day. I can't believe it! How neat!"

Chet leaned over as she started writing it down. "What's her condition?" he whispered sotto voce—a trick he must have learned in his television days when the mike was always on.

"What are you talking about?" I whispered back.

"Her condition. Does it have a name?"

"Fuck you, Chet."

What was left of his eyebrows stretched to take that in.

"What?"

"She's in therapy," I said, trotting out my usual lie. "She's got an eating problem, like a million kids. The therapist says she'll grow out of it."

That's the way the visit went—Elise asking him questions, trying her best to get him to talk, Chet reacting wrong or not reacting at all, me getting madder by the minute, tension rising all around. The climax came when it was time for her to leave. Rather than saying goodbye to her, kissing her on the cheek, tossing her a bone, he went over and sat back against his window, leaving the two of us alone by the door.

Elise cried the way she could sometimes, tears pooling up on those cheeks, then splashing down over her lips so she had to keep swiping them off in order to breathe. I thought it was the business with the doughnuts, but once I calmed her down a little I found out that wasn't it at all.

"He's such a *gentle* man," she said. "He's really good, I can tell."

That threw me. "You're crying because he's gentle?"

"Because he did *time!*"

"He murdered someone, princess. It was a long time ago, but he did."

She winced like I had slapped her. "No he didn't! He didn't murder anyone! I can see he's innocent, can't you?"

I put my arm around her, hugged her hard, and after fighting me a moment she hugged back. "I made it here on the bus alone," she said.

"There was the weirdest story that happened. You promise you'll listen tonight, no going off to your boring research stuff? It's about this purple-haired lady with packages and they fell on her baby and the driver got all mad."

Alan, of course, was a much harder proposition. He and Brenda were supposed to visit together, but Brenda had practice twice a day, the team was getting ready for their first game, magazines were already coming to do photo shoots of her, there was a holiday tournament in Boston designed to showcase her talent, and so Brenda was simply unavailable. Alan attended most of these practices himself—he wasn't going to let anyone near her without his okay—and getting him to agree to come was a real effort. "He's your grandfather for Christ's sake!" I shouted outside his room. "Yeah, grandfather, yeah *right*," he responded, and I didn't have an answer for that, not for his words, not for his tone.

But he played around with his appointment book, canceled some lunch dates, found thirty minutes when he was free. It wasn't hard to see him as a stranger when he came in—it was all too easy. He's a tall, suntanned teenager whose face is relaxed and settled enough to pass for thirty; his build is athletic, though he's no athlete, and he walks with the easy nonchalance of a good power forward. As for the rest, he has deep blue eyes and the family red hair, only on him it isn't an unruly shock or a bristly crewcut, but a wavy kind of bouffant sweep that would do an anchor man proud. His face is more alert than it is handsome, something to be reckoned with. He fell off his bike when he was seven and it left him with a Bogart scar on his upper lip, just enough to fascinate the girls, give his charm time to work.

Not your typical kid, not by any means, and this was emphasized by what he wore that morning: an expensive pinstriped black suit with a gray broadcloth shirt and an Italian silk tie. This wasn't because it was a special occasion—classy suits were his regular school outfit, his uniform, his trademark. He knew what he wanted to do in life, was certain he would do it, saw no reason to hide it, and dressed for what, in effect, he already was. "The CEO" they called him in school, and it wasn't said mockingly, either, but with deference, even by the tougher kids. It was only after this was well-established that we found out he had chosen the nickname himself, actually paid people to start using it—my son Alan, who leaves nothing to chance.

"Chester?" he said, stretching out his hand. "Alan Brown. A pleasure, sir. A real pleasure at long last."

Chet, who had been in one of his deepest funks before this, brightened instantly and shook Alan's hand. I thought I had heard his announcer's voice at its purest, but what I'd gotten so far was no match for what I heard now. "A pleasure on this end, too, by golly. Haven't had much of an opportunity to get to know the younger generation of late. And no one prompted me as to your hair coloring. A carrottop just like me."

"Dad tells me you were in television? I'd be interested in hearing about that"—he glanced meaningfully at his watch—"at a time when we can speak at leisure."

"Your father tells me you're in high school. Fine, excellent. I'm a graduate myself. What are you studying there? Carpentry? Metal work?"

Alan glanced over at me—was this a joke or what?—then cleared his throat. "I'm sort of marking time, frankly. I graduate in June. My career path is pretty much settled."

"Tell him what you're talking about," I suggested.

Alan ran his hand up and down his tie. "Sports agency. Representing athletes in negotiations, endorsements, signing situations, free agency. It's going to be one of the brightest careers in the new century. I'm doing it now actually. I represent my sister Brenda in her dealings with colleges. We haven't made a decision yet, but we're hoping to commit by January."

"Commit by January?" Chet pursed his lips.

"Of course, the NCAA doesn't permit actual representation, not at the secondary level, but let's face it—shit happens, right? There are thirty-one programs out there licking their chops to have her, all Division One stuff. She'd be shark bait without someone like me."

"Shark bait?"

"We want to make the right decision for her, do what's best. And of course I come along as part of the package, so it has to be a school that fits my requirements, too. Right now we're thinking strictly Big East or Ivy League."

Alan went into the details, who he was talking to, what kinds of offers were on the table, but the longer he talked, the more bored he seemed. I could see Chet struggling to understand, find a way to contribute, and I should have guessed what he'd finally come up with.

"Well, that's swell," he said. "I can see you're a wide-awake young man. But something you said bothered me, something you said earlier. You mentioned the new century. Do you realize it hasn't started yet?"

Alan fell right into the trap. "Hasn't started?"

"The first year ever recorded wasn't called zero, was it? It was called one. Hence the new century doesn't really begin until this coming year, 2001. What's more, because of changes in the calendar wrought by titular Church reformers during the Renaissance, the actual date of the new millennium's beginning is March seventeenth. I'm looking forward to it with a great deal of anticipation."

Smooth as Alan is, if you take him by surprise you can get him to listen. And he looked surprised now—looked like someone who was afraid there was a new, unexpected angle to things he hadn't considered. The two of them walked over toward the TV set, Chet going on with his theory, Alan nodding, buying time with that, trying to decide if he should be interested. He sat on the TV, folded his arms together, brought one hand out to brush a dust ball off his suit, then peered upside down between his legs at the Weather Channel as Chet droned on.

Me, I took the opportunity to do something I'd been wanting to do for a long time, go over to Chet's chair near the window and see what it was in the view that so fascinated him. There were oval smudge marks on the glass showing where he pressed his forehead and chin—it reminded me of those mounted binoculars you drop a quarter into when you're at the boardwalk. I put my head to the window, blinked, looked down. It was a sunny day and at first I couldn't see anything through the glare. I shifted position, looked again, but this time I was staring right into the corner of the building, where nothing existed but a solid brick wall. I shifted again, hunched up on the seat to see downward, but there was no view there either, the double glass was too thick, and all I saw was my own reflection leering back at me as if it were on the point of declaring its independence, a visage that was me in a way I didn't care to acknowledge just then, this stranger who was too middle-aged, too preoccupied, too intense.

I had my answer at any rate; what Chet stared at hour after hour wasn't anything outdoors, but his own reflection, staring at the face the glass broadcast back to him, trying to penetrate it, see through the mask, see through it to—what? Hadn't he spent enough time doing that in prison? What lesson could the glass show him that forty-six years hadn't already drummed in? Was it guilt mirrored there, writ so large he could read it despite his nearsightedness, or was it something entirely different, memories so complicated and personal I could have no conception of them, not from this distance?

It bothered me, sent up a burning sensation in my forehead—the thought of my reflection being pressed on the glass where his had been. When I got up again, crossed over to where they stood talking, I was feeling irritable, ready for the argument I had been preparing for ever since Alan came in.

He still sat on the TV. "I'd like to get your insights into various media concerns," he was telling Chet. "I'll leave you my card. You can blitz me if my fax is down."

"Time for a nap."

Both of them looked around, seemed surprised to find me still there.

"Nap for Chet, school for you. If you still bother with that."

Alan smiled, thinly. "Sure I bother." He swiveled around. "Good talking to you, Chester. We'll be in touch, okay?"

"I'll look forward," Chet said, equally smooth. But he must have sensed the tension, because he grimaced when he said it, started blinking like a nervous owl. "As long as the old superstructure holds out, that is." He patted his zipper. "I mean, the old infrastructure."

He walked off toward the bathroom, obviously in great pain, but doing his best not to shuffle or limp. Alan, once Chet disappeared, shook his head in admiration. "You know, I was a little doubtful before about that story you told us, him murdering that morning-show host he was sidekick to. But now I'm convinced. I can see it in his face, a ruthless kind of shadow. He did it all right. I respect him all the more."

That did it. Here I was, trying to keep everyone separate, not mix up the present with the past, and here Chet was charming the socks off everyone like my hurt didn't exist. I was no match for this, not with my son the CEO prattling on about toughness as he straddled the TV, the weather woman sweeping her stubby white hand back and forth between his legs.

"This must be a dream come true for you, Alan. You admire ruthlessness more than anything, and here's living proof that you have ruthless genes in your family. That should come in handy when you get around to negotiating your deals. I mean, what luck—a murderer in the family! What could look better on your résumé than that? Chet didn't just watch, didn't just pretend, he really did it! A pet murderer of your very own and with a few sugary phrases you have him tamed."

Alan bit his scar just like when he was little, but nothing in his face above that showed even the slightest trace of dismay. "Just for the record, not that you care, but I haven't negotiated anything yet," he said softly.

"No, and you're not going to, either. You keep your mitts off Brenda, you hear me? We're her parents. If any of those slick, lying recruiters wants to talk to anyone, they'll talk to us."

Okay, this was harsh of me, but I had learned it before—the only way to get through to him was to be even harder and more cynical than he could be himself. He was a killer's grandson? Well, fine, I was a killer's son, the gene was purer in me, less diluted, and for once he could be appalled by his father for a few minutes rather than the other way around.

"He's a convicted murderer," I said, reaching down to switch off the TV. "The state of New York didn't want the expense of burying him, that's the only reason he's here."

Alan boosted himself off the set, started pacing across the carpet with his hands behind his back—and it's a terrible thing to see a seventeen-year-old pace. "I don't care anything about him, all right? He's a leaky old man, pure and simple. It's what you said before. That other thing, the negotiating stuff. Who's going to do it if not me? Frankly, Dad, you simply don't have the skills. This is the big time, got that? The big time. You'd be in way over your head."

"I have a question. Why does someone with your compassion and sensitivity try so hard to disguise the fact you have either?"

"You don't care about money, okay. That's your generation. Mine is different. If you want to run an elitist radio station that lives in a tired countercultural past, that's fine, too. But we're talking your kids' education here, whether or not you'll be able to pay for their collegiate years. Frankly, as things now stand, if we're going postsecondary, it depends on Brenda's athletic talent plus my talent to maximize that talent's fair market value."

"The radio station you speak of so contemptuously has done well by this family so far."

"Yeah? Well, how come no one listens to it except baby-boomers who are this close"—he put his fingers together—"to going senile? You don't quite understand, Dad. Sure, maybe once upon a time people valued going your way, not giving a damn for money and all, but not anymore. Nonconformity is a luxury I can't afford. I have a sister to put through college and I have myself to put through college, and for that matter there's Elise coming along, who is truly gifted. If any of us are to ever have a chance in life it's only going to be through my own unaided efforts, simple as that."

He explained all this with admirable restraint, as if I were the kid, he the sensible, experienced adult. I was hopeless faced with that tone. I'd come this far as a father by always trying to be reasonable, but this is exactly where it had gotten me—a tendency, every time my reasonableness failed, to break out in these hot little bursts of indignation that left Alan totally unmoved.

And it wasn't just the generational bullshit, the tired old fight. All my friends were always telling me about arguments with their children, how they always ended up sounding like their own fathers had, hating that in themselves, being part of an endless cycle of point and counterpoint—and yet I would have liked nothing better than to ride that cycle myself. That was where the gap came in, for the hundredth time; I had no father to compare myself to, no echo I could call upon, no ready-made arsenal of tried and true clichés. Even half-true clichés—even any fraction of truth at all. What I wanted was to say something vital to my son, something that could only properly be said by clapping him on the back or hugging him, and yet there was nothing in my experience that permitted this, so the only recourse left was to sing the same tired song I had sung to him before, make a flapping motion with my arms that didn't even have the vigor to be a shrug.

"I'm glad you came this morning," I said quietly. "That's important, your coming."

He looked at me the way everyone was looking at me these days, trying to locate the calm, reasonable, friendly Alec Brown they knew and valued, and then, not finding it, he shrugged and started for the door. I had a pretty good look at him as he made his way out, or at least a good look at his suit. There on the back trouser leg, divided in half by the crease, was a thumb-sized stain I had to stare at before recognizing— peanut butter, peanut butter with just the slightest dollop of purple jam, and though I was going to call out to him, tell him it was there, I had just enough sense left to know it would be the wrong thing to do.

The following week, as promised, we took Chet to Brenda's first game.

A big night for all of us. The game started at eight. We told Chet we'd be by for him at seven. At five, Kim and I left Elise off at her violin lesson. At five-thirty, we arrived at our favorite Thai restaurant, found a line waiting for tables, decided we weren't hungry, got back in the car, and drove toward the river. At six, we were parked on what was probably the highest point in Springfield: an abandoned entrance ramp that led up toward the interstate but never quite touched it or merged—a place used by bikers, drug couriers, horny teenagers, and, in a pinch, repentant husbands who had been neglecting their wives.

"Romantic," Kim said, closing her window to the smell.

There are no hills in Springfield worth talking about, no panoramic viewing spots, no scenic vistas—nothing but this forgotten, weed-choked ramp decorated with pulverized malt liquor cans crushed into a luminous ring. Behind us the parking garages cut off downtown in layered seams of mud-colored concrete, and even if they hadn't, there was no possible way to see past the choke collar of I-91. In the other direction lay the Connecticut River, but that was invisible, too, blotted out by abandoned warehouses and abandoned railroad sidings and lots full of repossessed cars. That left most of the view straight ahead of us toward the north. These were the malls, and in the soft November twilight they looked like rectangles made of soft material, a child's squeezeable blocks.

We sat watching their lights come on as day faded from a sky that seemed weaker and smaller than what sky should be. It wasn't after-glow that rose in the daylight's place, but a purple dome that remained cherry black at its core, its fringes decorated by red, blue, and green Christmas lights, giving the effect of stars tethered low on the horizon against their will. Toward the center of the purple, probing like pencil flashlights at the thick pulpy mass, came the headlights of countless cars pouring off the interstate, searching for a place to park.

Anywhere, U.S.A., and it was a shock to remember all this still had a specific name, a supposed identity: Springfield, Massachusetts, third-largest city of the state it sat in, shire town of Hampden County, founded 1636, burned during King Philip's War 1675, center of Shay's Rebellion 1786–87, famous for the Springfield Armory, the Springfield rifle, one-time center of the nation's arms industry, one-time center of American lexicography, the city where the motorcycle was invented in 1901, famous railroad terminus, the birthplace of basketball and site of its Hall of Fame, home to Augustus Saint-Gaudens' famous statue *The Puritan,* two fine colleges, known in a different era as "The City of Homes," with a decaying downtown featuring discount sneaker stores, lottery outlets, and pawnshops cheek by jowl with a luxury convention center—the city, media researchers claimed, where more per-capita hours of television were watched than in any other small city in North America . . . not to be confused with Springfield, Vermont, Springfield, Georgia, Springfield, Colorado, Springfield, South Dakota, New Jersey, Tennessee, Missouri, Minnesota, or Oregon, and not to be confused, most of all, with Springfield, Illinois, home of Abraham Lincoln—Springfield, Mass., the place, for better or worse, I was born in, raised in, wherein I still dwelled.

"Horrible," I said automatically, not knowing what I meant.

Kim sat hunched away from me toward the door. "It's time to start thinking about Christmas," she said. I couldn't see enough of her face to know whether she meant it as a joke.

"Where those malls are was all countryside sixty years ago. There was a back road that had just been macadamized running between the tobacco farms and the river. In summer, the wildflowers grew so high along the edges that people called it Flower Road, and it was a favorite spot for Sunday drives."

"Nice," Kim mumbled, without much interest.

"It's along that road that on a warm June day in 1940 our pal Alec McGowan first met Lee Palmer, or at least first saw her. He was riding his bike toward downtown between his job picking tobacco and a job he had at Ryan's, the old Rexall drugstore on South Main. As he pedaled, trying to get there on time, he passed a girl walking in the opposite direction toward a big brown touring car—the girl had gotten out to pick an armful of flowers. This was Lee Palmer, out with her father for a drive with their chauffeur. After that first glance, Alec McGowan was never the same. It was the moment of truth for him. In his whole life, the one decisive moment of truth."

"Love at first sight?" Kim said, with a little laugh. "Did that really used to happen down there?"

"It's a long story, the next part. I'm not sure I have all the details yet, what happened next, but apparently he set off after the car on his bike."

"Like in silent films?"

"Yes. The plucky hero of an old silent film."

"She must have been beautiful."

"She used to be compared to the actress Teresa Wright. Now? No one. A style that's vanished . . . A smart girl, hard to judge. Rich. Lots of opportunities to be whoever she wanted to be. A girl with lifestyle options, as they say now."

Kim, still pressed in her corner, at least looked at me now, brushed the top of her hair back, tried her best to act interested. "How far along are you?"

"Halfway. It's hard without tapes, visual evidence. There's no inwardness left of the man—he wrote no letters, kept no diary. His life was all outwardness, and now even all that's gone."

"Does Chet know you're working on this? I would think he would have all the facts you need."

"That's just the problem. Facts are getting in my way. And no, I don't know what I mean by that statement either. It's what I'm trying very hard to figure out right now."

"Alan thinks you're writing a book for money. It's got everything, he told me. Celebrity, sex, jealousy, murder, and now, according to what you're telling me, romance as well, poor boy meets rich girl and falls madly in love. He told me he'd like to represent you."

That made me laugh all right, or at least pretend to. "With all deference to our CEO, he's got it backwards. No one remembers McGowan anymore. Sure, they're watching *Morning* every morning, but television has no history, it's all in present tense. Why should anyone be interested in the birth of something that never dies? And speaking of Alan, he and I had an argument the other day, did he tell you?"

Kim didn't answer, at least not directly. Instead, she slid over on the seat so she was closer now, but still not touching. "Tell me why you're doing this," she said softly.

"I've told you."

"Yes, but tell me again."

So I told her, or at least tried to, framing most of it in negatives. It certainly wasn't to make money, keep Alan in expensive suits. It wasn't from the restlessness of a midlife crisis, though God knows I wasn't immune. It wasn't to clear Chet's name, as some people thought, since I believed in his guilt right from the start. It wasn't a form of restitution, either, since it was foolish to think the scales could be balanced by anything I could do now. Fairness, justice, the American way? Nope, I was doing it for more selfish reasons, trying to correct an imbalance, all right, an imbalance in me.

This was getting closer; I started talking with more conviction, and I could see Kim's attention sharpen as a result. I had the feeling for a long time that I was stuck in the year 1950, the year I was born, a desperately long way from the new century, and I wouldn't be able to accept the future until I understood those years thoroughly, what happened then, what had gone wrong in the men and women who had control of that era. All those years when I had stumbled between paths, I had the feeling I was playing catch-up with the truth, and now it was receding from me faster and faster every year, undercutting what in other respects had become a happy enough life—so if I was going to catch up, it was only by racing backward, boring in, imagining, feeling, and then, once I grasped those years, the straight line to the past would instantly become a circle; blinking at the magic, I would be back again in the new millennium, ready to face it, ready to understand my kids and help them, ready to move on.

"And you know what the strange thing is?" I said. "The longer I go on with this, the more it seems like it wasn't my father who did the killing, but my father who was killed. Does that make sense? I've become convinced it makes perfect sense. Alec McGowan, the man I was named for, makes a better father than Chet ever did, and that was true from the moment the murder happened. I mean, who would you pick as a kid to have for your absentee dad? A shabby jailbird or a martyred celebrity? Without ever admitting it to myself, not in so many words, I picked McGowan, so what I'm writing about, trying to understand, is my father, why he was killed."

Kim nodded—if I couldn't get through to my kids anymore, at least I could get through to her. "How much longer until you finish?"

I shrugged. "Four months. Five maybe. There's a list of people I still have to talk to. The story's taken over now and I feel lost."

"That's about how long Chet has. Five months." She let that hang in the air a moment, then brought out her bombshell. "You got a phone call today, did I tell you? Someone named Martin Slisco calling from Long Island."

It stung, hearing that name so unexpectedly—it was like she had slapped me awake. "Slisco? He called when?"

"This morning. Who is he?"

"He was head cameraman during the McGowan years. A real bitter character who lives by himself in the suburbs chewing on his memories. I went and talked to him last spring."

"Why should he be calling you?"

"That's what I'd like to know. I had the feeling at the time there was lots he wasn't telling me. But if anyone knows where any surviving tapes are, he'd be the one."

"He said you and he needed to talk right away. He wants you to come down and see him on Sunday. He said he has something for you."

Sunday? I was ready to put the car in gear and race down there right now. Kim must have read my thoughts, because she put her hand on my arm, reining me in. "Don't go."

"It's only Long Island. I'll take the ferry and be home by dinner."

The lights from the interstate sliced through the car, illuminating her forehead, but leaving the rest in darkness. "Because of Brenda, I guess. Because it's Brenda's only day off the whole week and you need to spend some time with her."

"There's next weekend. I'm not doing anything, and she and I could take a drive, scout out some colleges."

"Alan's already taking her."

"This is important, Kim. Slisco very possibly has tapes."

Somewhere during this I could feel her turn away, literally turn, so she stared out her window toward the tenement triple-deckers that began just under the interstate, their windows blue with TV light and the first streamers of fog. I knew from her preoccupied expression what she was thinking about, what every school principal, every good one, is thinking about when they're fighting to concentrate on something else: fourteen-year-old girls having babies, sixth-graders bringing guns to school, a teachers' union blocking every attempt at reform, the board of education arguing over every dime.

"You know," she said, "if I ever get so wrapped up in my own work, so obsessed with finding answers, that it begins getting in the way of my personal life, my family, you, I'd like to think my spouse would be honest enough to tell me it's time to ease off, stay home more, even quit. You will be honest enough to do that for me, won't you?"

"There's nothing wrong with Elise," I said sharply.

She peered at me sideways, this time in real alarm. "Who said anything about Elise?"

I started the car, made a groping motion toward the windshield. "I'm not obsessed," I said, then, "What time did you say Slisco called? Did he want me to call back or was there just the message? He could be the key to everything. He just could be the key."

We were a few minutes late picking Chet up, which was unfortunate. He seemed a lot more nervous leaving the apartment than he had been leaving prison. He checked and rechecked the stove to make sure all the burners were off, went to the bathroom twice, stuffed his pockets with notes he had written, wrapped himself up tight in his coat, checked the stove one last time, tested the door lock, and only then seemed ready to leave.

He was no better in the car. It was cold, we were getting our first light snow, and he kept looking anxiously out the window, bracing his arms against the dashboard as if expecting us to crash. The traffic lights, headlights, the lights from store windows—in their glare you could see him blinking and sweating, as if they were searchlights sweeping across his face from a prison wall, him trying to get up the courage to make a dash.

I ignored this, or at least tried to. Behind me, hidden beneath her sunglasses, Elise chatted on about the game, stopping only to take a big chunk out of the bagel we had bought her in lieu of dinner.

"What are we expecting, Daddy? Zone or man-to-man?"

"Zone, princess."

"Diamond and one? Double team on Brenda?"

"Double team. Look for her to dish it off."

"Back door, Daddy?"

"First quarter. Then she moves out to shoot long . . . Are you okay, Chet? Warm enough for you in here?"

As always, the gym was packed. Bishop O'Meara was the best Catholic team in Massachusetts, the only one to have beaten us the previous year on our way to the state championship, and everyone was expecting a tough game. The volume of cheering, even outside the gym, was loud enough to make your heart thump, and inside, with the air horns and cowbells and bands, it was even louder—I had to all but shove Chet to force him in.

"This is crazy!" I yelled to Kim. "You get us a seat up high and I'll get the two of them settled down here."

I had decided before we arrived that Chet would do better on the lower, outside part of the stands where he had a clear path to the men's room. Coming in, tugging on my hand, Elise surprised me by telling me she didn't want to sit near anyone she knew, so I had her sit there, too.

"You watch out for him," I told her. "Explain to him what's going on."

"Play by play, Daddy?"

"Sure. Color commentary, stats—anything you want."

On her lap she had a pillowcase which she now unfurled, getting a bewildered Chet to hold out one end. BRENDABALL! it read. You could look up the risers and see a dozen identical banners.

I waited a second, studied the arrangements, had what I thought was a happy inspiration. "You watch out for her, okay?" I said, leaning over Chet's shoulder so he could hear. He nodded, nodded vigorously, pleased at having something to concentrate on beside the noise.

"Should I buy her anything?" he asked, putting his mouth near my ear. "Feed her?"

When I left they were pressed together with their knees touching, Chet doing his best to make sense of things while Elise whistled and screamed.

Warm-ups were just ending now. I made my way around the crowded perimeter toward the press table, where I could see Jimbo Elliot leaning over the microphone, his face all excited and flushed. Brenda, though I looked for her, remained invisible behind the heads, shoulders, and cameras that pressed against courtside, and all I could see of her was an occasional glimpse of the pink scrunchie that held up her hair.

"Dad! Glad I caught up with you. There are some gentlemen here I'd like very much for you to meet."

Alan wore a navy blazer and chinos this time, looking important enough that the crowd parted at his approach. With him were three men dressed exactly the same way; all three had the bland, mild-mannered look that passes these days for success.

"Dad, this is Ken Carr from the University of Virginia."

I shook his hand, gave him a plastic smile even phonier than the one he gave me.

"Atticus Rogers from Stanford."

A firm grasp I returned just as firmly.

"Ron Cutting from Yale."

I shook hands, smiled. "You have a fine daughter," one of them said, and the other two nodded. More must have been coming, but I shocked them and angered Alan by making a little shrug of apology and ducking past them up the aisle.

Jimbo saw me coming, put his hand over the mike and waved. He had his lucky madras jacket on, his lucky black tie. "Am I supposed to talk to you?" he shouted, while I was still some distance away.

"It's a sabbatical, not a retirement. How are things going?"

Jimbo looks like a sports announcer should look—red-faced, scholarly, and more than a little nuts, though there's no finer radio man in western Mass. "Not so good," he said. "You want numbers? You want gloom and doom?"

I waved toward the microphone. "Everyone in town's listening tonight."

"Of course everyone's listening tonight. It's the other twenty-two hours of the day we're talking about here. Frankly, Alec, folk music fans are getting a little long in the tooth. Jazz lovers, too. As for classical, I believe there's one ninety-year-old woman who still cares for it, but she lives three miles beyond our signal. An outfit called Soundburst Inc. called the other day. They're interested in whether or not you'd be interested in selling out."

"What did you tell them?"

"What I always tell anyone. That there's no way you'd be interested in selling a station that's been in family hands for well over sixty years."

"Did you take their number?"

"I may have scribbled it down somewhere," he said cautiously.

"Call me with it when you get a chance. How's it look tonight?"

For Jimbo, this was much more comfortable ground. "Warm-ups were a show. You see Brenda sink that one from half-court swish? I could see the Bishop girls all but faint."

Everyone was on their feet now, rhythmically clapping as the introductions began. I fought my way back up the risers to where Kim held a space open, stood there with the rest of them, trying to glimpse Brenda in the ring of players that surrounded the bench. She was introduced last, the gym erupting as she trotted out to center court. There were so many high fives, pats on the rump, energetic pumping of fists, last-minute stretchings, nervous little hops, that it seemed odd to have it all suddenly freeze into the familiar tableau of the national anthem. Motionless, Brenda's height seemed even more exaggerated compared to the other girls'—she's six foot three, and seems taller. Other than this, and the size of her hands, nothing distinguished her from the girls standing next to her. She's slender, straight-bodied, with legs that seem too skinny for a player her height, making her appear oddly delicate and fragile. The sportswriters liked to talk about her poker face, which is another way of saying her expression doesn't betray anything, neither talent, nor arrogance, nor even interest. I could see why they said this—looked and saw a pretty enough teenager who took after her mother, someone who exuded quiet confidence and yet at the same time invited you to underestimate her, smiling imperceptibly at the surprise she would give you the moment you made that mistake.

She won the tap, got the ball back, banked in a turnaround jumper from her favorite spot just off the key. The noise, which could not have gotten louder, now got louder as everyone started stamping their feet. Girls' basketball was everything in this city, the boys hardly counted anymore, and it wasn't tough to figure out why. In the century since the good Dr. Naismith had invented the sport as a way to shorten our miserable winters, the boys had mastered it completely, so what they played was goonball, one on one, but for the girls it was still a team sport, or a ballet, or whatever analogy struck you as you sat on high looking down. I always thought of women washing clothes by a mountain stream or harvesting grapes or weaving; this was something ancient and communal and patterned, but definitely *labor,* the kind, when finished, that would lead to merriment and celebration, but which while under way must be taken as seriously as possible, the fate of the world riding on weaving the patterns right, with beauty, delicacy, imagination, and skill.

In this labor, in this ballet, Brenda was the dominant figure. She was the fastest girl, the most delicate shooter, the fiercest rebounder, and seemed to understand the geometry better than anyone else on the floor, the diagonal shortcuts that always brought her to the right place first. She did all this with an understated, sober kind of competence, the only sign of flair being her famous pink scrunchie, the bobbing ponytail it barely controlled, and the decorative little flourish of the wrist with which she finished off her shots.

It was complicated what I felt watching her. Most of the time I felt so proud my chest literally swelled, but at other times I couldn't help feeling the sadness I experienced during warm-ups—the sense that each new jump shot, each dazzling assist, was taking her further away from us, away too fast.

As for the game itself, it was clearly no contest—by the end of the first half we were up by twenty-eight points. I made my way down to check on Chet and Elise, and saw them sitting exactly as I'd left them, only now the banner was wrapped around Chet's shoulders as a shawl. He shivered, looked even paler than he had when he came in, flattened into himself by the noise, and I realized it was a serious mistake to have brought him. What was stranger was that Elise looked the same way—looked frightened of something, though I had no idea what. I started to go over to see what was wrong, but the crowd was so thick, so many people wanted to congratulate me about Brenda, that I was unable to get there before the second half began.

It was largely a repeat of the first, only now Brenda, rather than shooting, kept dishing the ball off to spread the points around. Once, open in the corner, she hoisted up an old-fashioned hook shot, the one I had taught her in the backyard when she was eleven, and I could see her staring up toward the stands trying to find me, as if to say *that one's for you.* A few minutes later, alone underneath, she went up for a layup and for no apparent reason staggered—it was as if an invisible hand had jammed her, though there wasn't a Bishop player within ten feet. So slight and harmless-looking was this hesitation, I don't think anyone noticed but me—me and Alan. I saw him down near the scorer's table, and I could see him grimace, jump to his feet, but a second later he was sitting down again with his pals the recruiters, smiling expansively, laughing. Five minutes later, the score being ridiculous, the coach took Brenda out to a standing ovation.

There didn't seem to be much reason to stay after that. In the great oval windows at the far end of the gym snow was falling, lit by an outside spotlight, and people were pointing at it, pulling on their coats and scarves. Kim volunteered to bring the car around to the entrance, and I went down to collect Chet and Elise. They weren't there, which didn't particularly worry me, not at first. Elise had probably decided to buy herself a last hot dog at the refreshment stand or Chet needed to visit the men's room, and in either case I was sure to find them in the hall between the gym and the classrooms, and so that's the way I headed.

The hall was a green concrete passage that smelled of cigarette smoke, urine, and chalk. It was deserted, or at least that's what I thought, but then I came fully into it and saw down at the far end near the woodworking shop a ring of eight or nine people centered around something I at first couldn't make out.

I was slow to grasp the significance of this, and then I grasped it all too quickly. The men's room was beyond the ring and the refreshment counter immediately to its left. They're not here, I decided, but a vague, ominous something made me continue through the green light of the hall. I could see now that the ring was comprised of middle school kids, the older, paler ones, boys and girls equally, dressed in baggy flannel shirts, reversed baseball caps, and jeans that ballooned out over their ankles. They were chanting something loud and insistent—for one ludicrous moment I thought they were practicing a new sort of cheer—and then I was up to them, and what was in the center of their ring became plain.

Elise, crouching down like a frightened animal, her hands pressed tight over her ears, her body dipping down on her knees like she wanted to jump clear of the ring and couldn't find enough bounce to do so—it was Elise, and the kids were throwing popcorn at her, hard bits of candy, lighted cigarette butts, shouting the same thing in a high nasal nagging that doubled itself off the walls.

"Fuckin' fat lesbo! Fuckin' fat lesbo!"

I had two coherent thoughts—*Do they have guns?* and *Where's Chet?*—and then I saw him standing to the side near the men's room entrance, so my first horrible impression was that he was part of the ring, the actual ringleader. But in this I was wrong, brutally wrong. The only sense I could make of it was that, remembering my instructions, he had followed her out to the hall or she had followed him—that Elise had been surrounded by the kids loitering there looking for trouble, and that Chet, coming out of the men's room, had arrived there one instant before I had.

I started forward to pull her away but Chet beat me to it. With a quickness that was startling in a man so old, he stepped into the ring, turned around, located the biggest of the boys, took a step toward him, put both withered hands around his windpipe, and pressed in hard, so the boy's head snapped back and he gagged. There was something elemental and horrible in the suddenness of this transformation—it was like seeing an old scarecrow hop off its fence post and jerk its way to life. The boy gurgled something, made as if to break free, but Chet, jutting his chest out like an angry pigeon, bumped him back against the wall, then moved in and kneed him in the groin, once, twice, three times, his leg making a blurring motion in the garish green light.

He'll murder him, I remember thinking, with a clarity that mocked my previous obtuseness.

The boy prone and helpless, Chet lurched toward another one, but the ring broke now and ran. They prided themselves on hardness, worshiped nothing else, had no trouble with someone like Elise, but they'd never seen anything like what they saw in this old man's face, not on television, not in their videos or comic books or games. The boy staggered to his feet, went sliding and crouching away, holding his arm up to fend off new blows, but by then Chet was back against the wall, panting, breathless, old again, his face the pale mask I had seen in the prison hospital, making it impossible to imagine that what had happened had really happened. Elise, who had watched this, bent over in a crouch, now spotted me and came running over, crying hysterically, and I hugged her for all I was worth.

"Why, Daddy?" she sobbed. "Why?"

I looked over her head toward Chet, but he didn't see me, didn't react in any way, other than to hang his head down and stare mildly at his hands, and then he suddenly brought them up to his temples, pressed them in as hard as he had pressed in on the boy's throat, screamed and screamed and screamed again, the rich announcer's voice exploding into thin reedy shards, going falsetto, the echo reverberating down the cement hallway toward that lesser, weaker echo— the buzzer sounding to end the game.

Six

Cheers, whistling, applause—the accordion-sweet wheeze of words that aren't intended to mean anything. It all sounded louder, more metallic on the ferry than it did normally, a canned soundtrack canned in turn by the iron resonance of the enclosed deck. The girl working the refreshment counter reached high to change channels, then came back to push coffee across to passengers who had descended from the morning chill. It was the first boat of the day and there weren't many aboard. Once served, they wrapped their hands around the Styrofoam to warm them, then stepped back to get a better angle on the screen, looking up with a rigid, lockjaw kind of stare, their eyes and foreheads coated in an amber radiance that thinned, widened, and blinked across the empty white screens of their expressions.

I ordered some coffee, stepped back, and stared up at the television along with everyone else. It was the weekend edition of *Morning,* with the second-string host—a handsome young black man with an easy, engaging manner, boyish and serious in alternating flashes, so smooth he was immune to any cynicism, even one as strong as mine. I tried remembering where he came in the succession—was he the eighth after McGowan or was he the ninth? He had a sidekick, a woman, pert and pretty and intelligent, very much in the Lee Palmer mold, and I wondered if she would recognize the name as the style's inventor.

I finished my coffee, ordered a refill, climbed the stairs to the open deck. Now that the fog had burned off, the morning was glorious, with the kind of warm November sunshine that seems left over from August and just enough breeze to set the water dancing, bring it to life. Behind us on the Sound, set low and brown against the ferry's wake, was the Connecticut shoreline; ahead of us, just as low but greener, was Long Island, airy and insubstantial, pinned down by water towers and transmission lines and smokestacks that seemed placed there to keep it from floating away altogether.

There was no one outside in all this but me. I sat down on a bench that faced forward, watched as the Island left off being a line and became scalloped and curved. As beautiful as the morning was, something in me still resisted, refused to give way. I thought about my car phone on the lower deck, wished I had brought it in order to call home. Yes, things had quieted down there. Yes, the situation seemed to be under control. Yes, the present and its problems would remain on hold for one more day at least, and yet for all that I felt like a scuba diver plunging through the roiled surface of the sea toward its placid bottom, felt like I was abandoning something, selfishly escaping—and then I remembered who I was going to be talking to, realized my analogy was only partially correct, and that if I was diving through a troubled surface it was only to descend into even murkier depths.

The drive across the Island didn't take very long. That early in the morning there was little traffic; with the foliage gone, the houses seemed closer together than the last time I'd been there, a shapeless kind of city-suburb mix. Levittown itself wore the seedy look a once vibrant place takes on when it's leaving middle age—placid and neat and orderly and anemic, as if it were lacking an essential vitamin to give it oomph. The basic Cape Cod–style houses had all been expanded years before, and they all looked too big now for their tiny lots, their driveways crowded with four and five cars. In front of every third or fourth house was a pickup truck and trailer, lawn crews attacking the fallen leaves with noisy vacuums they wore looped around their shoulders, giving the effect of specialists removing hazardous waste while the population remained indoors.

Slisco lived on Lindbergh Street, in what had to be the smallest house left in town. His lawn wasn't cut like the others—there were blades high enough to have tassels. Set in the middle, where I had noticed it the last time, was an old rusty hand lawn mower, its shaft slanting obliquely through the weeds. On the way to the door, on an impulse, I detoured over to try and push it, discovered with surprise that it wouldn't budge—that it was mounted on a little cement pedestal buried in sod.

"My monument to a vanished epoch," the lawn mower said.

I turned around, but there was no one there. I looked up toward the stoop—no one there, either.

"Years ago everyone cut their own lawns. Sunday mornings you'd see them out there, working away. Good men all, working up a sweat, getting a little nature in, showing their kids how it was done. Now we have mercenaries. You know about the Roman Empire, how it started to decay once they invited the barbarians in to do their dirty work?"

Between the hoarseness of the sound and the force of it I realized it was coming from a speaker, but I had to kick through the grass to actually locate it, there toward the base of the lawn mower, round and button-sized, with a wire leading toward the front door.

"Enter. And wipe the dog shit off first."

There was a buzzing sound, the front door creaking slowly open as in a haunted house. Entering, I immediately started coughing—the cigarette smoke was so thick, so ancient, it formed a second door, one that was hard to penetrate without choking. In the smoky light I saw what I had seen last time: a house straight out of the early fifties, reeking of linoleum and Naugahyde and Formica, and the kind of stream-lined spic-and-span efficiency that once upon a vanished time had seemed so compelling. It was museum quality—none of the appliances seemed used. As hazy and dark as the house was, none of it seemed used.

I found Slisco slumped on the couch beneath the yellow halo of a weak and stuttery lamp. He seemed gaunter than he had been last time—wiry, but a stripped wire, what little he had for insulation all but gone. Like almost everyone from television's glory days, he had a noticeable pallor, making it seem as if those early lights, rather than tanning him, had bleached out every pigment except white.

It wasn't the look of a healthy man—if it wasn't for the glasses, the raccoon darkness beneath the rims, I wouldn't have recognized him. The only parts of his face that seemed solid were the thick metallic flanges of his nose, and the rigid smile that tightened across his lips just below—the smile of a bitter, intelligent man who's finally getting his chance to deliver lines he's been rehearsing in solitude for years.

"This is the last one left, the last original Levitt house. People from the Smithsonian came, asked me to donate it, said they'd send a crew to take it apart and reassemble it down in Washington. I told them to scram. They got all mad with that, said they'd take it by eminent domain. Out in the carport is six hundred gallons of unleaded gasoline. They ever come back, I'm going to blow the house up to kingdom come."

His hand pressed down into his lap, like there was a plunger and he was practicing. "Funny," I said, and then "Why did you call? I have problems at home, lots of things going on. You better have something for me better than that."

He rubbed his hand across his forehead, examined the sweaty residue, then smiled, as if this was just what his bitterness needed, to have someone it couldn't easily push around.

"I moved here in 1950, just after McGowan hired me. Ask me why."

I shrugged. "Why?"

"I work in TV, I figured what better place to live than in the middle of the ignoramuses who would be watching. Old man Levitt sold it to me personally, last house left on the block. I had to lie about having a family—oh sure, I told him. Two brats and an old biddy, no problem there. . . . That was then. Nowadays? Young people, so scared of each other no one goes outdoors except to scuttle to their cars. You go out for a walk at night, all you hear is the sound of alarms going off, burglar alarms, car alarms, the sirens all talking to each other, that's what you hear. Fucking hicks, that's all they are. They're products, not people. Each of them a brand. You want to hear my fantasy? I invite everyone on the block for a barbecue, just like in the old days, and when they assemble here I set the gasoline off and take a hundred fucking yuppies with me straight to hell. . . . I have a lot to say, so you better sit down."

He reached behind him toward the lamp and pulled. In the added light his face seemed as blue as his arms—stubbled, shadowed, shrunken. "I had a visitor last week. I may have mentioned him last time, Albert Forster Brinning. Calls himself 'America's leading public television documentary maker.' "

"I know the name."

"A nice young man, Mr. Brinning. Good manners, very slick. He's done documentaries on Pearl Harbor and football, and now he wants to do one on the early days of television. He seems to have gotten it into his skull that I have tapes of those old *Morning* shows. He's willing to pay for them, and pay quite well."

"Then you'd be crazy to say no."

Slisco smiled his thin metal smile. "You're much more intelligent than your father, you know that? Your mother fool around? . . . Okay, this Mr. Brinning, he got me talking. What I told him was about the old days and how I was suckered into leading the charge for a union and how they fired me for that and how I was blacklisted and how the goddam union never fought for me and how they've been fucking over this country ever since, them and their pals the liberal do-gooders. Mr.

Brinning listened politely enough, though I believe he took exception to the part about liberal do-gooding nigger sons of bitches. Big mistake on his part. I could see then what he really was. One of these bastards who makes believe he's one of the guys, then laughs at you the moment he leaves. He had a blonde with him, did I tell you that? She had an ass you could strike a match on, and I could tell by her expression they had just fucked."

Wait long enough against that kind of bitterness and it turns back on itself, gets sloppy, finally has no choice but to get to the point. But maybe I had listened to too many other witnesses, the patient ones, men and women who took delight in drawing you back with them on their memories, coloring things in, elaborating, taking pains—had too many good experiences there to put up with this.

"You said something about tapes," I said. "Do you have them or don't you?"

It was blunt enough to at least get him moving, break him loose from his mood. He got to his feet, limped heavily to the window, peered through a crack in the blinds, came back again, tapped his finger against a pretzel-sized microphone there on the end table, sat down.

"You know what a Huston camera crane was?"

"I'm asking about tapes."

"Maybe this is the way to ask."

"A tripod mount."

"An X-shaped crane. Also called a Sanner dolly. It was a big innovation, something I invented myself so as to get some fluidity in the establishing shots. Everything was too static before that. Took three men to operate it. One guy moves the boom up and down and around. Second guy moves base around the floor shoving and grunting. I'm up on top doing the focusing. It would take me so low I was looking up at people, or it could bring me high, maybe twelve feet, and I'd be up there shooting down. You got so you felt pretty cocky riding that, finding angles on people. You got so you could see things no one else saw."

"Everyone tells me you were a hell of a cameraman, maybe the best. Good eyes, quick reflexes, good instinct for composition."

He frowned, though I could tell he liked hearing that. "Damn straight good eyes. Eighth Air Force in England. Bombers, B-24s. I could make out those Messerschmitt cocksuckers before the pilots could even see them as specks. But that's why I felt comfortable up on that Huston. It was just like bombing again, up there in the wild blue yonder above all the flak."

He shifted on the couch, brought his hands behind his head, let the silence last long enough to set me up. "I guess you're getting pretty far into your book," he said, almost pleasantly.

I shrugged. "Pretty far."

"I guess you must know the truth about a lot of things, even more than I do myself. You probably don't need me to tell you nada. You probably would be pretty good at a history test on those days, right? Do good on it and who knows, I might just have a surprise for you, some goodies you can take home. So, here goes. Marilyn Monroe's first appearance on national television was on *Morning,* true or false?"

I smiled at him, didn't answer.

"Humor me," he said.

"July 1951. Easy."

"Very good. What color dress was she wearing?"

"You tell me."

"Red, whore red. I spent the entire morning trying to get low enough on the Huston to see underneath ... A famous show. McGowan wouldn't have anything to do with her, he was laying better than that every night, so he assigned her to your pal Chet. She was too much for him to handle. He was sweating, his glasses were steamed up, and I made sure I focused on that, the steamed-up lenses. He had an erection, too, this pointy little boner under his pants, and I could have focused on that, but I didn't. Later, just before she left, I got up high and shot straight down on her boobs. I could see in pretty deep from up there—she had nipples like erasers, and they pointed sideways, like this. She slipped one out just before the commercial. Kind of rearranged her dress and accidentally on purpose one boob spills out. No one believed what they were seeing. All across America they had a subliminal flash, but no one believed it and we didn't get a single letter. You know about what happened with McCarthy?"

I shook my head.

"Okay, Joe McCarthy comes on and McGowan is gunning for him. He isn't famous yet, just starting to make a name for himself, but McGowan knows he's a yellow lying bastard and so he decides to get him drunk before the show goes on air, make him look ridiculous. 'Come on, Senator, let's limber up a little,' he says, and there the two of them are, in the greenroom, McGowan nodding like he's taking him seriously, McCarthy downing Bloody Marys like they're water. But it didn't work. Drunk, McCarthy only acted more serious, more solemn . . . sober he came across as a nervous pansy . . . and that became the secret of Joe's success, drinking himself into self-importance, and McGowan always hated himself for teaching him that trick."

I bought this, at least partially—I was stupid enough to take out a pencil and pad—and that only got Slisco talking even faster.

"True or false, you tell me which. John F. Kennedy appeared on the show in 1950. His old man arranged it, leaned on one of the network vice-presidents. McGowan was furious. He lit into him right from the start. 'So, Senator. What's it like to be born with a silver spoon in your mouth?' Kennedy chokes and sputters, manages a sickly laugh. McGowan's just warming up. 'So, Senator. A handsome young buck like you must have lots of girls chasing him, right? Tell us what that's like.' Again Kennedy looks around like he's looking for papa, but McGowan doesn't even blink. 'So, Senator. How'd you get a glamorous job skippering a PT boat while lots of guys had to do the war's dirty work?' "

"False. Kennedy wasn't a senator in 1950."

"Yeah? Well, you should know, you're the bio-grapher. How about this. Jackie Robinson comes on, only right away there's trouble. This dolly pusher name of Al Coates is a Phillies fan, a cracker right out of

the Alabama hills, and he yells 'Hey, nigger, smile!' just before we go
on air. McGowan comes over, hauls Coates out onto the set where the
light is good, smashes him in the mouth."

"True," I said, guessing.

"Yeah? Well, it must be true then. Hell, Slisco was just the guy with
the camera, just a poor slob riding a crane, what does he know? Then
that time with Einstein, you know all about that probably."

"Albert Einstein?"

"Hey, great! So you've heard of him! Okay, Einstein is a big fan of
the program, we're told that on good authority, watches every morning before he goes to work in his lab. McGowan finds out, decides
what could be better than to have him on, only he won't come on, said
he'd talk but only if the show came down to Princeton, talked to him
in his study. Who's going to pass on an offer like that? We go down
there on the train, set up cameras and lights, five thousand watts'
worth, and in he comes in his baggy sweater, puffing on a pipe. White
shirt underneath—bad for flare—but none of us had the guts to tell
him to change into a blue one. McGowan is all nervous, only time I
ever saw him that way. He asks about his boyhood, his moving to
America to escape the Nazis, what his work day was like, and so on.
Einstein's answering kind of from left field, in his thick German
accent, but it's great television and McGowan sits hunched over by his
knee like he's praying. Follow me?"

"Go on."

"I can see he's getting up the nerve to ask something big, and sure
enough he pops out with it. 'Professor Einstein, sir, many people
throughout the world regard you as the wisest man now living, one of
humankind's true sages. Can you tell us, can you try and tell us, what
the secret is of life?' Einstein thinks about this, puffs on his pipe,
thinks some more, brings his fist up and points a finger, is about to
answer, when there's this hissing noise, a little puff of smoke—the
goddam incandescent's blown, the one we used for highlighting. Losing that causes the Photicon to go. We could have kept shooting with
number two, but Einstein hops up, gets all excited, fishes a screwdriver

out from his sweater pocket, but he doesn't have the slightest idea what to do—a guy like that, all those brains, all that reputation, and he couldn't even fix a ten-cent fuse."

"Fiction," I said. "A clever tall tale."

"Yeah? You sure? If there was some tape around you could see for yourself. Too bad there isn't. Well how about that time McGowan walked off the program, you must know about that."

"A dispute with the executives, second year of the show. Yes, I've heard something."

"Heard, sure. Hearing's cheap. Seen?"

"Of course not. There's no tape."

"Right. There's no tape . . . Okay, they wanted him to do commercials. They wanted him to do laxative commercials and car commercials and they kept hammering him, the vice-presidents and the sponsors and even General Fucking Big Cheese in person, and it got to be too much for him, his saying no all the time, them not backing off. He agrees to do an air-conditioner commercial, insists on ordering forty tons of snow they find in Canada somewhere and truck down to dump on Forty-ninth Street in one huge pile. Once they did, he balked—he sent Chet out to do the ad. It was a joke anyway, because kids left the window to piss on it and instantly the snow turned yellow. But the executives wouldn't let up, because they knew McGowan could sell anything if he turned his mind to it. . . . One morning right in the middle of the show he turns to my camera, shrugs, says 'There must be an easier way to make a living than this,' turns around, grabs Mike the Muffin, who was there making a delivery, says, 'Here, Mike, you're in charge today,' walks off the set. Next day thousands of letters come in demanding he return, and the network had to send detectives to find him, out in New Mexico, where he'd gone on a plane, bring him back. From then on the bigshots had it in for him, no matter how successful the show became."

All the time he talked he sank lower in the sofa, became thinner, bluer, until in the darkness his voice hovered near the ceiling unsupported by any flesh. Of course I must know all that, he said, me being his bio-grapher, having all the facts at hand, knowing true from false. He was just the cameraman, his job had been merely to transmit pictures, aim the electron gun. There was nothing he could tell me probably, why even bother—for instance that story about McGowan being the illegitimate son of an exiled Russian prince, or his being a big-time drug user, a joy popper, or about the time Winston Churchill came on and sipped brandy out of a teacup, or how McGowan had Slisco come to parties at his mansion and film 16mm movies of his orgies, him getting off on that, that and Ferris wheels which he took a kid's delight in and had one especially erected on his lawn—or what about the time McGowan took the show to New Orleans in time for a hurricane and Chet got swept out to sea right on camera and screamed like a girl for help, or about McGowan being called up by Eisenhower for advice on his television manner, or how McGowan was the only star who ever knew squat about how everything worked and could take a camera apart and put it back together blindfolded, only at the same time he was convinced some machines had it in for him and he would grab a mike he didn't like and yell, "You better shape up! You better shape up!" as loud as he could . . . and how he worshiped his mother, kept her body in a special mausoleum out in Queens where he could visit with her and talk with her and keep in touch, or how as a young man he had prospected for gold in the Yukon, or his taking up with whores after he got tired of bluebloods, his drinking, his staying up late, and how they didn't make men like him anymore, not even close to what he was in his prime, good and bad, he was beyond all that, the plain facts couldn't contain him, TV at its most basic was nothing more than pictures obtained from contrasting shades of white and gray and no one ever had more contrast in him than Alec McGowan, who for four solid years had carried television singlehanded on his back until that clown, that imbecile, that bastard Chet Standish got jealous and did him in.

True or false, it was up to me to decide which, he was only the cameraman, a poor working stiff riding a Huston, what did he know, what did anyone know, there being no visual evidence left one way or the other? I listened to this without saying anything . . . Sure, great, if he wanted to taunt me it wasn't that much different than the taunting the past was giving me on its own . . . and I only broke in when the flow started slackening, his cynicism drying out into little hacking coughs.

"McGowan's codeine habit," I said, picking up my pad by way of encouragement. "Tell me about that."

"What codeine habit?" he said, almost sweetly.

"The one you just told me about."

"Who said I wasn't lying?"

I glanced down at my watch. "My family's expecting me. There's a boat at noon I just have time to catch. Thank you for your cooperation, Mr. Slisco."

That scared him all right—the threat of losing his listener. He started talking in an entirely different tone, one I'd witnessed before in the other old men and women I'd met with in the course of my research. At first their memories paraded out the tidy way they had filed them away, but get them talking long enough, prod them gently, and stories would start shaking loose on their own, rough and bumpy and disordered, and it was at that point you could start writing things down or tape-recording or really listening, even with someone like Slisco, who thought, when it came to memories, that he was the boss.

He pushed his glasses back on his nose, put his hand around his shoulder and squeezed hard, as if trying to force the blood back down toward his heart—squeezed and closed his eyes, the better to concentrate on what he was saying. McGowan liked to stay up late, he explained, and that was 99 percent of his problem. There were his women, who kept him hopping, and his love of Broadway and jazz down in the Village, and the fact he liked to walk to get ideas, and he liked walking at night best of all, enjoyed the feel of solid blackness on his face, and once he even got all interested in stars and used to go out to Jones Beach to study the heavens—and his drinking, too, though it never got serious, just enough to justify the time he spent in bars, watching people, studying them, trying to understand what made them tick. He was one of those intensely curious men who are afraid they'll miss an important clue as regards humanity if they sleep for even an hour, so he was always pushing against the limits, he who had to get up at 3:30 A.M. to get ready for the show. Sometimes it would be eleven and he would just be getting warmed up—the musical over, a woman to entertain, one last jazz club to visit, a fifty-block walk to clear his head, the whole island of Manhattan there before him like his own exclusive promenade. Often it would be one or two by the time he got back to his apartment, and then he would not only fall asleep instantly, but sleep solidly, as deeply unconscious as it's possible to be and not lapse into a coma.

The challenge was to snap out of this. At first he tried doing it on his own, using alarm clocks, six or seven of which he'd scatter around his bedroom, each one louder than the next. A windup Timex, the kind that had a brass hammer ringing back and forth between two bells; an electric GE that played reveille; ones that made a humming sound or screeching noise—even a special, when-all-else-fails model, as loud and penetrating as a fog horn. None of these could dent his stupor, other than to make him roll over and pull a pillow over his head, go on snoring.

The network grew concerned about it, his coming in late and groggy, and then toward the end of his first year he overslept one show entirely. They hired a service that made wake-up calls and didn't hang up until the phone was answered, and when that didn't work they ordered a husky assistant director named Pringle to go to the apartment and wake him up in person, which meant grabbing him by the shoulders and giving him a good shaking. This worked to a point, but McGowan soon grew balky. There were lots of informers in the network, detectives hired to keep an eye on the talent, professional snitches, and McGowan didn't like anyone knowing who he was sleeping with or anything about his private life.

"That's how I got started," Slisco said. "He trusted me, because when he stared into the camera's eye, he was always staring into mine right behind it. 'Well, Martin,' he said one morning after the show was over. 'I'm having this little problem and I think you're just the man who might help me out.' He knew I was an early riser, knew I had no family to worry about, and so I was taken on as his wake-up man with a steep raise to show me he took it seriously."

It meant taking the 2:30 A.M. train in from the Island, walking ten blocks through the quiet city, going up in the elevator, letting himself in with his own key. As part of his efforts to reform, McGowan made a rule that anyone sleeping with him had to leave before three, and so most of the time he'd be in bed alone, curled up naked under a comforter, a dreamy smile on a face that seemed younger, less troubled without glasses, a cowlick falling down over his forehead. There was a chair next to the bed where Slisco could sit and watch him, not making a move until the clock read 3:25. A lot of times, just before then, McGowan talked in his sleep, like he was subconsciously warming up his vocal cords, tuning them to the right pitch—but sometimes his dreams went in another direction, his face tightened, he would beat the covers off, even scream.

Most mornings he didn't scream. Most mornings 3:25 would come and Slisco would lean forward and say, "Time to get up, old tiger," or "You there, Mr. McGowan?" and touch him gently on the shoulder. That seldom was enough. It took getting up out of the chair, kneeling by the bed, bending down next to his ear, leaning over and saying the same thing much louder. McGowan would blink with that, flutter his eyelids like a woman, sigh, nod, roll over, and go back to sleep. That was when Slisco had to get physical. He would grab him by the arm and roll him over, do that twice, three times, like it was a game they were playing—roll, twist away, roll—and he'd always have to be ready to jump backwards, because in certain kinds of dreams McGowan would lash out with a fist.

After maybe ten, maybe fifteen minutes of this, McGowan woke up, at least partially. He would sweep the covers back, swing his legs to the side, stand up and stretch his arms out horizontally, do three fast knee bends, breathe in and exhale, all on fire to greet the day—he would do this, fool you so you would go over to the closet to pick out his clothes, and then when you turned around he would be curled back in bed sleeping even more soundly than before, and the whole procedure started over.

"Sometimes an hour went by before he was dressed. The limo sent
by the network would be down on the street blowing its goddam horn,
the phone's ringing off the hook, people back in the studio would be
wetting their pants. I could usually get him vertical inside thirty minutes, but it didn't get any easier after that. I tried everything. Cold
showers, brandy—a little hair of the dog—slapping him around, hot
coffee. Once he was so groggy he poured a whole pot of it right over
his hair, thinking he was in the shower and it was shampoo, and he had
to do the entire show with his scalp scalded . . . Massage was the only
thing that really worked. I'd get him stretched out on the bed and
straddle his legs and start right in on his back, working him as hard as I
could. He had soft skin, which was funny, he looked so square and
taut. It didn't seem to relax on its own. I had to knead it with my fingers, and I got pretty good at it. Ten minutes and he would get up on
his own and stretch, take a shower, get dressed, knock back some
orange juice, look himself over in the mirror, kind of laugh the way he
did, glance over at me, say 'Ready, old tiger?' and off we would go . . .
That was on good mornings. On bad mornings he was still asleep
when I shoved him in the limo and there was nothing on earth that
could get him going except one thing."

Codeine—only Slisco didn't pronounce it the usual way; *co-dyne,* he
said, slurring the syllables in a fake Southern drawl. He'd been using it
himself, having to get up so early, needing to be sharp behind the camera, and there was this druggist he knew in Brooklyn who wasn't fussy
about prescriptions. One morning when everything else had failed and
it was certain McGowan would sleep through the show, equally certain
Slisco would be fired as well, he poured out a couple of tablespoons,
put it in a little shot glass, pressed it into McGowan's hand.

"Try some," he told him.

McGowan, his eyes closed, waved the glass around until it was
roughly in the vicinity of his nose. "What's this?" he asked, sniffing
suspiciously.

"Sarsaparilla," Slisco said.

"Sarsaparilla?"

"Dr. Slisco's sarsaparilla."

"Yeah? Well, here's looking at you, Doctor."

He knocked it down in one swallow. There was no stopping him after that. Ten minutes later he was shaved, showered, and ready to go, talking a mile a minute, tossing ideas up in the air like a juggler, laughing, singing, snapping with such palpable energy it seemed risky to go near him. It got to be their regular routine after that—the morning sarsaparilla with coffee as chaser. The timing was tricky, he couldn't give it to him too early or too late, and eventually he discovered the best time was in the backseat of the limo on Fiftieth Street, just before they pulled over to the curb. It was like watching Clark Kent put on his Superman outfit—once through the studio doors he was dynamite for the next hour and a half.

He needed it, or something like it. He was under an impossible strain, not only the morning show to do, but documentaries and discussion programs and cultural events and the first Emmy shows and everything serious the network got up the nerve to offer—they wouldn't air it without McGowan as host. At the same time half the people working there were out to get him—underlings who resented his success, vice-presidents mad because he wouldn't knuckle under, advertisers who sensed his disdain, news people who thought he was too folksy, programmers who thought he was far too intellectual. His personal life, too. No one could fuck as much as he did and not need something in the way of a restorative. Sure there were rumors going around, and yes, Slisco would have to be careful about focusing too tight on his eyes, and naturally he was a little rocky when it wore off in the afternoon, but he needed some help, needed someone to understand, and there was a solid two years when he depended on Slisco for everything.

"You know who broke that up?" he said, jabbing a finger toward the dark. "That bitch Palmer broke it up. She and her henchman Chet. You get your pad out and you write this down because I'm telling you exactly like it was."

He stood up, as if to give his bitterness more force, staggered, grabbed on to the back of the couch, then disappeared in an old man's shuffle past the kitchen; a few minutes later came the sound of a toilet flushing and flushing twice more. It was a long time before he came back. Restless, I got up and paced around the living room, wedging the curtains back to admit more light. There was one trace of decoration in the entire room, a single picture, there on the opposite end table from the one he'd been leaning against: a black-and-white photo of a bomber crew below the fuselage of their B-24—a typical shot, the guys in back pointing up toward some flak scars, the ones kneeling in front displaying nervous, relieved smiles. Slisco wasn't difficult to pick out—he was the tall, reedy kid looking almost as gaunt as he was now, with that hard, brainy forehead jutting out from beneath his cap. What was different was his expression. He had a smile on his face, a cheerful smile—Martin Slisco the happy young airman, up to his ears in destruction.

He saw me staring down at this when he came back, grunted something I couldn't make out, sat back down. "You okay?" I asked.

"No, I'm not okay. I have colon cancer, the terminal runs. The doctor bastard shrugged, seeing how far gone it is. You know what he gave me for the pain?" He sucked his lips in. "Sarsaparilla. Sarsaparilla, my old faithful pal."

"I'm sorry to hear that," I said flatly. And, "Can I ask you one thing? You said everyone on the program was an informer. Who were you an informer for?"

That slowed him down all right, but that's what I intended it to do, the conversation was going too much his own way. Even so, I didn't expect him to answer.

"You know who BS was?" he asked, making his hand into a visor, pressing it against his forehead, peering down.

"Broadcast Standards?"

"He wanted to know everything about McGowan, who he was fucking, whether or not he was talking to anyone at the other networks, any bitching he was doing, who his pets were, who were his enemies. He knew I was getting him up mornings, helping him out. He knew about the sarsaparilla, too."

"So you went along?"

"If it wasn't me it would have been someone else and I would have been out on my ear. Once a week he'd have me up to his office, pour me a drink. He had a desk set up on a platform so he could sit there smiling down at you like Buddha. He was McGowan's godfather, the one who ran interference for him with the big guys—the only executive McGowan respected. He wanted to make sure McGowan wouldn't get hurt, that's all. Hell, I never told him the truth anyway. I lied to him like crazy. If he was stupid enough to believe my stories then that was his problem."

But he didn't want to talk about that, he said. He wanted to talk about how things were going along fine until Lee Palmer came on the show and then everything went to hell fast. She was a rich, stuck-up bitch, thought she was smarter than everyone else, started ordering McGowan around like she owned him, tried cleaning him up, which meant sucking all the juice from him, robbing him of exactly what it was that made him larger than life in the first place. Clipping his balls off—she may as well have used shears. And then what happened was that Chet Standish fell for her, got all jealous because she was so nuts about McGowan, started brooding on that, feeling sorry for himself because now his only role on the program was to play the clown. Between them they cut Slisco out altogether, kept him separated from McGowan so it was all he could do to get a word in edgewise with him anymore, he who had been his one and only ally when times were tough. McGowan was sagging without the sarsaparilla—you could see the pain droop his eyes down when he opened the show—and yet those two do-gooders had their claws into him now, and events started spiraling out of control.

"Were you there that morning?"

It was at least a minute before he answered, and when he did it was in a mumble I could just barely make out. "I was there."

"You didn't do anything to stop it?"

He stared at me so quickly, with such malice, it was as if he had thrown his eyes across the carpet at my face. "You don't get it, do you, Mr. Bio-grapher? My job was to sit on that Huston and focus the camera and capture what was going on. Period. It didn't matter what I was focusing on, I hardly even knew half the time. Champion twirlers and contortionists from Ringling Brothers and illiterate ballplayers and whackos McGowan dragged in off the street and reformed gangsters and generals and opera stars and Miss Americas and African chieftains and the whole fucking parade and it didn't matter, all I cared about was how they fit into the frame, keeping them there, panning across their kissers, making them look a hell of a lot sharper on camera than they looked in real life. McGowan lived in that frame, get it? Off camera he was a disaster, but once inside that frame he came alive. So of course I kept the camera on him. There was noise, confusion, a table falling over, people shouting, glass breaking, a woman screaming, these flat cracking sounds, but I kept the camera on McGowan, a medium wide shot, because the camera was life to him and inside the camera he couldn't be hurt."

He said this softly, the last part. He sat there with his head down the way a man will who wants to hide his crying, but he wasn't crying— that would be too much to expect.

"You have tapes, don't you?"

"Sure I have tapes."

"How many?"

"Four or five. I was going to be fired, they didn't want any reminders around of McGowan's bad old days, and I needed to have some samples of my work available when I searched for another job. Ordinarily we didn't save nada. We'd put the show on Kinescope sometimes, but in the afternoon they'd shoot the soaps over it just to save a few bucks. That's how serious we took them. Hell, anyone needed some string, something to wipe their nose off on, they'd rip off a strip and use it. Even the ones I have. They're not in what you would call mint condition."

"Excerpts?"

"Entire shows."

"The last show?"

"No." He glanced up at me. "Nice try."

"You mean the Kinescope wasn't saved or you don't have it?"

"I don't have it. The DA took it. It doesn't exist."

"But other tapes do exist? Where are they?"

"I put them away, never thought much about them, not until that videographer came by. He's offering plenty, ten thousand for each one, otherwise I wouldn't even talk to him. He's a smooth bastard, and I didn't like the way he showed off that blonde, but he knows a hell of a lot more about what I'm talking about than you do. You remind me of your old man in that respect. A little dim on the uptake."

It was stupid of him, that last line. Was it intended to make me blow up, storm out of there without asking more questions? Or was it just his usual bile, which, after that moment of softness, had now recirculated back to his throat?

"True or false, Mr. Slisco, your turn to tell me. You're making that up, about the documentary man. He never called you, never came. I'm the first person in fifty years to show any interest in your life. You're sick, you're going to die soon, you have no kids, no survivors. You're the neighborhood crank, and I bet on Halloween kids double dare each other to come knock at your door. Your only chance to be remembered is as a footnote to the life of Alec McGowan, and so you not only need me to hear you out, you need me to see those tapes, your best work. That's what I'm thinking, whether it's true or whether it's false."

"False in spades," he said, but there was no conviction in his voice. I shrugged, got up, went for my coat. "Stop right there," he said, once I was at the door. He was standing now, shuffling over toward the TV set for a crayon and pad. "You win," he said, without looking up. "I'm drawing you a map of where they are."

"No more games."

He looked pained this time, like I was breaking our deal. "Humor me, all right? I'd give them to you, but I don't keep them here. They need special conditions, humidity control—that acetate is fragile stuff. I have them locked away in a vault. This library place. A community college. It's over on the North Shore and you have to go right by it on your way back. This is directions and a note saying you have my permission to borrow them."

He handed me the paper—the writing was hurried and cramped, just barely legible. I was doubtful, there was lots more I could have pressed him on, but I shrugged, folded it in half, put it inside my pocket.

He followed me to the door, shrinking back from the daylight like it was a wave about to crash down on his head. "By the way," he said, just as I was leaving. "How's your old man?"

I shrugged, started to explain, changed my mind. "He's dying," I said.

"Yeah?" His eyes brightened. "Well, give him my best next time you visit him there in prison, okay? Tell him his old friend Martin sends his regards. Tell him I'll see him soon. Soon, real soon—straight down in hell."

I walked out past the lawn mower to the car. The lawn crews were done for the day, and without them the streets were deserted. A few houses down, a boy about Elise's age stood in the middle of the leafless lawn, tossing a football up in the air, but no one came out to play with him and by the time I drove past he'd already gone back inside.

There was a ferry at one, and I would have been in time to make it, but when I got to the exit mentioned in Slisco's directions the temptation was too much for me and I turned off. He was probably lying, but maybe he wasn't, and I could afford to waste a couple of hours and still be home by dark.

The road went through a residential area that wasn't much different from what I'd seen so far, then a long stretch with malls, and then I was up to the North Shore and the houses were bigger and further apart, their driveways sealed off by cameras, guardhouses, and gates. This was the backward-curving neck where McGowan had rented his mansion during his first summers in New York, which made me more interested than I would have been otherwise. The longer I drove the more complicated the directions became—I realized now that catching the first ferry was out, and probably the one after that, too—and I was cursing myself pretty good for being such a fool, when the road swerved to the left past a landfill, curled back on itself, turned to gravel, and abruptly ended on a high sandy cliff.

My first impression was that Slisco had sent me there to fall over—it was that high and sheer, much higher than anything I associated with Long Island. I parked on the flattest spot, pressed on the emergency brake, walked through poison ivy to the cliff's edge. Down below, shining flat in the afternoon sunshine, empty except for one stubby barge, was the full expanse of the Sound. Closer in, stretching into the water and partially encircling it, was a sandspit where some massive excavation work was in progress, even though it was Sunday. A nuke being decommissioned? A billionaire's house going up? It was hard to tell which.

It felt colder than it had been in the morning—as I watched, the wind left off scalloping the water, came up and whipped my face. I grimaced, plunged my hands in my pockets, turned and started walking toward the little clearing set back off the cliff under some scraggly oak trees. There was no sign of any library, not that I had expected one. Instead, I found the shabby remains of an old playground, with a broken seesaw, some rotted picnic tables, and a set of swingless swings. I walked around anyway, not feeling much except tired, trying to imagine it ever having known the shouts of children. Okay, it was Slisco's little joke and I was the butt of it, but I still couldn't understand the point.

That's when I saw it over on the highest, most exposed and windswept edge of the playground, near a rusted jungle gym: a granite stone about four feet high, embedded in the earth so it resembled a cross between a headstone and a historical marker. I walked over to study it closer. There were oak leaves and pine needles drifted around the edges, but when I swept them away I found a metal plaque bolted to the facing side, and on it, raised in salt-tarnished letters, an inscription so bold and legible even a fool, a credulous fool like me, could read it without squinting.

HERE IN THIS PARK DEDICATED TO HIS MEMORY LIES FREDDO THE CHIMP

STAR OF MORNING 1951

LIVE IT UP LITTLE FELLA!

LIVE IT UP!

Part Three

YOUTH AND
EARLY INFLUENCES

Seven

It isn't a mountain, nor a cliff, nor even a particularly high hill, and yet it seems the crucial dividing line between two separate worlds, two directions, two destinies. Toward the north the landscape escapes from the hills that so neatly contain it, widening into the great burnished tableland that leads to Quebec City and the St. Lawrence. Toward the north the feeling, even at this latitude, is of vastness and cold and strenuous possibility—and yet if you turn and look the other way the mood is entirely different, with green sheltered valleys that tuck into each other at their narrowest extensions, each valley set obliquely to the one next to it, but the thrust of them trending always toward the great magnetic pull of the U.S. border ninety miles away. It's not difficult to picture a young man full of energy and ambition standing here a hundred years ago, looking in both directions, carefully considering each, the strenuous hard way north, the deceptively gentle way south, shrugging, letting fate choose for him, flipping a coin, tails south, heads north, but making sure he flips it in such a manner that the coin lands tails.

Not a high mountain—even a middle-aged, out-of-shape biographer from the States can climb it without too much puffing, thanks to a graded trail laid out by the local hiking club. This early in December the fields are not yet covered with snow, and from huge mounds of brush in their centers columns of marble-colored smoke ascend toward a hard gray sky, like pillars supporting a burden that would otherwise collapse. Where the land is wooded there is evidence of a great ice storm, tree after splintered tree extending in an ugly band toward places named Asbestos, Drummondville, and Thetford Mines. Directly below, closer, lies the small rural village of La Chaussée, looking not much different—with its church spire, the whitewashed houses next to it, the patchwork of kitchen gardens, the tall wooded *calvaire* rising from a hill at the village's back—than it must have looked three hundred years ago, evidence of a style of habitation as old and unchanged as there is on this continent.

Explore closer and there are plenty of changes. Each house has a satellite dish set in front with the bird feeders; the old village road has been widened into a four-lane highway where traffic rushes by too fast on its way to Montreal; near the exit is a truck stop where a sign advertises *Le Striptease!*; there are enough abandoned snowmobiles lying about to equip an army of snowmen, and even the most pastoral of the meadows are dominated by massive pylons and sagging power lines bringing hydropower down from James Bay.

But from up high, on such a morning, most of this remains invisible, and what you sense most of all is how crucially placed the village is on that lofty continental divide of adolescence—the divide between a future that seems brave, daring, and strenuous, and a future that seems safe, timid, and soft.

The original stone church being too drafty for winter services, parish headquarters is now a massive concrete edifice on the east side of town abutting the hockey rink. The young curé, confronted by a visitor from the States asking to scan the baptismal records, is anxious to be helpful. What with the craze for genealogy, historians doing local research, scientists tracing genetic maladies, such requests are not as infrequent as you might expect. And yes, there it is—the name *LeBlanc* appended to a long list of first names. *Jean-Louis, Moïse, Abraham, Françoise,* the birth dates in a clerk's neat hand, twelve generations leading to the name on the bottom of the page, *Edgar,* born July 14, 1887 to *Henri* and *Gloria*—and the curé, examining the page, checking the next one, makes the obvious pun in better English than you might expect.

"None past this," he says ruefully. "After Edgar LeBlanc we draw a blank."

For all their history here, for all these deeply embedded roots, no one remembers anyone named *LeBlanc* being from La Chaussée. It's a different story with the name *Cormier*—there are still so many here it's hard to identify which particular branch of the Cormiers anyone is descended from. And so, when you visit the diocese's old citizens' home, bring out the name Yvonne Cormier, a lot of serious head-scratching goes on, connections made between various Cormiers, but none that seems flexible enough to include her. *Je Souviens* is the provincial motto, but it's obvious that when it comes to the LeBlancs and the troubled, passionate branch of the Cormier family, there is no one left alive who remembers them, nor the momentary celebrity of their last male representative.

Lyrical start—anything else to include here? Odd sensation Quebec gives, the detritus of our culture given a sheen of interest thanks to the French. I.e., girlie magazines in the gas stations, bustier girls, rawer headlines, cheaper paper. A mulish-looking teenager with professional breasts tries pathetically to proposition me, drawn by what can only be the allure of my Massachusetts plates, which can still exert a pull here. Asking at the cafe for a typical local dish, having the waitress bring me underdone french fries soaked in gravy. A French-looking cow loose on the road, moody and independent, a real Quebecois *vache*. The prevailing style in architecture: inflatable garages outside granite split-levels. Local color and may as well work in, point being, in 1910 you have to move to the dominant culture, now the dominant culture comes to you—and yet a certain gray loneliness remains.

Statistics ditto. Important to show larger forces. Young man fools himself into thinking he's making a decision on own when all along demographic digits suck him in. Quebecois immigration and causes, etc. Self-sufficient rural communities until 1870's, then the bottom falls out. Primitive farming techniques contribute to 70% drop in province's wheat production, while potatoes ruined by blight. At same time population explodes—over 670,000 by First World War. Textile mills booming in New England, places like Lowell/Lawrence/Manchester/Woonsocket. Agents from mills recruiting actively in province—fancy dressers/generous with booze/big promises/sign right here. Prospects of decent wages/compatriots already established there/cheap train fares down. "More often than not, the French Canadian fully intended to return home after earning enough money to achieve a modest objective, typically the purchase of a small farm or the paying off of a mortgage. At times, fed up with rural life, feeling they were a burden on their family, or simply wanting to become independent, young men and women struck out for themselves with no other goal than to be on their own" and footnote source. French Canadians fifth-largest ancestry group in U.S. The unknown minority. More than 20% some cities, including Holyoke.

Statistics, with their smug leering kissers you want to smash in the chin. The guilt, the impatience I always feel before them. Do they say anything, or include just to impress? Far easier to imagine a young man standing on that hill over the village with his hands plunged deep in his coat pockets, feeling all the strength, all the fear of youth. Brutal father? older brothers who bully him? no opportunities at all on the land, nothing to do but leave. Which way to go? Historical forces disguise themselves as burr in his gut and so he answers it the same way so many others do—toward the great lying promise to the south.

The one surviving photograph of Edgar LeBlanc was taken years later, at a factory picnic in Holyoke, Massachusetts. He's the tenth from the right, middle row, and from what you can see of him (the burly shapes crowd together to fit into the frame) he seems a capable enough man, with a broad forehead, blocky shoulders, and a slow and dreamy expression above a small feminine chin. As a young man he must have been observant and very impressionable, because for the next twenty years he would tell the story of his emigration to anyone patient enough to listen.

The train fare south was only ten dollars, but, disowned by his family, penniless, he had no alternative but to walk. Crossing the border into Vermont, he was accosted by an agent looking for men to work the log drive down the Connecticut River. It was brutal work, up to your waist in frigid water fourteen hours a day, the river boss charging you for drying your clothes out by his fire, the food tasteless, the men working beside you wracked by TB, coughing on you, leering, capable of stealing the boots off you as you slept, with drowning a real possibility and being crushed by logs an even greater one, so you could never relax. And yet the young Edgar LeBlanc loved it: the cold, silver river, the huge mass of chocolate-colored logs, being able to throw the full weight of his youth at something that—force it enough, curse it, outsmart it, poke, prod, and pry—would slowly and grudgingly *move*.

He became friends with someone only a year or two older named Philias Joseph Remillard, a happy coiled spring of a man who was the best riverman on the drive. Any tough job, any tricky piece of water to navigate with a bateau or a jam to break apart with a peavy, Philias Joseph would be the first one called. He was the best storyteller on the drive, too, and at night would keep the men entertained with descriptions of his adventures in bordellos all across the country. He was an atheist and made no secret of this. "Dat God shit," he would say, spitting contemptuously toward the fire, "dat's to keep de working man in his no place."

Edgar took to imitating Philias's swagger, his way of wearing his hat halfway back on his head—tried with only partial success to brave the river the same heedless way he did. At a bad stretch of water called Sumner Falls the logs piled up in a jam thirty feet high. The drive boss, cursing, offered a hundred dollars to the man brave enough to bury explosives in the jam's middle. Philias jumped at this. The men watched breathless as he leapt from log to log across the river, tamped the dynamite down with its wadding, lit a match on his fly, held it to the fuse, calmly regarded it, started dancing back toward shore, only to slip on the last log before safety, be sucked down into the current just as the charge went off.

The death of Philias Remillard took something out of Edgar, and not just temporarily. Reaching Holyoke at the drive's finish, he followed the other men to the whorehouses on the outskirts of town, where, after the usual frenzied groping, he woke up to find he'd been robbed of all his pay. For all his own brave talk of atheism, there was nowhere for Edgar to go for help but the local parish, where the French priest, Father Tremblay, working on commission, made a tidy profit steering such derelicts into the worst jobs at the city's worst mills. (Father Tremblay met a squalid end: caught as a pederast in 1935, he was quietly executed by the Springfield police.)

Edgar LeBlanc worked at the mill for eighteen years, stirring pulp. He joined the union, the only French-speaking local of the Wobblies. There are old pinochle players at the Franco-American club in Holyoke who still remember him—remember how when the great paper-mill strike came in 1924, Edgar, a leader until that point, took no part at all, and word went out that he had gone over to the bosses as an informer. Whether true or not, it was around this time he started drinking, drinking heavily. He soon lost his job. His hobby was carving replicas of the wild forest birds he remembered from his youth, but his hands grew too shaky for this. One morning in 1929, after a night drinking bootlegged whiskey with his cronies, he was found dead in the scummy, polluted shallows of the Connecticut where it came out of the dam, and it was thought that what he'd been trying to do was cross the river on logs visible only to him.

Only one other incident in his life is worth recording. In 1916 he met a young woman working at the mill as an assistant timekeeper who had been born in La Chaussée, her family having moved to the States when she was still an infant. Five months after they were married they had a son they named Philias, who was christened at Our Lady of Perpetual Truth, the shabbiest of Holyoke's three French churches.

Edgar was said to be a devoted father, when he was sober. He pressed his carvings into the young boy's hands, told him stories of the log drive, filled his head with atheism, and only hit him when it was necessary.

Of Yvonne Cormier's early life there is no surviving record whatsoever. Projecting backward from the woman she became, it's likely she was a clever, intense little girl, someone whose intelligence and imagination were totally incomprehensible to those who had charge of her. Like many French-Canadian children, she may have been sent to work in the mills at age nine; like most, she very likely grew up knowing the worst, rawest kind of discrimination. ("In cultivated circles," one historian writes, "the Massachusetts Brahmins, who regarded American culture as fixed, monolithic and Anglo-Saxon, viewed the French Canadians with suspicion and tended to confuse them with French peasants.") For many years, local newspapers would not even condescend to list "Canuck" births or deaths, seeing in these no significance at all.

There exists a wedding portrait taken of Yvonne when she was seventeen. The first thing you notice is her black hair coiled in plaits, thick and luxurious, almost too much for her small face to support. She's short, full-figured, and busty in the style of the day, so it's easy to picture her being pestered by men. Her nose is French and prominent; her cheeks have a raisin kind of tightness, but what stands out most is her eyes—they seem bright even in sepia, hot even, and make you want to place a compress on them to soothe them safely shut.

She was promiscuous, at least before her marriage, and Alec

McGowan grew up believing that Edgar LeBlanc was not his biological father. The birth of a child seemed to sober her in this respect; her considerable passion was transferred to the church. She was a fervent believer, went to mass on every occasion, knew more about the saints than even the oldest priest, and liked showing people the rosary beads that had turned from silver to gold in her hands. If anything, Catholicism wasn't severe enough to hold her; she began attending grubby, improvised chapels in the worst parts of the slums, where defrocked priests had grafted onto the traditional mass trappings of Southern fundamentalism, including the laying on of hands, speaking in tongues, even the handling of poisonous snakes.

And yet this was only the start for Yvonne LeBlanc. Even during her most religious period she was shrewd enough to sense that the authority of the Church was rapidly weakening and began looking around for a replacement. Finding a replacement, a stronger force, wasn't hard, even in the Depression. Materialism—that was what drove everything in her new country, the god people devoted their lives to, the tangible, easily comprehensible paradise on earth. Poor, with a husband who drank up his meager wages, and living in a cold-water flat that stank of fumes from the pulp mill, there wasn't much in the material world for her to worship, at least not at first; it was as if, having embraced this new religion, she couldn't find where the church was hidden, let alone gain admittance.

There were tag sales, bazaars, places where old furniture could be bought cheap, bingo games where she could sometimes win ten dollars, but these weren't enough to satisfy her. Through much scraping and saving she managed to buy a new Stromberg Carlson console radio, and she kept it on day and night, constantly fiddling with its antenna, never tuning it right, running to fetch a pad every time a sale was advertised, though she never had any money to take advantage of these. Her favorite occupation, her only hobby, was window shopping on Main Street in Holyoke, and she would apparently spend hours at this, pushing the baby carriage up one side of the street, staring with her face pressed against the window glass, noting each new display, memorizing the prices, comparing brands, their shapes and their colors, then going down the opposite side, doing the same thing.

Only a few more details survive. She was a compulsive liar. She herself had a drinking problem, though an odd one. Scorning alcohol as being for weaklings, she still possessed a powerful and restless thirst. Her drink was Moxie, the old New England cola, which she consumed by the caseload. Harmless, people said—and yet it caught up with her in the end. She died of pancreatic cancer two weeks after her fortieth birthday, by which time her only child, having renounced her completely, had moved out on his own.

All the evidence is that she was an indifferent mother during her son's early years, a smothering mother during his adolescence. Apparently the baby was left in a grandmother's care while Yvonne worked at the mill; she begrudged every expenditure the baby required, as it made even more unobtainable the consumer goods she craved. This seems to have changed when the boy turned twelve. Married to a failure, stuck in a dead-end job, with no other future than losing what remained marketable in her looks, she must have imagined that young Philias was her only way out.

He was good at numbers, counted early, and this gave her the first strand in the complicated scheme of hope she began weaving around him. Being good with numbers could mean only one thing: he would be good in business—and this is what she must prepare him for, right from the start. Other mothers she knew bragged about how their sons were destined for the priesthood, but she only smiled in quiet smugness at the depth of their naïveté. What was a priest in a doomed faith compared to an important businessman, someone who had his hands not only on the levers of power and riches but the country's very soul? Priests stuck wafers into people's mouths and made nothing on it; businessmen sold wafers to people and made plenty.

Of course this wouldn't be easy. Of course this meant changing his identity, starting over from scratch. Poor Edgar LeBlanc was the first

to go; even before his death she began speaking of the boy as father-
less. The French part of him was next. She took no pride in this
heritage, saw it only as an unnecessary burden. What point was there
in having him suffer discrimination he'd done nothing himself to
deserve? He wasn't a Negro, was he? He didn't even look particularly
French, not with those small features, that fair skin. She would invent a
new name for him as soon as she thought of a good one. In the meantime, she bought him elocution books (*Speak Your Way to Success, Twelve
Days to Vocal Power,* etc.), spent long hours sitting next to him at the
kitchen table, tearing his voice out by its roots and starting over from
scratch.

"It's not duh store," she would say, practically screaming. "It's *duh*
store!"

She grew so angry she reached into his mouth and lifted his tongue,
forcing it into the "th" shape shown in the books. But eventually, with
patience, her efforts began paying off. "How well he speaks!" her
friends would say, ashamed of their own accents. "Why, he sounds like
dose voices on duh radio even!"

A decent address was next. No one from the bad part of Holyoke
could expect to get ahead. No, it was Springfield where the opportunities lay, the nearby city where no one knew them and where, if you
lived in the right neighborhood, you could attend a good high school
absolutely for free. She took the bus there, walked the streets, gauging,
appraising. On Sabbaday Avenue she discovered that although the
numbers progressed regularly on the even side, on the odd side they
jumped from 137 to 141, skipping 139. That was the address she
invented for him, 139 Sabbaday Avenue, and to back it up she rented a
box in the nearest post office where his report cards could be mailed.
Sending him to such a ritzy school meant she would have to dress him
accordingly; there was a woman she knew who worked for the Salvation Army, had first crack at the trucks when they came in, selected out
the cleanest, freshest-smelling jackets and pants.

With a new voice, a new address, a new appearance, there was
nothing left to do but find him a new name. It's easy to picture her lis-

tening to the radio, jotting down names, assembling them in different combinations, trying to find something that sounded professional, dignified, and crisp. Victor F. Lodge. Trevor Tomlinson. Walter J. Honeycutt. Roderick Whitehead. But that was just the problem—the more formal they sounded, the more unnatural, and it wasn't until just days before the deadline for enrolling him in school that the correct name came to her in a flash of inspiration she had faith in right from the start.

Her oldest possession, the one relic left from her family's early days in Canada, was a thick wool trading blanket, the kind used to cover an entire Quebecois family on their sleigh ride in to mass. On one edge was a white silk tag; on that tag, sewn in delicate red thread, was the name of the firm that manufactured the blanket: *Alec McGowan Ltd., Dundee and Toronto.* She had loved that name growing up—by a natural enough process it seemed the name of warmth and safety itself—and that was the name she chose for him, *Alec McGowan* . . . and on the day she told him this, the change being complete now, he looked up at her with indifference, smiled very thinly, nodded, turned away.

New section here.

Big irony, etc.

Mother creates new identity for him, once assumed wants nothing to do with her. Quote from *Collier's Magazine* interview of 1/6/54. "My parents? Not much to tell actually. My father was a simple carpenter, originally from Scotland. My mother was a registered nurse with a large amount of Indian blood in her. They both worked hard and I seldom saw them."

Boyhood.

One of those who lie low and have no youth whatsoever. Okay, spell this out. Says to himself, not going to be loved, but not going to starve, so best course is to sit these years out, wait for better days. Obviously ruthless determination to escape mediocrity of surroundings or why else go along with mother's schemes? Other than that, an avid reader, a kid who keeps his eyes open, figures out early that school has nothing to teach him and must get his education entirely on own.

But wins decent grades in school—the kind of pleasant, easygoing personality a boy develops when he wants to keep everyone off his back. Quote from old school transcripts, still extant, the one written comment appearing over and over under teacher's remarks. "An engaging young man." "An engaging member of the freshman class." High school yearbook. "Our engaging and enigmatic member with the honeyed vocal cords and the wryest grin in town."

Handsome, judging by every photo—use the senior class photo, fourth from left, bottom row, looking younger than classmates and older, too. Younger in that others have no future beyond the boring usual, and he's still developing. Older in that his eyes have seen more, known more, anticipate better what's to come. Even without glasses he looks like he has glasses (use that line); something in the intent way he peers. Your finger taps out heads . . . accountant this one, cop this one, baker, banker, priest . . . then stops when it gets to him—*whoa, what have we here???*

Good dresser.

Lots of acquaintances, no real friends. No interest in sports. Too embarrassed to attend parties—how much does fear of exposure hold him back? Unlike everyone else, has no interest in movies, probably can't afford. Finds their dreams puerile/shabby/predictable/nowhere near splendid enough, not compared to ones he builds in secret.

Part-time jobs. Soda jerker. Tobacco picker (insert one-liner: the heyday of Springfield's politically incorrect crop). Apple picking in the fall. Works in Bible warehouse stacking crates. Every cent saved proves to him he has discipline, what it takes. At seventeen, still in high school, moves alone into rooming house on Sabbaday Avenue making one less lie to live down (abortion clinic as of 12/5/99). Summer he's eighteen works as lifeguard at tony rich girl's camp called Camp Metawee in Dublin, NH. How does he swing that?

Girls. Funny this part. How he has lots, but apparently all drawn from French-Canadian girls back in Holyoke. Tough ones, rouged/cigarette smoking/Hollywood sodden/early fuckers. One after the other. Segues into another pronounced trait—seeing things with old man's perspective, even as kid. Seeing *every* girl as pretty, knowing how transient it is, wanting to catch their blossoming in time. Avoids "nice" girls so he must have been diffident despite sexual precocity. Any of these girlfriends still alive? Kids by any?

First sign of future promise is winning essay contest sponsored by *Springfield American* on theme "What Is Pluck?" Quote entirely if room, otherwise emphasize main points beginning *Christopher Columbus had it of course. So did Thomas Alva Edison and Andrew Carnegie and Daniel Boone. It wasn't just courage, though they were brave when they had to be. It wasn't just that they were shrewd, though they were men with whom you wouldn't want to play poker. These were men who believed in their lucky star, knew just where it was located in the firmament, could actually look up and see it over their shoulders, even during the darkest night.* Go on to conclusion, him writing *What is pluck when all is said and finished? Pluck is luck spelled with a capital P. Pluck is the rare and precious ability some men have to spit fate in the eye and force luck to be on their side whether it wants to be there or not.* Written well, smooth, enough clichés to impress judges but obviously original. First prize savings bond worth $50 which he immediately cashes, in sudden desperate need for classy new clothes as will follow. Use photo of him accepting prize from publisher, head lowered like accepting knighthood.

Meets Chet Standish. Go slow here, four or five pages minimum. Exact meeting date still in doubt but in autumn 1935 CS is sent to military school in Pennsylvania to gain some backbone. Rebels via fainting fits on parade ground/throwing beets/getting stinko. Father allows him to return to Springfield High. Elected class president by buying everyone Hershey Bars and free sodas. "Affable" attached to him in every description. Spring of 1937 sees both CS and AM in same class. Bob Sasser (identify who he, where now, etc.) still remembers episode in history class one day. Smug teacher rails against unions and New Deal; AM, usually so quiet, rises from desk and launches into passionate defense of working people, what they have to put up with, conditions in the mills, drabness of housing, preyed upon by disease, no hope for kids, etc. Chet greatly impressed, more by passion and eloquence than anything specific. Catches his attention, is this what prompts introducing himself? Or does Chet envy him his slutty girls, wants in?

Insert crucial scene here when and if information becomes available. Impossible to imagine other than trite. "Hey I admired your little speech," Chet saying. "Saw your essay in the paper, real impressive piece of work. How come you don't speak up more?" Upshot is Chet offers him job on radio station father has just given him as birthday present. AM accepts, begins work there April 1, 1937, as evidenced by neatly typed entry in station's logbook still extant (photo).

Become unlikely friends—speculate on why here, trying not to slant it in retrospect with what happened. Chet class president/everyone's best pal/well connected/country club set/cotillions at Longmeadow/ good ol' Chet. Not a clown, though does a good Eddie Cantor, passable Buster Keaton. No problems with eyes yet. Rich but generous, the treat's on me. Enough touchy pride it boils over in quick snaps of anger he later apologizes for with lavish presents. Fashionably left, takes politics seriously, greets FDR as official representative of Springfield youth election of 1936. What he sees in AM. Someone restless/ ambitious as he is; someone who has talent in way he does not, but smothered under a barrel so he can pride himself on being his mentor/facilitator. Someone who will smooth out AM's rough edges and thereby protect him from his worst, most savage/retrograde instincts. Big brother in this respect; little brother professionally. On AM's part? Chet is first to accept his new self as genuine—not just tweed jackets/phony address/forced articulation, but new identity that will soon be too dynamic for a small city to contain. Hardest part of any dream being to sell it to that first customer.

Write this out briefly here, expand later, make sure to include first appearance of Margaret Osborne Pebble, Chet's sometime girlfriend. Dark-haired, serious expression, the best in the class when it comes to numbers, a no-nonsense kind who's pretty, but in the tight forced way of 35-year-old, though she's only seventeen. Explain how she picks out Chet as, not husband yet, but someone whose foolishness it's her duty/destiny to correct. Comes to help out at station soon doing all the books. Chet always trying to escape her domination etc., dumping her for dumbest blondes etc., always she waits out the foolishness and takes him back in steadily tighter hand. Quote from her letters, including "poor poor Chet" one where she maps out his personality and weaknesses like a detailed topographic map of Massachusetts.

Early radio as follows.

There is an exuberant, youthful quality to the halcyon days of station WSM that is reminiscent of those Andy Hardy films so popular with Depression-weary moviegoers in the 1930's. Fun-loving Andy, played by Mickey Rooney at his eager cocker spaniel best, always manages to get into jams with his parents and teachers, then has to face some imminent crisis, for instance the high school not having enough money to put on the junior prom, the solution to which always turns out to be one of the despairing friends jumping up and yelling, "Hey, I know! Let's put on a *show!*"

For a memorable period in the late thirties, WSM and its innovative programming was the hottest show in Springfield, the station everyone listened to, old people and youngsters alike. The station was founded in 1922 as the first licensed radio station in western Massachusetts; its owner was a millionaire gambler named Edwin Raugh, who became involved with radio as a pal of David Sarnoff, the brilliant innovator who put together RCA. (There is an old station legend that Raugh had been there on the roof of Wanamaker's in New York City in 1912 as a young David Sarnoff monitored the SOS from the sinking *Titanic,* his job being to warm Sarnoff with frequent cups of coffee as the long night wore on.)

Sarnoff, owing him a favor, got him to invest in radio, and offered to include WSM as one of the charter stations in NBC. Mr. Raugh had a stubborn streak and decided to keep the station independent, thereby establishing the quirky, maverick quality the station—all 10,000 watts' worth—prides itself on to this day. Unfortunately for Mr. Raugh, his gambling debts caught up with him at about the same time Wall Street crashed, and it was only the intervention of a wealthy friend, lumber baron Calvin Standish, that bailed him out. Standish, completely indifferent to radio, hired a caretaker-manager to run the station for a half-dozen years, then turned it over to his son, Chester, in hopes it would stimulate in him the business ambition he so conspicuously lacked.

Chester Standish, at least initially, looked upon running the station as a lark, not much different from being president of the junior class. His first move was to hire as co-manager his new friend, Alec McGowan; McGowan had no experience in radio either, but he listened to it a lot, and for Chet this made him eminently qualified. Then, too, though it wasn't quite clear yet where McGowan's talent lay, it was perfectly clear to Standish that the talent existed, and so it seemed a gamble worth taking.

To everyone's surprise, the station, rather than collapsing under the combined weight of the boys' inexperience, flourished as it had never flourished before. The first thing they did was give up the drafty shack out in the country that served as station headquarters and move downtown into a savings-and-loan bank that had recently failed. The second thing was to throw out the old-fashioned farm reports ("Poultry School on the Air" was a typical entry), and barn dances and hill-billy jamborees, and substitute in their place swing and big band and jazz; included among the latter were the latest recordings by all the black musicians that were just starting to be allowed air time—Ellington, Basie, and Holiday. More important, they reduced the hours allotted to music and began inaugurating programs that forty years later would become known as "talk." Interview shows, man on the street, commentary by local newspaper reporters—this formed the bulk of programming during the day, with high school sports on weekends and live church services on Sunday.

One of the station's happiest inspirations was the first call-in program in New England. They installed a microphone downstairs in the old bank's marble lobby, erected a sign outside inviting any passersby to come in and talk to Chet (sitting upstairs in the studio with earphones) about any subject at all. This was a huge success. Successful, too, and the ultimate secret of their popularity, was their eschewing the kind of sugary, happy-voiced artificiality that, along with grave pomposity, had dominated radio up to that time. The Chet-Alec team had as their rule that everyone, every announcer and DJ, just talk *normally*—quietly sometimes, exuberantly at others, but always intimately, as if their listeners weren't sitting out there in the ether, listening through ear trumpets, but sitting relaxed in the same room.

And they were lucky. When the great September hurricane of 1938 struck, the worst natural disaster in New England's history, WSM was the only Springfield station to continue broadcasting, though flood waters sent everyone scrambling to their roofs. Mayor Putnam came on air to order the evacuation of the South End, where the dike had broken; police used the station's transmitter to send out orders; with all the telephone lines down, the station offered anyone who could reach the studio the opportunity to broadcast messages to loved ones saying they were safe. From that day on, WSM became synonymous in most people's minds with reliability and safety; in bad times of any sort, WSM was the station to tune in.

Standish and McGowan quickly worked out an understanding of who was responsible for what. In a reversal of their later roles, Chet was the on-air star, the one who did the interview programs, the announcer on the most popular shows, the one whose voice, deep and velvety already, now took on a vein of steel that made it all the more compelling; so tough was his voice beneath the mellifluousness that he could broadcast twenty hours straight without being spelled.

McGowan concentrated on production, the technical end of things, and at first his voice was rarely heard over the air. The one show he enjoyed doing was the midnight show; he would play any records that were lying around, mixing them up, so that Caruso would come on next to Goodman next to Spike Jones next to the Carter Family next to Kreisler next to Ellington at his most suave. He wouldn't say much, except at the top of the hour, when he would deepen his voice, in imitation of the gravest, most pompous of the network announcers, and say, "Let's hear a report from our correspondent in Italy." Then he'd read a couple of pages from Edward Gibbon's *Decline and Fall of the Roman Empire,* about how the "Goths were

advancing to chastise the insolence of the emperor Glycerius"—and
when he didn't do this, letters poured in from all over western Massachusetts demanding that their wideawake correspondent Mr. Gibbon
be put back on the air.

When you try to picture those years, it's the youthfulness that jumps
out at you; you get the feeling that Depression-weary listeners tuned in
to the station just to plug into that energy themselves. Everything
seemed magnified—that's the other quality that comes through. Radio
was the first medium that enabled young men to project their personalities live at a distance, so it's no wonder they felt drunk on it,
everything coming to them with heightened significance. There in
the bank-turned-studio the two men sit in shirtsleeves at the huge
mahogany board-of-directors table they use as their desk, hatching up
yet another new program, another new promotion, another new twist
("You sit on the river, Chet, the ice is melting, and the first caller to
guess the exact time you fall in wins a month's supply of bituminous
coal"); the window is wide open, so the intoxicating springtime air
pours in at full strength—Andy Hardy times two, the chums putting
on their show, ready to wow them, and the only thing missing, the last
piece needed to make the resemblance complete, is the appearance of
their Judy Garland.

Set this up. For time being all goes well, but show how AM feels
need for decoration in his life, the hard core of it seemingly perfected;
needs something much larger than environment he finds himself in.
He turns edgy now, spring of 1940/war in Europe/out of high
school/charm of radio wearing off/bored with city/his sluts no
match for him. He's distracted, as if sensing he draws near to something determinate and final.

The meeting.

There now occurred what was apparently one of those chance
encounters beloved in melodrama, and yet surprisingly common in
real life—if not occurring with quite such intensity. The rest of
McGowan's life he referred to it simply as "The Meeting," and it's clear
he dated his life by it; before "The Meeting" was one life, a largely pas-

sive, preparatory one, and after it came his real life, marked by head-long and passionate pursuit. Not that he talked much about it, even to his friends; only a few ever learned who "The Meeting" involved, though it's clear the experience changed him forever, to the point where he worshiped the actual moment as a kind of totem, became exhilarated and depressed on its anniversary, reran the event continually through his memory, drew strength from it, and also despair. He believed in pluck, in forcing fate onto his side, but here fate had jumped out and snared him and he could never get over the surprise of this, the force and accuracy of that sudden spiritual punch.

The facts.

The facts. The facts as we know them are as follows. On a warm June morning in 1940, Alec McGowan was riding a dilapidated old bicycle he had borrowed from a field hand at a weekend job he had loading tobacco on one of the farms north of Springfield; apparently this wasn't for the money, but part of research he was doing for a documentary WSM was starting called *From This Valley*. He was late for a second job as a soda jerk at Ryan's, the old Rexall drugstore on Cypress and Main (this for money, since the radio station couldn't pay very much). His route took him along what was known locally as "Flower Road"—a long stretch of macadam bisecting two uncut meadows filled with wildflowers that would be at their most colorful and fragrant on a June morning like this one. It seems that somewhere along the way he was passed by a large brown touring car; it's easy to picture him being all but swept off the road as it sailed majestically past—then getting angry, maybe giving it the finger or raising a defiant fist. In any case, the touring car stopped and a young woman his age got out, walked back up the road with a basket and stooped down to begin picking flowers. McGowan, even from that distance, seems to have been immediately smitten; he put the bike down and walked over to her, but before he could get up the courage to say anything, the girl went back to the car which then sped away.

The facts. The facts as we know them. The facts as we know them are as follows blah blah etc. bullshit etc. Is this what it's come down to

at the crucial moment? Tone of cheap reporter on evening news.
Hardly know shit as regards facts and here I am parading them like a
marching band that's going to sweep all before it by sheer brass. Even
if there were facts, the more I have now, the farther/faster he recedes.
Not being able to give chase. Having to keep one hand (*best* hand)
behind my back and why? Okay, a bio's convention, everything exter-
nal going to be described hoping it hints at what's internal, but never
allowed to tackle the internal head/heart on. The convention sucks—
why bother playing? Up against a wall/barrier/edge. Deliberately
keeping myself behind the wall and why? When it comes to "The
Meeting" I know all about it. How do I know? I *know*. Plenty of lost
loves in anyone's life there for the tapping, my own sweet heartbreak.
Distill/extract/borrow. What a young man felt seventy years ago,
someone I never knew, or whose trousers I maybe brushed against
once in an NYC automat, all this happening in a vanished countryside
I never saw, and yet I know and why pretend otherwise—what's
gained? Why go to so much trouble resurrecting a life only to hide
behind these *apparently he felts, it's likely he wanteds, it's not hard picturings,*
those godawful impotent *seems to have beens.* Why hedge? I live with
him/study him/enter him and fucking *know*.

Write this out.

A perfect summer morning in June 1940. The air is warm, intoxicating—everything is given emphasis by contrast with the miserable New
England spring; anyone exposed to such lushness could feel only a
delicious sense of self-indulgence, self-reward. A young man pedals a
wobbly bicycle down an empty country road. Above him the sky
seems both softer and vaster than it has ever seemed before—not the
hard, remorseless ceiling it was for most of the year but a plush kind
of infinity the word *blue* can just barely begin to describe. It's a time
when towns are still separated by long stretches of farmland, so even a
short journey like this one takes on an air of adventure and expecta-
tion, giving a sense not just of pedaling into town but of pushing out
into the sea.

A sea, at this time of year, of flowers. He doesn't know their names, is too much a city kid for that, but he can see them spread out on either side of the road, orange ones, a purple spiky kind, little buttons of yellow, weeds that have creamy white tassels on their tips, so top-heavy they wave even without a breeze. He can smell them, too—a perfume baked into the good clean smell of macadam, part of the warmth that yields to him on the bike, then regathers itself behind him and seems to push.

He's in a hurry and in no hurry—he pedals all out for a minute, spreads his arms apart and coasts, closing his eyes in a little feat of daring that makes him smile. God he feels good. Good! An aching kind of good—the kind of good that can burst. Clouds of midges leave a gritty feel against his face, but he likes this, too—it's as if he's feeling the grain of the earth, and it's yielding to him, enlisted on his side. He'd gotten along well with the tobacco workers, black men from Jamaica, dignified and careful, who folded each papery leaf like it was a love letter they were sending to their women back home. There were bums, too, hoboes rounded up by the state police and ordered to work, funny and cynical, spitting on the tobacco as they stacked it just to show they had no use for any boss. He used to feel uncomfortable with such men, too close to their destiny himself, but he is beyond that now—he's a reporter, isn't he? A documentary maker, a radio man, someone who can talk to men like these, listen to their stories, jot them down on his pad, smile his broadest, turn the charm on, then borrow one of their bikes and pedal away into another world. The job at the drugstore was a joke, something he'd gone into expecting nothing more than a chance to pick up girls. Hell, he can play a soda jerk as well as anyone, those small-town girls with the big-city dreams are so easy it hardly counts, and no one took it seriously, life is short and sweet and you have to gather thy rosebuds while you can and seize the moment and what the hell it's all for fun and fun for all. Jesus he feels good!

The road was flat until now; as it nears the river the grade steepens, but so smoothly and gently it feels downhill more than up. He begins sweating, but this is pleasant, too, the dampness on his shirt cooling

him like there's a rider next to him just to fan. At the top of the grade
the river comes into view; from that distance it seems another road, a
watery kind of macadam lined with fruit trees and willows. A purple-
breasted bird darts down at him, protecting its nest, then another, then
a third, until he's surrounded by his own little halo of somersaulting
birds, rising up at him from the meadow, swooping, playing, urging
him on.

He believes in pluck, in forcing luck onto his side, but on a day like
this one no force is needed—all he has to do is touch the pedals the
merest fraction and the bike rolls on. Occasionally a car passes, swinging well to the outside to give him room, but for the last half-mile
there hasn't been a single car, and the road sinks far enough down into
the meadowland that he can't see anything but flowers. They sadden
him, or something does—always when his happy sense of well-being
reaches a peak it tumbles over into something darker—but by pedaling faster he's able to leave much of this behind. He reemerges on
another incline, this time riding above the flowers, doubled by his
shadow, which the noontime sun keeps folded in tight to the bike.

A biplane stutters and coughs on the horizon to his left—a crop
duster flying low, or a barnstormer showing off. Closer in, a cow shies
away from the bike, making a crashing sound in the meadow. In the
distance behind him, coming to him first as the faintest, finger-like
pressure against the damp spot on his back, a buzzing sound thickens
into a deep-throated purr. Soon he senses it's too close behind him; he
swerves to the right to make room, but the car sweeps by well over on
the shoulder, generating an outwash of hot air that spills him into the
ditch.

The old bike is so rickety it falls apart, tires going one way, frame
and seat the other, but he himself isn't injured. Mad—he's plenty mad,
and gets to his feet screaming in French. He can see now it's a brown
touring car, the long Daddy Warbucks kind, with a streamlined ele-
gance copied from the fastest locomotives. It stops a hundred yards
ahead—for a moment he thinks it's backing up to help him. But no,
the car is simply parking there. The back door opens, there's a pause,

and then a young woman bends her head down, glances to each side, jumps out.

This happens so quickly he imagines she's fleeing, running away—his first instinct is to rescue her from some unknown evil, and it's enough to cool his anger into something entirely different. He kicks at the bike, shrugs, then starts walking down the macadam trying to see better, feeling an odd combination of intensity and dreaminess he blames on the crash.

The girl holds a woven, oval-shaped basket. She walks into the meadow where the grass immediately hides everything but her shoulders, neck, and head. Still, he's had just enough of a glimpse to see she's tall, quick-moving, coltish—by the time she's into the first wildflowers she's moving faster, all but skipping. She finds the richest spot, begins gathering blossoms into her basket, her motions slow and deliberate now, so he can picture her frowning in concentration even before he's close enough to see her face.

The richest seam of wildflowers winds back around toward the road. In the distance the car sounds a plaintive toot, but she continues picking, the grass getting lower until finally all of her is revealed—it's as if the flowers have generated her from their midst. She's wearing a sleeveless yellow dress that compliments the light tan of her complexion; she's not as tall as he had first thought but holds herself in the erect, balanced way of a ballerina. He's motionless now, but something must be pressing on her as it presses on him, because she suddenly stops, looks up, sees him staring from twenty yards away. She's not frightened by this. She looks at him with more curiosity than surprise, a smile starting, but not quite managing to take over her face.

What can he see beyond the intense dreamy blur that becomes even more pronounced now that she's staring back? Someone who seems precisely balanced between the young girl she has just been and the woman she hasn't quite grown into—a girl-woman of seventeen, with short, curly, cocoa-colored hair that stops short of her shoulders, large deep-set eyes discernibly brown even from that distance, her skin freckled, gently suntanned across a face that is classically oval, something from a sculpture, and yet with so much vivacity it seems she's in motion even though she's not. A girl-next-door type, the All-American girl, a tomboy blossoming into womanhood—he recognizes the pattern even while he realizes there is no pattern that can possibly contain her. Her smile—and she's smiling now—is wide, almost a farm girl's, someone who's used to laughing, and it erases the touch of iciness that comes from her high cheekbones and small nose. Her throat is tanned like the rest of her, though it seems lighter, thanks to a simple necklace of scalloped white shells. Below it, beneath the thin fabric of her sundress, her breasts are small and high above a waist he knows, even from that distance, he could encircle with his hands.

Beautiful, of course, but there is something above and apart from all the other details he notices immediately, though it's a few seconds before he can find words for it. A windless day, a total calm, and yet she looks like a breeze has just crossed her face and she's about to close her eyes to the sheer sensuous pleasure of it, the sheer happy fun.

This is as much objectivity as he can manage—the rest comes to him, not through his eyes but as a deeper, surer kind of knowing; whatever that sense is, he pictures it as percussive, shaped like a hammer, striking him fast, repeatedly, and hard. He knows, with that old man's perspective of his, that this is a girl worth dying for. He knows, without any evidence, that this is a woman who is supple, strong, and intelligent—more intelligent than he could ever be himself. He feels, watching her, an exhilaration that bunches his shoulders together, a despair that buckles his knees. *Riven*—this is the word he will always use in trying to explain the moment, as if only the fast, piercing sound of those syllables can suggest the way the moment had come to him, what it had done to him, how things had changed.

How long could this encounter have lasted? No ordinary scale could begin to measure it for him, but say ten long seconds—ten seconds where the two of them stand there staring at each other without either saying a word. Behind them the car's horn begins beeping, this time louder, more insistently; the girl, hearing this, glances desperately back over her shoulder, then turns to face him again, her even, curious expression tightening into a look he reads instantly as beseeching. He starts toward her, but she turns and runs, holding the basket tight to her dress, the lightest, silkiest blossoms spilling out behind her like a yellow-purple ribbon tracing where she had been. Reaching the car, she stoops down for a moment by the side of the road, as if spotting one last flower she must have before leaving. The door opens, she vanishes inside, there's that purring sound, the car pulling to the left and coming again onto pavement, gaining speed, driving off.

It's only now that he's galvanized into action. He goes back for the bike, remembers it's broken, turns, starts walking after the car, bringing up his arm as if to pull it back by invisible strings, then—the string snapping—breaks into a run. Hopeless, he knows it's hopeless, but he has to press himself as hard as he can against the hard reality of this, drive it hot and choking down his throat until he knows it for what it is. He runs a half-mile, then keeps running though the car has long since vanished around a curve; it's not until he sees the church steeples of Springfield that he can bring himself to stop, by which time he is sweating, shaking from effort, the muscles spasming in his legs, his lungs burning less in exhaustion than from the pounding fate has just delivered. He walks slowly back toward where he had first seen her, follows the dirt left by the car's tires until he finds the sandy patch where it had parked. He remembers her stooping down for one last flower, looks down himself trying to identify which one it was that attracted her, doesn't see it, finds instead large letters drawn into the loosely packed dirt on the road's marge.

FIND ME they read. He steps back to see them from another angle, to make sure, but this time there can be no mistake. *FIND ME*. And left in the shady space between the words is her necklace with the shells.

It's not hard imagining what happens immediately afterward. A tired, beaten Alec McGowan forcing a smile, turning on enough charm that he can persuade a passing motorist to give him a lift back into town. Arriving at the bank to find Chet Standish broadcasting the sports news, waiting until he's finished, then immediately accosting him, demanding his full attention. Chet a bit alarmed at his appearance, his obvious desperation, but considerably bemused by this, and as always willing to help.

"Listen," Alec says, or something like this. "I just met a girl."

"Hey, what else is new!"

"It was on that road along the river. Flower Road."

"Great Scott! So you did it in the flowers?"

"Listen, skip that route, okay? I'm serious. You're the only person who could possibly know her."

Chet raises an eyebrow. "How's that, comrade?"

"She was in a big car, the kind you see at country clubs. Like in Northampton or Longmeadow, someplace ritzy like that."

"Longmeadow CC? I know all the girls there. What does this marvel of feminine pulchritude look like?"

"Brunette. Medium height. Freckles." He shrugs, appalled at how useless such descriptions are, then reaches into his pocket and pulls out the necklace. "Here, she left this behind. Have you seen it before on anyone?"

Chet shakes his head—he simply can't take his friend seriously, not when he's always been the one to beg Alec to find girls for him, not the other way around.

Alec, though, won't quit. "You must know her. She looks like someone who has a breeze passing across her face. Like there's a breeze and it feels good and she's about to close her eyes."

Chet sits up straight and smacks his palm against his forehead. "Oh *her*! Sure, I've known her since we were little. Lee Palmer. Why didn't you say that before?"

Eight

Who was this Lee Palmer—what had put that breeze across her face etc.? On one side strictly biographical not hard to answer. The Palmers a prominent Springfield family going back to the Revolution; evidence of their marriages/births/accomplishments/philanthropies. List some from sources here, establishing quietly ironic tone, as for instance: If Alec McGowan's life in Springfield is written in invisible ink on tissuey paper, then Lee Palmer's, at least outwardly, is etched in gold. As follows.

Her life started tragically. Her father, Matthew Palmer, was a Williams grad who forsook the family insurance business for an adventurous life as a mining engineer out west; among other exploits, he managed to be a member of the last party of whites ever ambushed by Indians, during the Ghost Dance troubles of 1890. At fifty, having made the family its second fortune, he returned to Massachusetts and built a mansion out in Longmeadow, the pastoral suburb south of the city. Somehow he met a young woman half his age—a typist named Ellen Shaw—and much to everyone's surprise, this resolute old bachelor became engaged. Judging by a surviving portrait, Ellen was an ethereal young woman with long auburn hair that made her resemble those Pre-Raphaelite beauties of an earlier era.

She had a difficult time with her pregnancy, and during the delivery her heartbeat became so fast and erratic that the doctors despaired of saving her. (This was 1921.) Her doctor, gravely shaking his head, approached Matthew out in the waiting room and put it bluntly—should they save the baby or his wife?

Matthew told them to save the baby, that this is what his wife would want—his wife who, losing the baby, would undoubtedly die of heartbreak anyway. The baby was safely delivered—a healthy, lively little girl anyone would be proud of, and yet right from the start she was saddled with the full weight of her destiny: spending her life feeling she had killed her mother, taken her father's love away from him, condemned him to a life of sadness.

Bearing this guilt, she must never hurt him again—this was her first rule in life, the one she would never break under any circumstances. In all fairness to Matthew Palmer, he did his best to be an exemplary father, *exemplary* defined by his own lights, which were no more rigid than any other member of his class and social position. Three days after her birth, he enrolled her in Mount Holyoke's class of 1943; arrangements were also made for a governess, a tutor, a good private school. He never married again. Every winter he would spend a month in Havana, where whatever high living he did apparently lasted him the rest of the year. He doted on his daughter, was smart enough not to smother her, and asked only that wherever her independence took her it wouldn't be so far from the line mapped out for her at birth that she couldn't swerve back.

And she *was* independent—people noticed that about her right from the start. "Poor Matthew!" his oldest sister, Barbara, wrote his youngest sister, Alice, late in 1927. "I'm afraid he has his hands full with little Lee. She's not stubborn, thank goodness, nor willful. But it's as if the air she breathes comes to her from somewhere other than where we get ours, giving her an energy that can't be constrained. I'm considering buying her a gymnasium set for Christmas. There is simply no other way to keep her out of our trees."

Pictures show a pretty child, with a much more approachable beauty than her mother's, thanks to the freckles. Her intelligence was as striking as her independence; she had a difficult time at Miss Porter's school, being so obviously smarter than her teachers that they resented her, even as they grudgingly gave her all A's. "Could do even better," is the kind of thin-lipped admonition that appears all across her reports, or "Some humility wouldn't hurt here." She must have had a social conscience (her father was the rich, as-long-as-it-doesn't-hurt-*me* kind of Democrat); at twelve, she had a letter published in the *Springfield American* complaining about how there were no parks along the river for poor children to play in. But what she loved best at this stage of her life was sailing; her father had a house in Castine, Maine, and she spent summers cruising on the family Herreshoff sloop, taking it out in all weathers, relishing gale winds most of all.

But other than this her adolescence seems to have been quiet enough. She is very similar to Alec McGowan in this respect, if in no other. Alec McGowan viewed his childhood as a bad one, but of no importance to his future; Lee Palmer viewed her childhood as a good one, but likewise of no importance.

There exists a scrapbook she kept the year she was thirteen. Toward the back, between pages devoted to autographs of friends ("Yours till Niagara Falls!"), is one of those lists adolescent girls are so fond of making.

Favorite color: *Yellow yellow yellow!*
Least favorite color: *Paleness.*
Favorite sport: *Ice hockey, if only they would let me play.*

Favorite author: *Willa Cather.*

Least favorite author: *Overly Ernest Hemingway.*

Favorite ambition: *To be a foreign correspondent like Dorothy Thompson.*

Least favorite ambition: *Everything everyone else lists.*

Favorite virtue: *Spunk!*

Support/enhance this with quotes from last surviving best friend distilled from as follows.

Helen Crouse (1921–). Graduated Mount Holyoke College 1944. Lists occupation as "socialite." President of Mt. Holyoke alumnae 1971–83. Interview of 1/23/99.

Lives in Quaker home for affluent women outside Philadelphia. Old and dignified sandstone building, very much like college dorm only with all the luxuries. Walks attached to a cart. Greets me in downstairs lounge by fireplace with coffee on end table. Daintily smacks lips after every sip—is coffee ordinarily forbidden? No one comes to visit much. Acts apologetic she doesn't remember more.

Lee married unhappily, she explains, once the history lesson (Depression/everyone's father going bust on the Street/horrors of war/the bomb/straitjacket of woman's role) is done with. *Married when exactly?* Well, it was right after she graduated, so that must have been 1944. I was maid of honor. *To a doctor?* Yes, Doctor Henry Coombs, who was a specialist in heart disorders and very prominent in Boston. *It wasn't happy, the marriage?* Oh I think not. *Did she tell you about it?* Only some. She was never one to talk about her feelings out loud. There's a myth that all women are comfortable with this and the ones who aren't are somehow cold. But she wasn't cold. Oh not at all.

We didn't keep in touch much except through letters, not once we graduated. She had her life, I had mine, but I know it was a loveless marriage. She felt hemmed in, constrained, like we all did, only she felt it with more force. I asked her once in a letter to tell me more, and she sent back a sheet of paper with a drawing of herself with a noose around her neck and the word *responsibilities* written up on end like a rope. Her husband expected her to take an active part in his world and she didn't want to and her father whom she adored was deceased by this stage and I think for once in her life she decided she would do exactly as she pleased and that's what made her decide what she decided. She was so beautiful you see and that always complicates things. Her father commissioned an Italian artist to do her portrait, and when he finished—this must have been 1939—he couldn't part with it and took it back to Italy with him, and then a Nazi general saw it during the war and brought it back to Germany with him, and an American colonel saw it and risked his life getting it back to her. She brought out men's chivalrous side—it was their only way to demean her intelligence. But she was always doing amateur theatricals, in college and after. Nina and Juliet and Desdemona, serious roles. She had lots of offers to go on stage professionally, but all she was permitted were amateur things to raise money for charity.

Harder to get her talking about Lee Palmer childhood, since knew of it only from stories they would tell each other in college. Knew nothing of AM relationship, apparently LP never speaking of it to her, though there was no question she was a girl who had been hurt and hurt deeply. Brings out scrapbook which Lee had given her. Goes over the list of favorites and laughs. Oh yes, she says, she had a whole wardrobe of yellow. Such a difficult color for brunettes, but her hair was so unusual. She did well in college. We were always making packages for the boys overseas, or going to officers' dances, and we probably had far too good a time of it, considering what was going on.

Attendant comes in, pours fresh coffee, checks her chart, fiddles with dial, leaves. Conversation lags, and she seems pained by this, really wants to help. Gives impression this is first time in long while she's thought of her friend, and is surprised at how powerfully remembrance strikes—so powerfully it seems to obliterate any facts that could be helpful. So she's rueful at end, despite my assurances. On way out takes my wrist and pulls me back in lobby for a moment, one thing more has occurred to her that I *must* know.

She was a girl, she says, her hand on my arm for support, whose heart was much larger than she ever allowed herself to realize. Hesitates, thinks about what she's just said, says it again for emphasis. She was a girl whose heart was larger than she ever allowed herself to realize, not until the very end.

Finish section with this quote after drumroll summation thusly. And so, on a perfect June morning in 1940, out on a Sunday drive with her father, listening for the fiftieth time to stories of his mining days out in Montana, feeling indulgent and sentimental toward him, but restless, too, Lee Palmer looks out the window toward the wildflowers, waiting until they reach the spot where they grow thickest before asking the driver to stop. At seventeen, she's about to confront the most impossible of transformations, growing from a lively and promising young girl into a polished and accomplished young woman, and the difficulty of this is very largely what her restlessness is all about. This is who she is, as best as can be determined. Someone who is independent at her strongest, capricious at her worst; talented in some undefined way that makes her scatter herself in a dozen different directions; burdened with more guilt than she deserves, though with a sunny, vivacious disposition; someone who gets furious at stupidity and unfairness; an athlete, full of that rah-rah kind of pep; brave when it comes to physical challenges, untested when it comes to moral ones; someone who is able to laugh at herself and take herself seriously in successive flashes; chased by the boys, but putting them off by lightly teasing; someone who is romantic enough to get lost in a dream and realistic enough to drop it. "A girl," as her college roommate Helen Crouse put it, "whose heart was larger than she ever allowed herself to realize," not until, in looking up from her wildflowers, starting back to the car with an overflowing basket, she hears a sound in the meadow grass and looks up to see standing there an even-featured, broad-shouldered, sandy-haired young man staring at her with an intenseness, curiosity, and restlessness she recognizes immediately as a match for her own.

Give Chet Standish credit. Pressed by his friend for information about this marvelous and mysterious girl, implored to arrange a meeting as soon as possible, he didn't laugh or put him off with evasions but came through for him big time.

Lee Palmer? Why yes, they had known each other since . . . well, since dancing lessons when they were ten, waltzes, quadrilles, that kind of thing, taught in the ballroom of the old Mohawk Hotel with that funny old fart Stanley Matthews for a teacher. After that came riding lessons in Hadley, and that would have been with Stinky Killum and Pete Boyle, and they were always chasing after her like she was the fox and they were the hounds. Her cotillion must have been—only a year ago, my god, he was *there,* but he must have been plastered, he didn't remember it at all. Boyfriend? No, he didn't think so. Dick Connors had been rushing her pretty hard, and Billy Edmonds had taken a shot at it, but she wouldn't give either the time of day. It was only the brashest ones who weren't frightened off by her beauty and brains, and she didn't like anyone brash. You'll have to watch yourself there, comrade Alec. Tone down that famous charm a notch or two. I'm not having you be slick on her just for laughs, eh wot? She's under my protection or else nothing doing.

It's easy to picture Alec McGowan staring at him in impatience and incomprehension as he droned on. He didn't care about any of that. He cared, but he didn't care *now,* he just wanted to know how he could go about meeting her. Leave that to me, Chet told him, and before the afternoon was over everything was arranged. Chet called her at home, talked casually about a dozen trivial subjects, not saying anything about Alec, and then, just before hanging up, like it was the merest afterthought, inviting her to the station on Monday for that personally conducted tour he had promised her the last time he'd seen her, which must have been at Betsy Merchant's dishy Christmas party, no?

Chet and Alec worked it out that the meeting should take place in the station's control room, which had recently been enlarged by punching a hole in the safety-deposit vault and linking it to the teller's counter. Speculate more on how AM feels here? How dressed, lines he rehearsed over and over in his head? Chet, as part of the tour, would bring her there, think of an excuse, tell her to wait for him inside, then close the door leaving the two of them alone. Invent dialogue and justify later, i.e., No one else was there of course, but it's possible to imagine and reconstruct the gist of what was said. Attribute where possible. Push hard on what's known. See what happens, how it goes.

No one besides the two of them were there, of course, but it's possible to speculate on what transpired. The studio is dark—over the windows hang curtains of monk's cloth, with a thick coarse weave designed to muffle extraneous sounds. In the corner, covered with an army blanket, is an unused organ, famous for the bass notes it would emit when one of the resident mice stepped on the pedal. On the one wall light enough to actually be seen (vouched for by Buzz Colgan, working there that summer as intern) is a large rectangular piece of construction paper, with handwritten commandments printed across it in stern black ink.

TRUTH'S ENEMIES ARE:

Gossip

Innuendo

Conjecture

Prophecy

Exhortation

Guesswork

Crusading

Slanting

Longing

Imagining

ANY ONE OF THESE CAN PUT HER TO FLIGHT!

Alec sits at the console, listening to the monitor playing Lionel Hampton on the vibes; it's lunchtime and they always like to play something bouncy at lunchtime, music that shakes the studio up, reverberates off the walls. Or maybe it's better to be standing, get a more energetic, forceful style going right from the start? He stands up, paces, presses his ear to the door.

There's the blurred sound of voices, Chet loudly coughing, the handle turning, someone coming in. Alec jumps back toward the console, deciding it's better if he's sitting down after all. He looks around absentmindedly, as if he isn't expecting anyone, pulls the earphones off, pushes his chair back, comes toward her across the room.

She doesn't bother hiding her surprise, so he doesn't bother hiding his delight—the frown instantly gives way to that engaging grin. There is something exchanged between them in that first glance that he is too caught up in the moment to analyze, but it's there working away all the time they talk, making the banality of their conversation largely irrelevant.

"I would have caught up with you," he says, just before the silence goes on too long, "if that bicycle hadn't collapsed."

She smiles—he takes the full brunt of her well-spaced freckles, the look she doesn't know is flirty and so is all the more flirtatious. Other girls he knew, so beautiful out in the open with the sun behind them, wilted when they came indoors, but if anything she seems prettier now and more focused, without the blinding halo where the sun touched her hair.

"I wish you had caught me." She hesitates the slightest beat. "I needed help carrying those flowers."

He laughs, feels relieved. "This is the control room," he says, sweeping his hand around. "Over there is the console and next to it is what they call a salt-shaker microphone because it looks like one and over there are the relays and the ugly black box is the voltage gauge and that dial goes right out to the antenna and those coin trays are left over from bank days, and nope, there isn't any money left though we keep looking. Chet told me a lot about you, silly stuff mostly. I don't know anything beside that."

All the time he talks she watches him intently, though he has the impression the examination is going on through some other means than via her eyes. She nods now, bites down on her lip like she's reached a sudden decision. "You're the voice on the radio. The midnight host. The one who reads from the history books, plays the strangest music. I listen sometimes." She frowns. "No, that's a lie. I listen all the time. I can't sleep, especially in summer when everything gets so—so impossible. I turn on the radio and lie in bed listening."

Alec modestly coughs. "How do I sound?"

"Oh, I always think of one of the Wise Men talking about this wonderful star he had seen. Gaspar or Melchior or the one I forget. Grave sometimes. Old. Other times there's more happiness there. Still a wise man, but a young one who works as a crooner on the side . . . A salt-shaker mike?" She turns it over, gives it a shake, pantomimes something falling out by waving her fingers—picks something else up, shrugs a question.

"That's my gavel," Alec explains. "I went to auctioneer school to learn how to talk faster because sometimes you have to in this racket. They gave me that when I graduated. That Bible over there was a gift from a Baptist minister. On Sundays I go around to different churches listening to sermons, trying to pick up tricks, what they do with their voices. The Baptist one tried to recruit me as a preacher—the Bible was a bribe."

"You work hard at this."

"I practice. Say I'm riding the bus in to work. I don't just sit there wasting time. I sit in the back where no one can hear me, practice describing things until it becomes natural. There's a woman in a very unusual blue dress walking down the sidewalk. It has pleats down the front, a ruffle around the bottom. Her hat is rather small for so large a woman. It's blue, trimmed with red. The dog she has on a leash is so well clipped you'd think it just came from a canine beauty parlor. Why is she sobbing like that, dabbing her eyes? . . . I also whisper ten minutes a day, which gives your voice urgency."

He continues with the tour, talking a mile a minute, yet feeling all the while that he's speechless—he's never been so conscious of the impotence of words. Still, she listens with great interest—she breaks in now and then with an intelligent question—and he has taken her around twice, three times, is starting his fourth, before they both realize how silly it is and laugh at the same time.

"I guess you've got to be going?" he asks.

"No, not yet."

He puts his foot up on the stool, reaches down for a broken microphone, an eight-ball this time, round and black, taps his finger there, pretending he's talking to it not to her. "I had a dream about you last night," he says softly.

She tilts her head. "A nightmare I bet."

"I was asleep in the dream, dreaming—does that make sense? I was sleeping inside my own dream and you were there with me, only I couldn't see your face because there was a sheet over me or a blanket and it didn't make any difference, because I saw you perfectly. Not saw you, *knew* you. It was like everything else had disappeared from the dream, even the black haze that surrounds it normally, and yet you still managed to be there at the center right beside me. When I woke up from that I felt . . . I can't tell you how I felt." He shrugs. "And I'm supposed to be pretty handy with words."

Well, there it is—risking it all on one throw of the dice. She remains by the wall looking at the memos tacked there with pins; through one long minute's worth of agony he's sure she won't respond.

"That's funny you said that," she says, turning back to him, staring down at the same mike herself. "My dreams are boring and tame usually. But I dreamt about you last night. Oh, I could see you perfectly. You were riding that ridiculous bike and I was running alongside you holding on to your back to keep you from falling."

Alec reaches down and moves the mike aside so she has no recourse but to look directly at him. "What happened then?" he asks, meeting her eyes.

"Nothing." She looks away.

"Nothing?"

"You fell!" she says, and covers her face with her hands.

They both laugh—he leans forward and takes her arm, tugs her gently back toward the console. "This is where you'll be working mostly. We see you as our morning announcer, the dawn patrol. Chet's a bear waking up, so we need someone who starts fast. How's that sound?"

She puts her hand up in a whoa-there gesture. "Hey, I'm just visiting!"

He shakes his head, leans down to shield his hand with his shoulder, pretends to write something down. "How can that be? We've already penciled your name in the log. You start tomorrow at six sharp it says here. You're working for WSM now."

She pretends to pout. "And just whose idea is that?"

"No one's. That's just the way it's meant to be."

"Isn't there usually an audition?"

"Sure, if you want. Repeat after me. She sings sibilant slumber songs as she saunters sensuously along the shaded seashore."

"Where she sells seashells?"

"You're hired. Six A.M. sharp. Wear something that doesn't cause static. Yellow would be good. Yellow is the color that sounds best over the air. And roomy, so you can breathe."

She salutes, smiles, turns to go, feels the bond come tight, stops, turns back to stare at him, frightened, begins to say something, but he beats her to it.

"You won't want to forget this."

He reaches his hand into his pocket, hesitates, hesitates a longer second, winks, then brings out her necklace of shells.

Yes, only slightly darker in rewrite, less gee-whiz in it—they're both in awe of fairy-tale beginning, scared at coming to perfection so fast. Justify invention by making it work—no other justification needed. Continue with new section starting: The next year and a half, for all three of them, was to be the happiest interval in their lives. None of them wrote memoirs, the one surviving member of the trio has no use for inquisitive biographers, and except for one elliptical letter, the hints that can be gleaned from old station logbooks, there is no written record of those fifteen months at all. And yet WSM still survives, if barely; it's possible to visit the old bank downtown, take the ancient caged elevator up to the offices on the third floor, ask politely and receive a tour of the premises conducted by whoever isn't too weary from overwork and underpay to show a visitor around. Downstairs is the old safety-deposit vault, with modernized controls, but otherwise little changed from the days Lee Palmer swept in and began making order out of chaos. The very first thing she did, once she learned the ropes, was to cover up the bare plaster walls with wallpaper, novelty wallpaper, FDR in profile with the famous cigarette holder jaunty in his lips, repeated over and over so there are hundreds of him. Though the paper has faded over the years, become covered with doodling and hastily scribbled notes, it's still there holding up the walls, making it possible to imagine the three of them laughing as they bought it, laughing as they pasted it up, three young New Dealers brimming with confidence, the Depression be damned.

There's other evidence as well. The station has a collection of photos of staff members taken throughout the years, and dozens are from the thirties, showing the trio with their arms wrapped fraternally around each other's shoulders, mugging, hamming it up. The three of them at a fire, boy and girl reporters out on the beat in glossy fireman's coats. The three of them at a Shriners picnic, the Bohemians in the enemy camp, sashes across their chests, funny hats set askew, laughing at their own impudence. The three of them right at home now, posed in the studio dressed in evening clothes, each bending back a skinny floor mike, swaying in synchronization to the beat.

Lee Palmer went on the air immediately and immediately became a hit. This was a time when having a woman's voice on radio was a rare and risky thing. It was felt that people would resent a woman trying to sell them anything, and the few women who were on radio tended to sound like teachers lecturing a class, but listeners seemed to take to her instantly, since advertising revenues shot up dramatically from the day she began. This was all part of the McGowan-Standish plan to make radio more approachable, true to life—every other station offered the same boring parade of baritone eunuchs—and by offering something different, not only did they get women to start listening in greater numbers, relating to Lee's confident, direct manner, but men as well, snared by the vaguest of tremolo somethings at the bottom of her girlish voice, a sound you couldn't help but feel would soon deepen into something huskier—a sound that, on one level, reminded them of happy innocence, on the other went straight to their groins.

Soon they had her doing everything: interviews, record spinning, remotes from jitterbug contests, jalopy racing, and agricultural fairs. By the time autumn came she was so wrapped up in the work that she put off going to college for a year; there must have been a serious scene with her father over this, but (was he secretly proud?) this once he gave in. One of her greatest worries was whether she was overly pampered and spoiled, and proving she could make her own way in the real world must have been a source of great satisfaction and pride.

That winter, inspired by her energy, the station branched out in a dozen new directions, including, at Halloween, an on-air haunted house with such realistic creaking, moaning, and screaming that, to this day, old-timers in town shudder at the memory of it; an interview program with famous dead people, Chet acting as host, Alec posing as George Washington and Lee as Martha and so on, the three of them talking about how gloomy the prospects looked for the Revolution (but maybe that dependable General Arnold could be called upon for help?); a radio beauty contest, Chet trying to describe contestants over the air by words alone, having trouble when it came to their figures, stuttering out *pulchritude, statuesque,* and *stately;* and then the enormously popular midnight show on weekends, "Our Place," Lee and Alec playing their favorite jazz records, talking to each other in between about things great and small ("Hey, Alec, you see that moon tonight?" "Sure I did, Lee, and I made a wish I'm not going to reveal"), the two voices in the darkness sounding like lovers talking cozily in bed—Lee probably not realizing this, a shrewd and savvy Alec knowing exactly where the appeal of the show lay, luxuriating in it himself.

Radio served as the great neutral ground that made his relationship with Lee possible. Without it, it's hard to see how the differences in their upbringing and backgrounds could have been surmounted. Where could they have met? What could they have talked about? Both

of them regarded each other's past as nonexistent, it simply didn't
matter to them, not at this stage, and not because they deliberately
blocked it out, but because when it came to radio—this demanding
new technology into which they poured all their exuberance, dedication, and imagination, and heard it pour back out at triple the original
strength—someone's past simply didn't matter.

Having fallen in love at first sight, they now proceeded to fall in love
for real. It's not hard to understand the pull. Both were exceptionally
attractive. There's an alert, intelligent something in Lee's expression
that can be found replicated in the quickness of Alec's—glancing at
their photos, your immediate assumption is they're brother and sister.
They were well matched in the most salient aspects of their character—their both needing to find something much larger and richer than
what they found in the ordinary circumstances of their extraordinarily
different lives. Both felt a wild impatience with anything trivial or
humdrum, and to find someone who shared this, understood this, suffered this, must have been exhilarating.

Even their differences were of a kind that only made their love
more desperate. She was good with people, though not particularly
interested in them unless they were exceptional; he was still rough at
this stage, with a deep, random curiosity about every variety of human
condition. He was one of those rare persons who is entirely capable of
living inside a dream, if he ever had the chance; she was the kind who
could go and seize a dream with every bit as much determination and
ruthlessness as he could, yet maintain at the same time an intuitive
kind of prudence, so the vertigo that comes with living a dream would
never overwhelm her, dash her back out. And more than this. Loving
her was for him the last step in his complicated self-transformation;
loving him, for her, was the first step in the same process.

So there were dangers—right from the start there were dangers.
The secrets in Alec's past (a father drunk on Sterno, a mother dead of
Moxie, a name stolen off a blanket), and the expectations that weighed
so heavily on Lee. But—trying to understand how they viewed this
themselves—what possible difference could any of this make when

what counted was what happened when they looked at each other, the magnetic way fate had located the other, the understanding established without either one of them ever willing it, what happened when they touched.

What happened when they touched? Did they become lovers, in the physical sense of the term, that first summer? Knowing his sexual history, his background of casual pickups, it's hard to imagine him holding back very long. Clearly, based on what happened later, she was capable of being an ardent lover herself. But even with this, the evidence is almost entirely circumstantial. If you study those old photos in the station's file cabinet, you get the sense that something is going on between them in the pictures taken later that first year that wasn't going on in the earlier ones; you get the feeling that when they're standing by the station's Christmas tree they're nestled tightly side-to-side, even though it's clear—study the picture closer—they're not actually touching at all. This comes across in picture after picture. There's a kind of easy relaxation in the way they exchange glances; the photographer calling on them to smile for the camera, they turn and smile knowingly, comfortably, at each other.

One piece of evidence goes beyond this, though its meaning is somewhat elusive. Among the letters Helen Crouse saved from her best friend is one written in 1944 shortly before their graduation from Mount Holyoke. Though it doesn't mention Alec at all (Helen never learned of his existence until later), the context seems to suggest it was of him she was writing. In other respects, it's a typical letter for Lee— rambling, exuberant, intense, girlish one moment, wise beyond her years the next.

"You'll hardly recognize the campus," she wrote her friend (who had taken a semester off to recuperate from a bad case of measles). "Soldiers everywhere, sailors, marines. All officers, of course—they wouldn't risk having enlisted men near their precious little darlings. No one has explained what enemy they might expect to find lurking in Mt. Holyoke, but I suppose they want to guard against parachutists . . . Went to a talk last night at chapel, yet another talk, by a refugee who just managed to escape from Poland. This one was different. A homely little Jew with a voice of iron. He had us crying, with what he described. I can't write about it, but it was true and it's horrible and we all felt very small and insignificant and hateful when we came out . . . But what I wanted to tell you. Dean Williams spoke to us first and managed to make an even *bigger* fool of herself than usual. It was a warning more than anything. About how during wartime there was much more temptation around and we had to be careful about becoming engrossed (her exact word!) in unhealthy relationships. What smugness! What *hypocrisy*!!! They tell us not to live for the moment, to save ourselves for the future, at the very same time they're doing everything in their power to cut our futures off. And they think it's so easy, too—to live for the moment—that we'll all rush right off and bed someone (forgive me, dear Helen!) just for fun. . . . I know something about moments. For most people it's always in the future, the moment they've been waiting for, and then it slips past without their recognizing it, then they spend the rest of their lives regretting not having seized it when they had the chance. Seize the moment? That's the easy part. Recognizing the moment when it comes, that's so much harder. Your only recourse is to seize *every* moment, not miss any— and yet that's so impossible, too. I had a friend once who could do that but he was the only person in the world that could. I was always failing him because I couldn't live that intensely, not constantly, not at the pitch he demanded. I think that's why sex is so terribly important (forgive me, Helen mia!) and so terribly beautiful. It's the only way you have to make the moments stop . . . I became dizzy and confused and needed certainty, needed respite from that terribly sweet rushing feel, and it's the only way that's possible, isn't it? Most of the time life doesn't ask enough of us, but sometimes it asks too much, and then you have to make a decision about how brave you are or hide from the truth you aren't. But what a cold lonely virtue truth is! To be able to stare it in the face. Truth isn't for lovers, it's for one person alone . . . Well, that was all so very long ago now. I had nerve then, daring— those puny substitutes for courage. My father should have named me

Prudence Play-It-Safe Palmer. I expect I'll be one of those women who sigh a lot as they go through life. But all that seems petty and insignificant now, compared to what is going on in this world. . . . Have you heard the news? Henry and I are all but engaged. He's in the navy, intelligence, and so he won't have to go on a ship. They have him stationed in Boston, and he's going to try and sneak in some pre-med classes while he's there. What are you supposed to feel? A good man, I think. I suppose we're very much in love etc. We're thinking of Castine for the wedding once the war ends. Of course I want you to be maid of honor, will you *please*??? Hope you're feeling better now, with no permanent scars. Roger (picture me salutin'), wilco and out, your loving friend Lee."

It was never a smooth relationship, even at the best of times. Conflicts, misunderstandings, jealousies—bitter recriminations followed by desperate, passionate reconciliations. In all these one person served as their peacemaker, their go-between, duenna, confessor, faithful confidant, and ever-loyal pal: Chet Standish.

He had brought them together, introduced them, seen to it they had the radio station to do with as they pleased, and almost all the time the two of them were together Chet was there, too, to the point where there isn't one surviving photograph where he isn't just off to their side, looking absurdly happy, avuncular and content. It's easy to picture Lee and Alec becoming lovers that first summer; what's harder is imagining how they got rid of Chet long enough to be alone.

Their relationship needed someone like him. It was so unlikely in so many respects that without someone to act as their facilitator their love would have imploded long before it did. Chet leapt eagerly into this role. He spent hours alone with each one of them listening patiently to their side of things, doing his best to explain Alec to Lee ("You have to understand he's a genius who hasn't found what he's a genius at yet, so he's bound to be difficult"), or explaining Lee to Alec ("The rich are very different from you and me—well, *you*, anyway, comrade pal").

He tried to be evenhanded in this, but he must have sensed the duplicity that underlay Alec's talent, the part of him that was invented so recently it hadn't yet become real enough to depend on, and he worried about this, saw it as threatening. Alec's sexual prowess was a danger, too—he knew how often and how carelessly Alec had scored. Then, too, some of it could have been plain old-fashioned snobbiness. Alec was fine on radio, acted like someone who was to the manner born, and yet—well, there was that poor white Canuck past, and you never knew when that was going to lash out and hurt Lee in some undefined and yet horrible way.

Chet was quite capable of following Alec around the station—studio, office, record library, john—hammering him with warnings, injunctions, cautions, advice. More hours for Lee on top of what she's already doing? That's pushing her, Alec, pushing her too hard. Of course it's fine for you, you're a glutton for punishment, but for Christ's sake she's only a kid. I see the way you're beating her over the head with all that talk about excellence. Excellence? You're a fascist of excellence, Alec, I hope you realize that about yourself. You want people to fail, you're so near failure yourself it gives you a perverse delight if someone else fails first—they're *it*, so you're safe for another day. I won't have it, understand? Hey, you're my best buddy, and hey, I hate playing dictator, but it sticks in my craw the way you slave her around. Which reminds me. Saint Valentine's Day is next week and did you get her anything yet? Hell, I'll loan you the money, but get her something decent, okay, not just fudge. And slacken off on the intensity while you're at it. That Hamlet act wears thin. She's precious and vulnerable and far too good for either one of us and I won't have her hurt.

Chet felt chivalrous toward her, felt he had earned that by the force of his renunciation. After all, he could very well have fallen in love with her himself and he would have been able to offer her someone much closer to what her upbringing had prepared her for. And yet he hadn't done this—he had magnanimously stepped aside to let Alec have room. Didn't this count for something? He made them understand this, not in so many words, but by his grave, never-failing patience, deepened by the hurt he was big enough not to mention, but not big enough not to feel. For when all was said and done, he was by far the most romantic of the trio, the one most capable of surrendering to a great idea. What he seemed to be in love with was *their* love, the fairy-tale rightness of it, the summertime perfection.

They were inseparable—for fifteen months they were almost constantly together. Occasionally Margaret Pebble would be invited along to make a fourth, but she didn't have the imagination to sense what was going on or how to accommodate herself to it, and so most of the time it was just the three of them, laughing over old jokes, improvising new ones, Chet always happy to make a fool of himself, Lee and Alec respecting him for that, being careful never to laugh at him too meanly or too long. There were long drives in Chet's roadster, Lee behind the wheel as Chet's eyes were already starting to go bad, Flower Road their favorite destination, even in winter. Going for swims out at the quarry north of town—Lee lithe and athletic in a brown two-piece suit, doing Olympic-caliber dives from the highest ledges to Chet's coaching, while Alec, a nonswimmer, sat applauding on a rock. The station "adopting" an orphan from the Catholic charities (a boy named Tommy Strong who is still alive, a retired Ford salesman in San Diego), the three of them spoiling him shamelessly, buying presents for him, letting him have the run of the station. A famous night when they went to Worcester to hear Father Coughlin speak, the fascist priest who had an enormous following, Chet getting so mad his face turned red, heckling, getting in a fight, being arrested, going off to jail. Talking shop in the old Workingman's Cafeteria in the South End, the darkest, coldest, dingiest eating place in the city, parking themselves at their favorite table in back where over endless cups of coffee (Lee, teasing them, flavoring hers with scotch from a flask) they talked radio, brainstorming, planning new shows, talking about how if revenues kept climbing they would soon be able to start buying up other stations and form their own network to rival the giants.

There are few hints of trouble in all this, not real trouble, not until late in the spring. The actress Bette Davis came to Springfield as part

of a promotional tour. Lee, assigned to interview her, started by asking how she felt having managed by sheer will power to transform herself from homely-looking to beautiful. Davis exploded at this, as Alec
later did, too, lecturing Lee on the proper decorum.

"I wanted to make her *real*," Lee insisted, defending herself.

"These people aren't real," Alec yelled back at her. "They're made
out of tissue and they rip at the slightest touch."

The station log shows Lee Palmer gradually less of a presence;
often beside her name is the single word *missing* written in Alec's handwriting—*missing,* as if he were reminding himself of that first message
she had scratched to him in the roadside dirt. The station still has a
calfskin guestbook that distinguished visitors were asked to sign. One
of these in July 1941 was her father, Matthew Palmer, on what must
have been a difficult visit. Why was he there in the first place? As a
potential investor? As a friend of Chet's father, the old man showing
off what his son had accomplished? Did Alec meet him, shake hands?
It's not hard to imagine how galling this must have been for him—to
meet Lee's father and have to hide everything. And for Lee. How difficult to have the two men she loved most in the world be standing there
next to each other, her father taking no more notice of her lover than
if he were the janitor, a menial nonentity not even worth the effort to
charm.

There were probably more quarrels that second summer, more
desperate reconciliations . . . speculate on details? More in-depth
analysis/shrewd insights/philosophical asides? . . . Time pressed hard.
Her father had allowed her a year to do what she wanted, but now it
was her turn to honor the bargain and go off to college . . . Any examples of erratic behavior under stress to insert here, either one of
them? . . . There seems to have been a separate dynamic at work as
well, adding its own pressure. Their relationship had lasted a year, it
had been dizzying, maddening, wonderful, and yet it had reached the
plateau that inevitably comes, when without some firmer commit-
ment, the sharing of greater responsibility, love's energy can grow stale
bewilderingly fast—and aphorisms like that?

Late that summer, as the time drew near for her to go off to college, Alec desperate at the thought of losing her (and realistic enough to know that no passion could span those separate worlds), Lee herself driven almost insane by the rival tugs on her heart, the two of them apparently decided to elope. The evidence is sketchy—what other course was open to them, given the circumstances? Once, years later, in talking with his drinking pal Barbara Jay, the subject of elopement somehow came up, and Alec became hysterical—he started sobbing, clutching his hands to his head; it was, in Barbara's words, as if she had pressed a button on him marked *Pain*. Then, too, there is the more certain evidence of his having quit the radio station in September without telling anyone, leaving town in the dead of night to enlist in the army, all this happening suddenly, without any apparent premeditation. Something extreme must have precipitated this and it's difficult to imagine what else it could have been.

Their plan could well have been as follows—make up friends, make up letters, make up documentation if that's what it takes? . . . They were going to meet at the bus station downtown. . . . Biographers, ordinary ones, scratch their heads and give up here. . . . There was a bus at six A.M. for New York—why bring them to life only to abandon them because what was most important in their lives precisely the things history can't record? . . . Bring nothing, he told her, not even a suitcase—we'll travel on sheer nerve . . . sheer nerve/gumption/balls? The truth is there, why not seize it? (*TRUTH'S ENEMIES ARE: Literalness/Fact/Detail/Documentation*) . . . He had $250 cash in his suit pocket, enough for three months' rent, a grubstake to get them started. Add richer layer of details, dropping last vestiges of formality. I've already taken big steps—genie out of bottle, no going back. He arrived there while it was just barely light, the station so quiet and deserted he could hear not only the chirping of birds but the busy scratch of their claws on the tin roof overhead. Truth always forcing you to make up facts to support it, story demanding similar. AM/LP ungraspable by any other means. The platform reeked of urine and cheap dago wine, but he could detect a honeysuckle kind of sweetness wafting in from a nearby park. Worked before, been working all along now, have crossed line no going back etc., understanding demands it playing out on its own.

Invent this whole.

According to people who know the story, their plan was as follows. They were going to meet at the bus station downtown in time to get the six A.M. bus for New York City. It was important to leave early—Alec wanted to ride that morning surge of energy, capture the tide at its fullest, let it bear them away to their new life. She made lists of what she should bring, but he made her tear them up—bring nothing. No, they had their youth, their confidence, their talent, and nothing else was needed—they would start from scratch in the city once they found jobs. A justice of the peace could marry them, he had enough money to find an apartment, they would make the rounds of the radio stations, and everything after that would fall naturally into place.

But it's 5:45 now on the big station clock and still there's no sign of her. As always, he hides his agitation by devoting even more energy to appearing calm; anyone happening by him at this moment would have seen a handsome, sleepy-looking young man dressed better than anyone else in the station, whistling softly to himself like he hadn't a care in the world. Across from him, what few passengers are waiting begin to board the olive-green bus, which rocks slowly from side to side. One of the families—tubercular father, dark-skinned mother, two gaunt and silent kids—carries what seem to be all their worldly possessions in three great pillowcases; they make him think of Okies who had somehow gotten it backwards, gone east rather than west. He watches them board, reminds himself to ask Lee what she makes of them, strolls casually over to the driver, asks him the time.

"Six o'clock," the driver grunts. "Going with us?" Alec looks over his shoulder toward the glass door that leads into the waiting room. "No, I'll catch the next one," he says calmly. "Suit yourself," the driver says. He spits on the pavement, slaps the door, disappears inside, the bus backing out of its slot with a great screeching of gears that sounds like the mechanical equivalent of what's going on inside Alec's gut.

He waits until 6:10, then checks his one piece of luggage and heads out to the street. "Where to?" the cab driver asks when Alec leans down to the window. He's finishing an egg sandwich—a young Negro who looks capable of something desperate.

Alec tells him the address, the one he's memorized but never said out loud before. They pull out from the station and head through the deserted streets. It's going to be a hot day. Steam rises off the pavement and mixes with fog rolling in from the river, but the sun is up there now, a yellow finger prying away at the haze. The driver knows a shortcut through downtown, and a few miles later they emerge in a residential zone of lawns and fences and dignified-looking homes. This is Longmeadow—this is the town where Lee lives. The driver slows down to read the street signs. Sure, he comes out here lots, he explains, rich college kids coming home on vacation—and after a few more turns they come to the right one, Sheep Meadow Drive.

He pays the driver, then walks steeply uphill looking for number five. The houses are even bigger here, spaced farther apart. There's a child's red scooter lying on one of the lawns, but it's the only sign of actual life. Her house turns out to be just barely visible from the street—a three-story Tudor mansion with heavy beams crisscrossing stucco walls the color of cream.

Imposing and castle-like as it is, he's relieved to actually see it after wondering about it for so long. He smooths his jacket down, wipes back his hair, walks up the driveway as slowly, as casually, as if he lived there himself and was coming back in from fetching the paper.

The driveway curves and splits around a formal garden. He's alert, ready for anything, but what happens next takes him completely by surprise. There's a squirting noise behind him, a sudden wet feel on the back of his neck, and he jumps around to see it raining upside down.

It's a few seconds before the shock wears off. Sprinklers are shooting water into the air across the lawn, something he has never seen before, sprinklers everywhere, so he has to skip backwards to avoid getting soaked. For an absurd moment he remembers his father—how angry he would have been to learn rich people employed machines to

water their lawns—and then something happens that changes everything very fast. He's walking toward the house, trying to figure out
what he's going to say, when he hears a wet purring sound on the other
side of the driveway, where it hooks back to the left. He cuts across the
garden just in time to see a long brown touring car with shades pulled
down driving fast toward the street.

"Hey!" he shouts, in total impotence.

No one hears him, or if they do it only makes them drive faster. He
starts running, his shoes slipping on the tread marks left across the
wetness by the tires. There's a hedge that obscures things, and when
he reaches the street he has to look in both directions before he sees
the car pulling away toward the left. He wishes he had made the taxi
wait—a big mistake—and in his desperation, he remembers the kid's
scooter lying abandoned on the lawn three houses down. It's still
there. He picks it up, kicks dirt off the tires, runs furiously on the sidewalk with it until the hill tilts over enough that he can put both feet up
on the scooter and coast. Okay, this was rotten of him, a terrible thing
to do, breaking a little rich kid's heart, and yet he *must* do something
like this and do it immediately, shove away the desperation pressing
down on him with a desperate act of his own.

By the time he reaches the bottom of the hill his speed is so great he
falls off the scooter and goes rolling across the pavement, tearing his
jacket, bloodying up his face. Instantly, he's up and running again,
managing to keep the car in view just long enough to see it turn left
again toward the city.

He runs three blocks, the sweat pouring off him, sees a bike on the
grass near some kids playing in a park, experiences the same flash of
guilt he experienced the first time, picks the bike up, ignores the kids'
yelling (they pick up rocks, hurl them, start to cry), and pedals, twisted
like a pretzel on the too-small frame, toward downtown. He has no
doubts whatsoever that Lee is in the car behind the drawn shades, and
all he wonders about, wonders in a way that makes his heart pump ten
times faster, is whether she's being borne away involuntarily or going
on her own.

There's traffic now, people driving in to work—he has to dodge his way between cars, does this so heedlessly, with such quick and unexpected swerves, that horns start beeping at him from all directions. Collisions become inevitable—dead ahead of him an old woman throws her hands across her face in horror—but always at the last second he manages to swerve around the pedestrian or delivery truck or hydrant or dog. A cop sees him, blows his whistle, lunges forward to grab him, but this only makes him pedal faster. The morning air is hot and salty on his face, like a bitter cream an invisible hand is smearing on just to slow him down, but then he recalls scratching his face when he fell off the scooter, tastes the blood on his lips, swipes at it, keeps on.

He remembers chasing her the first time on that long-ago June afternoon, remembers the desperate sweetness, that agony kid stuff compared to what he feels now. He tries holding the word *love* between his lips, as if the tactile feel of it can summon her back, finds this difficult, but holds the word there in his mouth until it loses all meaning and there is nothing but a black bitter taste where it mixes with the blood, sweat, and spit. He remembers the sounds she would make when he held her, urgent and yet so soft they could barely find their way to his ear as he lay against her breast, a sound for him alone—how it was his responsibility to nurture that sound, keep it burning like a flame—and the remembrance of this nearly drives him mad.

He bumps across a railroad crossing, almost falls, straightens, speeds on. To his left is the bus station, but there is no chance whatsoever the car will head there; to the right is the train station, and this is the way he turns, the bike tires scratching against the hot pavement, the front tire sagging, then blowing out. He jumps clear of the bike before it's even stopped rolling and runs across the street to the station, just in time to see the brown touring car pull out from the unloading zone, its shades pulled up now, but no one visible inside except the ancient, putty-faced chauffeur.

He's guessed right, brilliantly right, but there's no comfort in that. He runs into the station, which is high-ceilinged and cool, dominated by a sharp metallic smell that makes it seem built of nickels, quarters, and dimes. It's empty, ominously empty. When he rushes up to the ticket counter he hardly knows where to begin.

"Which train just left?" he demands, startling the ticket girl with his vehemence.

She composes herself, lapses into gum-chewing indifference.

"Lots of trains leave here, mister. You'll have noticed this is a train station?"

He looks up at the departure board, tries through the sweat to read the white letters, turns back.

"In the last half-hour."

"One to Albany, one to Providence, an express to Portland."

"Portland, Maine?"

"You think maybe it would be Portland, Oregon?"

"When's the next one?"

"To Portland?" She looks down at her timetable. "Tomorrow. You want a ticket or are you just window shopping? Next!"

He could slap her—she has no idea what kind of desperation she's dealing with, what he's capable of in the fury of the moment. But he's judging everything by the need for speed now, and slapping her, whatever the satisfaction, would slow him down.

He hurries over to the waiting room, hoping by some miracle the train has been delayed, but the steel doors down to the tracks are already barricaded shut. There's no doubt whatsoever that the Portland train is the one she's taken. She spoke of Maine often, told him how she'd like to bring him there, walk with him on the rocks or go out in her sailboat to visit the islands, and her face would get all dreamy with that, though to him she might have been talking about Mars.

He walks out to the street, passes a phone booth, has a sudden inspiration. Chet! Of course! They hadn't told him anything about their plans, not wanting to burden him with worry, not wanting—if they were honest with themselves—for Chet's protective side to make things complicated. But he's just the man now that it's an emergency. Chet with his money, his contacts, his willingness, could fix things in a flash.

He calls him at the radio station, rehearsing his explanation as he listens to it ring, but after twelve rings no one has yet answered. He calls him at home, but no one answers there, either. He waits five minutes, pacing up and down the sidewalk, then tries again at both places without any luck. Where could he be off to? A minute before his eyes had all but watered with gratitude at the thought of Chet helping, but now his emotions slam back the other way and he feels furious that he isn't there when he needs him most. The bastard! The rich stupid blind fool!

But now his luck changes. A black Studebaker, the kind of car a hoodlum would drive, pulls over to the curb and two people get out— a fleshy man and a fleshy woman laughing hysterically as they hurry arm-in-arm into the station. One must be seeing the other off, because not only do they leave the car running, but the driver's door remains open, inviting him in. He slips behind the wheel, kicks at the brake until it releases, hesitates just long enough to notice what's lying beside him on the seat—a pornographic comic book, a flask made of silver, a child's baseball mitt—and then he puts the car in gear, lurching and jerking out into traffic as behind him, from the fog of a distant world, comes the sound of a woman's furious scream.

There's a more immediate problem. He can hardly drive—when would he ever have gotten the chance? Chet's roadster, sure, but even there Lee would do most of the driving while he lounged in the passenger's seat telling them stories. He manhandles the steering, pushes the clutch in too hard and too often, and the car stalls three times before he's even reached Main Street. But once past the worst of the traffic he begins to get the hang of it and he drives out of town toward Route 2, the only highway he knows that runs eastward toward the coast.

The towns are smaller there, lifeless—they seem designed, in their August indolence, to soothe the hurry out of him, drift him to sleep. To fight this he drives faster—every field, every patch of wildflowers, makes him more reckless, until it's all he can do to keep the car on the road. He's been far too rushed to stop and consider things, but now questions jump out at him like concrete roadblocks shoved out from the trees. He can no longer sustain the illusion she is being taken away against her will—there is no conception of her he's capable of that includes her doing anything she doesn't want to do. She's fleeing him, then, fleeing him deliberately, and that leads around to why. Is it on account of her father, her devotion to him being so great she can do nothing to hurt him? Okay, he can accept this, deal with it, wait longer, but why hadn't she told him that right at the start? He remembers their talking it over, the tears, holding on to each other so tightly uncertainty couldn't find a way past, and how frightened and unsure she had been, shivering with it, until something vital had suddenly kicked in beneath his warmth, a quality at the core of her, the courage he loved—her saying yes, entering into the plans with double his own excitement. Yes, New York. Yes, an apartment there. Yes, the jobs in radio, the making of a new life. Yes, together. Together. *Together.*

An hour goes by, two hours, three. The traffic gets thicker as he nears the coast, families off for an early weekend, trucks hauling milk cans, men driving as fast and recklessly as he does, consumed by— what? He sees girls hitchiking by the side of the road, peroxide blondes in shorts, recognizes them as his own type—tells himself he should pick them up, have fun with them, go back to the kind of escapade he was good at—and this becomes part of what he speeds away from, the past sucking him back so fast there's nothing he can make the car do that can escape it. Still he tries. He stays in high gear even in the built-up sections, ignores every stop sign, sideswipes a farm truck, becomes blinded by hay—outraces a police car, enters Maine, follows road signs toward the coast.

It seems harder now—it seems as if Maine isn't just a name but a real and solid force on the windshield, pressing him back. The sun is strong enough he has to squint to see, misses a cluster of road signs, backs up to read them. Portland, they say. Portland Downtown, Portland Center, Portland Ferry, Portland Station. He crosses a bridge over anchored fishing boats, passes a section of tenements, counts the blocks off, turns.

The station is smaller than Springfield's, outdoors, with two tracks flanked by shedlike waiting rooms and long macadam ramps. He parks by a sign that reads TAXIS ONLY, dodges around some abandoned luggage carts, stops the first person he sees—a newspaper vendor packing away his unsold morning papers.

"Has the Springfield express come in yet?" he demands.

The vendor looks at him and laughs. "Express? Hell, mister, ain't no one ever called *that* train an express. Lucky if it gets here by midnight, tracks being so bad."

Alec rushes up the steps to the platform, leans over to peer. Only a few people are waiting. A man pushing a girl in a wicker wheelchair. A woman tapping her shoe in impatience. Two college men wearing Harvard jackets, even though it's sweltering now, close to ninety. These last two snigger as he approaches, and it's only then he remembers how shabby he looks, with his torn pants, blood-clotted forehead, sweat-soaked shirt. Still, there's enough bitterness in his mood that he would willingly get into a fight, smash their insolence all to hell, and it's only the sudden whistle of a train that prevents him from ramming into them with his shoulder.

A bell rings as the crossing gate swings down stopping traffic. The locomotive coasts along the platform; it's dirty-looking, besmeared with insects and dead birds, all but limping—the gray passenger cars bump into each other as they clatter to a stop. Conductors reach their arms out to unfasten the doors, leaning down with their little stools to make bridges to the platform. Passengers disembark. They look prosperous, happy to be on vacation, already tanned; some are dressed in yachting clothes, and one man carries a leather portfolio on the end of a polo mallet like he's mimicking a hobo.

Lee Palmer is the last one off. There's a slight, graceful ducking motion by the door—the conductor makes a little bowing sweep with his hand—and then she is alone on the platform five cars up from where he stands watching, a distance of no more than sixty yards. She's wearing brown slacks that emphasize her small waist and long legs—above them is the yellow blouse with embroidered neckline he bought for her in the spring. There is no wind, but she stands there sweeping her hand back over her hair as though there is.

He's too far away to read her expression, but there is something in her posture he recognizes immediately, and it sets her apart from everyone else who's gotten out. She is not happy, not glad to be there, not lighthearted and carefree. Something else is working on her, something that makes him feel perversely lighthearted himself. She turns, sees him, stifles a gesture her arm seems to want to make on its own. He is ready to run to her—has already ducked around a fat man toting golf clubs—when he sees the two college men come up on either side of her, take two small suitcases from her hands, press in on her like a pair of crimson shoulders added to her slim form. They laugh, laugh loudly, laugh in possession, then, as she hesitates on the lip of the stairs, looking behind her with a kind of desperation, all but force her down the steps to their waiting roadster.

He knows what he should do—move quickly and he can be up to her in three fast strides. But he stands there, motionless, as if there are nails in his shoes driven into the platform, allowing him only to teeter forward in a pathetic imitation of a run. He tries to call out to her, throw his voice around her like a lariat—there is nothing his voice can't do, hasn't he proven that a thousand times?—and yet nothing comes out, there's a rag in his mouth stuffing the words down so he stands there choking. Always before his greatest gift was staring truth in the face, confronting it, sizing it up for better or for worse, but now, here, truth is staring him straight in *his* face, sizing *him* up, and he has no stomach for it at all. The truth is this: she hadn't been forced down the ramp, hadn't looked back at him with the beseeching look he tried so hard to find. She had looked back at him in alarm, had turned away frightened, had hurried away from him down the steps of her own free will—and this is what nails him to the platform, unmans him, robs him of his voice.

It hardly matters. Being stuck there, being powerless. It hardly matters. He's sure there must be a difference between something imagined and something real, but he's so tired now, so silly with fatigue and disappointment, he can't find the strength to make the distinction. As lassitude overcomes his body, his mind races ahead, compelled by something much surer than will power alone—a dream layer which in him isn't flighty and insubstantial, but the deepest, hardest layer, the fastest part of him, and so why not go chase her with that?

Dream chase or real chase, it doesn't matter. It's a yellow car they get into, yellow verging on gold, and he keeps them in sight for the first few miles, but then his car begins sputtering, steam shoots out horizontally from the radiator like the snorts of a cartoon bull, and it's only by pressing the gas pedal all the way in that he manages to keep pace. They race over bridges, cut around the inside edges of bays—at one point the roadster detours through a cornfield just to shake him and he has to do the same thing, the bumps making the hood fly open, so for several seconds he drives blind. He hits someone, a biker, a hitchiker, a farmer—bodies fly past the bumper in waves. At one point the college men set a trap for him, birch logs spread across the road, and he revs the car up so it goes flying over in a somersaulting leap— but they're outdistancing him now, and out the window one of them shoots a tommy gun at his tires, the golden bullets chomping bites out of the concrete, forcing him to swerve.

The road swings out along the coast and for the first time ever he sees the ocean, shining in the afternoon sunshine, appropriated by encircling headlands, a fancy blue and white carpet owned by bigshots, nothing that could ever be his. There are mansions everywhere, cedar-shingled, weathered, dominated by huge porches, their gables topped by enormous American flags. He gets lost here, the sun is too blinding against the windshield, and it's only because the roadster leaves a golden exhaust behind it that he picks it up again, follows the sparkling ribbon to where the road ends in a dilapidated wooden pier.

He sees the taller, handsomer of the Harvard men stoop down to pull in a dinghy. Lee balances out along the pier and sits herself in the middle seat, puts the oars in their locks, pushes her sleeves up, starts rowing. By running out the pier and jumping he can catch them, but he's forgotten something, something vital, and a second before he can remember what that something is the second Harvard man jumps out from behind a pile of lobster traps and socks him in the jaw. Alec is staggered, but recovers quickly—he jabs him in the stomach, manages a hard right cross to his forehead, finishes him off with three swift kicks in the groin. But that's not enough, because from behind the rocks a whole gauntlet of college boys emerge dressed in tennis flannels, each one wielding a wad of money that they beat him with as he races beneath—thick folds of paper money, hard sandbags of coins—and he has to hold his hands over his neck and dodge their kicks in order to avoid going down.

He races clear, but he's lost valuable time now, the dinghy is pulling fast out into the harbor and he has to run along the beach until he finds a dinghy he can use himself. He's never rowed before, but he's a fast learner and he jerks it through the garbage-flecked waves at a speed double the other boat's. But no matter—they're already up to a long, sharp-bowed sailboat, scrambling over its rail, hoisting sails. It's a golden boat with golden sails—the mainsail, as it catches the wind and billows, looks as if it's made out of yellow dust. He blinks the sweat away, tries making out the name raised in elaborate brass letters across the stern: LEE'S LOVE. He sees her leaning backward over the edge to balance the boat's tipping, sees her silhouette, the tracing she leaves in the air, which is unlike the tracing anyone else could leave, the delicacy, the firm way it indents, straightens, curls, convincing him as it had a thousand times that this is the only line he could ever love in the world, down to its slightest scallopping detail—a line she hadn't inherited but had willed for herself, imagined, spun, and deliberately set against the waxed amber backdrop of the sky.

He's almost up to them—he is reaching out to grab a line that trails from the side—when they surprise him one last time, turn on a hidden motor and surge suddenly ahead. The wake catches the bottom of the dinghy just as he's reaching and spills him out into the ocean. His lungs fill with water, forcing him down. He kicks wildly to the surface, tears at his clothes, trying to escape their weight, calls out to her with all the force left in him, but this only allows the saltwater to suck its way in. His lips feel it, then his chest, then his heart, then his groin.

"Lee!" he calls, coming back up again to the surface. "Lee!" he cries, bobbing up a second time. "Lee!" but this is the third time, that's all anyone's allowed. He knows what's tormenting him, realizes his peril, understands perfectly the truth of his predicament, but he's caught in a backspinning whirlpool of garbage—broken lobster shells, discarded condoms, dirty money, and crap—and the weight of it sucks him down.

He stands there on the station platform, unable to move. "Excuse me?" someone is saying. He looks around. It's an attractive woman in her forties, looking up at him with a flirty pout. "Do you know what time the train leaves for Bar Harbor?"

"No, ma'am," he says, very politely. "No, I'm sorry but I don't."

He gets in the car. He retraces his exact route from Portland back to Springfield, stopping only once to siphon gas from a parked Chevrolet. He drives to the bus station, retrieves his suitcase, drives the six blocks to the train station, where he'd first stolen the car. He buys a ticket on the next westbound train, then drives the car around the corner to a deserted street of warehouses and pawnshops. There's an alley piled with garbage—he parks so the car is on the sidewalk nudging the biggest of the trash-filled bins. He leaves the car running, pulls some newspapers out from the trash pile, makes a little teepee on the backseat, lights it with matches from the glove compartment, waits until the upholstery starts burning in candy-colored flames, stands back to watch.

He has fifteen minutes to make the train. In ten minutes the engine catches fire with a sudden whoomph, then a louder explosion comes as the gas tank ignites. The fire spreads to the garbage bins and sets their metal to sizzling, but it doesn't seem hot enough to spread any further. He stands there watching anyway, concentrating on the brightest flame, the hottest flame, the most ardent, the one that leaps and dances with most energy and determination—and though it licks at the brick of the nearest building, jabs, sucks, kicks, recoils, and kicks again, there is only one soul to feed it and against the cold asbestos weight of a city it can make no impression at all.

Part Four

THE GOLDEN AGE

Nine

Connections, linkages, sutures, threads. They came easily now, not strands that had to be forced together, but parts that merged seamlessly, joining past and present on their own. Youth wants to burn? Well, my kids burned plenty, the house hardly required any extra heating even in winter—burned, though what young people burned for now wasn't love, but fame, riches, celebrity. A gauntlet of money? I was running through one myself—not wads that pummeled me, but dollars that stroked, tempted, and teased. The miracle of radio? It was on now in the kitchen, our antique RCA sitting venerably on the countertop in company with its over-vitamined descendants, the television, the fax, the computer, machines so arranged that I sat in the immersion zone at their center, the sardonic campfire ring of our time . . . me the relic, the one who must ignore all these and concentrate on his morning paper fetched from outdoors in its blue plastic sleeve, sit down, and spread it ceremoniously across the breakfast table, weigh its corner down with my coffee mug, begin perusing the news of the day: an article explaining how by the end of this new century, thanks to the latest discoveries in biochemistry, *life* as a term would be meaningless, there would be so many versions of it, half-states, quarter-portions, and hyphenated in-betweens that by the year 2100, *man* and *woman* and even *person* would be nonsense words you couldn't use without extensive qualification.

Morning at our house, two days before Christmas, the wayward biographer, the deep-sea diver, rising early after a hard night's imaginings to see if he couldn't catch a glimpse of his family before they scattered their separate ways.

And a glimpse is what I got, at least of Brenda. She had apparently been the one to turn the TV on, draping it with a wet dishtowel so it was muffled by a scrim. Of Brenda herself all I saw was the red of her varsity jacket as she disappeared down the icy driveway, her ponytail bobbing awkwardly above her collar as though it limped.

Of Kim I got five minutes' worth. There had been a bomb scare at her school the day before, the third in three weeks. She was edgy on account of this, distracted—my attempts at conversation, once she sat down with her own coffee, were met with shrugs, and after three absentminded sips she was back on her feet again, scanning e-mail, punching out messages for the kids, pulling together her things.

"Any suspects?" I asked.

"Someone good with voices. That's what they used when they called it in—a Bugs Bunny voice."

I went over and held the door open for her, we kissed, she strode off into the brown viscosity that passed for morning, and then I was alone again in the kitchen, priming myself for whoever woke up next.

Elise—and that gave the morning a jolt all right, blasting the darkness apart with a laser beam of energy. She ran in with a Superman kind of flourish, a towel around her shoulders like a cape, went over to the TV set and twirled it around like a matador daring the television to charge, checked the computer screen, frowned, hurried over to examine her backpack to see what Kim had left for a snack, smiled, saw me, blew a kiss in my direction, went over to the refrigerator, pulled the door open, stood there studying the contents motionlessly, with great intensity.

"How's about a hug?" I said.

I got one—as always, I teased her about having to beg. She had on her Alaska T-shirt with her favorite musher on one side, his lead dog on the other, white silhouettes against the jet-black fabric. It and a Santa hat with a floppy pompom that drooped over her eye.

"Class party today?"

"Uh-hum," she mumbled. She put her hands together in a praying gesture. "Waffles?"

I glanced at the clock. "Frozen okay? You need to drink some juice with it."

"Can I have eight?"

"Two."

"Six?"

"Three."

"Five?"

"Four."

I shoved over to make room for her, sat there trying not to watch her eat but watching her anyway, feeling the complicated mix of emotions I always felt when she was chowing down that way—pleased she was happy, whatever the cause; frightened of what the waffles were doing to her, thickening the burden she already carried. And yet, as always, I couldn't bring myself to say anything. Don't put an emotional overlay on the food issue, all the therapists said, especially with pre-adolescent girls; don't put an emotional overlay on *anything*—and here I was too cowed to challenge them, though I felt like shooting my arm out, knocking those wretched waffles to the floor.

Elise reached for the syrup. "Can I go to Grandpop's this afternoon?"

"You were there yesterday afternoon."

"Yeah, but I need to go again."

"I'm taking him to the doctor's this morning for a checkup. Can we wait and see?"

I didn't tell her what really worried me, that at one of these check-ups—and soon now—the doctor would order him into the hospital and that would be that.

"You need a ride to school?" I asked, trying to change the subject.

"Ride?" She saw through that at once. "I'm not afraid of them any-more."

"Well, no, I know you're not afraid of them. You've handled this like a real trouper right from the start. It looks like snow, though, and I thought maybe since I'm going that way anyway—"

"Trouper?" The word made her giggle, so I wasn't prepared for what she said next. "Grandpop calls me fatso."

"What?"

"Grandpop calls me fatso. He says if that's how I want to go through life, I may as well get used to it. He says he'll leave me five thousand dollars of his life insurance money if I lose ten pounds by New Year's."

"That's in a week."

"The genuine New Year's is March seventeenth. You didn't know that? It's the genuine start of the new millennium, too."

That was enough for about an hour's worth of interrogation, that fatso business, but I knew I didn't have that kind of time. "What else do you do at Grandpop's?" I asked, pushing the juice toward her.

Elise flipped the pompom out of her eyes, twirled her fork around, speared it into a waffle's soggy middle. "He listens to my stories, I lis-ten to his."

"Which are about . . . ?"

"The olden days. Being on television. The best ones are about this man he used to work for. Not work for. You know—he was his sidepal."

"Sidekick? You mean Alec McGowan?"

"Yeah, like that. He talks about him for hours at a stretch. Hey!"

Alan, sneaking up behind her, had tugged her cap off, kissed her quickly on both ears. They wrestled a minute, Elise giggling hysterically, and then, glancing at the clock, she grabbed her backpack and her coat. I walked her to the door; she said she wasn't scared, but I noticed, before starting down the sidewalk, that she looked carefully both ways to see if any middle school kids were around.

Three down, one to go. Alan sat hunched over the table spooning cereal into his mouth, staring back over his shoulder toward the towel-draped TV. His red hair, for a change, was uncombed and curly; his expression was sleepy and unusually relaxed. Even stranger, he didn't have a business suit on; he was wearing jeans and an old flannel shirt, making it seem the straps that bound him together had inexplicably come undone.

"Seen Brenda?" he asked, once I sat down.

"A glimpse. She was up early."

"Physiotherapy." He had to insert his finger in his mouth, rearrange some cornflakes, in order to pry the word out. "You'd be amazed at how crowded it gets before school starts. A whole line of girls clutching their knees."

"You seem to be taking it better than the rest of us."

He glanced up at me, sharply this time. "Hey, I'm her twin. Her knee hurts, my knee hurts. I heard her crying the other night—and it's not Brenda's style to cry."

"I was watching when it happened. Just a kind of sag. There was no reason. It was like her knee said, 'I'll carry you just this far in life but no farther.'"

Alan shrugged. "No one comes back from an interarticular cartilage. She's determined, a brave kid, but—not in time to do her any good."

"Your pals the recruiters?"

I didn't mean that as a taunt, but he must have taken it that way. He stirred his spoon around like he was considering whether it was worth an argument. "The hell with them," he said. "I've got a better plan, anyway."

I waited for more, but the stockmarket reports from Japan had come on now and he craned his head around to listen.

"Some interesting fluctuations," he said softly.

As a kid he had watched television for hours on end, hardly moving, showing excitement only when someone was murdered, and it had been a long time before we had managed to break him free of this—and if it had taken naked, in-your-face capitalism to do it, programs about Wall Street and investing, then hurray, I suppose, for naked capitalism. A fast, contemptuous glance was all he ever gave TV now; he tore from it what he needed, as quickly and heedlessly as a caveman ripping off a hunk of mastodon.

I had news of my own. "The deal looks pretty solid for the station," I said, automatically falling into his tone. "It's a serious offer and it's going to be hard not to say yes."

We discussed it for a good fifteen minutes, Alan listening attentively, jumping in now and then with a pertinent question, supplying, when I finished, some sound and sensible advice. How much longer would it be before I relied on him for all my business dealings? I wondered. But then, if I took the money, there would be no business to advise me on. The irony was enough to make me smile, though I tried not to. Seventeen years of trying to bond with my son and here we were bonding like hell over a business that was about to vanish.

"I guess the upshot of all this is that you might not have to worry about college," I explained. "Losing those scholarships, Brenda's bad knee. There should be plenty of money for college for all three of you."

Was I looking for gratitude, Alan throwing his arms around me in joy? He smiled at any rate—a bit condescendingly, but at least he smiled.

"That's what my plan's about," he said, moving his bowl aside, swiping off some crumbs. "We won't be needing any parental funds. I've noticed there's a huge resource out there that's not being tapped whatsoever. Elementary school athletes, the good ones—kids of nine and ten who are already awesome, particularly girls. They're starting to be heavily recruited by parochial schools, prep schools, places like that, and it stands to reason they need an agent to represent them, negotiate the best deal. A few of them will develop into college potential, future pros, and if I can get in on the ground floor, get myself positioned—" He plucked at his shirt. "That's why I'm dressing this way. I'm going to games, courting kids, talking them up, and I need to relate to them on their level."

I expected him to look at me for approval—I was trying my hardest to summon some—but he caught sight of something on the counter, jumped up and hurried over in that direction. "My God! Elise forgot her reindeer cookies! She'll be crushed."

He got out the cellophane, tenderly wrapped them, went to fetch his car keys, started toward the door.

"I noticed those bad-mouth kids haven't been tormenting Elise lately," I said, following after. "Your middle school contacts have anything to say about that?"

He nodded vehemently up and down. "Sure they do. I bought them off. The ringleaders. It wasn't cheap, but I figured it was worth it for Elise's sake."

"You bought them off?"

He looked at me like I was five. "You don't think they would have quit on their own, do you?"

"No. They're little racists."

He shook his head. "Race has nothing to do with it. The one time they yelled nigger at her, this one kid who did?—the others beat the shit out of him. They want to be fair in that respect, and besides, they're integrated. The only thing they care about is her body size . . . which reminds me. You know what the most important issue in this new century is going to be, don't you?" he asked, the door open now, Alan teetering on the steps like a sprinter in the blocks.

And that was my role in life now—to hand him his exit lines. "I give up," I said. "It's your century, not mine."

He pursed his lips together, made as if to say something, winked, zipped his finger across his mouth, winked again, spun around, and—

deliberately messing his hair up, pulling out his shirttails—disappeared out the door.

The malls were gridlocked with holiday shoppers, and though I tried every shortcut, I was still running late when I pulled up in front of Chet's apartment. Our routine had been for him to be waiting there on the sidewalk all ready to go, but we'd shrunk back on this the last couple of weeks: from him standing in the lobby to him sitting in the kitchen to him lying on the couch.

I buzzed his doorbell, then let myself in with the extra key. I usually went through the motions in a businesslike rush designed to shut out every concern but the job at hand—getting him to the doctor and back—but this time, maybe because of the grayness, the nearness of Christmas, things felt different even before I went in. Here we had this miserable comedy of a relationship, putative father and putative son, and rather than finding a way around this wall, we had only managed to build it higher, with thicker plaster, tougher studs. Alan and I had moved half a millimeter closer over breakfast. Maybe it was time for movement here as well.

"I'm here!" I shouted, loud enough for him to hear me, and then, while I waited, went over to look at his latest messages.

There were three, taped to the last patch of virgin territory left in the apartment: the outside of his microwave oven. He'd switched from black felt marker to red, and it made the messages seem absurdly bright and merry. The first one was short: *Ask K. to wrap presents for E.* The second was longer: *Don't strain over stool Relax and CONCEN-TRATE and go Naturally.* The third, compared to the other two, was big as a mural, and it ran from the door of the microwave around onto the side: *Long is the way and HARD that out of HELL leads up to LIGHT.*

I was reading these when Chet came in. Kim had bought him a sportcoat for an early Christmas present and over that was the parka I'd gotten him for winter, yet he was already shivering, as if his chills were being generated internally and all that the insulation accomplished was to keep the cold from escaping.

He had deteriorated badly over the past few weeks. The rusty baldness had darkened into purple splotches that butterflied down his forehead toward his cheeks; his eyes, so small already, seemed like dots added to a stick figure drawn by a child. He coughed all the time now—hard and desperately, interrupted by frantic suckings as he tried to find enough air to cough again. I was hoping he had reached a stable, drug-supported plateau from which weakness would gently claim him, but he had slipped from that plateau now, and it was clear nothing was going to be spared him, no indignity, no pain.

He saw me staring at his messages, pushed and poked with his hand until his fingers escaped the parka's sleeve, pointed to the longest one. "Milton," he said. "A lot of people might think it's from the Bible, but if it were it would say leadest, not leads. I became very enamored of him while living upstate."

Upstate? "Yes, I can see that," I said.

He tried pursing his lips together, but they were so emaciated, all that happened was that a little bit of flesh got a little bit thinner. "Some men there you wanted to hug they were so innocent, but the others were ignorant savages."

A sentence—and yet it was the most he'd ever said about his experience in prison. And his voice was still strong; if anything it seemed deeper and richer than before. It was as if his head was wasting away down toward his body, and his body was wasting away upward toward his head, the only gainer in this being his throat, his vocal cords, sucking in the strength he was losing everywhere else.

I got him down to the car okay, but the traffic was even worse than before, so that was another twenty minutes added to a drive that should have taken five. By the time we arrived at the clinic its parking lot was deserted; when I walked around to the entrance I found a sign printed in Gothic lettering saying they were closed for Christmas, wishing us a good one, listing a phone number we could call in the event of an emergency.

Chet had enough medication to last him through the weekend—what made me mad was having brought him out in the cold for no reason. I climbed back into the car, explained the situation, started the wipers against the rain, put the car in gear but stayed right there.

"Listen, this is just an idea. Do you feel like seeing anything? Taking a drive? I planned to stay with you at the doctor's all morning, so there's not much else I have to do."

It wasn't the first time I had asked him that. After every appointment I would mention something about going out for coffee or taking a drive to see his old haunts, but he always insisted I drive straight back to his apartment. And so it surprised me what happened. His head stayed hidden in the folds of the parka's hood, but there was enough movement to be read as a nod. "Drive," he said, and then another word came out in between coughs, something that sounded enough like "river" to make me head in that direction.

There wasn't much left for him, even if he could see normally. The strip we were on had nothing that wasn't built yesterday, and the North End, the vibrant heart he might remember, had all been gutted in the urban renewal of the sixties. So the river, for someone who remembered the old days, was not a bad choice. It was cut off from the city center by I-91, but past it were warehouses and railroad sidings that went back to the turn of the century, looking no more dingy and squalid than they had ever looked, and in between them you could get a glimpse of something the color of a playground slide, with just enough of a breeze on it to suggest motion and flow.

Chet leaned against the window trying to see—it was hard to know how much he could bring into relative focus. Still, he seemed interested, alert, curious; he had left off coughing now, and, just as I was wondering about his eyesight, surprised me by bringing up the subject on his own.

"I see a set of kids' blocks. No detail, no color. It's like everything in the world is coated in gray fur."

"You want me to try and go closer?"

"Is there still a bridge over to West Springfield? The old bridge?"

"Yes."

"Take that. I want to motor north along the bank."

The bridge was hung with netting for repairs, not much was visible below it, and the other bank had the same mix of warehouses and junkyards as the Springfield side. But there were longer glimpses of the river now—sagging old docks, boats forgotten and swamped along shore, ice floes out in the middle bobbing and rolling like kids enjoying the slide. "We motored up this way once," Chet said, speaking to the glass more than to me. "Late summer."

There was silence after that—for a moment I wondered if I was hearing things. The grayness made me feel stupid, slow, but not so stupid I couldn't recognize it as a crucial moment, one I had to handle gently or it would melt before my eyes.

"'We' meaning Alec, Lee, and you?"

He nodded.

I pushed on the moment again, a little harder. "The summer of 1941?"

"Yes."

Chet brought his face from the glass and closed his eyes, focusing inward. I wasn't sure what to say next, but I was certain that getting him to talk more depended on staying close to the river.

"This must have been pretty then," I said.

"Much uglier. Sewers emptied into it and people threw garbage out from their back porches and there were tin cans ten feet deep along the banks. Up north was pretty. That's why we drove that way."

"On a picnic?"

"Lee brought a hamper from home. Her father had a French chef named Henri, only he wasn't a Frenchy at all, but an old Portuguese baker from Chicopee named Johnny Medeiros. But he could pack a picnic hamper all right. Foie gras, wine, petits fours. But this wasn't just a picnic. This was something very different indeed."

All this, compared to his usual silence, was like a wave of volubility, one I wasn't sure how to ride. And so I didn't say anything, not for a few minutes. The road along the Connecticut ended at the interstate ramp, and I had to go north whether I wanted to or not, but you could still see the river from up there, and by the time we reached the next exit we were past the malls, out into the country, and I felt confident enough to press again.

"I'm trying to picture what it must have been like."

"She was never more beautiful. We drove with the top down and then when we got to Northampton we had to switch places, put her in back, because men would see her in the front seat and turn to stare and we were always dodging collisions at the last moment. So we put her in back for safety's sake. She had on a sundress, a new one, and sitting next to her made you feel like a king."

"Was it a yellow sundress?"

He made a brisk motion with his hand across his nostrils. "Of course it was yellow. It was always yellow with Lee. On a day like that one she outshone old Sol himself."

He shifted position in his seat, made a lurching motion, began coughing. It wasn't as bad as some of the spells he suffered, and yet, in that confined space, the staccato wheeze made it sound like he was hacking out his guts. It was unbearable, I realized now, because it did violence to the tempered beauty of his voice.

We lost sight of the river, but the clouds were darker and more elongated to our right, so I could still trace its course. We were past Deerfield, coming upon the first signs for Vermont, and I was wondering if we shouldn't turn back because of the weather, when he started talking again—softer now, as if he were very conscious of what energy was left him.

"It wasn't just a lark, either. Lee thought it was, but Alec had other plans."

"Plans?"

"Intentions. Motives. Call it what you will. He had never told her the truth about who he really was, how he had been brought up, his forged identity, and he wanted to tell her, and he wanted to tell her in a special way."

I sensed his rhythm now, the pauses that were meant for me to pick up and carry. "Which was?" I said.

"He had heard stories all the time from his father about a riverman named Philias Remillard, the man Alec was originally named after. About how he was king of the log drive, a hero, a prince among men. About how he died in a logjam and how they buried him with his spiked boots there by the river under a little stone the men chipped in to erect. Alec knew where this was or knew where it was supposed to be. The plan was to go up to Vermont and find the stone and use that to explain to Lee the truth about who he really was."

"She didn't know until then?"

"She never asked, sensed she shouldn't. Their present was so perfect, everything before that seemed like an empty blue hole."

"You mean a black hole?"

He closed his eyes, concentrating. "No, it was blue. Their love was built around an icy core . . . She knew nothing about his past. And she didn't learn then, either."

He explained about their drive—how it was so hot the radiator overheated and they coasted to a stop near a stream, the three of them, while they waited for it to cool, wading hand-in-hand through the shallows until they reached the deepest, richest part of the shade, like a cathedral it was so quiet, the friends standing in the center, not daring to say a word. How later, back on the road again, they came upon a cow that had bolted loose from its fence—how with much yelling and laughing and yodeling they helped the farmer shoo it back. A little later they saw farm kids selling lemonade and they bought out their entire stock—real lemonade, squeezed from fresh lemons, so tart it was like taking the breeze down your throat. Then came a store that sold funny postcards; corn so high it formed tunnels along the roadway; a state trooper who stopped them for speeding but only gave them a warning once he caught sight of Lee; hawks drifting on the updrafts forcing you to squint to make them out—and all along, the big river in reaching distance to their right, like a highway itself it was so flat, a silver one leading north toward coolness and clarity and perfection.

The longer Chet talked the slower his words became, until I glanced over and saw him slumped against the window, sound asleep, the hood of his parka wedged against the glass like a pillow. He looked harmless there, baby-like, swaddled—it was easy to see why Elise defended him from murder. I'd seen the violent side of him the night he protected her from the mob, and already, a month later, I couldn't believe it had ever happened. But maybe that was the secret—that even weak men, when things are doled out at birth, are allotted two spasms of fury in which to lash out hard at the world. One had happened fifty years before, one a month ago, and now that they were discharged he could sleep soundly—there wouldn't be a third.

The clouds became thicker once we crossed into Vermont, but I found it impossible to turn around. For company, I switched on the radio, curious to see if our signal reached that far. It did, a scratchy pulse that flickered in and out according to the syncline of the hills. It was the eleven-to-noon slot, the amateur hour, when we let almost anyone sit in as guest announcer—a show that went back to the thirties, one of McGowan's innovations, and still the most popular program we had. It was the mayor this time, Springfield's mayor, playing corny Christmas music while reading the Nativity; with the distance, the softening of static, he almost managed to sound homey, generous, and kind.

At the third exit past the Vermont line I dropped down to the old highway that ran closer to the river. It was a much leaner, sparer kind of land than was visible from the interstate, the hills leaving only a narrow strip into which were pressed the frozen Connecticut, the snowy highway, a few scattered farms. Most seem abandoned, their yards empty and scraped clean—survivors of everything the last century had thrown at them, only to succumb here in the first few seconds of the new one to forces I could only guess at. The houses came a little thicker toward the villages. Fifties style, most of them, erected back in the days when everyone dreamed of the suburban life, weathering horribly now, beyond rescue by paint or carpentry or TLC. Most had satellite dishes mounted on their roofs, cold black dials under which the houses stiffly spun. Most had some attempt at decoration—a plastic wreath, a string of lights—but they looked like neglected leftovers from previous years, making it seem as though Christmas were a much darker kind of celebration here, something that spoke of sternness and not joy. But it suited me, given my mood. The grayness, the flinty farms, the sagging lights—the feeling that morning was limping along with the old year on its back. Suited me and cradled me in.

The frost had gotten under the pavement and the bumps woke Chet up—or maybe he had been awake all along. We were in one of those gaps in the hills where the station came through clear. He leaned toward the radio, made a twisting motion in the air as if trying to turn it louder, coughed, then sank back into place against the window.

"I've been listening a lot," he said. I was peering out the frosted window trying to see. "I've been listening a lot," he said again. "When I have a free moment."

"How's it sound?"

"Well it *sounds* fine. We always did have that champagne signal. But I'm concerned at the programming. It seems old-fashioned to me. All that eclecticism. People nowadays are looking for a seamless whole. I think you're pushing that nostalgia button a little too hard."

"It's not nostalgia."

"Well, no, not nostalgia. I didn't mean to say actual nostalgia. But I think we need a slicker, more contemporary sound. I'm not tickled pink with our direction."

"Speaking of which"—and I grinned my phoniest. "I'm stopping for directions."

"For what? For the rapids?" He stared out the window. "They must be out there."

"Windsor, Ascutney, Hartland. Any of those names ring a bell?"

He closed his eyes. "Hartland, I think. Yes, it was Hartland. I'm positive. Heart and land. Lee made a joke about it and we laughed. We felt it must be a fine place to be so denominated."

We stopped at a bakery that catered to skiers. None of the teenagers working behind the counter knew about any rapids, of course—it was stupid of me to even ask. I pumped myself some coffee, drank most of it waiting for Chet to finish in the men's room. I was just about to go in and see if he was okay when he came back out again, his fly open, his cheeks freckled with brown bits of paper towel. He didn't see me, started down the wrong aisle toward the rear of the store. There was a shelf piled with holiday pies, and his shoulder brushed against it hard enough to set it wobbling so that it very nearly toppled over on his head—a shelf with a hundred apple crumb pies. I grabbed his arm, steered him outside again, parked him in the car while I went over to ask who I should have asked in the first place: two men unloading Christmas trees from a rusty half-ton truck.

"Sumner Falls," the older one said, when I explained what I was looking for. "Only place on the river the dams haven't tamed. Two miles north, then take the gravel road down to your right. Stop when you feel the earth shake."

He was right, especially about that last part. The dirt road led through hemlocks to a terrace above the river, with a parking place near some overturned picnic tables and a dirt ramp leading into the water. I parked, told Chet to wait there, walked the rest of the way through three inches of sandy snow, and felt even through that insulation something beating strong and steady beneath my boots. WARNING, read a big orange sign, DANGER!—and just past this the rapids came into sight. They stretched away at an oblique angle toward the New Hampshire shore, a hundred, a hundred and fifty yards of pounding whitewater that contained a good amount of silver as well, so that it seemed the river was being poured from a foundry that specialized in turmoil, brilliancy, and chaos. There was enough declination at work that I could see the river level was perceptibly higher upstream, see the water crest over on itself and tumble even before reaching the granite reef that tore it to shreds.

On the highest rock, unconcerned, three gulls sat watching a raven that slanted back and forth above the highest spray—against the whiteness of the horizon its black was riveting. The bay downstream was a wide one, completely frozen except for the channel gouged out by racing water. Closer to shore, the ice was piled with driftwood the color of old antlers.

I took a step or two out onto the ice. The pounding came to me, not just through my boots now, but as a deep-throated roar in my ears, and this was much more intimidating than any sign. But the rapids themselves, the actual dance of water, seemed the only thing in that frozen landscape that was alive and vibrant and healthy, the ice nearer shore the part that was dead. It was hard picturing it the other way around—seeing the rapids as representing death to a young riverman, the shore representing safety. And yet, managing the somersault, it wasn't difficult at all to picture the river crowded bank to bank with logs, the current forced to work by clever Lilliputians armed with double-bladed axes and ironshod sticks. The sky that framed everything was so gray and motionless it seemed lifted out of an old book, a faded illustration not so much of any historical detail, but of the grainy heart of time itself—and even someone as dull and slow as I am could feel the percussive surge that came with recognition, even if it had to enter me through my feet.

There was no wind, but it felt as though there were. The raven slanted back toward shore; in following it, I spotted something red and happy-looking embedded in the snow, walked over, picked up a fisherman's plastic bobber, which I pocketed for Elise.

When I got back to the car Chet had the window rolled down an inch, sat there with his head against the crack like a kid putting his ear to a seashell. "What's there?" he asked, without taking it away.

I sat down in the driver's seat, turned the heat up, but kept the car right where it was. "Bait buckets. Beer cans. A soggy campaign sign. Someone dragged a picnic table over to the ice like they wanted to make a causeway."

"I remember cables. Big cables twisted around the trees where they held in logs during the drive. Lots of spikes, too, rusty ones. We walked barefoot to the water and we had to tread carefully."

"No cables now. Where is Remillard's stone?"

"He was the one who drowned in the logjam. Alec's father's closest chum."

"Yes, I know."

"Remillard's father was called from Quebec to fetch the body. He showed up in a buckboard wagon, pocketed the pay that was owed his son, then left without the body—he didn't give a damn about that, just the cash. So the other rivermen chipped in to put the stone up. Philias was everyone's hero. . . . We didn't find it. We looked and looked. Alec told Lee what he was searching for, but he didn't say why. He was going to later, after we found it. He couldn't tell her the truth about his background unless he was convinced of it himself, and he couldn't convince himself until he saw the evidence with his own eyes. . . . We must have searched for an hour, going deep into the wildflowers, prying them apart. After a while Lee and I drifted on back to the little sand beach while Alec kept searching on his own."

He described the way the shadows from the big maples kept the sand cool, but how just a few steps out into the river the sun came back and it was hot, gloriously so, making it impossible not to go swimming. He described what Lee and he talked about as they waited for Alec to give up and join them—small talk at first, radio talk, talk about what they could see out across the river, the birds, the drifting cornstalks, the shimmery dance of water toward the clouds. Lee talked of how being born to money gave you a sense of power, but that was nothing compared to the sense of power that came to her when she thought of her talent, her vocation, so strong and sure now it had scrubbed that money sense, that hateful sense, clean—and then, tired of waiting, she pulled her sundress over her head in a smooth, totally unselfconscious motion, handed it to him along with the little strap of her bra and the silkier handful that was her slip, waded out into the river, and, smoothing back her hair, making a little ducking motion, dove gracefully in.

Alec came back and they sat on the bank watching Lee swim, not saying anything, neither of them having to, knowing it was the most beautiful sight they had ever seen. She swam out toward where the current spun around in a cream-colored whirlpool, let it catch her, hold her, then rolled away from it and swam backstroke toward the shade. She was fifty yards away; Alec, taking pity on Chet's eyesight, began trying to describe her out loud, what she was doing, what stroke she was using, where she was in relation to the bank.

"It was all so natural," Chet said. He had his face to the window now, not just his ear—whatever he was taking from the river, he was taking directly through the parchment of that feebly veined skin. "Lee swimming, the two of us watching, Alec trying to let me share it. 'She's coming this way,' he said. 'Backstroke now. The water is yielding to her shoulders, tapering past her breasts, re-forming over her legs' . . . We were one. Lee was merely another part of us, the beautiful part who could shape water into her own image. Alec was our brains, our daring, our courage. I was—what? 'Our connective tissue,' Alec used to say, and he said it seriously . . . When Lee came out I took my shirt off so she could use it as a towel. She wrapped it around her shoulders, lay down on the sand with me sitting next to her while Alec went off again to look for his stone."

As he talked, I pressed my own face against the glass, like it was a screen I only had to touch to see clear, and I could, but only out to the snowy launching ramp, the frozen relics of summer, the deadness of ice. Always before with Chet, remembrance had come in choked and miserly bits; I wasn't prepared to have it flow this way, and it made me feel an unaccountable kind of anger, knowing my imagination wasn't equal to weaving together what he was telling me, not then, at any rate, not staring out at that snow.

"A cloud came across the sun behind us. Not an ordinary cloud—it was slate blue and dark, like a shutter pulled down across the afternoon. Without that cloud I don't think she would have told me. She started shivering and I had to go over to the car and find a blanket. When I came back she was sitting with her arms around her knees. 'I have something to tell you,' she said, staring at her hands. That struck me more than anything—she was always a person who looked you right in the eye. 'We're eloping,' is what she said. 'Alec and I, next week, to New York.' She told me what few details they had thought through. Alec had bought a ramshackle old Ford for fifty dollars and he was going to meet her at the park across from the station and this was all happening on Monday, which meant in three days."

There was a pause here, a dramatic pause—I looked over, saw him watching me, remembered that this was a man who had spent his life waiting for cues. "What happened then?" I said.

"I listened to her, realized she was terribly unhappy and terribly scared. There was no question but that she loved him—the questions were about everything else. She didn't ask me for advice, not in so many words, but I knew this is what she wanted. I was always giving her advice, it was as normal as her swimming au naturel before us, and so I mulled for a while and then I told her what I thought."

"Which was?"

"That it was madness. What kind of life could they possibly have had together once the initial exhilaration wore off? They were from totally opposite worlds—that would have caught up with them very soon. Alec was unreliable when it came to that kind of thing. He'd had hundreds of girls and left every one of them and that kind of pattern is impossible to break. They were lost in a delicious fantasy and it was my job to protect them. What they planned was impossible, and what's more, it was impossible to tell Alec, he was so determined there was no telling what he might do, and so I arranged to pick her up at her house Monday morning and take her away in secret to somewhere she could find peace."

"Was it to Maine?" I asked, hoping he'd say no and smash my certainty to bits.

He nodded. "Of course Maine. She had a summer house there. It was the place in the world she loved best."

"And so you took it upon yourself to make the decision for her?"

"There was another reason, though I didn't tell her that. Alec was at a point in his development where he needed to be hurt, needed it badly. He was talented, extraordinarily so, but there was something artificial about it, a fundamental shallowness that worried me quite a bit. He needed real pain in order to achieve his full potential. I could see this very clearly. Losing Lee would sting, of course, but he would get over it and when he got over it he would be a much larger, more formidable kind of man. As so it proved."

I thought about the phrase a moment before I felt what it described—*it took my breath away*—and phrase and feeling, lumping together in my throat, all but made me gag.

"And so you decided their fate for them?"

There wasn't enough skin left on his face for a grimace, but he tried. "All I did was explain to her the truth."

"You're a real specialist in that."

There was a grimace this time all right—his lip borrowed flesh from his chin in order to tighten. "What do you mean by that statement?"

"I mean your telling Elise she's fat. Your bribing her to lose weight. What could possibly be the motive? No, don't bother telling me. It's to hurt her and bring out her talent, right?"

He put his hand to his mouth like he was talking sideways into a microphone, used it to scratch a scabby spot on his chin. "Someone has to tell her what the facts are. Prison is full of people whose fathers were too pamby-namby to tell them the truth."

"Yeah? Well, I wouldn't know about that. What fathers do or don't do with their kids."

"Elise could have my eyes. Did you ever notice her squint? It skips generations, macular degeneration. At thirty she could be legally blind."

"She's adopted, for Christ's sake!"

This didn't stop him. "I'm going to give her back her dignity, and if I have to do this through shock tactics, then so be it. It's the only task I have left to accomplish . . . Alec became a codeine addict, a sybarite, a lecher. I helped him gain his dignity back, too."

"Right. A good one, Chet. You took a gun and dignified him right out of existence."

"I just meant to warn him. It was an accident, what happened. The Kinescope showed it clearly, but the DA's office destroyed the evidence. I just wanted him to stay away from Lee."

The words seemed old as they came out, arthritic, lame—they shouldn't have been enough to anger me, but they did. "Your advice to Lee about not eloping. That didn't have anything to do with your being worried you would lose your precious radio station if both stars left, did it?"

That hit him hard—his chin jerked away, then jerked back again.

"The doctor you found me," he said slowly. "He takes too many vacations. You should have found me a harder worker. All he does is prescribe medicine with giggle juice in it to shut me up."

"Giggle juice? Is that the best you can do?"

"All you care about is your biography. You see me as a pet canary who's going to sing. I'm not going to sing."

"Listen, Chet—"

"You never visited me. Not once in forty-six years. You left Lindy to take care of me, washed your hands of all responsibility."

All right, a hard jab back for a man his age, one that hit me square. I had one punch left in my arsenal, a secret from the past I was certain he didn't know about, my roundhouse punch that would floor him, and yet angry as I was, I couldn't use it, shouted instead the most obvious and tired thing.

"You stay away from Elise, you hear me? You fucked up my life and you're not going to fuck up hers."

I got out of the car, slammed the door, stomped off through the snow. There were some birch trees behind the picnic area and I headed for their middle, needing motion, not thinking about where I was going. The path ran uphill through deep snow and it was good to feel the resistance, have a force I could shove my anger against and feel it shove back.

I'm not sure how far I went. A half-mile probably. The path stayed by the river and where the trees gave way it came back in sight—the rapids, this time from high above. They seemed tamer now, shrunken, the snow muffling their roar. A sharper sound came through, a quick metallic slamming, but I didn't understand its significance, not then. I walked some more, tried forcing away what I felt, couldn't, came to a cliff, stared down, kicked some rocks loose, turned back. I wasn't angry anymore. I was too cold to feel anything but a vestigial hankering for a cigarette.

It was then I saw the sign, nailed high on one of the dead birches. There was no lettering left—it looked like an arrow-shaped piece of driftwood that had been impaled there for centuries—but I followed it deeper into the woods. There was milkweed, just high enough the flame-shaped tassels escaped the snow, and then a band of spruce that acted as a wall to hold the snow back. In their center was a small clearing and in the middle of the clearing was a pewter-colored headstone, or something that resembled a headstone, hard and flinty and weathered, and not much bigger than a book wedged vertically into the ground. I walked over, bent down, took my gloves off, ran my fingers along the face of it trying to clear away the lichen. There were letters—I could feel the indentations under my fingers—but they were worn and illegible, and the only thing I could make out, even after scraping away at the gouges with a stick, was a zero.

Was it the zero in *1910*? Did the letters above it spell out the name Philias Remillard? It was hard to know what else it could be. This wasn't a graveyard, just a single stone, and it was on the highest spot overlooking the rapids, so it made sense as a location. The spruce couldn't have been much older than thirty or forty years, and before that the knoll had probably been covered with wildflowers and raspberry vines, so it might have been impossible in the summer of 1941 to have found it beneath the vegetation.

I knelt in the snow, rubbed my fingers along the gouges a second time. As rough and hard and unreadable as the stone was, there was a kind of comfort in those qualities—the roughness and hardness and illegibility being exactly what truth would bury itself under in order to stay remote from the likes of me. I knew now why Chet shut his eyes in the presence of the past, and I shut mine instinctively, trying to feel past the stone to what lay beneath. I knew why Alec felt he had to touch adamant stone in order to understand the truth of his identity— that was the first layer I came to, the easy layer, the smoothest transference. Here I had been struggling so hard to make communion with a man who had been dead half a century, seizing his identity, wrapping it tight between covers, and here—closing my eyes, pressing my fingertips so hard against the stone the pain shot through the numbness—I could do it, or come damn near, not by reaching toward the ghost of a dead riverman, but by plunging through that to McGowan's story, which rested underneath, the deepest layer, the one that lay beneath snow, stone, gravel, and dirt, the one I was as close to touching in that moment as I ever would be.

Ten minutes, fifteen—I knelt there as long as I dared, and the longer I knelt there the more certain I became I had found Remillard's grave, and the more certain I became the more excited, to the point where I wanted to rush back to the car and tell Chet. The contrast with my anger was so extreme, so dramatic, it made me laugh. Here I was, the aggrieved child storming away in a fit of anger, and now here I was, the child again, needing to show his parent the marvelous treasure he had found in the woods.

The car was empty when I got there—the passenger door open, the front seat powdered with an inch of fresh snow. I looked up toward the privy, but there were no footprints in that direction. I turned, looked the other way toward the river and spotted him instantly, a hundred yards out on the ice. His parka was brown and too big for him and it made it seem a pelt was lurching across the ice with the inner animal removed—a ghost animal, wounded, hunching over in submission to the snow. He was moving downstream, parallel to the open water, but then I saw him bring his hand up, sweep his hood back, swivel his head like a periscope, swerve off to his left so that he was making directly for the rapids.

"Chet!" I yelled, and the weight of the cold stuffed the word down my throat.

I started running. At first the surface was dangerously slick, but the farther out on the ice I went the grittier it became, so it wasn't long before I was up to him. It was close enough to the rapids that the spray had formed a jagged mound of what looked to be frozen coconut, and he was trying to scuff through this and gain the open river; when I grabbed him, his boots kept windmilling in the air, kicking up shavings as the ice sagged beneath us and almost broke.

"Stop it!" I yelled. I put my arms around his neck, or where I thought his neck should be, then pulled him back like a lifeguard with my other arm around his chest. He resisted—I felt a surge of desperation that made him squirm in my arms—but then, between one second and the next, he went limp. I squeezed in harder, expecting to find a hard core of bone or muscle that would fight back, but there was nothing. For all the time I carried him, during that long trip back across the ice, I was certain I carried a dead man—that he had snuck away from me just when I held him tightest.

I cradled him with one arm under his legs, the other under his back, so he stayed in close against my parka. There was no weight to him whatsoever, and yet it was a hard enough journey—the sagging ice, my frozen fingers, the blowing snow. Three times I fell with him and three times I got back up, and each time it became harder for me to understand what I was doing, why I hadn't just left him to walk on in the direction he craved.

I got him to the car, slouched him down in the front seat, went around and turned the heater on full blast. He was alive—the parka caved in on itself, then convulsively expanded—and in another minute his eyes flashed open and immediately clamped shut, as if he didn't like what he saw, didn't like it at all.

Was there a hospital anywhere close? If before I felt like an angry kid, and then an excited kid, now I felt like a scared and lonely kid, very far from home and not at all sure what to do next. My first thought was that he was going to die of exposure right there on the front seat, and my second thought was that maybe that wasn't a bad thing, to die before he could suffer further, and then a moment after that I was relieved to see him breathing normally, sleeping, or apparently sleeping, and I decided the best thing to do was get him back to Massachusetts as fast as I could.

It took two hours, driving through snow back into rain. Somewhere along the way he wet his pants and the smell was terrible, but there wasn't anything that could be done about it. I turned the radio on, hoping it would comfort him. I put my arm around his shoulder, tried rubbing in the warmth. It was almost dark by the time we reached

Springfield. I drove past his apartment and continued on to our house, put my arms around him again, carried him through the garage into the kitchen and then up to the guest room, where I laid him down on the extra bed. I pulled off his clothes, cleaned him up as best I could, heard him mumble something without being able to determine what it was. Then I covered him with a quilt, turned the light off, and tiptoed, exhausted, back downstairs.

No one else was home. A third-grade party, extra physiotherapy, recruiting ten-year-olds, a meeting at school—I was so tired I couldn't remember who was where. There was a note in the kitchen from Elise—*The package truck came for you no peeking until Christmas*—and on the table beside it was a plump manila envelope plastered with stamps.

A letter bomb—in my stupor I could think of nothing nicer—and I unwrapped it gingerly. Inside swaddled in tissue was a black plastic something that it took me longer to recognize than it should have. Not a bomb part but a videotape cassette, a fat one. Attached to it with duct tape was a handwritten note on a piece of yellow scrap paper.

Can't take a joke? No hard feelings. A Xmas present. One more to come once you watch these. Stay tuned, old tiger. Slisco.

Ten

It was a tape of two separate *Morning*s, with something much darker spliced in between.

What comes on first is the window on Forty-ninth Street, the faces staring in, so it seems the same footage preserved in the broadcasting museum, and it's a few seconds before the difference becomes clear. It's raining, heavy drops that pearl on the window and smudge the faces, the camera keeping everyone in a much softer focus, their bodies, their raincoats, blending into a single black, broad-shouldered entity beneath a hundred and fifty separate heads. Perhaps because of the rain most of the signs are of places where the weather is extreme. *Cordova, Alaska. International Falls, Minnesota. Caribou, Maine.*

The film quality is much better than the fragment in the museum, except for an occasional flare-up of bright gray light. Even with the rain, the black-and-white, there's a remarkable clarity at work, so it seems as if it really is a morning you're staring at, one that's far fresher and more promising than anything that passes for morning today. Eight A.M. on a sodden midtown street circa 1951 and everything is visible—the whorled bamboo shafts of the umbrellas, the taut convex fabric covering, the sandstone gray of the buildings that serve as backdrop, the warts, tics, and scars on the gaping faces.

The camera lingers on the window, just as in the museum fragment; as with the museum fragment, you expect the tape to suddenly snap to an end, so the shock is all the greater when, to the upper right of the screen, a single word appears, scrolled in the stark, understated kind of lettering you see at the start of foreign films: *MORNING.* A shock, a small one, just enough to prepare for the bigger shock that follows. Against the window, coming in from the right as if from out of the massed onlookers, and yet most definitely on the inside, the camera side of the glass, appears a very young, very handsome Alec McGowan.

The sleepy face that seems evenly split between good-natured boyishness and world-weary irony. The horn-rim glasses. The shock of light hair over the intellectual forehead. The bow tie. The breadth of his shoulders beneath his double-breasted suit. The surprising grace and athleticism of that simple motion in from nothingness and down on the stool—sitting sideways, his hand cupped over his knee like he's hiding something there, his body half-turned in a posture that suggests repose and motion simultaneously.

He sits with his back to the window, smiles, says nothing. He hunches around, looks out at the faces on the street, the raindrops pearled on the window glass, seems lost in contemplation, turns back to the camera, smiles again, opens his mouth in a quick and stealthy yawn. He opens his mouth and yawns again, then a third time, then a fourth—it seems like he's yawning or chewing gum or humming, and yet there's no sound to go with it . . . and then the truth becomes clear: the tape is soundless. Whether because of technical problems, audio decay caused by the years in storage, or another of Slisco's mordant tricks, what comes from the monitor is video alone, just McGowan chewing on words that get lost in his mouth before they emerge. It's cruel, a terrible joke—yet maybe not so cruel, since it forces the focus onto the original miracle everyone fell so quickly, so overwhelmingly in love with: seeing people who were a thousand miles away appear in front of you, right there in your home. *Seeing,* not hearing—by then, thanks to radio, hearing was old hat. Seeing is where the freshness comes from even now, the scrubbed sense of morning. It's McGowan, he's alive, you're seeing fifty years into the past, and so the silence doesn't wall him off but accomplishes just the opposite, resurrecting him in a way that rivets your attention right from the start.

At first the camera angle is slightly oblique. McGowan stares toward something just to the left of the camera and slightly below it, and then, suddenly, he looks directly into the lens, as if by this quickness to take it unawares, turn it inside out on itself, focus it outward. He blinks— he seems, in the open way he does this, with those feminine eyelashes behind the heavy glasses, the only person who has ever blinked on television before or since—and then squints, the corner of one eyelid tightening into manly wrinkles, the other actually shutting so that he seems like a person who is about to put his eye to a powerful telescope. The camera, anticipating this trick, immediately bores in, and what he seems to put his eye to is the TV screen itself, in a way that stops just short of being ludicrous. Seeing this, your first reaction is to jump back, and yet immediately afterward you feel flattered, as if these eyes, out of all possible subjects they might focus on in the enormity of the country, have found your eyes, and your eyes alone, worthy of consideration.

He wants to see out—in those first few seconds he desperately tries—and then the camera draws back again and he withdraws into his sleeply, contemplative look, sitting there on the stool, as if, having tried once again, and failed once again, he can, without any hard feelings, go back to letting the camera watch *him.*

His opening monologue is triple the length anyone would be

allowed now. As he talks, he decorates his words with a whole range of facial accompaniments; he squints, wryly smiles, turns to look at the faces behind him, turns back, winks, lets the overhead lights flash off his glasses, moves his eyes upward, stares at the camera again, this time like a wise old man peering over his specs, looks shyly away, talks to his hand, the hand that still rests on his knee. It's his famous trick, holding something with one hand, a small prop—and yes, here it comes now, he raises the hand from his knee still clenched in a fist, brings it higher, shakes it like it's holding dice, then turns his hand over and uncoils his fingers to reveal what's hidden inside.

A cannon—a brass toy cannon, the souvenir kind sold at old battle-fields or historical sites. He holds it up to the camera, makes his face grimmer than it's been so far, talks directly to the prop itself, as if he's scolding it in the mildest, most gently reproachful of ways. Without words, there is no way to determine what this is about, what the subject is, why the cannon. After a minute, a minute and a half, he tosses it up in the air and catches it again, pockets it, gets up from the stool and strolls over to the left, away from the window.

He's followed by a camera—the heavy pedestal kind, cannon-like itself, short-barreled and massive, the network's logo prominent on the side. A man in shirtsleeves pushes it with what looks to be real effort, his legs bent and stubborn like a mule's. Visible now, as McGowan walks slowly across it, is the famous open set. Baby overhead spot-lights aim down like blossoms in an upside-down garden. Armored wires coiled on the floor force stagehands to detour. Chalk marks for positioning make it seem like kindergarten students have been let loose to decorate. A dozen people mill around in what at first seems total chaos—half of them shout directions at the other half. The effect is of taking something by surprise a few moments before you're supposed to—of plunging directly into the experience before it can be framed or neatened or smoothed.

It makes your eyes greedy to see everything—you have to blink to keep up—but very quickly certain details begin to stand out in a not quite motionless tableau. A pleasant young man stands peering down at a book while a makeup assistant, reaching up on tiptoes, runs a brush down the back of his hair. A pretty young woman with gamine features talks to an old black woman who keeps looking over her shoulder as if she wants to bolt. Carpenters are on their knees pounding away at what looks to be nothing more than a large box mounted on sawhorses. A young boy wearing a big flat cap runs up to McGowan and pushes a newspaper in his hand; McGowan takes it like a runner accepting a baton, reaches into his pocket, extracts a quarter, flips it backward over his shoulder. An older man in suspenders comes over, says something to McGowan, sees the camera, squats, waddles under it, disappears. There is no small talk, no chitchat, no gab. These are people who are comfortable with each other, professional, focused strictly on the job at hand.

McGowan sits down in a padded swivel chair with studded arms behind a counter-like desk. Above him are six clocks showing the time in Tokyo, Moscow, London, New York, Chicago, and Los Angeles—all have third hands that sweep together around the dials, counting off the seconds, giving the effect of precision and unity and the universal march of time. Under the clock labeled *New York* is lettering with the date, *November 11, 1951,* and so that explains the little cannon—that it's Veterans Day, Armistice Day, and what McGowan's opening monologue must have been about was war.

He points up toward the date, makes a little checking motion with one finger, looks off to his left toward a monitor, and (just on the monitor at first, then filling up the larger screen) on comes the feature known as "America Wakes Up": short little clips blended, one into the next, showing various locales around the country where, later on in the day, significant events are scheduled to occur.

At a cemetery (is it Arlington?), Marines in dress uniform roll a narrow carpet across the grass while behind them other Marines arrange chairs in neat rows. In a shipyard, workers looking very small lean over scaffolding to pin bunting to a passenger liner's side. In the chamber of the U.S. Senate, pages pour water into pitchers, which they then place on each desk. At a racetrack, a lone exercise rider leads his mount across the wide dirt track as the rising sun casts their shadows out across the infield. At a hospital, nurses coming off the night shift sip coffee as they give report. In an empty classroom, a teacher breaks chalk into a tray and readies the inkwells. At a city firehouse, bone-weary firemen bend the kinks out of frozen hoses, the pumper behind them coated in ice. At a bakery, a beaming baker with a homely and lovable mug holds up to the camera a tray of hot cross buns. Cars cross the Brooklyn Bridge on one half of the screen while, on the other half, a solitary truck crosses the Golden Gate through the fog.

America wakes up, gets ready, prepares for events great and small—and then it's back to McGowan behind the desk, a head shot now, smiling benignly, splitting apart his index finger and the middle one saying (it's easy to read his lips) *Back in two.*

You brace yourself for the commercial—there's a white frothy blur that looks like soap bubbles—but then the whiteness darkens into a heavily marbled gray, making it seem as if the camera has demurely turned away to stare at the floor until the two minutes are up. Just as there is no sound on the tape, there are no commercials, and it's hard to know whether this is because whoever did the original Kinescope decided they weren't worth recording or the result of Slisco's own impatient editing. But it gives the effect of a hole in a doughnut—the outline remains, but no filling.

Back to McGowan, who sits at the desk looking vaguely impatient, but sleepily so, as if he's used to this kind of interruption and is nothing worse than bemused. He's flanked by the man and woman seen in passing earlier. The woman is elfin-looking and pretty, with short black hair and enormous eyes—another in the famous revolving door of *Morning* girls. She glances at McGowan with that little-girl pout too emphasized, turns to the second man and bats those eye-lashes too obviously and too fast.

It comes as more of a surprise than it should that this second man is Chet Standish. He's much more broad-chested and substantial than anything the still photos show. He wears his hair in a crewcut with stiff upward bristles; below it, his face is rounder than it later became, the small eyes happily centered above plump, chipmunk-like cheeks. Like McGowan, he wears glasses, only his are small, rimless and pale; around his neck hangs a microphone as long and thick as a clarinet. He seems perfectly comfortable there by McGowan's shoulder, accepts the camera's close-up scrutiny with good-natured pleasure, although he seems marked by some secondary stamp right from that first appearance—and yet secondary in the very highest way there is to be secondary, a secondary genius, secondary first class.

The camera comes back to McGowan, who points his index finger to the left. Frank Stannard, standing behind his own desk, reads the news—a Frank Stannard who looks no younger, no different, not one whit less craggy than he would forty years later. He reads for longer than a contemporary anchorman would, shuffles through sheet after sheet of white paper, bobs his head up and down trying to keep eye contact with the camera, and only after three minutes of this does what he's saying begin to be illustrated with clips. These aren't live—it's film, of a lesser quality than the Kinescope. The first clip is of a railroad train lying sideways along a trestle (a gentle look to it, the poor train weary, needing to sleep), ambulances rolling up, men in hard hats carrying stretchers . . . and after that comes a shot of what must be the Supreme Court steps, pompous men walking ponderously up them, a reporter talking breathlessly off to the side, a gangster's fedora slouched over his forehead . . . then something much stranger, a long establishing shot of a tall oak tree somewhere, broken glass on the ground beneath it, beer bottles, chicken bones, litter, the camera closing in on the longest, thickest, straightest branch and there tied around the middle a frayed remnant of manila rope . . . and then quintuplets, their beaming mother, their beaming father, who, as the camera bores in, clasps both hands to his head and makes a *Mamma mia!* kind of grimace . . . and after this a long, very distant shot of a basketball game, the players small and obscure in a haze of cigarette smoke, lobbing up graceful two-handers that fall like mortar shells, shredding the net.

Chet comes on to do the weather. Standing in front of a big schoolroom map of the United States, he takes a pointer, begins pointing. It will be forty-one degrees in Casper, Wyoming. Chicago comes in at forty-seven. Down in the Texas Panhandle highs will reach seventy. The remnants of a tropical storm are causing trouble down in Florida—there are curlicues scrawled all over the state—and up in Maine an early snowstorm is marked by little crosshatches that extend out into the Atlantic. *Button up your overcoats!* Chet mouths. Between the fullness of his cheeks and the way he moves his mouth for emphasis, his lips are easy to read.

McGowan stands alone now, everything dark behind him, so that he's centered in what seems a cathedral-like light coming down from a mullioned window high above. It's a stark light and it suits him. His expression is sober. His hands remain clasped behind his back. He talks for a minute, no longer. He finishes, turns to look to where the light seems to be coming from, and you see it's yet another monitor mounted high on the wall.

The monitor picture expands to fill the screen entirely. It shows a field somewhere, flinty, a stubble of dead grass just escaping a snowy crust. The sun is coming up, slowly, stiffly, its light just barely able to penetrate the gloom cast by the rocks. In the distance, toward the top of the screen, there is motion—a peasant woman, a yoke around her neck, carrying buckets, her head bent toward the ground in concentration and woe—and then behind her is more motion, the camera focusing long toward a jeep bouncing over a rutted road, with too many soldiers perched too precariously on the sides, making it seem as if they are fleeing.

A close-up next, of high black infantry boots, fatigue pants tucked into the tops, laces doubled, and just in front of them the lower third of a metal spade—and above this nothing more than one mittened hand around the spade's shaft and a dangling triangle of jacket. To the right of the frame, forming its corner, are five layers of sandbags and the butt end of a rifle. There is no motion at first, but then the spade meets the frozen ground, knees dip, a dusty little cloud envelops the boots.

In the distance are bare hills that could be in New England, only they are shorn of all vegetation, older-looking, folded, and inconceivably worn, stretching into the distance without end. Korea—it can be nowhere else. The camera pulls back to frame five GIs wearing quilted parkas and Russian-style fur hats. They're smiling, most of them, at least while they're together in a bunch. One points to himself—*Me?*—then steps aside. He's twenty, no older; he has jug ears and quick eyes and looks like the kind of kid who back home was good at fixing trucks. He's talking, his jaw working hard, and it's not difficult to imagine the kinds of things he's saying ("I am Staff Sergeant Michael Schwartz from West-by-God-you-better-smile-when-you-say-that Virginia. Hello, Mom. Keep the farm up, 'cause I'll be home *mo sukoshi*"). His face dissolves into another face, a black man's this time, wearing his fur hat at a rakish angle, a three-days' growth of beard across his chin ("I am Private First Class Bog Daniels from Denver, Colorado. When I come home I'm gonna really celebrate the leaving of Korea. When nighttime comes you're really shaking, but mornings ain't bad at all"). The first GIs look cocky, happy to be filmed, but the longer the camera watches them—the more they forget about its presence—the more frightened they look, bewildered, like they want to be anywhere but there.

There is no reporter visible in any of this, just the metallic hills, the palpable cold, a handful of GIs doing their best to smile for the folks at home. The segment lasts fifteen minutes. The picture becomes smaller, the monitor darkens, McGowan turns away from watching it and walks, without comment, into the blackness on his left.

Revealed where he had stood is the simple wooden box the carpenters were hammering together at the start of the show. A muslin curtain hangs down the open side—and there, it's parting now, drawn back in the jaws of a snaggled-toothed dragon and then fussily bunched and neatened by his pal, a mouselike creature with a clown's round nose. It's Kukla and Ollie, the famous Kuklapolitan hand puppets, one of television's earliest sensations. Ollie, the dragon, flaps his protruding jaws open and closed. Kukla listens, seems to dither, then plops down below the stage and reemerges with a beautiful poppy-shaped flower.

Ollie, rather than thanking him, snatches it from his grip. Kukla, usually so gentle, rips it back again. Soon they're fighting, locked in a furious clinch. The little box of a theater goes dark as they disappear; miniature searchlights sweep against the backdrop, there are jagged explosions of vivid light, paper silhouettes of marching soldiers, and then Beulah the witch goes flying back and forth on her broom high above the action, her head tossed back in cackling glee . . . finally, when all is darkest, the war at its height, Kukla and Ollie emerge again, wounded, bandages over their foreheads, lame, with just enough strength left to stagger to the edge of the stage. Ollie prods Kukla with his snaggle tooth to see if he's alive. Kukla stirs, barely, and from the way he tosses his head about, you can see Ollie is crying. At last Kukla manages to stand upright again; Ollie rummages in the debris of war, finds the flattened flower, and, using his tooth, plumps it out until it regains a semblance of its former shape. This accomplished, he hands it over to Kukla, who holds it to his big round nose and sniffs.

The stage goes dark—the muslin curtain falls and then immediately goes up again. McGowan steps back into the picture, looks behind him at the box, and then Kukla is resting his chin on one shoulder, Ollie on the other, and McGowan, after patting them affectionately on their heads, mouths very clearly the words *Thanks, old tigers,* then spreads his fingers apart in the V-gesture he used last time for a commercial.

It's coffee-break time when the show comes back. You see the open set again, technicians working on the cameras (one cools his off by waving a towel), script girls clutching sheafs of paper, assistant directors pressing earphones to their heads trying to hear. In the center of the confusion, sitting slumped in director's chairs (an overhead mike shaped like a beehive coming down to listen in), McGowan, Chet, and the *Morning* girl sip coffee from porcelain mugs as, behind them, a quick, cocky-looking man in a deli apron fishes around in a big paper bag and pulls out various wrappers. Mike Rinaldi, Mike the Muffin. It seems a genuine break, not a staged one—a welcome break in the intensity that has come before. As McGowan chews on his bagel (visible is the melted butter, the dollops of jam), sips at his coffee cup, he waves Rinaldi over, points to another bag that Rinaldi has left on top of a camera. Rinaldi reaches in and pulls out, not bagels this time, but an old-fashioned leather scrapbook, which he spreads open on McGowan's lap. A camera sweeps in behind them, focuses on their fingers as Rinaldi taps out what's there: snapshots of him in the merchant marine, standing proudly on the deck of a tanker with his shipmates, sitting forlornly in a lifeboat somewhere in the ocean, standing with his hand around the waist of a pretty South Pacific girl, a big shitkicker grin slapped across his face.

The break lasts five minutes—McGowan himself cleans up the debris. Just before ending, appearing only for a second, Martin Slisco (young, skinny, gum-chewing, intense, his arms tattooed from the elbows up) is flung ceilingward aboard a blocky-looking crane.

The second half of the show now—Chet leads off by interviewing an author. This is a young man, his face a club boxer's, with cauliflower ears and tough-guy lips, and it's apparent from what follows that he's an ex-GI, an infantryman-turned-novelist. He's at ease with the camera, more so than Chet, who seems momentarily taken aback by the young man's fervor, but then recovers; in an impersonation that seems instinctive, he begins copying the soldier-writer's mannerisms, his pugnacity, the way he gestures, shadowboxes, grimaces, and squints. Chet dutifully holds the novel up toward the camera, only something is wrong, because one of the assistant directors scuttles in from the right, taps his shoulder, reaches in front and gently turns the proffered book right side up. But now Chet's hand is in the way—the title remains invisible throughout.

They're still talking when the picture dissolves into another conversation in progress over to their left. It's the *Morning* girl talking to the black woman seen earlier, who still hasn't taken off her coat. They're standing behind the high counter used in cooking demonstrations, only the counter is piled with material—ribbon, wire, crepe, perhaps for making wreaths or bouquets. The girl handles this interview all wrong. Her face is so busy being cute and adorable she can't remember to keep the condescension out of her expression; she has no sense of the woman's dignity, and the interview, the demonstration, goes nowhere—you can see that the wreath woman responds only in monosyllables. A second before this breaks down completely, McGowan wanders over, as if he's just happening by. He looks down at the counter in interest, says something to the *Morning* girl, who, bubbling and vamping, disappears off to the right. Alone with the wreath woman, the first thing McGowan does is help her off with her coat, and he watches as she ties a wreath together, her hands moving with the utmost economy, even tenderness. They talk while this goes on— McGowan picks up various bits of material and asks her what they are. It's apparent now (the black crepe, the little American flags) that what this woman does for a living is make wreaths to place in veterans' cemeteries. When she's done she holds up the finished wreath to the camera, but even after that, they continue talking—she seems to have forgotten there's a camera there at all. She reaches into her pocketbook, takes out a picture, holds it up for McGowan to see; the camera comes in behind her to focus down on a photo of a very young, proud-looking Marine smiling out from beneath his helmet. When the picture widens again you see the wreath woman is crying.

Too intense—it's almost too intense for the screen to carry; there are more gray flares here than anywhere else on the tape—and the next segment, flowing directly out of this, lightens the mood gently. Terry Hodges now, the resident quintet. Hodges is pirate-like, swarthy, a waterfront thug who happens to play a mellow clarinet. The group behind him, integrated, tuxedoed, bend easily to whatever they're playing. A minute of this and a vocal trio steps up—three WACs in uniform who launch right into song. It's a bouncy tune, judging from the way their heads sway ("Mister Sandman"? "Boogie Woogie Bugle Boy of Company B"?); your fingers want to snap to it even without sound, and they're still singing when the camera draws back into the frothy gray blankness of a commercial.

The big surprise is next. Expecting to come immediately back to the show in progress, it takes you a moment to realize something strange is going on. The picture stays dark . . . the tape seems broken . . . and it's only gradually that it lightens again—an effect that, in its lifting from an enveloping blackness to a striated gray, perfectly mimics the coming of dawn. It's film, not true Kinescope, but the quality is excellent. What becomes visible is a statue alone in a field, or what seems to be a statue. As the camera dollies in closer, the statue walks slowly to the right and stands staring at a distant ridge, which, in this light, you can just barely make out. The camera comes around to shoot a medium-distance shot from the front, and you see it's McGowan, wearing a trench coat, his hands plunged deep in the pockets, and he's brooding, staring out through the cold morning grayness toward something the camera itself can't quite reach.

A battlefield—the realization comes a moment before the little identifying title up in the top right-hand corner of the screen. *GET-TYSBURG* it reads. *A Morning Essay by Alec McGowan.*

There's more light now. McGowan stoops, rubs his hand back and forth in the wet meadow grass, comes up holding a bullet, a minié ball. Like a flattened marble, it looks so harmless. The camera focuses in closer as he pockets it, talking easily, stopping now and then to point out a monument or to stoop down to read an inscription, but it's clear he's less interested in giving a tour of the battlefield than he is in using it as the starting point for a talk on war in general, what it does to a land, using the unspoiled perfection of this pastoral scene to make his points for him.

He visits town, pokes his pinky through a bullethole in an old wooden door, strolls through the cemetery where Lincoln made his speech. Devil's Den, Cemetery Ridge, Little Round Top. They're easy enough to identify—and then he's walking across the field where Pickett's men made their charge, angling toward a lonely clump of trees that have just taken on some sunshine, so their tops flare like matches above a landscape that is gray and lifeless and still.

Only one other person appears during all this, shot in tight close-up—an aged assemblage of wrinkles so deep and so convoluted they seem to furrow up the screen itself. A last surviving veteran? A boy from the village who remembers the day the soldiers came, the sound of cannon, young men crying for water, the scream of disemboweled horses? McGowan talks to him patiently, the old man smiling, proudly holding out his arm for McGowan to feel his muscle . . . and then the picture softens back and again we see McGowan walking alone toward that lonely scraggle of bare trees.

By the time he reaches it—by the time he crosses the field so many thousands of young boys couldn't cross—the sun is past the Round Tops and the little knoll glows with morning light. The camera swings around behind his shoulder and catches the sunrise proper—a clichéd shot, full of redemption, forgiveness, and renewal, and yet it works, it works beautifully. The camera backs slowly off and McGowan becomes small and smaller, still and stiller, a statue himself now, no different from the other stones that, this early in the morning, guard the battlefield alone.

Back to the studio. Chet and Alec sit at the desk beneath the clocks, which sweep toward the top of the hour. Chet, turning back from the monitor, reaches across to shake Alec's hand, then brings a finger up beneath his glasses to scratch—or is it to wipe away a tear? This is good television, there's nothing phony about it, and McGowan, genuinely moved himself, puts his arms around Chet's shoulder. Sitting next to each other, touching, you notice something that wasn't fully apparent before: these men aren't just pretend buddies, but old friends, comfortable and relaxed in each other's presence, forming a composite that is larger than either man alone—the strongest face that America, to meet morning, could possibly put on.

The camera moves in closer, on McGowan alone. He hesitates, peers out with curiosity and need, and then the right hand goes up from the elbow, palm outward, fingers touching, like a cop stopping traffic, a witness swearing an oath, a president at his inauguration, a chief at a pow-wow, eyes on the camera trying to see into the soul of whoever is watching, the simple word said a full beat after the hand goes up, said quietly so the viewer has to lean in to hear, perfectly readable through the motion of his lips alone . . . the unimpeachable hand, the soft voice, the eyes staring out through miraculously clear glasses, the single word that comes a pledge, a promise, a benediction, all wrapped up in a sound people remembered as so deep and solid it seemed to emanate from the upraised hand itself.

Truth, he mouths—and with that the first tape ends.

Eleven

The other parts come faster, as if the film, as if the reality the film is recording, is moving at an accelerating, ever more furious pace, leaving you less time to focus, consider, react—and this starts immediately with part two. The splice isn't perfect, not quite. It's meant to blend in seamlessly with the first part and thereby gain even more irony than it would have independently, but there's a bump where the original film skips, a hesitation where things go from mud-colored to sand-colored to silver.

It's taking place at night—this is the difference that comes first. A camera focuses out a large bay window, the kind that would front a mansion or castle, and outside the iron scrollwork you can see figures holding up hand-lettered signs. The film is of a lesser quality than the

Kinescope that came just before; it's grainy, blistered with little white bubbles and wiggly floaters, making it look as though what's being filmed is a boiling molecule of water, complete with its paramecia and amoebas. And it's in color, not black-and-white—a very primitive and faded color, as if the water has osmosed into everyone's clothes, washing them into the same purple dampness decorated by the occasional crimson spot.

A home movie—a movie shot just for fun. The camera focuses out the mullioned window where men and women in party clothes hold up signs scrawled in lipstick across outstretched white sheets. *Dullsville, Nebraska* reads the closest. *Ass Hole, Montana* reads another, and *Hix Ville, Tex.* The longest, the one in back, is held up by three people, like a Chinese dragon: *NONE OF YOUR BEESWAX WHERE I'M FROM DAMMIT!*

The men and women—young, summery-looking, beautiful—act drunk, mildly so, at the stage of a party where things start to get silly very fast. They jab their signs up and down, chant something in unison, make Nazi salutes, give the camera the finger, make like a conga line and snake away into the purple-red darkness, leaving the film to its amoebas and blisters.

The camera (hand-held, judging by the jerky way it swings about) pans back to film the interior of the room. It's crowded—the party is in full swing—and one of the guests who is immediately recognizable is Martin Slisco, dressed in an elegant linen suit, skinny in it, reedlike and saturnine, holding a 16mm camera that must be similiar to the one that's doing the filming: a leather box with a stubby lens and a windup dial. Between one scene and the next he disappears, after which the camera work becomes steadier, the pointing being done by someone who isn't drunk like the others, almost certainly Slisco himself.

A man in a cowboy hat sits behind an improvised desk made by turning a chair upside down onto another chair. Framed by the upturned legs, his head between them like a cartoon felon peering out through bars, he's doing a remarkably good imitation of newscaster Frank Stannard. He squints like Stannard, looks grave like Stannard, rustles through his notes like Stannard, and just before you think it *is* Stannard, he leers and spits tobacco juice directly toward the camera, which dodges back to keep from being hit.

Chet Standish comes on next. He acts drunk, more so than the others—he carries a fluted champagne glass and bobs his head down to sip like a pigeon on the rim of a birdbath. He's the only one there who isn't dressed formally but wears a Hawaiian shirt open to the navel, baggy shorts, black dress socks held up by garters. The other guests must be applauding—he curtsies in acknowledgment, then goes over to a wall where someone has hung a sheet with a crude outline of the United States. He proceeds to deliver the weather, pointing toward the Northwest and holding his arms in front of his chest, shivering, pointing down toward Arizona and fanning his hand across his face—*hot.* You can see what's going to happen a moment before it happens. He points to the Northeast, is about to say something, when from the edge of the frame someone throws a pitcher of beer that soaks him over the head. He smiles ruefully, stands there licking the inside of his arms as the suds roll down, then, facing the camera now, mouths very clearly the words *Over to you, Alec.*

The camera has to cut across a dozen faces before finding McGowan standing alone and forgotten in the darkest corner of the room. He's the only man there who seems at home in formal clothes, and yet he's sweating, his face glistening with it, burning with an inner restlessness that is all the more apparent from the fact he hardly moves at all. He takes no direct role in what follows—when the camera finds him it's always within touching distance of his corner—and yet he remains the central and dominant figure; all through the movie you can see the others glancing in his direction, checking his reaction to their hijinks, playing for his eyes more than for the camera. With the tuxedo, he resembles a circus ringmaster, one who has his cast so well trained he can do all his directing from the wings.

The focus swings across the room past the jutting *Heil Hitler* arms, the bodies poured into black sheath dresses, the sparkling red and blue sequins that adorn them, until it settles on the most boyish-looking of the girls, the one with a stylized curl licking down over her forehead like a sharp little tongue. Is she supposed to be a *Morning* girl? Someone hands her an alarm clock and a yellow cardboard sun. She drops them to the floor, closes her eyes, sways back and forth to some inner music, begins peeling off her long white gloves in a languid and very sexy striptease.

She's good at this, though nothing comes off except the gloves. The camera, disappointed, pans over to where an interview is in progress: a very serious-looking Chet sitting on a bar stool talking to someone covered in a long white sheet. But it's not a sheet, it's much plusher than a sheet, it's genuine Ku Klux Klan regalia, complete with narrow eye slits and a high conical hat. Chet is asking questions, nodding; the Klansman, as he answers, keeps reaching out from under his robe to pick his nose through a special slit. He's got a cross with him, fashioned of cardboard; when he has trouble lighting it with a match, Chet reaches into his own pocket and produces a lighter. This goes on for five minutes when suddenly a husky black man, solid as a linebacker, comes up behind the Klansman with his arms folded menacingly across his chest. Chet gulps, points—the Klansman turns, leaps up in fright, grabs his stool and rushes off in panic.

The camera pans across the room to get everyone's reaction. No one laughs or even smiles—no one looks as though they're having a good time. There are forced smiles, thin as ax blades. For a moment you see McGowan standing beside a fireplace with a phony-looking fire, holding a whiskey glass, bored, unamused, and the camera hurries back to the center of the room, hoping to find something worthy enough to entertain him.

Chet comes back on to seize the initiative. He arranges the girls in a chorus line facing the camera. He pats and positions them just so, making sure they're exactly the way he wants them. Over on the left stand the pretty younger girls; on the right, the more glamorous, harder-looking pros. The camera focuses in so all you see of them are medium close-ups, their torsos from waists to necks. The first girl peels her dress down over her bra, and then the second does similar, and then the third, and so on down the line—only this isn't enough, because the camera sweeps back again and each girl pushes down her bra in what seems an expanding ripple of pink-white heat.

A contest is under way and Chet Standish acts as emcee. He walks around behind the first torso, twists his head down into the frame so we see him smiling, then cups his hands under the first girl's breasts so they stand out as if mounted on a shelf. He holds them, jiggles them, judges their weight, looks up at the onlookers, asking for applause. He does this with one girl after the other, moving right down the line, stroking his hand over the smaller breasts to get the nipples erect, rubbing an admiring pinky along the larger of the aureoles, cupping his hands under the roundest ones, pulling his hand back like it's been burned when he grabs the pointiest nipples. When he comes at last to the largest pair, the ones that get the most applause, he steps around in front of whoever it is, reverentially kneels, and starts sucking greedily on the nipples.

The film quality changes in a scarlet flare that's temporarily blinding, then settles back into a sober, workaday black-and-white. From out of the breasts, as if its contours were nestled there for warmth and safekeeping, appears the skyline of Manhattan. The skyline of Manhattan, cantilevered back to vertical, gloriously jagged, unabashedly phallic, seen in the early morning light from one of the bridges to the east. The camera focuses westward as if commuting on the sun's rays in from Long Island—very slow past La Guardia, a little faster past the piers, descending over the East River, tunneling between buildings, so fast now that it smears the skyscrapers into a mercury color that makes the city seem molten. And then, just when you're caught up in the rush of it, falling, the focus stops and in the resulting clarity, walking three abreast in the center of an empty midtown street, are Chet Standish, Lee Palmer, Alec McGowan, their arms linked, so the first, the inevitable comparison is to Dorothy, the Cowardly Lion, and the Tin Man waltzing down the Yellow Brick Road toward Oz.

They obviously know this—for a second they swing their legs back and forth in unison (*We . . . 're off to see the Wizard!*) and manage a teasing kind of skip. They're on their way to work, this is the premise, and the camera follows them as they cross Forty-ninth Street, enter the network building through its revolving glass door, brush past the assorted ushers and script people hurrying to meet them, take their coats off, put their briefcases down, and, smiling and laughing, disappear through the plush padded doors of studio 8-H.

MORNING reads the caption that scrolls across the screen; the letters begin as horizontal stick figures that struggle valiantly, as an alarm clock goes off next to them, to reach the vertical, yawning and stretching themselves into position to spell the word out. There is no window on Forty-ninth Street this time, no hometown signs, no opening monologue, no clocks from five different cities, no "America Wakes Up," no regulars wandering in off the street, just the three of them sitting there at a long desk in front of a backdrop that in its spic-and-span whiteness, its coy suggestion of decoration, could be a kitchen, an office, or a bedroom.

The three of them smile at the camera, act reluctant to break off their conversation, but at the same time seem happy to get to work. Lee is the one you focus on first—the other two, perhaps because of the party footage spliced onto the beginning, seem vaguely sleepy, mildly hungover, creatures of the night who aren't fully there yet. Lee, by comparison, seems fresh, alert, energetic, exactly the person morning would designate as its spokesman if morning could talk.

This must be 1954 (no date appears), the early spring. Lee had written her famous letter to Alec that winter, breaking the silence of twelve long years, asking, in so many words, for a job—the letter that led to Alec's last and brightest inspiration. Once she moved to New York—divorced now, free, determined to succeed—he had worked her in gradually, letting her do an interview here, a feature there, until they were both confident she could handle the pressure of being on air full time. Here there are few traces of awkwardness—it's as if she's born to be there, a round peg in a round hole, the vital feminine link that had been missing for so long. Once or twice she forgets where the camera is, but this only adds a spontaneous flavor, as if she's content to let the camera find *her*.

She's the same Lee Palmer as seen in the radio station photos, and yet different in a hard-to-define way (the motion? the live quality? the confidence?) that involves more than her looks. She isn't drop-dead gorgeous like the other *Morning* girls, the failed ones, the ones the camera never quite believed in. Her hair is still curly and short, but instead of the tomboy quality she had when younger it suggests a defiant, going-her-own-way kind of independence that is more mature—as does the suit she wears, the trim jacket, the businesslike skirt. Her smile is still wide, a farmgirl's, someone who's used to laughing (no, who *remembers* laughing, is enjoying being able to laugh once again), and her face has broadened just enough to dampen the prominence of her high cheekbones. Her skin has gone from flawless to textured—watching her, you feel compelled to move toward the screen and touch it, and it takes a real act of will not to try. She's attractive in the way many women aspire to be—not unreachably so, not a movie star, but something they might approach themselves in their very best moments before the mirror. This partially accounts for her enormous popularity with female viewers right from the start, whereas all the other *Morning* girls, the overdressed, over-lipsticked mediocrities, had been the kind of women other women love to hate.

Her manner backs this up. She's sitting there talking with the men without deference, as an equal—as more than their equal, the center of interest, and they know this, defer to her, all this being evident even without sound. She's big sister and little sister in alternate flashes, sophisticated one moment, homey the next, smart, but not too smart, a cheerleader who isn't snobby but a pal to everyone in class, telegenic in a way that defines the term—someone who is likable in the very first second the camera catches her face. This is the foundation, the blend—and topping it off is just the right note of wistfulness, as if the breeze that had once ornamented her face has moved off now, leaving her just the slightest trace weathered, saddened, deepened, a woman who isn't out ahead of her destiny anymore, but the slightest trace behind.

It's hard to take your eyes off her, bring them to the stolid book-ends formed by the two men. When you do there are surprises. Across Chet's open, friendly-priest's face is a look that at first seems nothing stronger than puppy-like devotion; he stares over at Lee and can't bring himself to turn away, even when, judging by the way his lips move, it's time to address the camera directly. With (you imagine) directors gesticulating wildly off-camera, trying to turn him back, he simply can't take his eyes off her, not for a second. The convention here is that he chats with her and with Alec and now and then remembers to include the viewer in the conversation by turning to face the camera, but the convention is no longer strong enough to hold him. What does hold him is a wholehearted, passionate, desperate kind of emotion, the force of which is scrawled across his Rotarian kisser like he's pantomiming pathos, and pantomiming it perfectly. It's not brotherly affection this time, nothing protective or sheltering. He's in love with the woman he stares at. In love. On live TV with millions watching he's caught being in love.

A shock, a real one, and then the camera, faced with his stubbornness, glides across the desk to focus on Alec. His appearance has changed since the first tape; he wears a striped regimental necktie, not a bow tie—his glasses are thinner, lighter, less square, and above them his hair sweeps down across his forehead in a stylish wave that makes him seem, not ten years younger, but like a man trying to *appear* ten years younger. It's as if he senses the viewer's restlessness, is trying to disarm it, stay three steps ahead. When he looks over at Lee it's all very natural, and the only emotion on his face beside the good-natured camaraderie the scene calls for is an obvious pride that his protégée should be comporting herself so well . . . and maybe a trace of something more complex that is harder to read. He moves his lips in a slow, very precise way, as if he's lost faith in their ability to form the words he's searching for; he blinks and blinks fast, the man who was famous for never blinking. Stunned might be the best word to describe this— not stunned in a bovine sense, but stunned like a man who's been surprised to the core of his being and hasn't decided yet whether this is for good or for evil.

Back in three, he mouths. Where his face has been comes the frothy gray doughnut ring of the commercials.

Frank Stannard reads the news, looking more like a granite monument than ever. Negro demonstrators march outside a concrete building surrounded by police dogs. A rocket sits on a launch pad, then falls slowly to the side. President Eisenhower wearing pajamas lines up a putt. This is followed by Chet doing the weather. There's a new map, a fancier one, with electronic lights that blink on as his hand sweeps across the states. He spends no more than thirty seconds over this, then reaches into his jacket's inside pocket, takes a letter out, begins to read, putting the stationery so close to his eyes it covers his chin like a bandanna. Finishing, he reaches out of the camera frame and pulls back a gift-wrapped package, which he unwraps with great care. Inside is a beanie with a propellor on the top—*Kalamazoo* it reads across the front. He smiles with effort, puts it on, twirls the propellor to get it going—and all the while he does this, keeps stealing glances offscreen to his left at someone who remains invisible.

Lee is up next, interviewing a bigshot, a man in his sixties wearing an expensive suit crossed by a watch fob and with an expression that manages to exude goodwill and slyness at the same time, like a child molester disguised as a pediatrician. John Foster Dulles, Eisenhower's secretary of state—the face looks peeled from a history book, juiced with electricity so it twitches. He's talking slowly, earnestly; he leans forward with his baggy hands between his legs, making his expression go folksy. Lee is still smiling, still engaging, but you can tell from the unflinching way she stares that she wants answers, not bullshit, and if Dulles can't read that then Dulles must be blind.

A demonstration follows, one of *Morning*'s never-ending attempts to show Americans how to work their new toys. It's air conditioning this time. The man doing the demonstrating wears a white lab coat and has the kind of mad-scientist look that pitchmen of the day favored. He has a whole bank of machines set up in a mock wall, streamers pinned to their grilles, along with a huge thermometer he wheels over to where the jets converge. The mercury plunges, of course, but too abruptly, making it seem someone is hidden in the bulb pulling a string. What's new is that Alec McGowan handles all this himself, or at least

summons up enough energy to stand there watching while the pitchman dances his little dance. He looks bemused, nothing worse—he
sleepwalks through the first few minutes. The pitchman tries valiantly
to get him to stand in front of the jet stream; the pitchman himself
stands there, wraps his arms around himself and suggestively shiv-
ers—but he must be saying the wrong thing, because McGowan suddenly wheels around and says something out of the side of his mouth
that makes the pitchman gasp. He'd become notorious for that—using
sarcasm to put imbeciles in their place, a dangerous game, but here it's
something instinctive and angry and over with quickly.

Lee Palmer is back after the break (double the last one, the demure
blur hiding God knows how many ads) with an actors' roundtable.
The camera dollies back to reveal, sitting around her in canvas-backed
director's chairs, the stars of *On the Waterfront*. They're easy to pick out,
even with all the years intervening. Karl Malden looking serious and
intense, hands clasped before him like he's praying. Rod Steiger leaning back like a riverboat gambler, a cigarette loose between his fingers,
his eyes half-closed. Eva Marie Saint, looking ethereal in a simple
white dress. A short, nervous Elia Kazan sitting a bit off to one side,
smoking, the cloud from his cigarette finding the smoke from Steiger's.
They talk animatedly, without prompting—all Lee has to do is break in
when it's time for a film clip. There's the scene with Marlon Brando
and the pigeons on the tenement roof, when Eva Marie Saint realizes
there's a tender side to him and they fall in love; there's the brutal beating Brando gets as he tries to organize the longshoremen, the famous
stagger as he weaves his way across the docks to lead them back to
work. It's good television, and Lee, surrounded by all that talent, blinking in a girlish, gee-whiz way that seems totally genuine (yet making
sure no one actor hogs the limelight), more than holds her own. *We'll
take a break here,* her lips say, and with that she seems to take control of
the program's entire flow.

Commercials—and then a marching band, a high school band.
They can barely fit on the set, and the ones on the edges have to
wedge shoulders in order to cram in. They all act terrified, but that dis-

appears once they pick up their instruments and begin playing. So much gusto goes into this, such a great swinging of horns and flailing of drums, it seems strange it can't be translated into actual sound— the camera jumps back from what must be an overpowering blast. Halfway through the number, three baton twirlers prance out and start twirling—and right behind them comes Chet Standish, wearing his beanie with the propellor, twirling a baton himself. It goes well at first, he manages to do it, but then, following the girls, he decides to throw the baton in the air and catch it on its way down. He tosses it up, loses sight of it in the lights, ducks, but too late—it hits him right smack in the middle of the forehead. Behind him all the kids start laughing, but you can see it really hurts. Chet blinks, blinks as if he's crying, reaches blindly for the baton lost on the floor, says something that can't be made out, turns, bows toward the band members, and points them offstage.

Lee comes back for an exercise feature, with an improbably muscled man in a leopard-skin bodysuit going through some stretching exercises. The man seems to be having fun doing all this; he doesn't breathe hard, and midway through his push-ups he begins doing them one-handed. Lee, dressed in a plain gray sweatsuit, keeps up as best she can with the exercises. Her figure isn't as perfect as her face, seems average in bust, waist, and hips, but this only makes her appeal greater, emphasizing the everywoman quality. The exercise man is patting her on the back in encouragement, lying down to start another exercise, when Chet Standish appears from the right. This must be unscripted—both the exercise man and Lee seem startled, not sure what to make of him. Chet mugs, raises his hands above his head like a prizefighter entering the ring, gets down on his hands and knees (his suit jacket flopping over his legs) and begins to do push-ups, showing off. But he can't do them, his stomach goes down independently of his shoulders, and instead of making a joke of it, he tries again, this time just managing to squeeze one off—and then immediately glances up at Lee looking for her approval.

Commercials, the blank frothy grayness dancing with so much agitation you feel that an actual picture must surely blink forth, but it never does, not until the break is over. Chet, Lee, and Alec sit behind the desk where the show began. If it's easy to read Chet's lips, it's even easier to read his expression. It seems defiant, hurt, resentful, so your first reaction is that the man must be drunk. He sucks in his cheeks the way a fat man sucks in his stomach, trying to make himself hard; he glances over toward McGowan's direction, grimaces, then tightens his eyes into an actual scowl. What's ludicrous is that a tuft of hair sticks up from the back of his head like a feather, and Lee, catching sight of it, smiles and reaches to stroke it gently back down. This soothes him enough that he remembers where he is, what he's supposed to say. *Be happy,* he mouths, looking right into the camera. Lee nods, smiles, very much the mother here, the one in charge. *Be good,* she mouths, then looks expectantly to her left.

It's Alec's turn—Alec who by this point you've forgotten is even on the show. Marginalized, shunted to the wings, he at least has the camera at the finish and seems determined to make the most of it. He stares out like the McGowan of old, trying to see clear—you notice, watching him, that there was more sinew, more toughness, more tension in his face than you ever realized, and you only realize this because now it seems gone.

He says a few words, then pauses, so you expect that hand to go up—expect to see that hand upraised from the elbow palm outwards fingers together, the famous gesture, the famous slogan. But this is not what happens. Yes, the hand seems perceptibly to lift from its position on the desk, but then another hand reaches in from just off the frame, a womanly, affectionate hand, one that comes down taking his hand with it—a gesture so instinctive, so real, so tender, it can only be impelled by an emotion much deeper than the camera can ever understand.

It seems to soften him, just there at the end. He looks away from the camera, keeps his hand down under Lee's, turns back to squint at a camera that suddenly seems very distant. *Be safe,* he mouths. Nothing more.

The picture, in a reflexive spasm, starts to roll horizontally while at the same time the focus blurs on McGowan's face, stretching his features until their rubbery mask fills the screen, blending into a blackness crossed by skipping white lines. The skipping gradually slows, and where the gray faded away into the edges of the screen in little rivulets, gray now returns, coming in from the corners and finding other rivulets like a tide running up a darkened beach.

The rolling stops. The picture takes on a reddish tinge and arranges itself into a rectangle that flashes like a mirror, though it takes another second to understand why. It's a pair of eyeglasses seen in close-up— glasses in still life that seem placed on a man's toupee, so what is visible beneath the lenses is a tight and very coarse black hair. A joke of some sort, like Groucho Marx glasses over a fleshy nose, but it's hard to get the point. The camera moves in toward a vague suggestion of fleshy lips, only they're sideways, askew, and it's one beat more before the joke comes into focus—that you realize the hair is pubic, the whiteness on the sides the plump flesh of a woman's thighs holding apart the earpieces, that what is directly underneath the eyeglass lenses is a woman's vagina.

The camera pulls back, takes in more. The woman becomes visible, lying on her back with cushions under her shoulders, peering down through her breasts, which she holds apart to watch herself being filmed. She widens her legs inviting the camera in closer; her long nail-polished fingers come down and remove the glasses so there is no barrier left at all. But before the camera can get there, a man steps between her legs, hiding everything with his flapping suit jacket, so the effect is oddly demure, as if a curtain has been pulled down at the climactic moment.

A party again, a party in progress, and what strikes hardest is the beautiful, professional quality of the film. The color is excellent, equal to any used today, with erotic reds and misty blues and silky blacks. The walls are hung with satin sheets that billow outward (is there a fan?) as if to suggest a sultan's tent; there are candles set on little tables, and their creamy light gives a lambent quality to the entire room, making it seem as if everything, bodies, lounge chairs, sofas, sway to a rhythm that can't quite be heard.

Guests mill around. Some of the men wear suits and ties like they have just arrived from work; others are already down to their jockey shorts. The girls are several stages ahead of them; they're the hard ones from last time, the professionals, and they're wearing work clothes, garter belts and push-up bras and transparent panties and stiletto heels. They go over and select men to be their partners, like a kind of Sadie Hawkins dance where the men are the chaste virgins, the women in total control.

The fucking begins. A man holds a girl up to his waist as she clutches him with her legs. A girl sucks another girl, while a third kneels down to use her hand. Twins, women who look like twins, take turns licking a man's cock. A photographer goes around taking snapshots where the bodies lie thickest. It's not as phony and mechanical as a stag film would be, but it's not spontaneous fun and games either. The camera keeps up a methodical, businesslike sweep—panning to find buttocks or breasts, lingering for a second, zooming in for a closeup, then drawing back to resume working the room. What's odd is that there's an air of expectancy and build-up to all this, not climax—people keep looking up no matter how involved they are, as if they're waiting for someone, and the camera itself keeps swerving over toward the satin curtain, expecting it to lift.

McGowan is invisible, at first, and then suddenly there he is, the one person still dressed, standing a bit to the side looking on with an expression of dreamy benevolence. Is he high on codeine? Drunk? The sharpness in his eyes is gone; he stands there in a white linen suit and a kind of planter's hat that makes him look like he's in costume. For all the grappling, the twisting, the humping, the others remain very aware of his presence—all this seems an elaborate demonstration staged for his delectation alone. Two of the youngest girls, catching sight of him, push away their partners, come over to start pulling on his clothes—one, the more inventive, nestles her face against his pants and uses her teeth on his zipper—but he brushes them away and resumes watching alone. As central as he is, he's not the one everyone is waiting for—the backward glances continue, even with him there.

When exactly is all this taking place? Before Lee Palmer reentered his life or after? There are no clues as regards date or chronology, and five minutes of watching makes the fucking itself seem dated and old. You expect to see bodies that are different, of another era and style, and the usual fleshy patterns seem unimaginative and plain. What's more, the participants seem bored, too, so they're all concerned to increase the shock. A man takes a hypodermic needle and punctures a girl's outstretched arm. A blonde takes a condom and snaps it up and down like a yo-yo. Martin Slisco appears in the pathos of a long shot—thin, pale, old-looking, as if he's journeyed there from the present, his penis weak-veined, cold-looking, just barely rigid. He sits in a canvas and steel lounge chair with a girl on the arm—the girl is crying, struggling to get up, but he holds a toy knife to her throat and won't let her go. A mock commercial takes place, a woman's hand wedged inside a blender, a man plugging it in by sticking the plug between his buttocks, only this isn't funny enough, because two other men come over, take the woman by the shoulders, heave her against the wall, grab her arm and jam her hand in even harder, bending low with the cord to plug it into the nearest outlet.

The picture spasms, shudders—the focus blurs across the carpet as if the camera has fallen, spent, to the ground. When it clears again you're looking at the satiny curtain blowing outward under the fan. A spotlight flares creating a bright red circle; in the center of the circle the curtain suddenly parts. A pretty, dark-skinned girl comes out—she can't be more than eighteen—dressed like an Indian, with a war bonnet and a tom-tom and an orange loincloth. She beats on the tom-tom with a stick, crouches, turns to stare back toward the curtain. People have left off fucking now. They come around the side of the curtain and begin clapping their hands in rhythm to the girl's drum.

The curtain parts. Edging into the spotlight is an enormous ape, with curly brown fur, a black leathery chest, a thick rubber face. He comes out backwards, coyly, and then suddenly jumps around, revealing the huge dildo strapped to his waist. Everyone applauds, wildly, and the ape makes a little bow in acknowledgment (the tip of the dildo bending against the floor), then beats his fists triumphantly on his chest.

You can see McGowan off to the side, smiling with the others, though he doesn't applaud. The camera seems to be waiting for him to make some sign, and there it is—the briefest nod. With that, four of the girls run over and throw themselves down beside the ape's legs, grabbing him, fighting each other to kiss him first. The ape leans his head back and roars in ecstasy, shaking his bottom back and forth as the girls work him hard. He fakes ejaculation, falls to the floor in a swoon. Instantly, he's back on his feet, this time dancing with the little Indian girl, his hands under her arms. Faster and faster they dance, until it's too much for the girl and she falls away, dizzy, leaving the ape to dance on wildly by himself, holding his arms above his head like a ballerina, then snapping them rigidly back down like he's dancing a flamenco, spinning around again, even faster now, until he twists so violently, the top third of his costume—the shoulders, mask, and face—comes unscrewed and goes flying off to the side, revealing the man underneath.

It's Chet of course. It's Chet, and the only surprise is the startled way he blinks at the light, as if he's convinced he is an ape, is shocked to learn he isn't. But the look doesn't last long. In a moment, the applause continuing, he seems nothing more than a rather ordinary man who is happy at being drunk, happy at being sweaty, satisfied with his performance, ridiculously happy, even proud.

The camera watches him too long and he seems to know it. He makes a sudden waving motion with his hand, snaps his head down, vomits all over his fur. His head jerks in reflex and he vomits again, and this time the camera isn't fast enough to pull back—thick bits of fluid splatter over the lens. The guests fall back in disgust, and the only one who doesn't is McGowan—McGowan who steps into the frame and takes Chet by the shoulders, shakes him, seems to be asking if he's all right. Chet grabs him in turn, lets his head fall on his broad shoulder, so for a moment the two men waltz. The girls who were suck-ing the dildo, seeing their chance, now start tugging on McGowan's clothes, and this time he doesn't resist. Once they have his jacket off they start on his shirt, and when that's off they start pulling on his belt, tugging down his zipper, pulling down his pants. Slowly, wearily, he turns so his back is to the camera and then, as his pants and under-pants come off, leans over and thrusts his buttocks out backwards directly toward the lens, filling the frame with a white, doughy color that seems as harmless, as innocent, as bread.

The tape freezes on this—for a full minute there is nothing on the screen but his motionless moon—and then this too disappears into a watery blackness. The tape, finishing, makes a sound that is part plastic sucking, part plastic purr, and jumps out of the slot it was pushed into three hours before. In the quiet, in the darkness, I walk over to the television, make the little curtsy the height of the set requires in turn-ing it off, place my hand against the screen, spread my fingers out so my palm flattens and I can feel the afterglow of warmth that, in ebbing increments as I press it, turns into the glassy equivalent of dust.

Part Five

STAINED GLASS

Twelve

I had my biography now, illustrated, juiced with motion—as much story as I would ever have unless Chet relented and spilled the beans. If I was going to make a try at finishing, it would have to be with what I had, basing it partly on hunch, partly on evidence, leavening it with the empathy I felt for the man, whatever understanding I'd managed in my stumbly way to seize. And just because I'd been forced to reach so hard for this understanding, I felt a new confidence in what was there, realized the time had come to risk staking out my ending—to imagine Alec McGowan a few days before his final show, alone in the room just off studio 8-H that served as his dressing room, office, hermitage, and cave, the last morning of June 1954.

No one is allowed there without his permission—a permission he never gives. Even Lee had been hurt when, after the first show, flushed with her success, she had followed him back and he mumbled some excuse at the door, turned and quickly kissed her, then disappeared inside. For ninety minutes he was watched by 23 million people, and for the next thirty minutes he needed to be watched by no one. He tried explaining this to her—she had listened, confused—but now it was her turn to be stared at, analyzed, and critiqued, and she knew all about that herself.

The room is filled with unread newspapers, a typewriter covered in black carbon paper and yellow foolscap, a record player, a hot plate with naked wiring, an antique rolltop desk with memos speared to its wood on the nibs of fountain pens used just for this purpose. In the early days he had kept his office bare and spartan, as if to prove he was doing the show on inspiration alone, but things have changed since then; it's so crowded he has to make a sideways motion to get past the door, and there's only one spot, there in the center of the room under its one weak light fixture, where he can find enough space to perform the little ceremony that in the course of the last twelve months had become his habit.

He stands there and brings his feet together, closes his eyes, lifts both arms until they stretch parallel to his shoulders and he can feel the heavy tension in his armpits. Like a plane coming in for a landing, he makes a dipping, gliding motion, cranes his head back, laughs out loud. Yes, it's like flying, he's defeated the physical laws that govern everyone else, done it exuberantly, at full throttle, for ninety minutes of flight, though what he feels during the show is even more exhilarating than flight, it's like walking a tightrope over a shadowy chasm, his talent so real and palpable and instinctive it's buoyed up by the danger, not sucked down. And yet that never lasts a second longer than the program does, the feeling of balance. He stretches his arms out, not to fly anymore, but only to stay on the tightrope, the rope growing thinner and more frayed with each moment, the chasm deeper, his feet having to frantically dance merely to remain where he is—dancing on tiptoes, dancing madly, though his feet move not an inch.

He has to let himself back down onto gravity's shoulder, but he has to do this gently or he will fall into the chasm, crumple upon impact, shatter into so many thousands of shards that all the network's horses and all the network's men could never reassemble him. He's cut back on the sarsaparilla, takes less each morning, and yet the soaring sensation has only gotten more intense, as if it has nothing to do with sarsaparilla, the fuel coming from something stronger, more potent, older. He can stand the headaches, the nausea, the dizziness, and yet there's a new feeling it's harder to withstand, not just that gravity is sucking him down, but that it's jumping gleefully on his sternum, pressing his shoulders into the ground, pounding on them with a mallet. Always before, if he waited long enough he would touch bottom and be done with it and begin the struggle back up, but now there is no bottom— no bottom, just at the moment in his life when it's more important than ever to prove to himself he can stop falling any moment he chooses.

He brings his hands down to his sides, crosses them over his groin, feels his left pulse with his right hand, brings the same hand up and places it over his heart, checking the rhythm. Too fast, and yet in a moment it will be too slow, and so he keeps his fist pressed there to stop it right in the middle. To prove to himself he can stop—that's the challenge for him now. The night was easy, he wouldn't bother with night much longer, had already cut back hard on the partying. Always before, he had felt the need to keep one cynical step ahead of the network's own cynicism, give his mordancy its head, prove he could plunge into blackness and reemerge into daylight without any aftereffect at all. All those millions who woke up to watch him thought morning was easy, something that required no more effort than opening your eyes, and yet he knew morning was something you fought toward, paid for, achieved—that was what drove him, what the sarsaparilla, the girls, the wildness supplied.

But he'd take less, much less—he'd quit entirely, and quit soon. It's stupid of him, he doesn't need that anymore. He has his nights with Lee, and it isn't like night at all, not the struggle he was used to, but something that brings peace and solace and fullness, and from that kind of night it should be easy to roll unscathed into morning, without experiencing the terrible leadenness he suffers now. Thirty minutes since the show finished and he feels worse, not better—he's already planning what excuses he will make when noon comes and he cancels his first appointment. He needs to change that, adjust his calibrations. It takes ninety minutes to come down now, not thirty; every minute of exhilaration has to be paid for with a minute of despair.

He uses various tricks to try and steady himself. One has to do with letters. Each day the network is flooded with them, a thousand on slow mornings, eighteen thousand on busy ones, three or four thousand on average. When the program first started, the numbers were much smaller and he would try to answer them all with a handwritten note, and then came a time when he at least tried to read them before handing them over to a secretary, and now that had become too much for him, too, even to glance at them, and yet he still insisted the mail be brought into his office each day, three rolling hampers full, four hampers, five. He would keep them there a week, until the room was filled, every space taken, and the air took on a sweet papery aroma of arsenic, lilac, and ash.

He knows what they contain now, he doesn't have to read them. There are requests for money or promises of money or questions about money, letters asking for advice about love, asking for love, pleading for love . . . *I just lost my wife, my husband doesn't understand me, I see in you a fellow spirit, I'm so lonely I'm losing my mind, I can't find anyone worth cherishing, if you're ever in Sacramento or Milwaukee or Greensboro or South Bend* . . . demands to be allowed on the program, promises to reveal secrets, prove theories, solve problems, right wrongs . . . letters berating him for saying something or not saying something or attacking this or praising that . . . letters that weigh him down with despair, though many are from people who love the program, understand what he's trying to do, tell him how much it means to them, encourage him to go on. Sometimes he dreamed about bringing in a set of huge industrial scales, divvying up the happy and sad letters, weighing them in separate piles, letting the scales decide which is the larger force in the world—and yet he knows he doesn't have to, that the happy far outweigh the sad, and the only conundrum worth thinking about is why, if this is so, the overall weight of the letters still saddens him to the point of actual tears, drives him with gravity back toward the ground.

He looks at the overflowing hampers, the rectangles and squares jumbled in star-shaped overlaps, the postcards folded over the edges like pie crust, the whiteness giving him the sense of a great continental swirl of motion, at the center of which is this room. At times he would dip his arms into the hampers up to the elbows, pluck out handfuls, deal them out like cards across his desk, taking a childish pleasure in the different envelopes, the delicate stamps honoring genuine heroes, the purple postmarks with the small-town names he loved saying out loud, Bird-in-Hand, Tugaloo, Smackover, Cape Fear . . . He would even go further sometimes, would take the letters out and rub them over the bare skin of his wrist, enjoying the feel of the stationery, the tickle of soft pink notepaper, the manila stock that was heavy and scratchy, the postcards with their smooth, cool facings.

Intoxicating, and yet dangerous, bringing him too high again, tempting him to stay there by taking another, even larger dose. The muscles along the top of his shoulders ache, his armpits feel cold, his head pounds right back from the temples. As it peaks, as it becomes intolerable, he stumbles over to his dressing table to find some aspirin.

He stands there, looking down at the bottle, feeling dullness in its thickest, most viscous form—it's as if the light, the very rays of it, comes to his eyes slathered in butter. So it takes longer than it should to notice something he should have seen before. On the mirror in front of him, the mirror he doesn't care much to look at anymore, are letters scrawled in lipstick so they cover every inch. He stares at them without seeing, looks back at the aspirin, takes a step backward, and, holding his head between his hands to steady it, tries looking at the mirror again.

YOU VILE MALEVOLENT LECHER

YOU CONTEMPTIBLE PIECE OF WORM SHIT

KEEP YOUR BESTIAL HANDS OFF HER

And it's funny, but as big as the letters are, as real and palpable their hatred, he can picture Chet Standish squatting with his face pressed close to the mirror, squinting, trying with great pains to fit the letters in, like a Japanese artist brushing in venom with the most delicate of strokes. Had he snuck in during a commercial? Other than this, there was no sign of his having been there at all.

It tips him back again, just when he thought the looping roller coaster had stalled safe at the top. He paces along the narrow alley left in the center of the room, glances up at the wall clock. Eleven, which means one hour until his first appointment, which means one hour to pull himself back together, whip himself into shape. He has another trick he uses when the first trick has lost its power—a better trick, one that, if he plays it correctly, has an astringent quality, like aftershave splashed over his face, bracing him, sharpening his acuity to the point where he can cope. He sits in the leather armchair that fronts his desk, drapes a towel around his aching shoulders, leans his head back, closes his eyes . . . closes his eyes and tries remembering all the executives who had been there during his own tenure, what their names were, what they looked like, what kind of agony they had caused him, how long they had lasted before being let go. It's a long list, it takes a real, puzzle-like effort to pull the names back—the vice-presidents in charge of programming, the vice-presidents in charge of sales, the vice-presidents in charge of the news division or the entertainment division or whatever division had the job of reining him in.

There was Donald Lattimore, who enjoyed telling him he wouldn't last a week—Donald Lattimore, who walked slumped like a man without a backbone, a miracle of spinelessness, a man of mush. Armel Phillopson, who wanted the show to include on-air bingo games, prizes, jackpots, and who later became the mortuary king of Arizona. Harold Thoringer, who insisted they include horses on the program, swore by horses, had horses on the brain. Todd Lean, who crapped in his pants once, stood there looking at a ratings sheet and crapped in his pants. Tony Creager, who always got up in meetings to talk about the importance of "boobs, fannies, blondes." And Boice, Andrew F. Boice, who liked screaming at underlings, actually took vocal lessons to increase his stamina, and who went to the hospital once when one of Thoringer's horses, sensing a phony, kicked him in the balls. Patrick Grisson with his lisp, his hungry furtive look, the way he would steal food when no one was watching, leftovers from the cooking demos, wrapping them in his handkerchief and having them for lunch. Jerome Pardy, who couldn't finish a sentence without the phrase "cost per thousand" in it, and who would have gladly recrucified Christ if the General had asked. Shep Williams, who wanted the show to origi- nate from Hollywood, wanted the news eliminated, loved dogs like Thoringer loved horses, always insisting what they needed on the pro- gram was a "resident pooch." Jason Hoving, who favored wing-tip shoes and plush serge trousers—a man who liked saying of television that it was "the bland leading the blind."

They're marching past, strutting their little struts, trotting out their pet phrases, taking their best shots at him, ranting, raving, falling by the wayside, dropping away. But something is wrong now, there at the end of the parade, where the laggards marched. Usually he was able to picture them entering a prisoner-of-war camp, a German stalag, each and every vice-president holding their hands in the air begging to be a stoolie, a collaborator, a Quisling—picture them with their arms upraised, going over to kiss the naked ass of the German comman- dant. And yes, he has them there, takes pleasure in picturing them beg- ging, only the parade isn't over, there's one straggler left who swerves away from the barbed wire and keeps sauntering alone toward the horizon: Walker Halford, tall, banker-like, silky, with a habitual smirk that came more from his forehead than it did from his mouth. He was famous at the network for being the one vice-president who had ever quit of his own volition instead of being fired; one rumor said he had gone to Wall Street, where the real money was, another that he'd chucked everything and moved to Maine to raise poultry. McGowan had gotten along fairly well with him, Halford pretty much leaving him alone, but there was a dispute once about the book-review segment, a programming director named Firsten who was giving him hell because the ratings showed a pronounced dip whenever a serious author came on.

They'd argued back and forth. McGowan digging in his heels, Firsten blustering and threatening, Halford standing a bit to the side, his forehead bunched in that ironic smirk. Did he do it with his forehead in order to stand apart from the implications, have it both ways, compliance in the mouth, chin, and lips, arrogance up higher? It was a good trick, and McGowan admired him for it, only this time Halford hadn't backed him up.

"No more literature shit," he said, after the other two men had their say. Then, as McGowan looked over at him, pained, he shrugged his shoulders, came out with it. "The numbers, Alec," he said, spreading apart his fingers. "You'll have to accept it, and you may as well accept it right now. There's only one principle in television that is ever applicable. One is in all circumstances better than zero, and two is in all circumstances better than one, and three is in all circumstances better than two, and that's the only truth worth talking about here, everything else is the merest vanity. You'd be stupid, criminally stupid, to butt your head against that."

Is that why Halford is marching back now, to dispute that point again? McGowan had spent a lot of time since then finding arguments to rebut him. Okay, maybe one was better than zero if you looked at it his way, but zero had certain qualities you couldn't belittle, being round and simple and innocent, though, if pressed, he would grant him that one was better than nothing when it came to getting your point across. One was a start. One was a good start, because you couldn't convince two unless you convinced one; otherwise there'd be nothing to get the numbers rolling, they would be stalled at zero forever. One—that was the hard digit, the big step, and there were legions of people who, when it came to convincing, never managed to get that far at all. But was two intrinsically better? One was solitary, alone, unsupported, somewhat icy, but two was a partnership, two was multiple, got dialogue started, so he could understand the argument that it was better in certain respects than one. Not always, of course. Sometimes. And three was community—three you got conversation going, disputation, give and take. With three you could have three disciples, three believers, three converts, and if they each went out and found three more you were up to nine and then eighty-one and then up into the thousands before you even broke a sweat. But who was to say this was good, or even necessary? You could spend your life appealing to one and make of that life something real and serious and daring, and maybe because it was real and serious and daring you shouldn't expect much more than one.

For if you went further, bought into Halford's logic, then where did it stop? Okay, nine was better than three, and ninety was better than thirty, and 900 topped 300, and 9,000 had 3,000 beat solid, and sixty million was better than any of them, the best number, the number that radiated the most beauty, the one that corresponded to the number of television sets in the land. And yet a beauty like the sun's, impossible to stare at, blinding, impossible to achieve—if by some miracle you managed to draw close to it, nothing would happen except you would burn. How come they didn't see that, the Halfords so hungry for more? Well, sure, they could all march toward the sun, be incinerated together, the innocent zeros turned into obedient slaves marching in lockstep behind the fat imperial six with its whip, but why did they have to insist the only way to get there was to pile number on top of number in a huge digital pyramid that was mounted in quicksand wrong side up? He could ride the number one if he had to, light a fuse on its bottom, soar toward the heavens free of all that ponderous weight. One was better than zero and two was better than one and three was better than two and because of that notion vice-presidents screamed at him and advertising directors screamed double, and whatever he did wasn't good enough, there was always a better number just over the horizon they had to race toward and yet somehow they never managed to grasp it, and all it left in him, even when he pursued it hardest, joined in the chase, was an overwhelming longing to flee from these sordid increments back to the scoured, self-sufficient purity of one.

Not that he disdains Halford's philosophy entirely—Halford strutting off in the distance past the POW camp, making a tsk-tsk motion with his ass. Yes, it might be one you were after, and to reach that one you might have to strain sixty million through the filter. But if they wanted more millions they could listen to him for a change, not fight him at every step. He could picture a show where all the celebrities and politicians and pitchmen were chucked overboard, the airwaves given back to real people, people who would come on the show and tell their own stories, without any shaping or editing or intervention. You could visit them at work or at home, go to beaches and find them there, or parks, or hospitals—the camera would always be moving, never in the same part of the country longer than a morning, always restless, always hungry, and yet when it found someone special, someone whose story made you weep or laugh or marvel, it would settle on them, take its time, let the story come out at its own pace, without the noose of brevity, this terrible choking. Okay, three was better than two, and sixty million was better than thirty million, and if he was given his way they could have their sixty million, they could reach their goddam sun on the back of their goddam pyramid—and somewhere in that sixty million would be the one he was after, and so everyone would be happy, art and commerce would blend in perfect harmony, the lions lie down with the lambs, peace come to the airwaves, joy to the world.

Fat fucking chance.

With a fast, sickening lurch, the roller coaster starts up again, immediately dropping, so he has to choke back the bile not to retch. It's always this way. The sarsaparilla went right to his head, exhilarated him, got him flying; then, as it wore off, the nausea would take over again, weighing him down with a feeling that was much worse than the dizziness alone. He tries giving in to it, letting the first wave dash over him unresisting, but there's something different this time, it comes not in waves but as a rapid-fire pounding on the lower third of his ribs, and it takes him a few more seconds to realize where it's coming from—that someone is pounding furiously on the door.

He weaves his way past the letter bags, gets there just in time to hear a squeaking sound, see a stiff edge of wood being pushed under the crack at the door's bottom. It just barely fits; he knows he could help by tugging on the emerging corner, but he stands there watching like a man transfixed by a cobra, until the board is all the way through, lying right there at his feet.

It's a cue card, a small one, coming in upside down, and he has to square it around to make the letters out—the chalky letters that are smudged, as if they're blowing in the hot breath of whoever scrawled them.

SHE LOVES ME NOT YOU
.
IT'S THE SHADOW OF YOU SHE'S GOOFY FOR NOT YOUR DESPICABLE

REALITY

RELEASE HER OR FACE THE CONSEQUENCES

A chalkboard—and yet it acts exactly like a mirror sticky with instant memory, so he can picture in its reflection Chet holding his face up close, printing out the letters, getting down on his hands and knees by the door to grope for the crack, shoving it under with both hands . . . getting back up again with chalk on his nose, walking down the hall with great dignity, oblivious to the stares he got, his face pancaked with white.

Chet. Well, they would have to have a talk about things, that was all there was to it. He'd neglected him, hardly talked to him outside the show. They needed to get away together somewhere they wouldn't be bothered, maybe out on the Island, do something simple and different and corny, like packing a lunch and some beers and going out on a party boat, catching some flounder, getting sunburned and seasick, laughing this off or puking it off but shedding it once and for all.

There was lots to explain, they would have to start way back in the past, scrutinize everything, see if they couldn't identify what had gone wrong in their friendship and when. Chet couldn't possibly love Lee, that part was all invented, could be nothing else *but* invented. He had plenty of girls, he had a wife back in Springfield, he and Lee had always been like brother and sister. Sure Chet hurt, anyone could see that, but he hurt in general terms, and if he had chosen jealousy as his particular brand of pain it was because that was the handiest pain available.

Or something like that. The truth is he's too wobbly yet to concentrate further—he walks slowly, rigidly, back to his desk, sits down in the leather armchair, glances up again at the clock. It's 11:30, which means 7:30 in Moscow and 4:30 in London and 10:30 in Chicago and 8:30 in L.A. He tries, as he often did, to picture what it's like in all those places all at once, but it doesn't work; as was happening more and more now, he gets stuck on Chicago, the city he knew in detail, the place he'd gotten his start.

The best two years of his life now that he looked back on it. Television was brand-spanking-new, no one understood what to do with it, no one bothered him, he had figured things out on his own. They were crazy, some of the stunts they pulled. A friend at police headquarters gave him a list with the names of the most corrupt Chicago judges, and he would call them up right on air, deepen his voice, and say, "This is your conscience calling, Superior Judge Peterson, this is your conscience calling, do you accept the call?" Other times they would truck the camera out to O'Hare, pack it in blankets to keep it from freezing, point it at planes taking off and landing in the snow—not saying anything. They were always amazed at how many people enjoyed that, just the planes there in the darkness, the lights flaring on the end of their wings. When it was time to sign off they'd get Lilly Vesco wearing men's pajamas, have her wink at the camera and then very slowly roll up her sleeves—do nothing more than that, just roll up her sleeves, and it was the sexiest thing ever seen. They'd go to bars, get the camera set up in a corner, talk to whoever was there—those were the best shows, the ones that were truest, the kind of thing you couldn't do anymore. Even that time slot was vanished now, no one bothered with it. They came on late, after midnight, so, technically speaking, it was a morning show, too, the forgotten kind of morning where anything was possible. "And remember this, folks," he would say in signing off at one-thirty. "It's always dawnest before dark," and people would puzzle on that, send him letters asking what he meant, even philosopher-bigshots out at the university who pressed him to explain.

To remember this helps, and yet he worries about it, too, the precipitous retreat his head is making every time it's faced with anything hard. Always before, pressured, he had looked toward the future for comfort, not the past. It was where his passion came from, his drive, and he recognized this as clearly as if it were cogs, gears, and levers he was talking about, not spirit. He doesn't want to give up on this, throw them too soon into reverse—and yet something desperate is needed to get him ready, he has only twenty minutes left now before he'd have to go through the charade he had come to hate, put on not the plastic smile but the plastic impassivity everyone at the network expected.

Only twenty minutes left, meaning it's time for the big one, the sure shot, the certain cure. He moves the chair around until it faces the letter bags in their hampers, regards them, makes no move to actually fish one out. It's in these letters where salvation lay, one in particular that seemed as if it were the condensed distillation of all the millions of letters that had come in over the years, the mass of them pressing downward like glacial ice to compact together an incredibly thin layer of richness wherein all the weight of the country, the dreams, hopes, and fears, had combined in the exact words in the exact order that melted a way into his heart.

The letter itself he keeps in a book behind him on the desk, but there's no need to fetch it since he'd memorized every line. The book is about birds, left by an ornithologist who had come on the program to talk about robins dying from DDT. Why he had put the letter in a bird book for safekeeping is one of those small mysteries he enjoys mulling over, but there's no time for that now—it had seemed important to hide the letter inside a book with pictures of birds, and beyond that he won't delve.

Hello, Alec, the letter began. *It feels right to be sending this to you, so maybe it won't be a total surprise. I hope it isn't—that there's still some linkage after all these years. Maybe you get lots of letters like this. I hope you remember me—no, that's just me sounding like a bashful young girl. But watching your success from afar (I confess it's not every morning, but I try), I feel as if no time has elapsed at all, and that if I just start talking to you it will be as though we never left off, and so here I am talking. Your show is an inspiration, what you're trying to do, gather the whole country for better or worse right there in one meeting place, that little screen that suggests so much. I can remember when all you wanted to gather in was lil' ol' Springfield, so you've really come a long way. Me, I feel like my own life has hardly begun yet. It was beginning, with you, and I was foolish and frightened and thought it wasn't, and ever since that time beginnings for me have been lost I don't know where.*

This brings him up all right, out of the sticky-sweet cloud straight to the top of the roller coaster, where he can see things plain. He had not spent twelve years of his life waiting for this letter to arrive—that was the miracle of it, the thing he can't stop marveling over, the best test of its reality. In the course of that midnight train ride from Springfield to Albany he had hardened himself to losing her, renounced his youth, driven away happiness as a notion that never need concern him, and, finding he could survive, had gone on with his life. The hurt he carried was as much a part of him as his shoulders, and yet he had never wasted time wishing she would return to remove the pain, start over. He knew men who did that. Men who yanked success in like it was a line leading back to their past and on the end of that line the idealized girl who had originally spurned them—men who would go to great lengths to persuade time to roll backward, deliver up their lost love on a silver platter.

And yet with the arrival of the letter life had pulled its rarest trick, startling him so much he isn't sure how to take it even now. Who would think fate knew how to do that? It could only be a perverse kind of switcheroo joke, resurrecting one love in the world to counterbalance all the millions that were crushed. He's a prop in a magic trick, only he hasn't figured out yet if he is meant to remain passive while the magic works, or, waving his hands about, to perform prestidigitations of his own.

You don't have time for all the details, and already I feel they're dust behind me. I'm divorced, I'm alone now, and it's no one's fault but mine—my hands have been the ones doing the choking, my throat shows the scars. But sometimes I think of our radio days together, how hard we worked, how we overflowed with ideas and energy and determination, all three of us. I like to think I was good at this—that I would be good at this still. Talking to people. Thinking on my feet. Bringing out people's stories. I've acted quite a bit here and around Boston, small potatoes really, but I think it's an attempt to bring that part of me back somehow, or maybe just to get experience being in front of an audience. I get offers to do more, but it's not acting that interests me, but being back on radio again, or better yet, being on television ... There, I've said it. You probably get hundreds of letters asking for jobs. But I'm not asking for a job, not really—at least that's what I'm telling myself now. I can see very clearly what you are up to, the ambition that drives the program, and I wanted to tell you there's one person out here who understands what this is and that even if you don't connect with anyone besides me—well, there's a connection going on, and it's very strong ... I plan on coming to New York as soon as I finish with things here. There's nothing left for me, and I remember your telling me that's where my future was and I was too silly then, too girlish, to see you were right. I plan on being there the first week of February. If you're not too busy I would love to get together and talk. Do you remember the Groundhog Day broadcast we did, Chet, you and me, burying the microphone in sand, making our voices go squeaky? We could celebrate Groundhog Day together at the finest restaurant in town.

He hadn't expected this, begged fate for favors, so it's only natural that his emotions lag behind events. Things had gone wonderfully well, they had walked over to each other in the lobby of the Plaza as formally as strangers (Lee in a brown wool suit with a yellow scarf, tugging it nervously as she turned in a circle, trying to locate him), and then, a yard apart, had run the last steps into each other's arms. He offered her a job immediately—they had talked and laughed and cried all through lunch, oblivious to all the stares—and before the week was out they were lovers again, as if no time had passed at all. Alone for so long, she was starved of affection; alone, amid all his women, he was starved, too, and so even touching hands across the table had seemed an overpowering act of union, let alone the passion that followed.

Every night now they're together, at least when she isn't off speaking at a gathering of professional women or university women or these other organizations that seemed to have sprung up solely to welcome her, but he knows this isn't forever, that in time she won't need this adulation. Things, all in all, had gone wonderfully well.

No, what's needed now is for him to get back to the man he once was, fight it out alone before talking about marriage or making definite plans. The sarsaparilla is part of it, of course—she had begged him to slow down. The courtiers will have to go, likewise the jesters. He'd given up the partying entirely. He'd started working out at a gym over on Fifty-second Street, has plans to whip his body back into shape playing handball. His blood, his whole way of seeing, reeked too much of night, and he has to wring that out drop by bitter drop. But who's to say he can't? He's only thirty-five now, still young, his recuperative powers still intact.

Their love will come back to where it was originally—of this he is certain. One trick he had learned when younger, the old trick, was to pretend you felt something until the feeling became real. He pretended he belonged in a top school in Springfield, pretended he was as sophisticated and classy as any of the snobs. With Lee he'll proceed similarly. He will act like he loves her, say the right words, tell her he loves her every opportunity he gets, do his best to remember the way it had been for them back in the past, before the war, and thereby create a bower beneath which the pretense will blossom into the real. He sees this happening by autumn—by autumn the feeling must be restored one hundred percent or damn near. He will have to cut back some on his expectations, sure. Who is he to go around asking for an ethereal, idealized, world-championship kind of love, when at the end of everything, behind the hundreds of women he'd had, whose names he couldn't remember, the affairs doomed to disaster right from the start, the drunken nights he couldn't recall without retching, the long years when he felt totally alone—when behind all these was the person he had missed the first time, a real woman, a real love.

Not that any of this will be easy—he knows he's facing the hardest fight of his life. There was the old Lee he loved as a boy, the new one the whole country had discovered, the future Lee he will fall in love with again given time, and it's up to him to keep these three Lees together, not have them splinter apart in his hands.

In the night I can't sleep, Alec, so I pace this empty house trying to remember. Sometimes I do. I remember how I always felt the world was something I had to force myself through, something that stood against me. The slant of the earth, the slap of the wind, the current that comes off strangers as you brush past them on the street. They presented a grain that always lay opposite to my grain, I could never see a way around. And yet that must have been an illusion, because the moment we came together everything changed. I wasn't frightened anymore, the breeze was still there only now it brought tidings of constant joy. I wasn't ever frightened with you, I was always brave. Nothing has changed that feeling for me. Even in my weakest, most solitary moments, part of you still prevents me from being crushed. And does more than that. Turns the world in my favor.

How foolish this must sound. I don't even know if this letter will reach you, and so here I am tossing it in the air like a message the wind must carry just the right direction. If it reaches you, if it just seems old and tired and desperate like the thousands of other letters you receive, that's all right, too, for at least it's made me acknowledge the truth of something I've hidden for too long. I love you still, Alec. I love you.

Find me.

He walks slowly over to his dressing table, stares into the mirror past the smudged lipstick that's already melted in the warmth of the lights, sees himself there, striped and decorated by the melting letters of Chet's poisonous message, decides he looks presentable—decides, after a longer moment, that he actually feels good. Twelve o'clock now—the worst is over. His head still hurts, as it will for the rest of the afternoon, but it's nothing worse than the guilty tap-tap feel of a minor hangover. He rummages on the table until he finds the aspirin, pours himself some warm ginger ale, swallows five pills. A headache is nothing, not against this renewed steadiness, the way he feels centered now, ready to go on.

Out in the corridor all is quiet, at least at first—so quiet he can hear the hum of the fluorescent lights overhead, the echo his steps make against the spotless linoleum. He turns the corner over to the elevator bank and immediately is surrounded by a laughing, smiling mob that seems almost to have been hiding there just to surprise him. Everyone wants to get his attention, needs to slap him on the back, congratulate him, shake his hand. Hey, Alec, how's the old boy? Alec! Wonderful to see you! She's brilliant, Alec, a tonic, just what the show needed! What a natural, Alec, everyone's talking about her. Great find, Alec. Great find! A breath of fresh air, Alec! Everyone's in love with her out there. America's new sweetheart! He shakes hands, smiles in acknowledgment, even mumbles a few words in response, all the time feeling as if this is another part of the hangover, something he has to suffer that will all soon go away.

He takes the elevator to the seventy-ninth floor, realizes, once he steps out, that this is the highest in the building he's ever been. There are no mobs this high, no backslappers. At the end of the hall a door flies open, someone runs in, panting, as if he'd raced all the way up the stairs. It's a page in uniform, with enough braid on the shoulders for a South American general. He rushes up, clicks his heels together, produces an envelope.

"A message for you, Mr. McGowan."

McGowan is feeling good enough to snap off a salute. "Aye aye, sir," he says, making the boy blush.

He opens the envelope. It's a single sheet of yellow paper. On it, written in red so at first it seems like lipstick, are two rows of words.

GIVE HER UP

THERE WILL BE NO MORE WARNINGS

He stares down at it, rubs his thumb and forefinger along the edge, finally remembers the boy standing there, waiting for a reply.

"Mr. Standish give you this?"

The page nods.

"Give him a message for me. Tell him flounders. Sheepshead Bay. Next Saturday. Long talk. I supply the beer."

The boy looks confused.

"Here, I'll write it down."

He hands the note back, but the page still stands there clearing his throat. "I wonder, Mr. McGowan? If there's an opening? As assistant director? I'm going to night school to learn production. Everyone tells me I have what it takes. I'm a fast learner and I think on my feet. Slaughter's the name? Franky Slaughter?"

McGowan is about to make a joke, thinks better of it, nods to get rid of him, and continues along the hall, looking for number 29. The carpet is threadbare, the lighting weak, and mixed in with scruffy offices marked *Personnel* or *Rights & Permissions* are offices that aren't connected to the network at all. He reaches the end of the corridor, has turned to retrace his steps, when he notices a darker hall branching to the right. There is only one office, number 29. The door is closed, but in the center mounted on a silver plaque are the words BROADCAST STANDARDS.

He rolls his knuckles against the door speakeasy fashion, lets himself in. What hits him first is the odor—a mix of chicken broth and old plaster that makes him think instantly of school. The office itself is small and shabby, taken up by metal file cabinets that look too rusty to open, a flat metal desk. BS stands near the greasy window with his knees slightly bent, as if contemplating jumping. He turns, looks down significantly at his watch, smiles, advances with his arm out straight like a spear.

"Alec, me boy! How's the old tiger? It's been far too long!"

McGowan does his best to smile in return. "Three years, isn't it? Your office was . . ." He strains to find the right word. "Elsewhere."

BS smiles, thinly, pulls a folding chair over for him, goes around behind his desk to sit. He looks the same as he did that long-ago night when he delivered his famous speech, the night a despairing, worn-out Abramsky had died. Silver hair cut long like an artist's, leonine features, a patriarchal way of squinting, decisive lips. What's new is the way he is dressed, in the kind of tight-fitting rayon suit that's all the style now, designed to make businessmen look streamlined, lean and hungry—only on him the effect is exaggerated, making him look emaciated and starved. BS they call him. McGowan struggles to remember his real name—Ned Custer—smiles when it clicks into place.

Custer leans back in his chair, his fingers touching each other in the shape of a church. "Yes, elsewhere, as you so tactfully put it. My last office was on the fifty-second floor. It was slightly less shabby than this, but otherwise had no virtues. The year before that I occupied a corner office on the fifty-first floor that was dignified by carpeting. Two years ago I was on the fiftieth floor with two rooms, one for my personal secretary."

McGowan isn't sure how to take this. "You've been on the move, then."

Custer is peeking into his hands now; he draws them back until his nose enters church. "Yes," he says, smiling even wider. "On the move. A regular odyssey. Do you have time?"

Custer lowers his voice the way someone does who's settling in for the long haul, starts a recitation that seems honed by much practice— not for public delivery but for some private, inverted kind of delecta- tion. He describes each office in increasing detail, moving back from the shabby ones on the higher floors to the plusher ones on the lower floors, retracing every step of his banishment, his exile, his humilia- tion. His tone isn't sardonic, but something a hundred times harder, as if the recitation, the remembering, is sharpening his brain into an ax blade he intends to use for some imminent cutting. McGowan lis- tens patiently for the first few minutes, then ceases to listen at all. Custer likes remembering offices as a way of shaping himself up, as McGowan likes remembering vice-presidents, and maybe everyone in television goes around brooding over such lists—maybe, for that mat- ter, everyone in the world.

McGowan turns his attention to the window. He's sitting close enough that he can see out below the sash. It's not the best view of the city, not the fabled Midtown canyons with their toy cars and antlike pedestrians, but a narrower, quieter view through the flanking build- ings out across the waterfront toward the cinnamon-colored Hudson. In the distance, just barely visible, so that at first it seems no more sub-

stantial than a greasy brown smudge on the glass, are the first low hills
of New Jersey—and yet this captivates him immediately, much more
so than a city view, giving him a sense that right outside the window in
the center of that smudge begins the wide and exhilarating expanse he
fell in love with years before.

That's what he'd like to do someday. Have a new show and have it
originate from out west. New York is tired, stale, too isolated in its
cozy little pocket. He has to shake himself free, get himself centered
deep in the country with the country wrapped around him, tap some
of that expanse, start fresh and young and strong. What kind of show?
He hasn't thought details yet, he wants to cherish the idea in its early
stages when it's still pumping from deep inside his imagination. It will
be a show that belongs to the people, not the sponsors. It will be a program where people can come on and say what's on their minds and it
will show them where they live and work and play and it will turn its
back completely on celebrities and sports heroes and politicians and
the other superficial gods whose time now was past. Ordinary people
would be the stars, working people, people who won some battles, lost
most, but who hadn't given up no matter how fierce the battering. It
would focus on their faces—thousands of homely ones, thousands of
plain ones, Negro and Chicano and Pole and Indian and immigrant
Greek, the whole glorious stew, their faces, their stories, blending into
an impressionistic montage that would be television's finest hour, its
masterpiece, its justification for being. Chet could be one host and Lee
could be the other and he would be there directing, acting as the middle
man between the idea and reality, making sure nothing interfered with
that feel, that sheen, that spirit. *Morning?* That's shabby, too narrow and
specialized. All day is what's needed now. The whole goddam day.

That's the big dream, the one he needed to bring him all the way
back, make him feel like the Alec of old. The first program he had
achieved on his own, and it had damn near killed him, but this one he
would accomplish with Lee by his side. She sensed the drama even in
ordinary people, that was the magic in her—on radio, on television, in
the most artificial and pressured of circumstances she could still home

in on what people aspired to in their largest, bravest moments, and there was no need to seek further for the secret of her success. He isn't immune to that kind of charm, not by a long shot. And not just with big dreams, either. There are plenty of small ones they can keep busy with while the big one approaches. Travel, he'd hardly ever traveled, never just for fun, never outside the country. They're already shopping around for an apartment to share, but maybe in the future there will be more than that—maybe a home out in the country, a patch of land where they could get a garden going, plant some apple trees, be alone. Okay, maybe now she's too busy for that, too caught up in her success, but this will wear off fast enough, she'll see things more evenly, be more than happy to escape. Kids? Well no, not yet, but he likes to think of it just this way—kids with a question mark, the possibility popping up over the horizon in hazy double silhouettes. He pictures Lee in blue jeans hanging up dresses on a clothesline stretched between apple trees, her hair streaming out in the morning breeze—pictures her and falls in love with the picture and almost weeps with the sense of peace this brings him, the sense of beauty. He will act like he loves her as passionately as before, say the right words, hold her desperately, and if he acts like that and pays attention to the smaller dreams, the larger dream will come.

How foolish this must sound. I don't even know if this will reach you. If it finds you, if it just sounds old and tired and desperate, that's all right, for at least it's made me acknowledge the truth of something I've hidden for too long. I love you still, Alec. I love you . . . Find me.

Something—a motion, a change in inflection—makes him focus back on Custer, who, having finished his monologue, sits staring out between those pale, self-supportive fingers, looking at McGowan the way someone looks at a screen. It makes him uncomfortable, being taken unaware like that. If he talks first, it's because in whatever game they are playing he senses he's already lost.

"I remember what you said in your speech," McGowan says, making his voice even softer than it is normally. "About television being for ordinary people. How it would grow with its audience given time.

How it should aim for the high middle ground. How it would bring into the world a new sense of community."

Custer arches his eyebrows, as if they're the muscles in him in charge of remembrance. "The speech?" He smiles. "Ah, the speech."

"I listened with my heart beating. I found it inspiring."

Custer swivels in his seat so he's facing the window, makes as if to put his feet on the desk, thinks better of it, stares off toward the glass. "Television's time will be very brief," he says. "People will quickly come to their senses."

He says this quietly enough that Alec thinks he's misheard. "I'm sorry?"

"The golden age is already over. Your friend will be the sacrifice, or, if you prefer, the first victim."

"Lee?" he says automatically.

Custer shakes his head the barest minimum. "No, she's a remarkable find, Alec. Everyone sings her praises. You've heard the rumors surely? She's been negotiating for her own show. With another network, of course. I don't think she'd stoop to asking for yours. She intends to start her own morning program."

"That's bullshit. A deliberate lie."

"Well, it would be nice to think so. I have it from her makeup assistant, and I've found them in the past to be very reliable sources of information. This is as may be. But that's not why I initiated our little chat."

Custer swivels back to face him, puts on his tight little smile mask. "I'll be honest with you, Alec, as befitting old friends. Your sidekick has become an embarrassment. This Palmer woman has raised standards wonderfully, but in the process she's made him look even more like a relic. He's a myopic buffoon, an erratic buffoon, a loose cannon who's turned ugly. This morning's show was his last."

McGowan isn't surprised; when that mask comes over a man's face, he's prepared for anything. He even feels a little more assurance now—he at least knows what game he's playing in, even if he's badly behind.

"His last?" he says, playing dumb.

"There will be no melodramatic on-air farewells. You're to call him this afternoon and tell him to clean out his office by five o'clock sharp."

"No," McGowan says. "No, Ned, I don't think so."

What surprises him is that Custer has been chosen as their emissary—what lies had he invented to convince them he and McGowan were still close? And yet even here he has the sense this isn't the real motive—that the real fight hasn't begun. There had been a time when he would have welcomed such a fight, kept his guard up better, been prepared, but that time was gone; now all he wants is to get that other agenda out on the table without any more of the shadowboxing he'd come to despise.

"He doesn't go," he says, this time with more force. "We've been together through too much. He's as much a part of the show as I am."

Custer thrusts his chin forward with peculiar emphasis, as if fitting it into a brace suspended inches before his face. "It's funny you should mention that," he says mildly. "Another change is being contemplated as well. Your ending, Alec. The sign-off, your slogan. There are those who have come to feel it's old-fashioned and dated. There are those who have come to feel it is pompous, even arrogant. There are those who feel very strongly the time for you to use it is now in the past. I don't say I myself share this view, but there are many who do and they are not without influence in this corporation."

Okay, this is better, the sign has been made, all he has to do now is make the countersign and with that finished he can leave.

"Yes, I can see their point," he says, nodding. "I've thought along those lines myself actually. It's something I might strongly consider."

Custer beams—too soon, too eagerly, so for a moment McGowan feels pity for him, that he should play the game so awkwardly, even though he's won.

"Yes, I would strongly consider it, Ned. I would even go so far as to say I would agree to a change. Chet stays, of course. That would have to be a given."

"Of course he stays." Custer swivels around so fast he almost falls out of the chair. "I can guarantee that, Alec. Why, he's the best thing on the show as far as I'm concerned. A welcome breath of spontaneity. I told them that. I think they'll be pleased, quite pleased, at how reasonable you've been. And of course you'll still be allowed a sign-off. Just something a bit more modest and less confrontational is all they're asking for. And of course it will have to be cleared with me."

Custer snatches the phone up like it's a trophy, hums as he waits for his connection, begins arranging papers on his desk with a little herding motion, gathering them in. McGowan feels no need to listen. He gets up and walks over to the window, stands against it with his forehead against the ribbed fabric of the shade. He can see the same slight bump in the west that had seemed so significant minutes before—the little thumbs-up protrusion that suggests the entire breadth of the continent. Those were his best days, mornings during the war, when he had traveled the country on trains, fallen in love with the sheer physicality of it, the texture of the land, the way it unfolded, unrolled, gathered itself, and stretched. Staring at that first vague hill, tunneling his vision between buildings, imagining the continent, he feels an overpowering craving for the actual feel of it, a fold he can gather between his fingers and rub. After all the love he's poured into it, he expects the country to pour something back, actually closes his eyes for a moment, seeking a sign, an illumination, a dawning. And from the twenty-three million souls who watch him each morning—he expects a message from them, actually cocks his head, straining to hear.

Custer is a puppet, a clown a hundred times more pathetic than Chet, but maybe Custer is right—that the time for talking about truth out loud is over, at least temporarily, and he may as well face it. Maybe truth has to go underground now, as it has gone underground often throughout history, and not just in history, but even in the puny groove cut by his own passage. Sometimes truth is safer underground, sometimes it grows better robbed of light, only once buried you can't change the rules in mid-era, force it out just because you're sentimental and hungry. You have to have the courage to wait without expecting anything, years maybe, decades, even centuries. You have to locate where the cache is buried, memorize the coordinates, then turn your eyes deliberately away.

Television itself is just another stab at seeing—nothing new when you stopped and thought about it, not when it came to basics. It could last for a hundred years and still be just another station on the way to something clearer. He knows in time it will be superseded by a better way of seeing and in time there will be a better way yet, and the process will never stop, because with each step ahead something vital is lost sight of, so that what is gained in vision is balanced by what goes blind. This is something else he's going to have to deal with as the years go on, the implications. It's quite a list now. The questions he must ponder. The things he must deal with in order to survive.

Out the window, so small that at first it looks like a ladybug caught on the smudged glass, an airplane slants skyward, passing the little hill so fast and effortlessly it humbles the swell of it back into the ground. McGowan watches the plane until it's not even a speck and the gray sky folds in on itself without any sign of having been pierced. He feels, though he has no idea where it comes from, an overpowering loneliness that makes him blink to keep back tears. *Find me* is what she had written in the roadside sand on that summer morning so many years in the past, and he had hung his life around the message. But she had written it wrong, that's what he understands now. *Find us* is what she should have written. *For pity's sake, find us all.*

Thirteen

"Happy Valentine's Day!" the parcel driver said, handing it over, and at first that's what I thought it was—a Valentine that had been stored underground in cigar-colored packaging, giving off a dust that made me cough. Inside was a black cardboard sleeve with the videotape snug inside. There was no note this time, there didn't need to be. Valentine's Day, to someone with Slisco's sense of humor, must have been irresistible. And so its arrival that afternoon didn't surprise me as much as he intended. If anything, I sensed a controlling power that stood beyond Slisco's, a sardonic take on life far darker than his. Yes, he had his ironic little joke on me, but I hardly thought about that, wondered only whose ironic little joke in life he was, poor Martin Slisco.

I didn't watch it right away. I wanted to fight him a bit, take control. I could imagine him sitting in his small suburban house looking down at his watch, taking great pleasure in picturing me ripping the tape out of the packaging, my hands shaking in excitement, popping it into the television like a frozen piece of toast. That was part of the reason for delaying. The other part was simpler. The family was coming home now, things had gone from totally quiet to totally insane, and I needed everything quiet again before confronting it. And I couldn't watch alone. That was the real reason I waited. If my understanding was going to be completed I couldn't watch the last tape alone.

It was a school night, everyone went to bed early, but I waited an extra hour to make sure. The television was in the living room. I turned it on, pressed the sound low, fitted the tape in the slot, turned one soft light on, pulled a chair over, studied the arrangements . . . walked quietly upstairs.

We called it "Chet's room" now, not the guest room, and it was the last one along the hall. Outside his door was a dark tapered mound that, in the faint yellow of the night-light, could have been clothes left there for laundering. It was Elise—Elise who camped out every night in exactly this position. "It's just if he needs me," she said, in begging us to allow this. She acted like a sentry, marching up and down the hall when he first went to bed, sitting against the door with her ear close, listening, ready to run for water or towels or whatever he needed, then slowly, very slowly, slumping back down to the mound she was now, curled tight against the bottom of the door fast asleep, covered in blankets Kim brought from her room.

I eased the door open, stepped around her, and went in. Chet sat in a chair with his face against the window, peering out. There was no light on, and the only illumination came from the blue street lamp outside. I often came in late with his medications, so he didn't act surprised. He was sick enough now that the inner core of him must have been waiting for someone to come in and fetch him, the one from which Elise tried to protect him—the messenger who, for that first second as I came through the door, enlarged by the bluish halo, I must have resembled myself.

He got up and came over toward me, as if to make my task easier. On the table beside the bed was the full array of his medications. We had discussed these, Kim, Chet, and I, sitting down talking calmly, and had decided that once they couldn't keep the pain at bay he would enter the hospital. He wanted very badly to see the new millennium in, his own version, the one he insisted began March 17, but other than this, wanting to spare Elise any pain, there wasn't much left for him to wish for.

"I feel stable enough," he said, reading my thoughts. He had a johnny on, the kind you wear in hospitals, and he reached his hand in over his heart, as if to prove to me it was still beating.

"Are you strong enough to go downstairs?"

He looked puzzled, but nodded. I followed him over to the bed, helped him on with his robe. For all his weakness, he was still capable of surges when he seemed vigorous and strong; as I led him past Elise into the hall he clutched my arm for support hard enough that it hurt and I had to take his hand, reposition it lower down on my forearm where his thumb couldn't press in. He walked rigidly down the stairs—his face glowed in the darkness with a papery kind of sheen—and by the time I got him to the bottom he was holding my hand.

"Something came in today I want to watch with you," I told him. "I'm going to have you sit in this chair near the television and I'm going to sit here and we're going to watch this together."

"I don't see very well," he said, as if I didn't know this fact already.

"If I move it up closer, like this?"

"Yes," he said, nodding. "Yes, that's much enhanced."

The chair was close enough to the set that his knees touched the corner. He had never looked so small and feeble before, not even at his sickest—you could have fit three of him in the space left on the cushion. Here I had steeled myself for truth, and seeing him made me feel like a half-hearted inquisitor who was too soft to perform his duties. Whatever hardness I felt toward him had evaporated when I carried him across the ice.

"We don't have to do this," I said.

Did he sense what I was talking about? "Yes we do," he said quietly.

He blinked, tried finding me in the darkness, frowned—the first fully adult look he had ever given me.

"All right, then," I said, leaning forward toward the set.

Chet stared toward the screen with great interest, even smiled a little as I pressed the tape in and the light changed to white. Warmth came out before the actual picture—that little crescent wave of warmth that can soften you in the screen's favor.

"This was sent to me by a man named Martin Slisco," I said. "He kept it hidden in his house for fifty years. I want to know what you think of it."

My voice, in that silence, must have sounded brutal and harsh, but I had to reach through that now, all the spiky excuses truth studs itself with in order not to be seized by the likes of me. And I suppose I was already bracing myself for the usual denials—*an accident, just to frighten him, a tragic misunderstanding.*

"He was a cameraman," Chet said, leaning forward. "A lecherous bastard. You could always tell which girls he was going with because they would come in with bruises on their faces from where he hit them. He was a good cameraman in the early days, but then he got the shakes. No one knows why Alec retained him. He was a scoffer, a bitter scoffer. He always laughed at me and it came out coated in phlegm."

He shrugged like someone dragging his shoulders up in a vain attempt to warm his ears. "By then they all laughed," he said, so low I could barely hear. "The whole rotten mob."

I hesitated, knowing it was my last chance before taking the plunge. "There's no sound with this," I warned him. "I can rewind it if I have to. I can push this button and it will go back."

"Is there a way to stop it?"

"I can stop it any time you want. This will brighten it some. You tell me if you can't see."

The picture came on—McGowan and Lee Palmer standing together near the news wire, reading the tapes, talking to each other, getting ready for work. McGowan wears a plain business suit that looks too slick on him, too tapered and tight. Lee Palmer, a simple A-line dress with a wide sailor collar. The film quality was much worse than before, hazy, unfocused, with bite-sized holes that made it look as though the center had been nibbled by worms. And yet the haziness helped somehow—it made it seem more real than the other tapes, made you strain to see better, lent it the convincing imprimatur of decay.

Chet, hunching over like a man protecting his groin, moved his face closer to the screen. All the gauntness, every wrinkle, every manifest sign of weakness, seemed to have migrated to the deep puckers beneath his eyes, as if joining in one last effort they could manage only if they all squinted together. What could he have felt seeing his friends again? What overlay pressed down against his memory with what kind of sting? When he started talking it wasn't in the whiny, self-justifying tone I expected, but a voice that was simple, quiet, and clear, pitched to a steady level that served as the aural duplicate of the tape, making it seem that what I was witnessing was a long-postponed reunion—not just between three old friends, but between his voice and the soundless picture.

"That dress was"—he turned his face from the screen, sought mine—"you said there was a way to go back?"

I stopped the picture, played it back again—Lee reading the wire tape out loud while McGowan cocks his head, listening. They seem to be touching and yet, looking closer, it's clear they're not. Behind them, like a cloud over their shoulders, scroll the words *Morning July 3, 1954*.

"I gave her that dress," Chet said, talking to the screen, not to me. "It was her thirty-third birthday and I picked it out myself at Lord and Taylor and she wore it that day and it brought tears to my eyes, seeing her wear it just for me . . . There. They're moving over to the desk. I wasn't allowed on as part of the beginning anymore, I would come on later to interview the weirdos. That's all they thought I was good for now. The laughable stuff, the bullshit, and I had to beg to be granted even that."

"Who was calling the shots by then? Was McGowan?"

"There was a new director, Jimmy Burke. Alec deferred more and more to him, since he couldn't be bothered. He was looking elsewhere, had all these grandiose plans."

Chet made an impatient gesture with his hand—he wasn't interested in details. "He was taking her away from me," he said. "It wasn't jealousy. I wasn't jealous of him by then, it was all these millions who watched, everyone who had a piece of her now. Every day there were thousands more, they had never seen anything like her, a woman who could hold her own with men, who was intelligent and beautiful both, not a snob but a genuine person. A victory of brains over mannequin beauty—one critic said that and Alec had it framed. She got love letters, proposals of marriage—men would jerk off watching her, and everything Alec did only made it worse . . . He took me fishing, tried to sweet-talk me, thought he could buy me off with a few beers. I could see what he was doing. The show was failing before she came on, and he needed to turn her into a monster who wasn't Lee at all, but someone like those movie stars, someone invented. He let the network make up stuff about her to feed to the press—they squelched details about her divorce, made it seem as if she were a simple country girl without any past. I couldn't allow that. I couldn't allow her to disappear that way, into something invented. They were flying her around the country in a private plane, having her judge contests, give interviews, do guest shots on every two-bit affiliate there was. One more month and she would have been so far out there we wouldn't ever be able to bring her back again. I couldn't acquiesce in that—I couldn't allow her to disappear. My heart depended on her. Without her I couldn't go on."

On the screen, Lee and Alec are sitting at their desk and it's clear they're talking about what will be coming up later on in the program. There's a clip with a reporter standing on the Mall behind the Washington Monument, where a crowd begins to gather, and then a glimpse of a gnomelike man in the studio intently polishing a piece of glass with a cloth, and then, the camera panning leftward, a shot of Chet with a chef's apron high on his chest, standing behind a Formica counter.

"I was supposed to demonstrate an electric barbecue during the second half-hour, cook up some hamburgers. That was going to be the sum total of my involvement, just me grilling a faked piece of meat . . . I was happy about the apron, it fit right into my plans. There's a bulge there by my pocket, can you see it? There, right there. It was a .38-caliber revolver I purchased down on Fourteenth Street at an army-and-navy store called Leo's. The sales clerk was excited because it was nickel-plated—he held it by the barrel so I could see my reflection on the grip. They asked for ID and I gave it to them—by then I didn't care. I bought ammunition, took it to the docks, practiced shooting behind a warehouse where no one would hear. At first I only intended to scare him, but then I realized what would happen, that everyone would say I was such a clown I couldn't hit the broad side of a barn, and so they would only laugh more. I wanted to wipe the smiles off all their faces. That's all I could think about now. About taking the gun and using it as a kind of rag that would wipe the smiles off all their faces."

The camera shows Chet grinning, or trying to grin—it comes off like a man chewing glass. He looks to his right sharply, as if startled, and stares in bewilderment at something the camera doesn't see.

"What's that?" I asked. I stopped the tape, ran it back, watched him stare.

"Someone laughing. I hadn't even finished, this was just supposed to be a preview, and already they were laughing. Hey, Standish, make sure that's meat you're grilling, not your hand! Hey, Chet! Don't fuck it up! I was sick of hearing it . . . There. See? I'm tapping my pocket to make sure the gun is still inside."

The news comes on, Frank Stannard reading it, with more film clips than in earlier programs. Men in fedoras stand outside the Supreme Court building, which segues into a one-room schoolhouse, sharecropper kids listening to their teacher read from a formal-looking document, the kids gaping, trying to understand, which becomes a well-dressed family of four staring across their backyard through frosted 3-D glasses at a distant mushroom-shaped cloud, blending into peasants in coolie hats slogging through a rice paddy with bandoliers crisscrossing their chests, and a young old-looking Richard Nixon bowing his head at someone's funeral, into Grace Kelly kneeling on a carpet pressing her hands against wet cement.

The weather is next, Stannard doing it soberly, quickly, with no interest. Rain is forecast in the Pacific Northwest, sun in the Southwest, sun in the Northeast except for a boomerang-shaped band of thunderstorms off Cape Cod. It will be seventy-eight in San Francisco, eighty-two in Detroit, ninety-six in Philadelphia, ninety-five in New York.

"He's doing it too fast. What people wanted was a little flair with the weather, have you chat about it like they would chat about it riding to work on the bus. Rain? Looks that way, folks—take along an umbrella. Like that. They got eighteen thousand letters when they took me off the map, people insisting I come back again . . . I was in my dressing room here. I could feel the gun, but I remembered I had left behind the ammo and I had to go back without anyone seeing me and load it and come back again to the barbecue grill and I had to do this while the commercials were on, which gave me exactly three minutes . . . The bullets felt cold, I remember that. My fingers were clumsy, and it was hard to make them stop shaking. I could only manage to press two in, and then I heard Burke intoning my name, and I had to go back. I had the apron off now. I wrapped it twice around the gun so no one could see."

There's the doughy gray blur that blanks out the commercials, but through some fluke this time they emerge, looking crisper, cleaner, than the program itself. Remington Rand typewriters. Wonderbread. My Sin perfume. Ovaltine. Frigidaire. A stylishly dressed woman in high heels opens a refrigerator and strokes the back of her hand across the shelves. A football player eats Wonderbread, tackles six players at once. A man smiles in approval as his wife sprays My Sin on her throat. A boy sits typing, above him the academic awards his typewriter has earned him. Smokey the Bear warns about forest fires, a spade in one paw, the other turned palm outwards, blessing the forest creatures that scamper around his feet.

Chet watched these as intently as he did his own appearance, and I
realized that during the actual show he would not have seen them—
that commercials must have been the curtain behind which they could
all temporarily hide. Before they were over he started coughing, a bad
fit. I stopped the tape until he got control of himself, asked if he was
ready, pressed it in again. A promo came on, a teaser for a game show
later that morning, with a grinning host pointing to a dial with huge
numbers. "Where are you now?" I asked.

Chet stared toward the beveled edge of the screen, as if trying to
see around behind the picture. "There was a long wooden table just
off the set. Toscanini liked to spread his scores across it getting ready
for a performance, and it was all splattered with black ink. Alec stood
there turning through some memos. His glasses were off—no, not off,
resting on top of his forehead. He glanced up and saw me, looked at
me quietly for a moment, then did something he never did before. He
stuck out his hand. 'Good luck, old tiger,' he said. I mumbled something back, but my mouth was so dry I couldn't talk . . . Lee was just
the other side of him looking at a mirror. I remember that. All the
time I knew her, I never saw her look in a mirror before—can you
imagine that? A woman so self-confident she never looked in a mirror.
Only she was looking now. It wasn't to see how her hair was arranged,
either—I could recognize the curious, troubled way she peered. She
was trying to find herself there. She was losing her identity, those millions were sucking it away, and she had to search the mirror to find the
real Lee Palmer before it was too late . . . I watched her, deciding she
never looked more beautiful. She was staying young while the rest of
us grew old, and I would have given anything to have shared that with
her. I could even locate the spot where her youth was centered—right
below her hair on the back of her neck. I wanted more than anything
to put my hand against that coolness, pull her to me. I was going to tell
her that, but my throat was dry and I was afraid I might cry."

"And you went ahead anyway?"

"To wipe the smiles off their faces. I told you."

"Whose faces?"

"That whole leering mob. It wasn't just that. I wanted to bring Alec back to reality."

"By shooting him?"

"Yes. And to keep him from Lee."

"Did you think about your wife?"

"No."

"Your kids?"

"I thought how hard it must be for them, to have a father who was a clown."

"It had to be live, on camera?"

"Of course it had to be on camera. There was never any question about that. I had to tell myself it wasn't really Alec I was shooting but the man on camera. None of us was real on camera, not by that stage. Why do you think Lee was staring into that mirror?"

I waved my hand toward the picture. "What's going on now?"

"Lee always had the first segment. People wanted her now, this instant, and they'd get impatient if we saved her for later. That man there was from France, a hunchback who was the world's leading expert in stained glass. He was going around cathedrals in Europe that had been shattered by bombs during the war and restoring their stained-glass windows. It was the kind of thing Lee was good at . . . Here she comes. Watch this. The man's nervous, he could hardly speak English, but see how he calms down the moment she comes over? They put the glass up like that on sawhorses so he could demonstrate. The plan was to talk for five minutes, then the camera would come in from above and shoot down on him cutting the glass. Alec should be coming over right about . . . there. There he is. He wasn't supposed to do that, but he would come over if something caught his interest. He's asking the man a question, asking to see his tools. That's his chisel— Alec is feeling it to see how sharp . . . Here I come now. No, not yet. I'm around on the other side by the weather map and I have the gun out now, the apron unwrapped, the hammer cocked back. There. I'm walking quickly, because I didn't want time to think."

Lee and Alec stand with the little hunchbacked man between them and lean over to watch him cut the glass. Alec folds his arms across his chest, then brings up one hand and places it thoughtfully against his chin; Lee, beside him, looks down and tilts her head in curiosity. Chet blunders into them from the right, bent over like he's trying to become hunchbacked himself, bull-like in his impetuosity, on a straight-ahead rush . . . The tape is hazy here, wormholed, blistered . . . Chet still comes on, takes three steps more, his hand stuck out jovially before him like he's meaning to shake hands with all three. The revolver is visible as a second fist attached by a dark grooved cylinder to his real fist.

"Now," he said quietly. "I shoot them now."

Chet plows into the sawhorse with the stained glass, making Lee, Alec, and the hunchback jump back. Chet stops, startled, and while he looks down at the broken glass his fist jerks up like an invisible stick is knocking it aside. Alec, only a few feet away, lifts up on his heels and falls backward with his arms flung out. Nothing of his face is visible, there's a wormhole where it should be, but his arms are plainly visible flying open as he lifts off the floor and falls backward, jolted by the force of the bullet entering his chest.

I stared at the screen, reached forward, slammed the button in, ran the tape backward, stopped it, started it again. Chet comes in from off-stage, leads with his hand, trips over the sawhorse table, looks down startled at the shards of flying glass, and then and only then does the gun go off—when he's staring down at the floor, not at Alec. For the three or four seconds this takes, Alec's face remains invisible—what the screen shows are his arms flying apart as if he's trying to embrace the world backwards.

"You didn't see him," I said. "Look. You don't see him, and you don't aim. You hit the table, it startles you, the gun goes off by itself."

"I pulled the trigger. I meant to shoot him. From that distance I couldn't miss. Stop it there."

"It was an accident."

"Stop it there!"

The camera jerks back on its own, as if the sound wave from the gun has finally hit the lens, and the focus goes wider and blurs, with people making grotesque waddling movements in from the sides. Chet's face is confused, frightened, bewildered—his glasses have fallen off and he waves the gun blindly in front of his chest. Lee is closest to him. She looks down at the floor so fast her hair falls down over her eyes, looks back up, moves toward him.

"No!" Chet yelled, slapping his hand at the screen.

Moves toward him and rushes right into the gun. The bullet hits her in the stomach, so she's not lifted back but folds instantly, totally, with no struggle, like a little girl curtsying so low she topples. Immediately there are bodies surrounding both her and Chet, so it's like a pileup in football, the camera jabbing back and forth, trying to get to the bottom of things, find the ball. When it stops, the focus is on Alec, who lies chest down on the floor, his mouth pressed open against a snake-like cable, his hand reaching out toward the bunched fabric of Lee's dress. He manages to crawl all of an inch, reaches with his hand toward her several inches more, reaches one final time, doesn't quite manage to make them touch, his straining fingers and the motionless fabric . . . and then the stagehands surround the camera, someone clamps a hand over the lens, the tape goes dark, sputters, sends up wormholes, flashes white, stutters, ends.

"Daddy?" Elise's voice said from the top of the stairs. "Is everything okay down there?"

I went up to comfort her, which meant convincing her Chet was only restless, that he wanted to watch TV. Groggy, she didn't object when I led her back down the hall to her room, though I had to sit there waiting until she fell asleep. It gave me time to think, time I badly needed. What I tried deciding was what it would have been like for a kid watching as it happened—how funny it would have seemed, grown-ups wrestling, breaking apart the glass—how they would have run off to fetch their moms. I thought about adults watching the same thing, how it would have seemed shocking, not so much the murders, but television breaking its part of the implicit bargain agreed upon at purchase—that the family would pay on the installment plan, cart it tenderly home, place it in a favored gathering place, change its tubes at regular intervals, dust it off, arrange flowers on the top, treat it as a member of the family, and in return TV would never do anything to violate that trust—that it would entertain and amuse and frighten and titillate, but never for even one split second be real.

And I wondered what a jury would have made of the tape had they ever been given the chance to consider it—whether it showed a cold-blooded killer mercilessly carrying out his plan, or a confused, criminally negligent man playing clumsily with fire. First-degree murder? Manslaughter? Neither of them fit. How could you measure volition in the midst of those wormholes? Chet seemed a puppet controlled by chaos, a plaything, someone dangling, jerked about. To me, this was clumsiness, not intention, and yet there were Chet's own words to contradict me, the angry way he jabbed out with the gun. I had the feeling that if I went down and watched again, I would see something different—that every trick of slow motion, all the video enhancement in the world, couldn't put straight what the years had jumbled. Alec had walked into chaos at the wrong moment; Lee, in a reflex to help him, had gotten there, too.

Back in the living room, Chet sat slumped in the chair facing the TV. The tape jutted halfway out from its slot like a rigid black tongue—I pulled it out just to stop its mocking. When I bent over to help him up he started coughing, spasmodically, helplessly, the force of it using up every inch of him, and I didn't know which part to touch. It seemed forever before it eased off. I knelt down again, pulled him over to me, put my arms around his chest, trying to force warmth into those lungs, bring them comfort.

I knew we weren't finished yet, for all his weakness. The brutal part of me knew we weren't finished, that one last question had to be asked. "What happened then?" I said, when his shivering slowed. "Can you hear me, Chet? What happened next?"

His voice was low, broken—that was what shocked me most. His body was finished, his organs hanging by a thread, and yet his voice had always been indestructible. It flowed toward you, you never had to reach, and yet that's what I was doing now, leaning in to hear, pressing my ear toward his lips.

"I was surrounded by people, but no one touched me, not at first. My forehead was being pummeled against the floor—someone was lifting me by the hair and slamming my forehead down on the concrete, and then I realized it wasn't anyone doing it, I was doing it to myself . . . When I stopped, the cops moved in. They were local, they worshiped McGowan, they weren't concerned with being gentle . . . I remember trying to make out what time it was, praying there was a commercial so no one could see me . . . 'I wiped the smiles off their faces,' I said. I said it out loud, because I had to, it was part of my plan. 'There, that will wipe the smiles off your faces,' and after that I didn't think."

I lifted my head up, looked toward the cold TV and its temple-like squareness, realized, with an odd jolt of suddenness, that it was as old as Chet was—not the set, but the invention. Born at the same time, coming to maturity together, it seemed in that darkness as ancient as he was, weak and pitiable, something that would soon be covered by a shroud.

"What I saw there was a clumsy man," I said. "Someone who couldn't see straight, someone who—"

He shook his head, reached as if to clasp his hands over his ears—he didn't want to hear excuses, not now, when he had finally abandoned his own tired defense.

"I wanted him removed from the screen, and I wanted it so badly I took her as well. The rest doesn't matter . . . What I didn't know was how lonely it would be then. They took me to the station house on Fifty-eighth Street, kept me alone and incommunicado, didn't let me make phone calls, and so I got stubborn. I wanted to explain everything, tell them what I felt, but their leaving me alone made me change my mind. 'Come clean,' they said, just like in a movie, but I decided that's what I wouldn't do—I wouldn't say a word no matter what happened. At the questioning, the trial. Nothing. I was still a clown in their eyes, nothing had changed that. Some of the cops kept asking for my autograph as if nothing had happened . . . That was 1954, and now it's my turn, I want to be with them again, and the only way that will happen is if I remember them and talk. It was so lonely. In all my planning I never imagined the loneliness. 'Come clean,' the cops said. I wanted to tell them about the loneliness, but none of them were interested."

He sucked his breath in hard, as if he were going to start another coughing fit, but it was only to give his words more force. "For the first time I feel ready to face them. Hear me, Alec? I'm ready now. I clammed up at the trial, said nothing, and that was a mistake because I could have told the truth about this, *my* truth. Instead I clammed up— my tongue would be bleeding at the end of the day from all I bit back . . . If I tell you everything, leave nothing out, I'll see them clearer in your story than they ever were on that screen . . . Is it off now? Did you turn if off? . . . Sit next to me. There, sit closer. Touching. No lies now, no lies. You listen and hold on to me and I'll tell you everything you need to know."

Fourteen

It was a beautiful morning, he remembered, a real American red, white, and blue kind of morning, flags streaming in a fresh northwest breeze as he motored down Main Street on his way to work. This was the war's first autumn, but few GIs were dying yet, and the patriotic sheen hadn't had time to wear off. Shopkeepers cranked awnings out over their windows, then stood on the sidewalk, talking—a butcher leaned his head back and laughed uproariously at a joke told him by the milkman. A paperboy hawked the morning edition from a booth on the corner; shoeshine boys spread their polish cans out on the pavement, getting ready for business. Kids walked to school, tossing footballs back and forth; the girls lingered behind, pressing books to their bosoms, glancing shyly through peekaboo haircuts at boys riding past in their jalopies. Delivery trucks pulled to the curb—fruit and vegetables slid down ramps in tightly battened crates. The garbage was collected by strong men in coveralls; ice trucks squeaked to a stop in a cloud of their own mist. Over everything—over the stores, the streets, the people getting ready for their day—hung the earthy smell of leaves raked into the gutters in long pillowy mounds of orange, yellow, and brown.

He never felt so good—that's what he remembered. The station was doing well with advertisements taken out by the war industries, he had made some inquiries about joining the navy and it seemed a real possibility, and even without these he was still young enough that a surge of happiness would rocket through him each morning regardless of details. He drove slowly, carefully, not so much because of safety as because he loved this drive—the friends and acquaintances who waved to him, the evidence of a busy, prosperous, well-regulated city, the cinnamon smell of leaves streaming in through the open window against his face.

He was on his way to the antenna, not the station—he always checked it first thing. Squirrels used it as a playground, crows and hawks blundered into the top, and each morning there would be a pile of burnt carcasses to remove from the tower's base. To get there he had to pass P.S. 19, a public school built in the thirties and the newest in town. He had driven past—had heard the happy shouts as the kids lined up to go in to class—when there was a siren coming up fast on his tail, a flasher going off, a police car easing ahead of him, forcing him to the curb.

"That you, Mr. Standish?" the cop said, waddling over with his pad.

"Yes it is, Mike. Where's the fire?"

Instead of laughing, the cop shook his head. "Well, I'm having to give you a citation, Mr. Standish. You understand."

"Sure thing," Chet said—then, more hesitantly, "I was going that fast?"

"You drove right past that little crossing guard lad without stopping. He had his sign up. You went right past."

"Geezus, Mike, write me up. Don't know what I was thinking . . . Everything all right down at the precinct house? When it comes time for your raffle, let me know and we'll put on some ads."

I watched him drive off, turning my head to see better. The ticket didn't bother me—I had friends at headquarters who would tear it up. What bothered me was that I hadn't seen the crossing guard, though I had been driving no faster than twenty. I looked back up the street, started walking that way, but school was in session now and there was no one outside. I stared at the playground equipment, kept blinking and blinking trying to clear my eyes. There was a fuzzy dead spot in the center of everything. I could move my eyes to the right or left or turn my head and look sideways and things looked swell, but when I stared at things directly, there was a dead spot right in the middle where all was dark. It was as if shutters had come down, with latticework on the sides where the light shone through, but nothing in the center except solid wood.

I went back to the car. I had a jug of water in the trunk in case the radiator overheated, and I poured some in my hands and splashed it over my eyes, but that didn't clear them out. I stared in the mirror, pulled my eyelids down, thinking it was specks of dirt or ash. I got behind the steering wheel, put the car in gear, only now I was sweating, actually shaking, and I drove at a crawl back to the station, convinced that any second I would ram into a pedestrian and kill them. That cooks my bacon, I told myself, rubbing my eyes. That cooks my bacon all right.

That afternoon saw the beginning of the long round of doctors, ophthalmologists, osteopaths, faith healers, psychiatrists, and quacks he consulted in a futile effort to gain back his sight. His family doctor, consulted first, explained it was undoubtedly due to his never having had his tonsils out—he entered the hospital the next day. When that didn't work, his throat still burning from surgery, he tried a local ophthalmologist, who sent him to Worcester to see a specialist. The specialist had done extensive tests, though the one he kept coming back to was simplest—he had him stare toward a wall chart and read off the letters. "What wall?" Chet asked—and he wasn't kidding.

The specialist prescribed eye drops that made things worse. The next doctor was in Boston, a much shrewder man, and it didn't take him long to make a diagnosis.

"You ever drink any bootlegged booze?" he asked, when all the test results were in.

"Bootlegged?"

"Homebrew, backyard hooch—ever drink it?"

"No. Well, a sip."

"Sometimes we see that. This kind of thing caused by bad liquor. You see it in old people mostly, but that's to be expected. What's unusual is to see it in a man under thirty . . . What you have is a condition called macular degeneration. Degeneration of the macula, the center of your seeing. Your macula is a yellow area lying slightly lateral to the center of your retina, which constitutes, or should constitute, the region of maximum visual acuity—we like to call it the yellow spot. You see all right around the edges by tilting your head the way you're tilting it now . . . You're doubtless wondering whether or not it will get worse. Probably not. Possibly. You see poorly enough that you can be considered legally blind—you won't have to worry about the draft. Glasses won't help, but you should wear them anyway, the thicker the better. It alerts people to the fact you have a problem."

After that came the bewilderment, the adjusting, the compensation. The first phase didn't last long—there was no denying that mushy yellow haze in the center of his eyes. He decided from those first moments that he would never complain about his condition, never whine, never rail at the fate that caused it. He took a great deal of pride in this, it helped him cope, and yet it created a problem he couldn't have anticipated. He didn't *look* blind, even with the glasses—he could pass on the sidewalk for a fully sighted man—and so people always assumed he could function normally, that his clumsiness was just clumsiness. Not willing to be pitied, he had to allow himself to be ridiculed; there was no middle ground.

He couldn't bring himself to say, "I have trouble with my eyes," or "I'm considered legally blind." At a post office, having to fill out a form, he would tell the clerk he couldn't read. At Cape Cod that summer, playing in the surf, he had dunked a complete stranger thinking he was a friend and got socked on the jaw as a result; on that same trip he walked fully clothed off the end of the Provincetown pier. He threw out a bag with his wife's jewelry, thinking it was garbage; he flipped the wrong switch at the station, taking them off the air. Legends of similar grew around him like an exaggerated plaster cast, so he seemed, to most people, doubled—the affable, earnest Chet they remembered from prewar days, and the Chet who was now one hundred percent clown.

It wasn't so bad during the war, you forgot your own problems, but the late forties was a bad, a very bad time. I experienced depression, I couldn't sleep at night, I suffered impotency, and everything pierced me like my skin was made out of butter. I heard about a surgeon in Toronto who was operating on eyes, but when I went there he had just committed suicide over being caught fondling little boys. That made it worse for me—comprehending there was no hope. I remember coming home early one afternoon from the station, lifting you from your bassinet, sitting you on the sofa next to Lindy, who was dressing up one of her dolls. This is it, I told myself. This is my responsibility in life, providing for you, bringing you up, and how was I going to do that with only thirty-three and one-third percent of my vision? I remember you sitting there, nestling your head in Lindy's side—you were always looking for a pillow. I remember thinking how much I loved you both, deciding that I would do anything to keep you safe, that if it came down to it I would even steal. But then I realized there was something better than that. I wasn't totally defenseless. I couldn't see anymore, but I still had my voice.

My voice. Yes, it still counted for something. Fate takes away one tool, but supplies you with another, and makes it all the sharper for that reason—I read that in one of the doctor's offices, holding the magazine up close to my face, and it was a credo I repeated over and over like a prayer. Thank God for radio—and that hit me so strongly, watching you two play on the couch, that for the first time since my eyesight evaporated I broke down and cried.

What happened next, in his memory, lay so tight against this moment it could have happened the same afternoon. Since he couldn't drive anymore, he walked the thirteen blocks to the station, making sure he crossed only at corners where there were stoplights. He was on Main Street, passing Stassen's, the oldest hardware store in town, when he heard a faint throbbing hum emanating from the plate-glass window, making it seem as if the lawn mowers displayed there, the ax handles, the bandsaws, had suddenly decided to sing.

It was a television set, the first he had ever seen. He put his face to the window to see better, then went inside. "Hello, Chet!" Jack Stassen boomed. "Hello, Jackson. I see you folks have gone modern on me!" Stassen laughed. "Well, everything else is moving so slow. Damn that Truman. But this is the first time in a week we haven't had a line of customers waiting to look. Help yourself. If the picture starts rolling, give it a good whack on the behind."

Chet stepped around the nail barrels to get up close. It was larger than he thought it would be, at least the box part—you could have buried someone in it and still had room to spare. The screen itself was small, a sissy's face on a bully's body, and he had to squat right next to it in order to see. It wasn't just a flat screen, but beveled and curled around the edges, making him feel he could poke his fingers in beneath the metal rim and fasten on the hidden part of the curve, grab the electronic bits inside. What was on was a Boston Braves game, with Warren Spahn pitching. By peering, by getting up close, he could see his graceful trademark kick as he delivered toward the plate.

Everything I'd heard about television until then was negative. The picture was too small, it rolled too much, it snowed, the definition was terrible and the sound never matched the video. And it meant the ruin of radio—everyone predicted that. So I was prepared to hate it. But I couldn't, that was the remarkable thing. Right from that initial meeting I was interested, fascinated, enthralled. It wasn't like the movies, it was far more magical. This was taking place a hundred miles from where I stood watching, and it wasn't a week later like in a newsreel, but now, simultaneously. And what's more, I could see it, me who was legally blind. Before the war I loved going to Eastern League games, and it was one of the pastimes I missed. But I could see this game, get right in the middle. It was a clumsy box, it threw off so much heat it was torture to remain close, and the picture made it seem you were looking at things through sand—and yet if I put my face to the screen, squatted there like a catcher, I could see Spahn and the hitters and even the hot dog vendors in the stands. Because I was one-third blind I noticed the particulate nature of it more than most people—the picture danced in gritty motes—but that was hardly anything compared to the miracle of what was taking place. I could see. For the first time in seven years I could see like everyone else.

Before the week was out I'd bought our first set. I took cabs all over town searching for the best model—I even went down to Hartford. There was Admiral and Philco and Motorola and Crosley, but the best model by far was the RCA 630 and it was a bargain at three hundred and eighty-five dollars. I watched all the time, no one in those early days watched more. Roller derby, professional wrestling, Morning when it first came on, Milton Berle. I didn't care what it was, I just enjoyed being able to see after a day spent acting like a blind man. I didn't think much of myself those days, but watching television for an hour or two always made me feel much enhanced. It couldn't help but make you feel important. Here were these baseball games and variety shows and newscasts and they all seemed directed to you alone, making it seem television had no other purpose than to keep you happy and informed. I never thought about it much, at least not then, but I most definitely noticed it—I always came away from the set feeling better about myself, bigger about myself, than I did before watching.

It wised me up to a lot of things. Already revenues at the station were sinking fast, and it was probable we'd go bankrupt within the year. I decided what we should do is obtain a television affiliate and do it quickly before anyone in that part of the state got the same notion. Your mother was all for it and we'd gone as far as applying for a license, and then McGowan called and everything changed in the course of a few seconds. It was like an angel, him calling. I could see—looking at a TV set allowed me to see—and so it occurred to me I would see even better if I were on the other side of the screen, the curved inside beveled part, be associated with all this new technology, a part of the future, not stuck in a dead-end business that was about to become extinct. My voice was going to be what earned a living for my family, sure, but my throat got a lump in it whenever I thought about what the future held, and besides, my voice would still be important in television, Alec needing me primarily for announcing. They knew people watched Morning as they did their chores—they knew it was listened to more than watched, which required voices that could hold the audience through sound alone. So it wasn't just Alec McGowan calling, my long-lost pal for whom I'd do anything. It was an angel offering me back my eyes.

"I'm just going down to the big city for a few weeks," I told you the night before I

left. Your mother was furious and locked herself in the bedroom, and Lindy was away at Girl Scouts, so it was just you and me alone, sitting on the sofa, holding hands. "I'll wave in secret, okay? If you watch television I'll wink like this, and out of everyone in this great country of ours only you and me will know who it's for."

He was to be disillusioned fast. TV seemed flat and smooth when he watched at home—he pictured himself working on an expansive ballroom floor, with no cracks to trip him up, and instead he discovered it to be an obstacle course, a booby-trapped jungle gym, with so many things to bump into he could hardly take a step without ramming into something hard. Overhead mikes, power cables, cue cards, teleprompters, booms—there was always something waiting to strike.

And more than this, too. Here was this gigantic enterprise with unlimited resources devoted to capturing the world, reporters standing ready on every continent, sending in their film, a network webbed together by thousands and thousands of miles of coaxial copper cable, cameras that cost a fortune, of remarkable acuity, these resources wielded by, at least in the early days, the energy and drive of thousands of dedicated, sincere, passionate men and women—here was all this technology, money, and freedom placed in the hands of a few talented and imaginative people to largely do with as they pleased, and the result wasn't the new improved way of seeing everyone expected, but a hazy kind of blindess that was worse even than his own.

He could see it in staff meetings, afternoon skull sessions where everyone sat around a table, executives, producers, directors, and the on-air talent, discussing this huge monster with many million hearts, what it wanted, what it was after, what moved it, what it dreamed about, what made it watch, what made it buy. Would the monster be amused or offended if they had on a chimp? Did the monster like its news first thing or later, after it had time to wake up? Would the Southern half of the monster object too much if the bass player was Negro? How many commercials could they string together before the monster got up to crap? Everyone had ideas on this, but it was clear right from the first minute of the first meeting he ever attended that no one really had a clue, that it was all guesswork, that when it came to seeing into a viewer's heart they were blind men sitting around a table, taking turns trying to describe an elephant none of them had ever seen.

Only McGowan seemed immune to this—only McGowan seemed to know what was truly in an audience's heart. He always spoke last, in a tone that had the measured softness of true certainty—and there, the elephant would be described, in detail, with empathy, shrewdness, and insight, absolutely convincing, such that, in those early days at any rate, no one would dare follow him with a dissenting word. Whether the elephant he described so beautifully really existed was debatable, of course, but alone among those blind, groping pioneers he believed in what he sensed.

Disillusioning—and so I had to find new ways to cope. What I learned very quickly was how to go about taking yourself seriously, how to put a sardonic tone in your voice, shrug nonchalantly at everything, and yet constantly lose your temper over small things, throw tantrums, gain respect; how you did everything possible to let everyone know you were different from the people who weren't on camera, from the negligent way you strutted into the studio with your jacket slung over your shoulder to the preoccupied way you sat in the cafeteria sipping coffee. More than this, too. The way to surround yourself with flatterers, people who praised you to the skies even when you were lousy, did it loudly, smoothed out the details so you didn't have to worry. You needed your shirts washed, you gave them to so-and-so and they came back next day folded and starched; you needed some publicity shots, you snapped your fingers and they were on your desk first thing; you saw a woman you wanted and you woke up in bed next morning with her nuzzling your cock.

And what was odd, the more seriously I learned to take myself, the less account to me my own life became—I'd go on camera feeling it hanging by a thread. I had to play a role, from the minute I woke up in the morning to the minute I went to bed, and I learned to play that role so splendidly, with millions applauding, I soon forgot it was even supposed to be a role at all. That's what the drinking became, the parties, the wild nights. I'd forgotten the essential part of myself so easily I thought that by drinking and carrying on I could lose the invented part, too, match forgettings, come back to my real self by mixing poisons, pulling off a switcheroo.

That's when I started reading books I'd never even thought about until then, holding them close to my nose and reading one line per minute, spending another minute resting my eyes, thinking about what I'd just read. Emerson and Bishop Sheen and Norman Vincent Peale. What I wanted to find out was why our lives weren't real to us anymore, how easily we let them slip away.

I was disappointed with what I found. None of these thinkers had ever thought about television, not even Sheen who was on it all the time. I realized there were only two people in the world who could possibly understand what I was experiencing, Lee and Alec, only it was hard to see them off the show, they were always alone with each other, either that or Lee was off making special appearances, so it would have been just as easy to chat with Emerson as it was to talk to my two oldest pals.

But then suddenly there was time, a night near Easter when Lee invited me to a turkey dinner she was cooking us herself. She had an apartment on Eighty-seventh Street, three blocks in from the park. I went there almost every night—not inside, but to pace up and down on the sidewalk, looking up toward her windows. I would have dinner at a Child's on Lexington Avenue, eat a half-cooked steak alone, then make the hike uptown. Alec was in there most of those nights. I would see his silhouette against the glass and it would nearly kill me, wishing it was me there, not him. It would get late and the shade would come down over the yellow light from her bedroom, descend slowly right down to the sill, and I would have to bite my hand to stop from screaming and walk all the way home alone.

So it was the first time I was ever inside. It was a large apartment, the entire third floor, and there were paint cans in the hallway, ladders, sawhorses, since she was having it remodeled. There were stacks of pictures, too, waiting to be hung. Lee was interested in primitives—she was buying Grandma Moses before anyone else. I paced back and forth, feeling pretty miserable, since I didn't think I could survive the jealousy, what it would be like to see them together. After what seemed like an hour I got up the courage to knock on the door.

Alec came out first. He wore chinos and a baggy gray sweatshirt, and compared to his usual neatness it made him look naked. "I need to talk to you," he said, without any preliminaries. "Something important."

He sat down on the sofa across from me, folding his leg over his knee, but the funny thing is he didn't seem comfortable there, kept getting up to change positions. I felt more at home than he did—that struck me immediately. It was obvious he had something on his mind, but before he could explicate, Lee came in, dressed exactly like him, with baggy chinos and a big gray sweatshirt, over which she had tugged on an apron. Her hair was all messed up and curly and wet-looking, and she was patting it back into position, though I thought it looked just fine.

It was clear they had just made love. They didn't seem sleepy or sated, but you could see it in their expressions—question marks, evidence they'd been on their way to something important, passionate, and desperate and hadn't gotten there, and this confused them, made them edgy.

"I'm going to put a turkey in the oven," Lee said. It was beautiful the way she said this—she could have been saying "I'm going to have a baby," and she couldn't have said it with more pride.

Alec glanced down at his watch. "It's almost five-thirty, kiddo. Curtain is at eight. Do you really think that's possible?"

He had gotten us tickets for Carousel, *which had just begun its run. He was enamored of Rodgers and Hammerstein. Something tender and lyrical beneath all the schmaltziness got to him every time.*

I remember his eyebrows coming up when I ventured the word. "Schmaltzy," he said, like an echo. It seemed to make him angry, or something did—he kept drumming his fingers along the back of the couch.

No one said anything after that, not for the next long minute. Lee moved a bit in her chair. "Nehru on Monday," she mumbled.

Alec's expression brightened. "Need help?"

She tilted her head to the side, thought carefully. "No," she said at last, "I'm all prepared."

Alec looked disappointed, and I'm sure I did, too. A woman who needed no help with Jawaharlal Nehru—and what were we to make of that? He ran his hand along his eyes. "I hope people can see him okay."

Lee and I glanced at each other—we knew what was coming.

"People out there, you can't trust them on the controls. The instant anything flips, they reach for the horizontal, get us rolling, make us worse."

"Don't you think that's improved some?" Lee asked gently.

Alec put a lot of scorn in his expression, more than you'd think he was capable of; the only thing that made it bearable was that it wasn't directed at either of us, but out the window, toward the countryside, toward everyone.

"No one knows how to focus. No one! We've got to get manuals out there, teach people how to do it. What's the use of knocking ourselves dead trying to make the picture clear when those ham-handed morons don't know how to focus, let alone anything about contrast."

It was something he talked about all the time now—he was convinced everyone watching, every single person, had us tuned in the wrong way. He always had his minor quirks and obsessions, he'd had them ever since Springfield, but this one was the worst, and you had to figure the codeine had a lot to do with it. He'd cut down when Lee showed up again, but he was taking more now, even more than he did before, and it was apt to push his mind in certain directions, let alone what it did to his health. But we talked about it for a while, Lee trying to humor him and argue him out of it at the same time—sets were getting better, she explained, people didn't need to be video experts—and then, seeing it made no difference, made a little mock curtsy like a maid. "Well, I guess I'll just go and pop the bird in."

I followed her out to the kitchen. "I've something important I want to talk to you about," she said, but no sooner had she said it than Alec came in, and we got involved in a long discussion about whether the turkey should go in breast up or breast down and whether the pan should be covered with a lid. We knew we didn't have much time. Lee turned the oven as high as it would go in order to speed things up.

We went back out to the living room, sat down in three separate chairs, so we were all very distant from each other and our voices reverberated off the walls.

"Drink?" Alec asked. There was a decanter of bourbon on the end table and he poured me a double. "Obliged," I said, and before he sat down I had swallowed it and handed back the glass for more. Lee drank, too, which was a bad sign. She was drinking too much, trying to cope with an impossible schedule, and that was something that concerned me a great deal. Alec was always urging her on, sucking her down with him lower and lower—there were rumors of parties even wilder than what television people had grown used to.

We tried some small talk, but it went nowhere. The phone kept ringing out in the hall, but Lee didn't answer. It was hot outside, humid, and you could feel the pressure moving in from the windows building up to storm. Maybe that's what was wrong—something was. We couldn't laugh at ourselves, we who were always so good at laughing. The turkey burning up in the oven, adding to the heat, the thun-

derstorm moving in, the phone hammering away, three old friends drinking too much booze, and we couldn't have managed a laugh if our lives depended on it.

Alec wanted to talk about something—not the big thing he had whispered about when I first came in, but an idea he wanted to get our reaction to. He worried that the show had strayed too far from its original conception and we weren't as adventurous as before, not as courageous. He wanted to inaugurate more innovative features, as for instance taking a camera to one of those All-American cities with funny names everyone has always heard of without really being able to picture how they look, places like Oshkosh or Hoboken or Corpus Christi.

"We jump around, region to region. New England, the deep South, the border states. I pick the towns. What we do is set up a camera on the corner of Washington and Main. Every town has a Washington Street and it always intersects Main."

"Every town?" I said, raising my eyebrows. I was still knocking back the bourbon and it made me argumentative. "Every single town? That's a broad categorical statement."

Alec didn't let this stop him. "We set up a camera and we just let it film. No reporters, no voice-over, just the picture recording life as the town goes about its business."

He waited for our reaction—you could tell he expected us to applaud. I stared down at my drink, said nothing. Lee looked over at me, then back toward the kitchen, then finally accepted the challenge.

"It won't work," she said quietly. "A few years ago, maybe, but people want more than that now and they want it faster. They'd find it boring, having no one there to explain. They would turn us off in droves."

Alec smiled, just a flicker—he enjoyed being challenged. "You mean to say you don't trust our audience? You want to belittle them?"

Lee held her glass between her hands like a chalice—she swirled it around, made a little mist from the ice. "No," she said, smiling back just as evenly. "I'm just being a realist. You know, that boring old thing."

"That's what vice-presidents like to say, 'I'm just being realistic . . .' I'm going to do it regardless. I've already started the process of selecting which towns are first." *He hesitated, rolled his fist out from behind his head, separated out a finger. "Fuck realism."*

Alec couldn't curse—his voice was too soft—but that made it all the more effec-

tive when he did. Lee responded by making her voice go even softer; in an odd kind of way it made it seem she was cursing right back.

"You have a self-destructive side, Alec. It's the easiest thing in the world, you know."

"Self-destructive?" He smiled. "Then no one has to worry about me but me."

"You're still growing. That scares me. Everyone else is shrinking themselves to fit in the box. Your imagination hasn't gotten the message. It never has."

"You have me all figured out." He looked over at me. "She has me all figured out." He turned back again. "I'm way behind when it comes to figuring you."

"I'm just a real one hundred percent genuine American girl," she said lightly. Then, when he still didn't smile, "I'm confused and frightened and confident and certain, and my heart beats between those extremes so fast it makes me dizzy. I need someone to help me. Which is why I'll always"—

She didn't finish, left the phrase hanging. Love you? She acted flirty now, or like she was mocking someone flirty—with her it was always hard to tell. What she did is bunch up the top edge of her sweatshirt so she was all but nibbling on the collar, using the fabric like a playful mask, and it was the sexiest thing in the world. I wondered about that, drunk as I was. Wondered why she should have to remind Alec of her femininity just then.

Alec stared back at her as carefully as she stared at him, trading something I couldn't understand. Slowly, exaggerating the angle, he leaned his head to the side and sniffed. "I smell something burning," he said.

Lee and I jumped up. Smoke poured from the oven and we had to open the window to keep from asphyxiating. I grabbed some potholders, put my hands in, pulled out the pan. The skin was burning like there was Saint Elmo's fire on it, only underneath the meat was pink. None of us knew how to carve, but I was so drunk I took the plunge. The knife was dull, the meat so undone, blood oozed out with every stroke, so it seemed the turkey was alive and squirming there on the platter and I ended up having to tear it apart with my hands. Meanwhile the thunderstorm had broken right on top of the apartment and it was blacker than midnight, outside and in. Lee lit candles, but it didn't make it romantic, only shabby somehow, as if we were eating in a swamp. That was when we should have commenced laughing, but again, none of us could—it was as if there were pistons pressing our spirits down, and no one had the strength to fight back.

We ate in silence. Lee was quiet with whatever big thing she had wanted to ask me about, and seemed anxious about how everything tasted. Me, I wanted to ask them about a rumor I'd heard, about how the network was seeking to fire me, and how Alec himself was behind it. Fire me! If he had his way I'd be begging on street corners with a cup. I was mad about that, but embarrassed, too, so it festered inside like an ulcer. Alec seemed totally preoccupied—he kept glancing down at his watch. "I'm going to the theater," he said, before we even reached dessert. Without another word he pushed his chair back from the table, got up, grabbed his jacket. Lee ran to the door after him—not to stop him, but to say something I couldn't hear, her hands on his shoulders like they were dancing a cold and formal waltz. It was hard reading what was going on, I was so dizzy I could barely stand, but it seemed that what bothered Alec most was the apartment itself, the domesticity, the happiness. That seemed pretty profound to me. Thinking that what he was scared of most was happiness. When Lee came back to the table she looked miserable.

Feeling sorry for her made me think. Or maybe it was the thunderstorm, the booze—they made me dreamy. I decided that what I had just witnessed was the end of their relationship—that it was clear they no longer loved each other. That was the hard part, convincing myself of that, but once I did, everything else fell into place. Why Alec stormed out must be because he was jealous of me, which was also his reason for wanting me fired, and why Lee let him go was because it was true, she loved me now, not him, and it was up to me to seize this moment before it slipped past. Lee stayed in the kitchen, trying to clean up the mess, while I went out to the living room with a candle, put it down on the coffee table and crossed over to the sofa.

What I did there was take off my clothes—shirt, pants, boxer shorts, socks— and stretch out with my head on the pillow, waiting for her to come and join me. This was the moment I had been waiting for, and now I knew she wanted it, too, and so I just lay there waiting, with my head turned in toward the cushion so all I could see was the creamy dance of the candlelight against the fabric. I remember reaching up to touch the shadows, make them go still. I remember feeling warmth and confidence in my groin—how it seemed they were having a reunion there after being separated for so long.

It was a long time before she came in. I was naked, I had an erection, I watched the dancing flame, listened to the thunder, my head swimming in bourbon, thinking

*never in my life had I made love to a woman I genuinely loved . . . and then before I
even heard her footsteps, she was kneeling down beside the couch. I waited for her to
touch me, fold herself down, but this is not what happened. Gently, very gently, she
covered me up with a light cotton blanket, the fabric draping over my cock like it
was a tent pole and immediately shrinking it, the cool trim coming up against my
throat. I forced myself to press my eyes closed . . . and then suddenly I didn't have to
press them, I was asleep like a baby, the blanket tucked snug to my face.*

When morning came he was still there; the light coming through the
curtains jolted him awake. I have to get to the show, he decided, and it
was only after he started pulling on his pants that he remembered
it was Sunday. The turkey carcass lay cold on the dining room table—
the apartment smelled of onions and dried-out stuffing. He walked
around a bit, hungover and still in a daze. Alec's jacket lay folded over
the back of the couch with a playbill sticking out of the pocket. At the
end of the hall the bedroom door was closed and Chet stood outside,
crazy from jealousy and mortification. At first there was no sound, but
then, unable to stop himself, he moved closer to the door—and there
it was, Lee and Alec laughing in the soft, silken way only lovers can
laugh, as if the sound came filtered through sheets.

He walked home down Fifth Avenue, being careful to cross at the
lights, rode the elevator up to his apartment, poured himself a drink,
started brooding. It wasn't the humiliation that hurt most, but not having discussed the question he'd gone into the evening with, and which
only Lee or Alec could possibly answer. Why were our lives so false to
us? Why do we let them slip so easily away? Sure, television, but if it
wasn't television it would be something else doing the stripping, and
why was the fight so one-sided? Where had resistance gone, struggle?
Why this need to let our inwardness drift away like snowflakes? Why
were false lives so much more appealing than real ones? He had a long
list of questions, and with every drink he took the list got longer.

*It's everyone, I decided, we're all giving up, all I've done is joined the club—but
that wasn't true either, because it wasn't everyone. Alec McGowan had more justifi-*

cation than most to let his life slip away from him, and he never let go until I took it away by force. Or tried to take it away. Alec could see out of the camera that blinded lesser souls. He was so real the rest of his world crumpled around him as he stood erect, the central pillar, and I knocked him down with that bullet just because I wanted to be real, too. And it worked, because everything was real after that—real in spades. Prison was real. Cancer is real. Dying.

And he remembered one more thing about that final *Morning,* lying there on the cold studio floor surrounded by angry cops, people screaming, his forehead bleeding from where he'd slammed it down. There were signs on the walls, injunctions, reminders, commands, all written out on cue cards where anyone with a normal pair of eyes could read them without difficulty. He could never read them, it was one of the things people mocked him about, and yet lying there on the floor he could read them for the first time ever, at least the biggest one, the one pinned to the wall right behind the weather map, the one that read NO FROWNING ON CAMERA. It was clear, the letters miraculously pure and black and well-defined, and then he realized the reason he could see them was that his eyes were full of tears and the tears acted like wet lenses of just the right prescription and that was the only way, the last way left for him now, to get them to see.

Fifteen

Chet Standish, my father, wasn't satisfied with the new millennium everyone else was trying halfheartedly to believe in, but kept insisting upon his own right until the very end. He came close—he sent Elise out to buy streamers, noisemakers, cupcakes—but he didn't live to see it. The night of March 3, his pain was much worse than before, and for the first time he had hallucinations, moments when he called out for his mother and father and desperately sobbed. Kim sat on one side of the bed and I sat on the other, doing our best to comfort him. The truth is we were both scared, and not just about his condition. A storm had come up around midnight, with a gust of wind powerful enough to shake the whole house, and this was followed by torrential volleys of sleet. I turned on the weather radio, heard the meteorologist say, without irony, that this was another once-in-a-hundred-years storm, the third we'd had in the last six months. Our lights went out, we sat watching him in candlelight, and I went around pulling all the shades down, expecting the windows to shatter inward and drench us in glass.

There was one good thing about the storm—it kept Elise busy. She was frantic with worry about Chet, begged to be allowed to help, and Kim had the bright idea of getting her involved with the storm instead, this enormous and yet lesser thing. She was the one who fetched the candles; we had her fill pots with water in case the electricity went out again, listen to see if the station was still broadcasting, peer out through the curtains to check the trees, and this kept her occupied right through till dawn.

We were all exhausted by then. Chet's pain had slackened enough that he could talk fairly calmly, sitting there propped up by pillows. Yes, we agreed, a corner had been turned. Yes, it was time to go to the hospital now. Yes, it would be better that way, with no fuss.

Kim and Elise went downstairs to get ready. The moment they left, Chet tugged my head down close to his lips. "Call an ambulance," he said, closing his eyes as the next spasm drove through his middle.

"We'll drive you," I said. "You're doing just fine."

"Call an ambulance!"

It was the pain talking now; I had to sit there and help him through. He must have always pictured himself saying that in the end, *Call an ambulance,* kept those words ready at all times, like a syringe he carried strapped to his calf. His last cry for help—and once he made it he felt better, stronger, so I managed to get him up from the bed and dressed in the suit coat, trousers, and tie he insisted upon. The medication, like the pain, hit him in waves, and he must have been riding a good one now, because he managed to walk downstairs on his own without any other support than the rail.

Kim had the coffee going in the kitchen and Elise was already wrapped up thick in her ski jacket. She'd taken our warning about water seriously—there wasn't a pot, pan, or bowl in the house that wasn't full to the brim. Seeing Chet stumble, she pulled out a chair and held it steady so he could sit down. None of us could find his boots, but we discovered that Elise's furry ones would fit him and she helped pry them on.

I could tell by the way she wouldn't look at me that something was bothering her—not the big thing that was too huge to mention, but something below that, the next problem down. When she went back to the closet for an umbrella I followed her to find out what it was.

"I wanted to give him something," she said, frowning in a way that made her look too old. "I planned to give him something to take with him."

"A gift?"

"A keepsake," she said, proud she knew the word.

"Well, it took us by surprise," I said, lamely enough. "None of us knew it would be today . . . Listen, you can go to the hospital with us, okay? You'd be a wreck at school. I'll get Mom to write a note."

Kim and I managed a few minutes alone by the coffeemaker, not saying much, not having to. I knew she was remembering the same thing I remembered—the last time we had woken up early for an unscheduled trip to the hospital, when Elise was six and her appendix ruptured, and for a few terrifying moments we thought we would lose her.

"Is there anything else we should bring?" Kim kept asking, though we knew there wasn't. Outside, the sleet had changed to rain, and yet it slapped the house with even more fury, so we had to shout to be heard.

I was on my way out to warm up the car when there was a thumping noise in the living room loud enough to startle us, even with the rain. The kitchen door swung inward, but no one came through—we all sat there, gaping, even Chet—and then finally there *was* something coming through, a white plaster cast, rubber-tipped crutches, then, smiling sleepily, bashfully, beautifully, Brenda herself.

"Can I come with you?" she said, simply enough.

It was too soon to know whether the operation on her knee had worked or not, but it had immediately changed her expression. She looked younger, easier, unburdened—the poker face she always wore on the basketball court had softened into a shy, engaging grin that suited her much better. She hadn't given up hope of returning—she still wore her varsity jacket every minute of the day—but it wasn't a grim hope, and heavy as the cast was, she seemed to walk with more grace and confidence than she had with it off. *Go ahead and underestimate me*—that was still there in her eyes, a concentrated beam, only it was turning in new directions now, and it was going to be interesting to see where it stopped.

With the storm, the prospect of a depressing ride, we needed some-one to cheer us up, so I could have kissed her, appearing from nowhere that way. Elise, who idolized her, immediately brightened. Even Chet. You could see him preening for her, sitting straighter in the chair, genuinely pleased at this last surprise.

"Splendid to see you, Brenda," he said, making his voice deeper. "How's the knee coming? I don't want you missing school just for me."

"That's okay," she said. "Can I help you get up?" She swung across the floor with the crutches, making us all laugh.

"Well, I could use some help. Major help. But listen—and don't say no, Alec—I want to take you all out to breakfast. We don't have to be at the hospital at a certain time, do we? I want to go somewhere nice."

He looked over at me, expecting an argument. "Sounds great," I said, and "You buying?"

"If you go easy on me."

Kim walked us to the door. We had worked it out that she would go off to school, then come to the hospital later on to spell us. I explained this to Chet and he nodded. Kim, standing next to us, pointed toward the ceiling.

"I've always claimed Alan could sleep through a hurricane and I guess this proves it. I'm sorry, Chet. He stays up late working the Net. I'm sure he'll come visit this afternoon."

"Oh, that's all right," Chet said hurriedly. "No, no. He's a fine lad. He puts me in mind of myself at that age." He stared at her, hesitated, then came out with what could only have been a prepared speech.

"I want to tell you how much I value educators. They are the people who make this world a less barbarous place. I never had a good education and I always tried to make up for it through bluster. And I want to thank you for all you've done for me. Putting up with a sick old man, making me feel right at home. I'll never forget how—"

He stopped, leaned forward with a courtly kind of stooping gesture to kiss her hand. But he couldn't see it, couldn't find it, and so he stumbled toward her like a bear, threw his arms around her to hug her as hard and tight and desperately as he could.

Kim, when he stepped back, didn't trust herself to say anything—never have I seen her blink so furiously and so fast. She held his parka out so he could back into it, put her arm on his shoulder, guided him toward the front door. The down coat doubled him, padded him, made him seem safer. I had the car warmed up in the driveway, so he could keep under cover beneath the eaves of the garage until he got in. Brenda flanked him on one side, putting the crutches under her left arm, and Elise flanked him on the other, bigger than he was, even with his parka. They walked toward me through the rain—the blind, the halt, the lame—only it didn't seem that way at all, seemed the exact opposite. Most of the pain was in Chet's middle, but he wouldn't give in to it; he walked erect across the pavement, and Brenda and Elise, in unconscious emulation, walked erect and evenly, too.

"Drive carefully!" Kim yelled from the door. "I'll see you later, Chet, okay?"

It was more like motorboating than driving—the car sent up a wake that crested across the already drenched sidewalks. There was no one to be seen on the streets. The stoplights swayed horizontally in the wind, so it took nerve to drive underneath. Power was on—they still flashed green—but I didn't dare drive faster than twenty. Branches were down everywhere, trees sagged; we even spotted a pigeon flying backwards past the old armory. Elise and Brenda, of course, thought this was cool, and even Chet seemed impressed, to be embraced by something so powerful you felt squeezed by its pressure.

"Where shall we try?" I asked. "I'm open to suggestions."

Chet surprised me by speaking right up. "There used to be a place on the river called Link's Log Cabin. It was a drafty old place, but they served a bountiful breakfast. We used to go there all the time. I'm sure it's extinct now."

I turned around in a driveway, started back toward the river, but didn't get very far. The underpass beneath the interstate was flooded, and the next one down was obviously impassable. There were men out piling sandbags along the Connecticut, something I hadn't seen since I was a boy. "The Waffle House!" Elise yelled, and with every other option cut off, that's where we ended up heading.

It's a modern, sterile place in a mall, no different from a million similar. The menu is six pages long, which is why Elise wanted to go there, and the waitresses all know us and like to tease. If Chet was disappointed, he didn't show it—he simply wanted to play host. I helped him over to the table, ordered coffee for me, lemon tea for him. The dining room was empty except for one table close to the window, where a couple my age sat with a frail, senile-looking woman, staring out at the storm. Something about the motionless, silent way they sat there suggested they were embarked on the same kind of journey we were—that this was in the nature of a last meal.

Past the cash register is a room full of video games. The girls conned me for some quarters, then went over to play. There was one game in particular they liked—basketball, an arcade version in which by punching your fist on a little raised ball you shot baskets inside a brightly lit dome. They were having fun with it, Elise showing Brenda how it was done, the two of them punching away, getting the bells going, the lights flashing, each of them laughing hysterically, Brenda even more than Elise.

It was good watching them. It was good to sit silently with Chet, not feel uncomfortable. Another new stage in our relationship? Well, why not, I decided, why the hell not. Up above us in the corner a TV set was turned to cartoons; there were similar sets high in each corner mounted on shelves beside security cameras pointing down at us like short-barreled cannon. I wondered about that—whether the TV sets were meant to lure your attention upward so the security cameras could get a clear view of your face. And I wondered about my wondering—wondered if that was one of the minor fates in store for me now, to be the last person in the world to notice that the cameras had turned.

The girls came back to the table, Brenda swinging along on crutches, Elise pumping her fist in the air.

"Who won?" I asked.

"I did!" Elise said. "One second left on the clock. A long three-pointer . . . *swish!*"

Chet patted the menus. "You must be hungry. Don't forget, the treat's on me."

Elise had her own way of reading a menu, which was to start on the last page with the milkshakes and pies, then work her way back toward the potato skins and soup. Before she could finish, the waitress came over—Jory, our old friend. "Who's this handsome man?" she asked, making Chet smile.

"I'm buying," he said, once I introduced him. "You make sure you give me the check."

Jory saluted. "We have a special today on Belgian waffles. All you can eat, three ninety-five."

"Sounds good to me," I said.

"Me, too," Brenda said.

"Just the tea," Chet said, shielding the cup with his hand.

That left it up to Elise. I could see her looking at the menu with great intensity, then over at the serving counter where the waffle iron was set up near an overflowing bowl of strawberries and whipped cream. I could see a debate going on, a struggle—there was something concentrated in her expression not all that different from Chet's when he paraded erect down our walk.

"I'll have waffles," she said, putting the menu down.

Jory smiled. "Big surprise. How many, hon? Six?"

Elise folded her hands together on the table. "I'll have one," she said. "I'll just have the one."

Brenda, faster than me, reached over, grabbed her hands and squeezed. Chet, who had been watching Elise very carefully, closed his eyes and nodded up and down. Me, I didn't say anything, hardly dared move.

"Well," Elise said, when the silence grew noticeable. "I don't need *more* than one, do I?"

We all laughed, even Chet. So it was a happy enough breakfast, right through to the end. Chet made a great show of taking out his wallet, pretending it was empty, finally, with a little flourish, producing the bills folded up in a wad. The girls begged to play basketball again, so I left Chet alone at the table while I went to the men's room to wash up.

He wasn't at the table when I came back—he stood by the coat rack, holding on to it for support, cupping his free hand over his heart, fluttering it in and out like a trumpeter wailing his horn.

"The most remarkable thing just happened!" he said. "A woman came over—she was here with her son and daughter. She recognized me. She was Lucy Bridges, who I went to high school with. I remember her—Lucy Bridges! She was a cheerleader and the best girl in school in history. She said she always wondered what happened to me. Can you imagine that? She always wondered what happened to me . . . They're taking her to a home, poor dear."

Epic floods, quiet turning points, sentimental reunions. Big adventures for a morning's drive—fate wasn't done with Chet yet—and I worried that maybe we'd been too hasty in deciding upon the hospital. But after that first strong hour he seemed much worse in the car. It wasn't the pain—the medication was holding its own—but the pall cast by his realizing all such adventures were now at an end. We were all pretty quiet, even though the rain had slackened now. It occurred to me that there must have been many times during his trial and his years in prison when he must have pictured this trip or something similar— the tunnel-like darkness, the last meal, the long walk to the death house without the slightest chance of reprieve. As a kid in my loneliest moments I had pictured it, too, imagined me dashing in to save him from the electric chair at the very last moment, carrying him under one arm as with the other I fought off the guards with my sword.

So maybe that's why I did what I did next. The hospital was a half-mile ahead—already we could see the roof with its air scrubbers, satellite dishes, antennas—but before pulling off on the exit, I stepped on the brakes, checked the rearview mirror, swerved us around as if it were a getaway car I was driving, the coppers in hot pursuit.

It threw everyone sideways—the girls half-giggled and half-screamed.

"Where are we going?" Brenda asked, puzzled.

Elise stared out the window. "I know! Oh, Daddy!"

It wasn't a reprieve—I knew that as well as anyone—but I couldn't resist anyway, wondered only if he had the small amount of strength left that it would take. Main Street was deserted except for some day-care children walking together, holding on to a rope; the surviving stores weren't open yet, so I had no problem parking right in front. "I've got some papers I need to pick up," I said, lamely enough. "A few details to check on. It won't take but a minute."

Chet could see where we were all right—his face was against the window glass, his lips flattening in a painful grimace. Brenda got out first, then waited as Elise hurried around to help Chet. The bank is so old it has a marquee jutting out in front just like a theater, and it came in handy now, letting us get him in through the revolving door without being soaked.

"Look the same?" I asked, as we waited for the elevator.

He couldn't answer—he could only stare, blink, and nod.

I'd been there so seldom during the last year that I could understand some of what he must have been feeling. There's a sense to the station that's hard to put into words without sounding foolish, partly the smell of old coins that seventy years hasn't eradicated, partly the hum of tape machines and monitors filtered through our skimpy, tired old insulation, partly a vibrant, impossible-to-pinpoint kind of tingle that makes it feel as if you've stepped into fresher air than what's outside, a purer ozone, an atmosphere of vintage electricity that's only become more potent with the years. As we stood there waiting for the elevator to come down and fetch us, I breathed all this in pretty deeply, never mind what Chet was feeling. I'd been away a long time.

The office is on the third floor. The moment the doors opened the girls disappeared toward the record library. This had been their playground since they were babies and they were instantly at home.

"Hey! The prodigal boss! Come to see if we've been swept away, has he?"

Jimbo Elliot walked in from the lunchroom, wiping poppy seeds off his mouth. He looked as red-faced and dapper as ever, though unshaven and obviously weary after working all night. Next to basketball, storms were the great passion of his life: being in the station during a bad one, getting reports in from the worst-hit districts, broadcasting out advisories and reassurance. What he would have liked best was to be lashed to the antenna during a blizzard with a microphone taped to his throat—and once when I kidded him about this, he got angry because I wouldn't let him do it.

"I'd like you to meet my father," I said, waving him over.

That surprised him all right. He wiped his hand off on his shirt, stuck it out. "An honor, sir. A real honor, let me tell you."

Chet shook his hand—pleased, tickled pink, but too overcome yet for words.

"I thought maybe you could give him a quick tour of the premises," I said. "I've got a few things I want to check up on while I'm here."

Jimbo gave me a pretty hard squint—what was I up to?—but he didn't say anything, not just then. "The pleasure would be all mine."

Chet looked anxiously off to the right. "The gents' still down there?"

Jimbo nodded. "Lots of pictures along the way. What we call our 'wall of infamy.' You probably would recognize a lot of who's in them."

"We never had a gents' at first. We used to go down to Woolworth's, pay a nickel, use theirs. I was the one who installed the toilet. Or paid to do so. I wasn't much of a plumber . . . We used to keep the key right up there."

He couldn't reach the top of the door frame, so Jimbo reached for him, felt—came back down holding an old-fashioned brass key covered in dust.

"Well I'll be damned!" he said. We all smiled at the surprise of it—
and then Jimbo, after holding the door open for him, hurried back
again, anxious to get me alone.

"A remarkable guy! Looks like his picture, spread his features out a
little, pump some air through his gills. He looks like you for that matter. So, what's the verdict?"

I knew what he meant. "The verdict is, there's no verdict."

"No deal yet?"

"No done deal."

That gave him hope. "You mean you've changed your thinking?"

"I didn't say that, either. I'm going to decide once the new century
starts."

He screwed his eyes up. "That's ninety-nine years."

"A week and a half. Just ask Chet."

My office looked the same as always, crowded and disorganized,
and that bothered me at first, that the changes of the last year weren't
reflected there somehow. But I felt relief, too—the feeling you get
when you've put your life on hold and then sink back into it again, sagging down into the dusty indents left by long years of routine. The
truth is I needed five minutes to think about things before driving
Chet that last mile to the hospital. Here I was, the absentee manager,
the self-taught biographer, the clumsy father, the late-blooming son—
here I was, facing the rest of my life, which looked remarkably like
my past, and what was I going to do about that? I thought about the
station, what it would take to keep it going, wondered if I had the
strength, wondered, while I was at it, whether anything independent
and modest and different had any life expectancy now, or whether that
kind of thing was just for stubborn, punch-drunk martyrs who didn't
particularly care whether modern times clobbered them or not. Sell
out? Stay the course? The alternatives took turns jabbing at me and I
couldn't mount much of a defense.

And I thought about something I'd discussed often lately with
Kim—about how if there was one task this new century was going to
have to set itself to it was the task of reinvention, and whether I
wanted to put my own puny shoulder to the wheel of this, or whether

it was up to someone much younger who could fall in love with the small, forgotten corners of life, head over heels in love, at a time when that kind of passion was harder than ever to justify or sustain. Alan? Brenda? Elise? One of them? Maybe. Maybe no.

But it felt good, after staring so long at the past, to concentrate some on the future. For one perfectly balanced minute I felt like one of those Hindu deities with all the arms, one reaching backwards toward McGowan, another reaching to my kids here in the present, a third toward Chet straddling both eras, a fourth to my grandchildren, whom I could just dimly sense in the years to come. I was reaching toward all their spirits all at once—and then, really stretching, closing my eyes in effort, I felt the answering pressure as they all reached back toward me and with synchronous pressings seized my hand.

There, I told myself. *There.*

I arranged some papers on the desk, crumpling some up and tossing them in the waste basket, folding others, even sticking a few in my jacket as if they were urgent, knowing what I had to do now, at least as regards the station. But there was plenty of time to plan for that, all kinds of new projects we could talk about launching, only not right now. I had come to the station for my father's sake and it was time now to go and find him.

I caught up with them outside the glass partition to the studio. This was the older, smaller of our pair, the one made sixty years before by combining the safety deposit vault with the tellers' cages, slapping them together with that infamous FDR wallpaper, and it was still the studio the on-air talent preferred, being so cavelike and quiet. Jimbo had turned Chet over to Terri Cole, our morning announcer. She's small, she hardly came up to his chest, and yet she stood right up next to him, waving and gesticulating, explaining what was what, the ON AIR light draping them both in a tulip-red glow. She was dressed in thirds— the top part wrapped in scarves like a West African princess, the middle in a schoolmarm's prim blouse, the lower third in a tiger-striped leotard and pink sneakers. Terri always dresses this way. As Brenda likes to say, the only defense is that on her it all somehow works.

She was having a great time with Chet, that was clear. Terri treats people like microphones, gets right up close that way, and Chet wasn't so far gone that he couldn't be flattered by her attention. They were talking about the signal, the tricks it could do. "I used to hear you sometimes when I lived upstate," Chet explained. "When the atmospherics were just right. I aimed the antenna this way, just like a compass needle, and the signal seemed like a whisper directed to me alone. I always enjoyed that, the whispering. It was always a great escape."

As attentively as Terri listened to him, one ear stayed cocked toward the monitor—she's an expert at getting back into the studio two seconds before the music ends. "Hey, I know!" she said. "How's this for an idea? I've got this godawful cold, as you can probably tell. How's about sitting in for me for a few minutes? You know, for old time's sake. I'm playing mostly Dixieland this morning, just your thing, I'll bet."

She glanced a question mark at me, tilted her head to the side, smiled her sassy-cat smile—and smiled even broader when I nodded the barest minimum up and down.

"Three minutes left." She grabbed hold of his arm. "Come on, I'll get you settled in. An old pro like you, it won't take long."

Chet looked at me for help, looked down at her, didn't seem to know what to say. "Well, of course. Well, of course. I'd be honored."

"Honored? You kidding? The honor is all ours."

We all went in. The furnishings are plain enough—the control panel with its switches and dials, some overcrowded shelving, two rickety wooden chairs that probably dated from his own tenure. Terri held one back so he could sit down. He was wide-eyed at being there, if you can say that of a man whose eyes were so tiny—he wanted to look at everything, savor it, soak it all in—but there wasn't time for that now, and already Terri was clamping a black headset over his ears. In his fragile state, I was sure this would crush him, and yet he looked much better with the earphones on, even though he was trembling. His head seemed to expand, swell—in a good way, not a bad. He leaned forward and grabbed hold of the mike as Terri gave him his last instructions.

"I'll count down with my fingers thisaway. Five, four, three, two. Got that? This mike is sensitive, it will do whatever your throat wants." She glanced up at the clock. "Ready?" she whispered, bunching her hand up in a fist. "Five ... four ... three ... two—"

She nodded vehemently up and down, pointed to the mike, leaned back with an *all yours* gesture and Chet was on.

Or almost on. What I worried about immediately happened—he froze. He froze fast and he froze solid, holding on to the mike for dear life, like a student pilot suddenly asked to solo. For a moment it looked like Terri would have to grab the mike back—she actually started to reach—but then Chet made a violent shivering motion, dipped his head down, seemed, seemed quite literally, to take the plunge.

"Good morning ... everyone. This is ... Chester ... R. ... Standish. Chet Standish sitting in for my friend"—he closed his eyes, pressed the earphones tighter, thought hard, his chin trembling like a man who's about to stutter. "Terri Cole," he managed. "And glad to be with you. Back with you, uh, again ... This is WSM, the sound of greater Springfield."

His voice was scratchy and faint, nothing like his real voice, and it broke on the word *Springfield* like a thirteen-year-old boy's. He frowned, pushed the mike away slightly, winced as a new pain had its way with him, tried to concentrate, summon back something from the deepest part of his being.

"The time is now 8:33 A.M.—or should I say *ante meridiem*? It is a beautiful morning out there, folks. A wonderful morning. What I call a reee ... splen ... dent morning. What's a little rain in March? Gets the flowers growing, tops off the wells. It won't hurt you. You're not sugar, my friends, you won't melt—no sireee bob. We're going to be playing some records and bringing you some news and getting you started on what we hope is a swell day for all of you, a miraculous day, so stay tuned right here."

This was better, *resplendent* being the word that broke the ice, made his voice much stronger and deeper, so he suddenly sounded like the Chet of old. I understood now what the purpose of such words were, to lubricate the throat while it caught the listener's attention—the old broadcaster's trick, one of hundreds he could teach us.

"We'll be playing some Mr. Louis Armstrong and some Mr. Jelly Roll Morton and other surprises as the morning sails on. I'd like very much to send this out to my pal Miss Lucy Bridges with thanks for the memories and hopes that all goes well. This is WSM in Springfield, Massachusetts, ten thousand watts of pep, where the elite come to meet."

He was into the flow now, smiling, his eyes glancing over at Terri for her approval, but mostly sunk in that typical broadcaster's stare, looking out and looking in at the very same instant. Wanting to get a better idea of how he sounded over the air, I slipped quietly out the door and went up to my office, where I could listen on the radio, gauge the quality better, hear his voice the way it was meant to be heard, alone, a couple of feet from the box it came from.

"Good morning, Springfield," he was saying, really rolling with it now, caught up in the rhythm. "*Bonjour,* Chicopee. Good morning, Holyoke and Deerfield and Amherst, *buenos días* to you folks there in Worcester and Northampton. Good morning to all of you within reach of the sound of my voice. Good morning, Hartford and Boston and New York City, and wherever the wind may blow us. Good morning, Chicago and Dallas and St. Paul. Good morning, California, and we hope you're having as grand a day out there as we're having ourselves right here."

It was rich with years, a voice worth listening to—a voice like a weathered oak tree's, limbless and scarred, the sound emerging as the wind bores through the gaping cavities left by storms, pestilence, and rot—a voice that put a solid bottom on the first syllables of a word, then widened and brightened over the last. I played another trick now, tried imagining how he sounded at the very farthest reaches of our signal, places that could just barely hear us, maybe a farm out in the country where the rain came down as snow, or a distant city where someone hurt, battered, and lonely found him and feathered in on the buzz, trying to hear clearer. And I found I could imagine this without much trouble, the way his ancient voice must sound, surrounded by static, not sweet or syrupy, but coarse and gritty and pesky, something you loved and hated at the very same instant, so you couldn't turn it off if you tried. It was a voice that seemed wrapped in the wind it sailed out on, something that hit you with force on the side of your cheek— a gentle force, a weak force, but electric enough to turn you in its direction, take those fanlike aural rays full on the face.

And I knew what Chet was talking about, too, as he chanted it out loud—not the morning that comes with sunrise, but the tougher, harder one you reach toward on your own. His was the voice of that, or tried to be, as much as his strength would allow. I listened with all the distance I could imagine, heard a voice that sounded foolish, fluttery, and puny, a rusty, quixotic, doomed voice, a faint, weak, feeble one, something you grew irritated with in its repetitive insistence, to the point you wanted to swipe at it, block it, knock it away. *Good morning* the voice kept saying there in the distance. *Good morning good morning good morning,* the one detectable signal there against the background noise, something too remote and feeble to ever fully believe in—but you would do well to try.

About the Author

W. D. Wetherell is the author of twelve books, including the novel *Chekhov's Sister,* the story collection *The Man Who Loved Levittown,* and the memoir *North of Now.* He is the holder of the Strauss Living Award from the American Academy of Arts and Letters, and makes his home in rural New Hampshire with his wife and two children.